SPIRIT OF THE MERCURY DIME

BY KATHY SWOYER

Copyright © 2014 Kathy Swoyer
All rights reserved

ISBN: 061583941X
ISBN 13: 9780615839417
Library of Congress Control Number: 2013912104
Honsel Press, Issaquah, WA

Cover photo copyright Kathy Swoyer
Cover photo inset credit: Serge Timacheff/Tiger Mountain Photo
Pendant by Jewelry Garden
Back photo copyright Judy Corcoran

Spirit of the Mercury Dime is a work of fiction. Names, characters, businesses, organizations, places and events are the products of the author's imagination or are used fictitiously. Any resemblance to actual persons, living or dead, or events or locations, is entirely coincidental.

*To my mother, for teaching me the joys of reading,
the zing of ideas, and the magic of words.
And the Golden Rule.*

*To Rick, for his endless love, patience and support,
all shown to me in more ways
than I could possibly imagine.*

LOVIE
1850

The day the angel came for her, Esther was too sick to go. She had just birthed her perfect Lovie, but it was a difficult delivery and she was still nursing the slashes on her back. That morning, she had failed to address li'l two-year-old Billy as "Marster William" and enraged the Mistress. She felt hot, feverish, and weak.

"Go, Moses, be safe," she whispered. Harriet Tubman paused and considered, but not for long, and soon lit out.

Esther lay back on the thin straw mat and cuddled Lovie close. Another time would come.

PART ONE

CHAPTER 1

Spring 1995

Mallards had escaped their winter doldrums and returned to the lake. You never really see them fly in. Suddenly the icy, gray clouds part, and they're there. Springtime brings them out full force. The males strut and stretch their luminescent green necks; the demure, brown females swim placidly nearby. They show off their sweet, charming side as they wander off in pairs, stroll across the busy street, and waddle up the hill, blissfully unaware of the busy traffic (they seem to ignore the clear advantages of flying under these circumstances), just padding around willy-nilly, their bright orange feet flapping softly against the pavement. They emit soft, gurgling quacks as they search for that perfect nesting spot. Cute little hand-drawn duck-crossing signs border the streets to alert passersby of the mallards' haphazard travels.

However, springtime also invites other mallards that aren't quite ready to settle down. These portray a not-so-charming side. The drakes work themselves up into a mob-like frenzy of uncontrollable lust, feathers fluttering, and suddenly gang up on one hapless female, squawking, splashing, flying and landing right on top of her, a crowd of males, wriggling, struggling, one after another, until they have all had their way with her to their satisfaction. After the indignities, the female bobs to the top, shakes herself, and primps.

Eileen Hanley glanced up from her sketchbook and grinned. She could relate. But she was also struck by the beauty of the wings and the feather patterns, not that she could ever capture such a scene in her art, or would want to, for that matter. Imagine, a gang bang here in full view of the children. Nature's porno openly displayed. Thinking of her own workplace, her day job, her other job, Eileen imagined those ducks being marched into a sexual harassment clinic led by a dour-looking assistant manager duck who preaches against such displays and, stabbing the easel pad with her laser marker, sternly stresses, "This is not proper duck behavior."

Eileen had attended many such employee behavior sessions conducted by the hospital's venerable HR department. In fact, it seemed as if most of the hospital's problems had begun around the same time as those drab, mandatory meetings.

She peered up the hill where, nestled in the sycamore trees, the majestic, faded-brick Sunrise Hospital stood. She shook her head.

Serious trouble was brewing, and the magnitude of it gnawed her gut. Gas stations thrive filling up an endless parade of bloated vehicles, but something as essential as a hospital falters. After a long, tiresome rally, you could almost hear the poor old building letting out its final creaky sighs and giving itself up to its fate. Once the people inside had given up hope, there wasn't much the building could do all by itself.

Eileen's throat tightened. Heavens, it was just a building. In her old age—which, at thirty-four, was hardly ancient—she noticed that she was more sympathetic toward inanimate objects than, say, human beings. As a long-time hospital worker, she recognized this as not the most admirable quality. Still, it was true. She continued to drive her old Toyota, with its roughshod gasket, because she couldn't bear to give it up. She bought most of her furniture from thrift stores because she felt sorry for the abandoned pieces that had served their previous owners with quiet dignity. And this old building, regal and proud, didn't deserve this.

It had all started when the suits took over the place. First came the business suits, which were closely followed by the legal suits. At some point a few years ago, someone decided that the good old people who had been running the hospital for decades simply weren't good enough anymore. Workers needed "utilization review" degrees and specific "risk management" skills, and the government could only provide funding if a certain number of workers could prove that they had their "papers." Sort of like dog breeding.

Eileen remembered when she'd first met with Fern, the personnel director. Back in those days, they called it "personnel" because people knew how to spell it. In later years, they had to change it to "human resources." It wasn't really easier to spell, but there was spell-check now. Most importantly, the new department had to prove itself as an all-powerful, invincible organization—a secret society looming over all.

Its job was to handle all sorts of employee ills, real and imagined: sexual harassment, discrimination, disability claims, etc. These ills had become big business, and, by God, they had to be handled by a department with a real can-do name. Human Resources. These are *humans* we are dealing with. No, we aren't just dealing with them, we are providing *resources* for them, for humans! That's what we do! And don't forget the ever-important bible of the workplace, the employee handbook. Well-thumbed pages around sections titled Vacation and Sick Time. The key to HR hearts was razor-sharp memorization of this mighty tome. HR was an indispensable department for any business that wanted to take itself seriously.

Fern was before those days when you had to proclaim the reason for your existence to the world. She was just Fern, the head of personnel. And she already knew Eileen by name that day, many years ago, when she'd applied for the job of executive assistant to the president.

Nervous and unsure, Eileen had nearly bumped into a young woman leaving the office mumbling, "I just know it's irritable bowel syndrome."

"That Maribeth." Fern sighed and motioned Eileen into the office. "Eileen, come in, come in. Good to see you. How's your mother? I just love her; she's so funny." Fern had bubbled over with enthusiasm that day, over a decade ago. "She stopped in the other day when we were grumping around about the new cafeteria hours, and she soon had us rolling on the floor laughing, talking about her lasagna and her secret ingredient."

Hmm, they'd had lasagna the night before; Eileen figured she would have to inspect it more closely next time. But Fern's warmth had settled her nerves.

Fern was a stoutly built German woman, pudgy but with purpose. At the time, she was about forty-five, which seemed ancient to Eileen, who had just graduated from college. Fern had been dressed in a flowery shirtwaist dress, primly belted around her waist, slight bulges over both sides. Her chocolate-brown hair was neatly arranged in a bun on the back of her head, and from the base of her crown, a few tendrils had loosened, making a quite attractive frame for her face. She was a sweet old lady. Always had something nice to say about Eileen or her family.

"My mom is fine, thanks, Fern. And she'll get a kick out of your compliment; she thinks she's really a cranky old broad." Eileen's mother, Serena, volunteered twice a week in the physical therapy department.

"Oh no, how could she ever think that? She always makes us laugh."

Dear Fern. Of course, she was no longer at the hospital. After they'd paraded in the suits with their fresh, rosy faces and polished, plastic-encased business degrees, Fern's days were numbered. Everything was so complicated—so many government forms to follow, regulations to enforce, quotas to meet and exceed. "Efficiency, efficiency, efficiency" was the tony new phrase of the future. It was a nebulous term that no one could really define, but the suits all knew that Fern wasn't it. They didn't have to explain; it was simply known she couldn't hack it anymore. And if someone did need an explanation, then that person probably should go too. They all shared the same tunnel vision toward the future. The only thing they could see at the other end was a big dollar sign.

Somehow, however, in the midst of their efficiency, they'd missed the stacks and stacks of unbilled invoices accumulating in the corners of the billing offices. Progress was so fast—new technology, new computers, new departments. Everyone was so caught up in the excitement of learning all these new things, the billing fell behind.

Soon the suits' fresh, rosy faces had faded into pasty, pale blobs of flesh, bright eyes had turned stony cold. But boy, oh boy, were they making money for themselves, and making an impact! So many people let go—the suits were really doing their job! How dare those old-timers think they could coast on their laurels for so long.

Once Fern had lost her job, she tried working at the county nursing home, but she never could recreate the same joy and sense of loyalty there that she'd had for the hospital, Eileen knew. Every so often Eileen would run into Fern at the grocery store or bank, and Fern had just seemed to wither before her eyes. A wan smile outlined her lips, but no light sparkled in her eyes. Word was she'd contracted some disease or another.

Eventually, most of the middle-management people who'd been hired en masse back then had all been subsequently fired or "outplaced," another tony new word, and everyone was dressing like they used to, only now they were calling it "business casual." It would be ironic if it weren't so tragic, Eileen thought.

However, it didn't really matter what anyone was wearing anymore, because Sunrise Hospital's days were numbered.

Any day now could close a chapter of the hospital's history that dated to before the Civil War. Eileen had heard the legend, that the hospital had been part of the Underground Railroad that had provided safe haven for escaping slaves. And in this case, it was said, it was truly underground. The rumor held that beneath the morgue, long, twisted hallways branched out in five directions, tunnels that led to other safe havens. Eileen found the rumor far-fetched, as there had been several hurricanes and flooding that would most certainly have uprooted those structures, washing them away in a muddy mess.

Nope, it wasn't good enough that the hospital had battled its way through the Civil War, Reconstruction, floods, and more just to come crashing down due to the greed of a few bumbling businessmen.

Eileen couldn't let it happen.

CHAPTER 2

The ducks squawked in a frenzy again. Eileen looked over, expecting another rowdy avian brawl, but this time she saw Daniel holding a big bag of breadcrumbs. The ducks were ecstatic, surrounding him in a flurry of feathers and urgent quacking.

"Hey, ya bum, don't you know that's the worst thing for birds?" Looking down at the anemic pile of crumbs, Eileen scoffed, "White bread, no less. That's not fit for birds or humans."

"Hi, beautiful," he said. "These aren't birds; they're ducks."

"OK then, fowl. Speaking of which, it just binds them up into a gooey, pasty mess that eventually ends up in loose, smelly little piles plastered all over the banks of the lake."

"Oh, I know all about that. I eat the stuff myself, you know, and it has the same effect on me."

"That's why I love visiting you so often."

"Yeah, you just can't resist stopping over at least, what, twice a year? You're wearing out your welcome, you know."

Daniel Kensington was one of her dearest friends. He was her height and size, with the same focused blue eyes, and people often mistook them for brother and sister.

"You just missed quite a show," Eileen said with a sniff.

"Oh, were they doing that again? Shameless hussy."

"Hey, wait a minute. It looked to me like she was a bit outnumbered."

"Little tramp, egging them on so. Speaking of which, your beloved Gordon, Larson & Kammerer were in the news again. A couple of the attorneys were disbarred. One was a partner."

"*Disbarred!* A partner? I didn't read anything about this." She searched Daniel's face and caught a glimpse of that unmistakable tall-tale veil lingering there. "Wow. Oh my. An attorney can practice law while dead and not get disbarred. Who was it?"

"I think the Larson guy. And some associate."

"Adolphe?"

"Whatever."

"For what? Details, man."

"Insider trading."

"No! They all do that, don't they? I suppose they have rules—wink, wink—against it, but I thought those rascals all finagled their way around it. Offshore accounts and whatnot."

"Maybe so, but Larson's no bright bulb. It seems that a biochemical company was interested in testing some of the toxic gunk spewing out into the Susquehanna River from Amber Fuel."

"Good for them. It's about time someone starts worrying about the contents of that stuff." Eileen idly scratched her nose.

"Maybe so, but this wasn't to test it for toxicity. It was to test it for use as a possible cancer drug."

Eileen could not suppress a laugh. "Don't tell me. I suppose Larson bought stock in the biochem company knowing about their half-assed plan through his representation of Amber Fuel."

"Something like that, yeah."

"God, did the stock go up?"

"You said it. Through the roof."

They laughed merrily.

GLK was a law firm of deathly repute in the town, and, as such, considered fair game for morbid jokes. For Eileen, humor was often the best way to deal with realities likely worse than what the imagination could ever come up with. Whenever any industry in the area fell afoul of the law, its questionable emissions clouding the water or poisoning the air, Gordon, Larson & Kammerer was always there to support it and enthusiastically create terms to parse the word *pollution*.

Chemical stews of nightmare proportions become "environmental diversity." Yes, who are we to pass judgment on the proliferation of six-legged frogs and dual-sexed fish and wingless birds? These are the newly evolved creatures of the twenty-first century, and to look down on them is paramount to discrimination. Every creature has a right to live. What kind of heartless society have we become to look askance at these unfortunate beasts?

On and on, on their high horse about the rights of these disadvantaged creatures, clearly ignoring their own culpability. *Um, but it was your toxic stews that created these things.* Now, now, no one has proven that. Every creature has a right to live; don't you believe that? And so on. Suddenly, anyone who questions looks like the bad guy.

Daniel continued, "Word has it now that they're working on manufacturing a synthetic water. Just grab a little artificial hydrogen, a little artificial oxygen, and there you go."

"I don't think I want to hear any more."

Daniel reached out to hug Eileen, whose eyes suddenly brimmed with tears. Daniel held her tightly. "Oh, honey, I'm sorry."

"No, I'm sorry. It's just that…"

"Shh, I know."

Amber Fuel and Gordon, Larson & Kammerer together in a scenario again. Eileen's stomach knotted thinking about it. She had tangled with those characters herself a time or two.

It had been a couple of years ago now, posttreatment, on a Saturday morning, her favorite day of the week. That particular Saturday was special because it was a bright, sunny day in February, warm too, with the temperature already at sixty-two degrees. Birds twittered outside, squirrels scampered in a lively game of tag, and the barest hint of green buds peeked out on the branches of the maple tree outside her window. All were optimistically oblivious to the impending freak snowstorm that occasionally hammered the region in March, crushing the tender buds and chasing the wild critters off to the hills.

Eileen had settled in for her breakfast of a homemade chocolate zucchini muffin and hot coffee with foamed milk, otherwise called a latté when you forked over $2.50 for it in the city. She reached for the *Chronicle*.

What? She sputtered out her coffee—*ptooey*—all over the newspaper. She couldn't believe the headline: AMBER FUEL CHASES ITS DEMONS; HIRES SUNRISE HOSPITAL COUNSEL GORDON, LARSON & KAMMERER TO HEAD THE PACK

That did it. That was *her* hospital they were talking about. She was the executive assistant to the president. How dare they associate the hospital with the same filth that GLK, as they were fondly nicknamed, usually represented!

The filth that spurred this headline was Amber Fuel, a runaway-cowboy company that showed an appalling lack of interest in the fact that its product was leaking into the groundwater of the farmland in the middle of the county. Families were drinking well water reeking of petrochemicals. The company's response: "Oh, you must be mistaken. It's probably due to the fertilizer you all are using."

The company might just as well have said, "Your farm's not paid for anyway, what right do you have to healthy water? And just exactly when was your last payment anyway, hmmmm?"

Eileen shoved out of her chair and immediately called Winston, the hospital president and her boss. The line was busy. Oooh, how irritating that telephone lady is, saying, "The line is busy." As if I can't flippin' figure that out myself. She hit redial, once, twice. *Ring*. There.

"Winston?"

"Hello, yes. Oh, hi, Eileen. Boy, what a morning." Winston sounded tired.

"You've seen the paper?"

"Have I ever. And had I not, I've had plenty of people call and quite righteously point it out to me."

"We've got to dump those guys, GLK. They're nothing but trouble for us, Winston."

"They're a good law firm, but we can't take publicity like this."

"No kidding, Winston. We plead and cajole for coverage about our Senior Health Day and finally end up with a tiny two-point blurb on C-24, but when something like this happens, the press is gladly granting us a sprawling free headline."

"Hmm, yes, and we have nothing to do with Amber Fuel. Do we? Is Cassius one of our board members?"

"No, no, Winston. Remember? Some lunk on the board asked him, but luckily he turned it down. 'I demur' I believe was the way he put it."

"Well, that's a relief. Eileen, can you call the newspaper and tell them how displeased we are with that headline?"

"I'd be glad to, Winston." No, she wouldn't. She hated working on the weekend. But this was different and had to be done. "I'll just have to be careful how I word it. I don't want the story to be about Sunrise Hospital. We really have nothing to do with any of this."

"Yes, I'm sure you'll say the right thing. And we've got to get rid of GLK as our counsel. We'll work on that on Monday."

And that was it. It was up to her to gently diffuse the situation.

She made the call to the *Maple Leaf Chronicle*.

"What is the matter with you knuckleheads? Sunrise Hospital has absolutely nothing to do with that slime-spewing Amber Fuel. Why the heck did you implicate us—um, use the hospital's name in the headline? I'm calling as a concerned citizen and a supporter of the hospital."

"Oh, Eileen, knock it off, I know it's you," said Bob, the assistant editor, in an exhale of smoke. Eileen could practically smell it through the phone.

This town was too small.

"Come on, Bob, you know that's not a fair headline. What were you guys thinking?"

"Free press, baby, that's the name of the game. Y'all should be grateful."

"Give me a break, Bob. You could have said that GLK represents other industrial clients or other chemical-spewing creeps, but the *hospital*? Publicity like that isn't doing us any favors."

"Hey, GLK pointed it out to us. Nearly gloated about it. Would you like us to print a disclaimer, say, 'Sunrise Hospital, although admitting that GLK is its counsel, heartily denies any affiliation with Amber Fuel and its current situation. And, in an unrelated matter, the hospital's bed count is at an all-time high'?"

She shook her head and suppressed a laugh. "Yes, I suppose from chemical ingestion. That's not funny, Bob. And it's potentially libelous."

"Lighten up. I'm kidding. I'll do what I can."

She reread the article. In the midst of evaluating the environmental crisis, the *Chronicle* reporter continued, "While Amber Fuel is scrambling to find the source of the leaks, its counsel, GLK, is working hard to prove the company's innocence. GLK is a renowned local law firm that also represents Sunrise Hospital."

There it was again. Enough was enough; she would call GLK right now and leave a voice mail. Renee Sphincter—no, what was it, Finkster?—was the partner they usually dealt with. She looked up her name in the hospital's counsel directory.

"Hello, Renee. This is Eileen Hanley at Sunrise Hospital. Please call me first thing on Monday. We are concerned about finding our name in the newspaper apparently connecting us with the problems of Amber Fuel. Thank you."

That should get her attention. Think like a lawyer and insinuate liability.

Eileen let out a big sigh. Enough work for the weekend.

———

Sure enough, first thing that Monday morning at work, Eileen saw her message light blinking. Outside call, received 5:45 a.m. Someone was nuts.

"This is Renee Finkster of Gordon, Larson & Kammerer. Thank you for your call. Of course, we are disturbed that you feel compromised by the recent news article. I will be in the office on Monday at eight a.m. Thank you."

So much for a rousing show of support. What did she expect? GLK was used to dealing with clients who bred amoebae fungus in petri dishes, for heaven's sake. Eileen could hardly expect a gold-plated welcome mat. She couldn't wait to talk to her.

Winston's door was closed, and, frankly, she couldn't deal with his anxiety right now anyway. She idly looked through the phone book for law firms. She figured it would be better if the boardmembers had already selected a replacement, then they would be less willing to cave under whatever spiel GLK would spout to hold onto the hospital. She paged down through the list. There were only a few law firms in this town, and the board didn't want to go to the big city. Homespun was what they were searching for. They wanted attorneys who knew the town, knew the hospital, and knew the people.

Salto Duthie. The names sounded familiar, Neil Salto and Amos Duthie. Oh yes, theirs was the firm that donated big bucks to the Arts and Dance Commission. Their names were plastered all over the ballet and art show programs as corporate sponsors.

It sounded like the hospital couldn't go wrong here.

Just to be sure, she looked up Salto Duthie in the Martindale-Hubbell legal directory and ran quickly through the firm's client list. She liked to keep the MH around at work, just like she liked to have the Physicians Desk Reference and the really, really big Webster's. (If she were stranded on a desert island, those would be her book choices. Oh, and the complete Renoir Illustrated.) She saw nothing fishy in Salto's client roster. A couple of other hospitals, a few banks, department stores, the usual stuff. She checked out the firm's website. Nice design, creative yet tasteful. Sensible access. She clicked on the links to both Neil and Amos and gazed at their features. Nice, honest-looking faces. And laugh lines around their eyes. Yes, these guys looked like keepers.

She hopped out of her chair and ran next door into her boss's office. "Hey, Winston, you ever hear of these guys, Salto Duthie? They sound like the right bunch for us."

Winston looked at her blankly for a moment, then perked up. "Oh yes, they're pretty nice people. Have a great reputation in town. I see their names as heavy donors on the symphony and theater playbills. For a small firm, they must use their resources well."

"Do you mind if I call them? I'm on a roll here and would just as soon…"

"Oh sure, Eileen, I'd be grateful. We should probably have another firm lined up before we cut off GLK."

As if a hospital could be blacklisted by a law firm. Oh, Mr. High and Mighty Falconne Gordon, have you a nasty boo-boo in your major cardiac artery? I'm *soooo* sorry, but our hospital is packed right now. Full-capacity census; can't get you in, no way, no how. But you have a nice day, now, and enjoy that double bacon cheeseburger.

Yes, paybacks could be precious in this business. She made the call.

"Good morning. Salto Duthie. How may we help you?"

Very nice.

"May I speak with Neil Salto, please?"

"May I ask who's calling?"

"Yes, this is Eileen Hanley from Sunrise Hospital. He's not expecting my call, but I would really like to talk to him as soon as possible."

"Oh sure, Ms. Hanley, I know you. I bought one of your pictures at the flea market. Well, that doesn't sound so good, does it? But I love your style; it's so detailed. My daughter loves your stuff."

Sweet. "Thank you so much. Tell her that I really appreciate that."

"I'll ring you through to Mr. Salto."

The firm was earning gold stars already, and she hadn't even heard their pitch.

"Ms. Hanley, I'm so happy to hear from you. Your hospital saved my dad's life."

Neil Salto's voice was warm and gentle, thickly oozing self-assurance without a hair of arrogance.

"That's so good to hear, Mr. Salto." *Keep talking to me; your words are a creamy-smooth salve.*

"We thought he'd had a heart attack. My dad. We were lucky. It wasn't a heart attack, but he was in telemetry observation for a couple of days."

"Oh yes, CCU. Critical Care Unit."

"Yes. Well, Dad said your nurses were so charming, they'd give anyone the will to live. You can't underestimate that sort of thing in a hospital. The smallest detail can make a huge difference in the life of a desperately ill person."

"Why, Mr. Salto, I do appreciate your kind words. I must admit that we don't intentionally hire nurses based solely on their personality, but I'd like to think that our work environment is so pleasant that it brings out the best in our workers."

"Spoken like a true administrator. So, to what do I owe the pleasure of this banter?"

"Did you read Saturday's newspaper?"

"Straight to the point, eh? Yes, I did. I suspected there might be a connection between that and this phone call, but I didn't want to presume."

"Presume that we would be offended by GLK's publicly connecting us with their more, shall I say, sordid clients. Please, Mr. Salto, presume away. Our hospital is nearly fanatical about its image. These days, when all medical establishments are taking a beating from practically everyone, we must be particularly careful not to put ourselves in the limelight, or put ourselves in a position of sharing the limelight with companies renowned for maintaining huge profits no matter what the consequence to the environment or their neighbors' health."

"Nicely said."

"We were appalled."

"That's understandable."

"So, what I'm getting at is we will be asking GLK to withdraw as our counsel, but we would like to ask you first of your interest in representing us. We don't have any particular litigation matters pending right now, but there's always basic corporate stuff. And we would need a lawyer's presence during our board meetings."

Neil Salto had said that he would be honored to represent the hospital. He'd asked that Eileen fax or mail a proposal and he would check with his partners to make sure there was no conflict. When Eileen hung up the phone, she was smitten by Neil's easy manner - was he slightly flirting, too? *Oh, stop* - that was so different from the high-and-mighty grunting and harrumphing from GLK. She was also thrilled that this was so easy so far. So far—that was the key. Notifying GLK would be a chore. She knew they wouldn't, couldn't, give her a hard time, but there would be that wretched, underlying resentment. Like leaving a bad lover.

A quick board meeting was called and the members all grunted their agreement to can GLK. A couple of the members squinted and pursed their lips a bit but didn't say anything. It was final. GLK was out; Salto Duthie was in.

Eileen let Winston make the call to GLK. She had already done the hard work. And she figured it would be better coming from the president of the hospital.

Afterward a rift loomed large between the hospital and GLK. Nothing serious, just very clear snubbing at social events. GLK relied on the hospital as their most reputable client, lending the firm a certain prestige it wouldn't ordinarily have.

Gordon, Larson & Kammerer was a law firm steeped in tradition in the community. Maple Leaf's ancestors had been French immigrant soldiers who'd settled in the small Pennsylvania town in 1783 after helping Rochambeau's gang win the Revolutionary War. Once the smoke of war had cleared, young Falconne Gordon, Adolphe Larson, and Philippe Kammerer had the prescience to realize that the citizens of this new country would constantly engage in quarrels with one another, requiring barristers to sort through the confusion.

The hospital also had a history, going back to before the Civil War days. GLK had expected that these two old fogies of Maple Leaf—the law firm and the hospital—would be entwined together forever. So much for that. After the initial indignity of being *fired*, the law firm and the hospital settled into a comfortable compromise. They ignored each other. Seemingly.

CHAPTER 3

The ducks had settled into a sated clucking. Some circled and flew back to the lake, sputtering into the water like little dive bombers. Daniel stepped back from Eileen.

"What are you going to do now? Have they made their decision?"

Eileen pursed her lips. "Not yet. I'm not sure what I'm going to do if they close. I just know I can't let them raze this building for a stinkin' parking lot."

"Didn't you say that Virgil Ellingsworth was going to annex it to his manufacturing plant?"

Eileen paled. "I said no such thing. I couldn't care less what his plans are."

"Oh yes, I can see you're totally over him."

Eileen blushed. Dratted Daniel.

Eileen could hardly have a conversation with anyone these days without Virgil's name coming up, even now causing a fluttering in her chest. How irritating. Does he still grunt softly during orgasm? And lie back with his arms crossed on his chest afterward? She doubted that Daniel knew, although he had expressed appreciation for his tight little butt.

Oops. Daniel stared at her. Rolled his eyes.

"Uh, do you even need me around right now, or should I scuttle off into the bushes so you can continue your maudlin reverie uninterrupted?" he asked.

"Sorry, sorry."

He knew. He had been such a support. Since her parents had retired to Florida, she relied on her friends. She recalled his original question about Virgil and the hospital, hanging out there like a slash of lightning.

"Yes, that's the latest poop. So to speak."

Virgil wanted the hospital property for himself, undoubtedly for a brazenly opportunistic purpose that would further pump up his pockets. It was to become his own private carcass to discard as he saw fit. Over her own dead carcass.

"So, do you want to take a walk around the lake, take in some fresh air, clear out your head?" Daniel asked.

"No, I'm a little tired," Eileen said with a sigh.

Daniel said solicitously, "So, how are you feeling these days? You look great."

"I'm fine. It's just so much to think about."

"OK, hon. See you this weekend then?"

"Sure." Eileen managed a bright smile and hugged Daniel.

She trudged home, her head spinning with thoughts of Virgil. He's a one-man tropical typhoon, she thought glumly. There had been a commotion surrounding his nomination to the board.

―

The hospital had needed another board member. Shortly after GLK was discharged, Clyde Manville had retired from the board in disgust. He was chief executive of Convergent Modulators LLC, the company that had built this tiny town under the name Pete's Electric. The hospital needed another token "big gun." Virgil's name was suggested because he was young, rich blood. There was some question about his affiliation with Gordon, Larson & Kammerer; apparently, they represented his company, AGAF, but the connection seemed remote enough to not be a problem.

Eileen could never understand the rationale behind choosing board members. To perform properly on the board, it seemed obvious to Eileen, one should have a great deal of experience with hospitals. It seemed like a simple concept, but one that escaped the general consensus in choosing board members. Occasionally the board picked a token person from the volunteer organization of the hospital, but for the most part, the choices were men—almost exclusively men—in high positions at local companies.

Many emergency room patients critically injured in freak accidents on the job worked for the same companies whose executives graced the hospital board. One guy fell four stories from a scaffolding inside the electrical plant. Another accidentally hung himself in the ropes and pulleys. These incidents were rarely covered in the *Chronicle*. Yet the executives of those companies assured the public that they were completely impartial in making hospital policy that directly affected the treatments, and publicity, their injured employees received.

Not that there was any threat or suspicion that board members were involved with underhanded activity. Yet. It wasn't clear how they could influence treatment of their injured employees. But in this small town, there was still a good-old-boy network, and that was enough to make anyone nervous. Well, enough to make Eileen nervous.

Eileen knew that so much of how a hospital ran depended on legislative policy. Hospitals could not improvise on the fly. Still, there could be slip-ups—misplacing risk management forms, forging utilization review reports—couldn't there?

On the other hand, someone had to serve on the board, and it was mostly manufacturing-type people who lived around here.

Hospital board members were respected as godlike creatures. Ever since an incident back in the '60s in Charleston, when a young man had lost his leg to gangrene because hospital personnel ignored his complaints, hospital boards had been designed to oversee everything that went on in their facilities.

In the Charleston incident, a student had fractured his leg during a college football game. Emergency room doctors set his leg incorrectly in a cast, and the young man complained about pain and discomfort to several staff members who ignored him—and somehow also managed to ignore the increasing discoloration of his foot hanging outside the cast. He ended up losing his leg, and a jury awarded him thousands of dollars. Hospitals were, for the first time, held accountable and could be found liable for anything that happened to patients during their stay. Hospital board members were forced to evolve into more than figureheads and monthly poker players.

Like an adrenaline rush, Eileen's mind raced over the details of meeting Virgil. Why was it that sometimes she couldn't remember what she had for dinner yesterday but the tiniest details of her Virgil days were etched in gold in her brain? Eileen had been hustling around her boss's office trying to find his nail file kit. Winston had frantically asked her for it because he had a little loose cuticle flap that kept scraping against the papers, causing searing pain. He was preparing for that day's board meeting and trying to be as serious as possible, and he didn't appreciate a skin flap undermining his efforts.

"I think you used it last to pull out that splinter in your whatchamacallit," he'd said. Ew. Winston was always having little finger crises. Paper cuts, hangnails, cuticle flaps. The man's fingers were as delicate as a baby's derriere. He refused to go to a manicurist, although he could well afford it, because it seemed to him so extravagant and effeminate. So he simply chopped away at himself with his own nail file kit, and everyone had to suffer for it.

Suddenly, there he was. Virgil was so handsome it took her breath away. Boyishly so, yet with the smoothly groomed look of a well-maintained man. Impeccably-coiffed grayish hair (that was clearly blond at some point). The perfect spray tan—a little over the top, but what the heck. Nicely pressed suit. He didn't say anything, simply joined her in shuffling papers around and pretending to search.

After a bit he ventured, "Mind telling me what we're looking for?"

He grinned and she had to laugh. Then she got embarrassed. "M-m-may I help you?"

"Yes. I'm Virgil Ellingsworth, and I'm here for the board meeting. I'm the new trustee from American Grommets and Fasteners."

Eileen had seen his name earlier that month when she'd sent out the cards to board members with birthdays in March. It seemed like a silly thing to do; most of these men and women were kingpins in the community, and you'd think they'd scoff at something as trivial as a birthday card. But Winston swore it was important, and Eileen was sure there were several expensive focus groups organized to arrive at that most significant conclusion.

She had checked down the list. Virgil Ellingsworth. What a name. He was the new guy on the board. The chief executive of American Grommets and Fasteners. She loved the acronym, AGAF, and wondered if it was an accurate reflection of how they did business. She hoped not. The company had pretty much taken over the town during the past few years. Maple Leaf used to be known for its electronics and dog food industries, but now it was this grommets and fasteners stuff.

Separate folders were maintained for each of the board members, and Eileen had looked inside Mr. Ellingsworth's to see what sort of interesting tidbits she could discover. There were several of his company brochures. *Well, they design everything from flag holders to desk wiring to medical supplies*, she'd mused. *It seems the entire basis of civilization is grounded in grommets. What a feeling of empowerment for this Mr. Ellingsworth. Not bad for a Pisces. Happy birthday, Mr. Fish Man.* Grommets were also used in a special fish tackle, she noticed. *Let's just hope you don't hook yourself.*

On that day in her office, searching for Winston's nail file kit, Virgil Ellingsworth had cocked his head toward her.

"Oh, Mr. Ellingsworth, I'm Eileen Hanley. We're so honored that you're able to join us."

"Please, call me Virgil. Otherwise I'll wonder why you're talking to my father."

Breathless and feeling warm—ah yes, it took so little in those days—Eileen had walked Virgil over to the conference room where the rest of the board members were gathering. Loud murmurs of greeting filled the room as she left.

To no one in particular, she murmured, "He's obviously a popular choice. Got my vote."

As she headed back to her office to retrieve Winston, she heard "Eileen Hanley, we meet at last."

What was this? Another hunk-o-rama. Soft blue eyes. Dark blond hair, a little darker than that other guy—what's his name? Oh yes, Virgil. This man also sported just a little gray in the right places. How was it that men of a certain age wore it so well, while women with any gray looked like wretched hags? Lovely voice.

Eileen stood dazed. So many good-looking men, so little time…

"Neil Salto. We spoke on the phone a while back?" His smile could melt the candelabra. Should there be any.

"Oh, Mr. Salto, yes, I'm so glad to meet you."

She had forgotten that their new counsel from the firm of Salto Duthie would also be attending the board meeting. It was so easy for her to be flip and flirty on the telephone, but she was less confident about her wow-ability in person.

The handclasp was warm, firm, but not grippy. Nice gold band on the left. *Shoot. Oh well.* Hmm, Virgil hadn't offered his hand to her.

She walked with Neil into the boardroom and took a chair in the back. Oops, what about Winston? She jumped up to head out the door, but Winston rushed in and nodded to her. All was well in the presidential suite.

During that board meeting, like many others during those days, Eileen nearly nodded off listening to the treasurer's report. Fatigue still crept up on her at the most inopportune times, cancer's little bookmark. Thank goodness for board meetings; she could catch up on her afternoon naps.

She had found the lump herself, in bed. Those breast examination charts offered useful guidelines, but nothing beat old-fashioned self-love for discovering body anomalies. The woman's breast was beautiful, not to mention erotic; how could anyone, even oneself, touch it with such a calculating intent? You had to really get into it. Get passionate about it. *Believe me,* she'd always thought, *you'll still respect yourself in the morning.*

Her first reaction was "Oh, *that's* what one of those feels like!" Years of indoctrination of lumps, lumps, lumps—big lumps, little lumps, BB-size lumps, pretend-feeling them on those gooshy plastic boobies. Now here was one in real life, and it really didn't seem anything like those pretend lumps. She wasn't afraid; she was a little in awe of this out-of-place growth. Self-love turned to intense curiosity.

She kept feeling it and feeling it, trying to push it around. This didn't feel anything like a zit or a bruise or that little lump under her jawbone she would get during a cold. This was much bigger and more mystical that any of those. Her body had created this. What power. She immediately dived into her stash of medical books for an explanation. Of course it couldn't be cancer; her body couldn't betray her like that. It must be a fibroadenoma, a common benign condition, even though she was pushing the age limit for that. Fibroadenomas typically hit women in their early twenties.

She had reassured herself at the time, saying, "Well, I've always been young at heart."

CHAPTER 4

When Eileen returned home after leaving Daniel at the lake, she watched TV mindlessly for half an hour. Sometimes just the sound of voices was comforting. Voices she didn't have to respond to.

At Sunrise Hospital, Eileen was the president's right-hand man. She knew what was going on in the hospital before anyone else because Winston wanted her to read everything that came past his desk first.

Eileen was the executive assistant to Winston Kendall and privy to most of the hospital's operations, at least to the bidding of the board and the financial managers. Winston managed to do most of his own typing—he said he brainstormed through his fingers—so she wasn't bothered with that mundanity. She spent most of her day reading his reams of hospital reports, trade journals, and correspondence. She would summarize all of it, track deadlines, then pass it along to Winston. He eventually read it himself, but he found that her descriptions were pretty accurate, so he relied on her exclusively for her opinions and suggestions about things. Then she would draft responses for him. He usually made lots of changes, but he still respected her observations, and her work gave him a jump-start on the projects. Ordinarily, he would procrastinate until a project screamed for attention.

All in all, it was a pretty nice gig. Best of all, it didn't completely squelch the creativity she needed for her art, although it didn't leave much time for it either.

Right now, her paintings were beckoning. There were three that she had started and wanted to finish in time for Sunday's flea market.

She headed to her fancy art studio. It was that special little section between the kitchen and the living room. Other people would call it, well, the dining room, but she'd split it down the middle with an airy, Asian-style curtain. She was still renting, but she hoped to buy a condo soon. Miles, her ex boyfriend (they'd started during Springsteen's Julianne period but were over by Patti) claimed Eileen was waiting until she was unemployed—he had no faith in the hospital's future—and could really wow the mortgage lenders: "Yes, we must snap that girl up before she slips away." Her nest egg accumulated very slowly.

She carefully spread newspaper over the area of the floor where she worked and under her sketching table. She was very proud of that table. It was her first real purchase for her drawing business, a deduction even. Having deductions was so adult. So professional. One day she might actually show a profit. No more of this hobby stuff. Sitting on her artist's stool, with the bright light beaming on her fresh clean canvas and the brighter light streaming in from the window, made her feel like a queen. No matter that her kitchen table was two feet away and littered with crumpled half-read newspapers and magazines. She was doing the best she could.

She bent over her work in progress and squinted. There should be a brown dot right…there. She grabbed her teeniest brush out of the jar of gooey water and dabbed. Presto! Now the dog had a nose.

Painting her miniatures was her heart's work. Landscapes, wildlife, cavorting creatures, scenery, all on little three by five canvases. She had a perfect eye for detail and an extra advantage of twenty-fifteen eyesight. She figured her canvases were perfect for people who wanted an original painting but couldn't quite handle the thousand-buck price tag. Meaning the thousand-buck price tag of *other* artists.

She finally had enough prepared to display in tomorrow's flea market. It was the weekend go-to place. Not only was it a place to sell tossed-asides, there was a fine selection of antiques, furniture, and original arts and crafts, if you had the patience to slog through the junk to find it. It was a great way to display her work and get exposure in the community, cheaply. Rents for a display booth were little more than a handful of pocket change, and there was no obligation to show up every Sunday. It was possible to reserve your booth ahead of time, but mostly it was first come, first served. The loose arrangement was perfect for Eileen.

She framed her works in elegantly carved little frames and sold them for $75. People loved itsy, bitsy little things of art, probably because they were the only original artworks they could afford, so they pretended it was the most charming. Now she wanted to finish up a whimsical depiction of the Virginia reel, with little dancing dogs on one side and little cats on the other. The cats wore little dresses and bonnets, and the dogs wore little ties and vests.

And now for the coup de grace. She peered down at the piece and smeared the brush daintily over the pink paint. *Needs a slab of Smithfield ham, definitely. The kind with the little round bone in the middle.*

This was her trademark, adding one object that was completely out of place, like Hidden Pictures in *Highlights* magazine. Just dumb little things—a bumblebee, a copper penny, a peanut in its shell. Once when she felt particularly frisky, she elongated a particular bit of doggie anatomy. No one ever figured it out. With the tiny images so squished together, she could get away with it. Mainstream gift shops in town loved her stuff. She figured she would eventually settle on one particular trademark, but for now she enjoyed mixing it up. It was a good way to keep her skills honed. She didn't want to get stuck drawing the same scenes all the time.

When Sunday finally came, she bundled up her latest paintings, packaged them carefully between towels, and placed them in her Tupperware carryall. She might have to add to her once a month flea market schedule, she thought, especially if she was going to be out of a job soon. Winston had assured her that he would take her wherever he ended up—that is, during the rare times they dared discuss it in such negative tones—but there was no guarantee that even he would find another position.

The flea markets were also a great place to people watch. And get a tan. *Oops, that's right, get a tan. Break out the sunblock and heavy cotton cover-ups. Be afraid, always afraid, of postcancer residual side effects.* Life effects, as she called them. Tans were a no-no. She really needed to stay out of the sun, or if sun exposure was necessary, needed to slather on a couple centimeters of lotion or wear all-over clothing.

On this particular Sunday afternoon—not too cool, not too hot—she lounged in her comfy director's chair, handmade pillows for seat cushions, adjusted the umbrella, donned her shades, and readied herself for another great day of people watching. Lots of couples today.

Eileen had married in her early twenties because it was the thing to do. No woman hit her midtwenties in Maple Leaf, Pennsylvania, without being married, unless her flesh had sprouted oozing porcupine quills. Even then, she would have offers. At a rally following the Three Mile Island incident, she'd met Glenn, who had seemed brilliant and intense and the perfect man for her. His knowledge of hot fuel rods, vibration in the pumps, and relieving reactor pressure had her gasping for more, and she looked forward to a lifetime of stimulation with this man. But it was not to be. His intensity turned into fanaticism, and between passing out pamphlets on street corners and shouting garbled speeches on the square, he lost his archivist job at the York Public Library and began to dress like a vagabond.

Eileen had tired of it. She was working her butt off—at the hospital, at home, and with what little time she could squeeze in for her painting—and here this guy was moaning about not meeting his "potential." Not being "understood." Being a woman, she'd felt it was her responsibility to help him on his way, so she'd enlisted Daniel to help design and print some pamphlets. She'd submitted blurbs to the newspaper to advertise a few of Glenn's "talks." But that was enough. She'd bailed before reaching the martyr category and filed for divorce after three years. Telemarketing would become his destiny.

Marriage was highly overrated and too much of a sacrifice. She preferred to think of it as a license for subjugation of women, giving men a ready sexual mate, maid, and mommy, someone on whom he could shower abuse with impunity and at the same time expect his every need to be taken care of. Why so many women fell for it, she would never understand. Every time, it seemed, she got involved with a man and let her guard down, he started to bark orders: "Do you really want to wear those clothes?" "Shouldn't you wear your hair different?" "I don't want you to go out tonight after work." "I think you should eat this food." "I don't think you should eat that food." "Do you really think you should exercise so much? Or so little?" "I think you should wear different makeup."

Eileen shuddered. How did women ever allow themselves to get in that predicament?

And it was even worse now, she thought, because not only were women still expected to do the same things they'd always done—clean, cook, screw on demand, caretake a grown man and his sniveling brats—they were also expected to work full-time so he'd never run low on beer money.

Unfortunately, Eileen was OK-looking—nearly stereotypically so, she thought—with blue eyes; medium-length, faded blond hair that she half-heartedly "brightened" a few times a year; the much-touted symmetrical facial features; athletic body; and a wicked sense of humor. She should have sold laundry detergent on TV commercials. Men were always trying to poke their sticky heads into her business. She tried acting hostile to hold off the attention, but it was against her nature, and men adored her even more. All of those fancy pants, hovering over Eileen, flapping their sleek Armani jackets, waiting for her to sprinkle a few crumbs.

If she could find the man of her dreams who felt the same way about her and actually had something to offer her rather than draining her life's essence, she would get married again in a minute. She figured that was a lofty enough goal to keep her safe for a while.

She had thought she'd met such a man in Virgil. But he was already married and likely draining life's essence from another woman, which naturally freed him to be utterly charming to Eileen, at least for a little while.

OK, time to pay attention. People wanted to pay for her works of art, not watch her in a daze. A well-scrubbed, carefully coiffed couple pushing a stroller held out two paintings to her.

"We'd like both of these. Can you do better on the price?"

Eileen held back a grimace. It was a fair question, of course, but this wasn't like haggling over yard-sale lawn furniture. She always dreaded the question. Still, it never failed to come.

"Sure. How about $140 for both?"

The couple and their darling blue-eyed toddler all smiled with blond perfection.

"Deal."

It was a rough-straggle negotiation, won with perfectly honed strategic prowess. He might get some tonight, Eileen thought.

Eileen finished the transaction and hoisted herself back up on the chair.

She often wondered why a marriage license was the only state license that didn't have to be renewed periodically. Every few years or so, every couple should go to a magistrate, look each other in the eye, and repeat their vows. Rather than having to go through so much effort to dissolve it though divorce, a marriage should only be good for a specific period of time—with term limits, better yet—and the couple should be forced to go through at least a minimal effort to renew it. She couldn't see how it did society any good to force unhappy couples to stay together. Sure, divorce was always doable, but society had turned it into a monstrous, kid-mangling machine. Be real. What kid hasn't thought at some time or another about how nice it would be to have different parents for a change? And once a divorce is pending, the kid realizes how much benefit he can get by pretending he's miserable and playing one guilty parent off another.

The human brain was much too complex—wasn't it?—to be content with the simplicity of a lifelong, never-changing family unit. Wasn't the workings of the human brain comparable to the vast mysteries of the universe? As naturally as an explosive supernova scattering cosmic dust particles, as each couple split they would still have some responsibility for the kids. Eventually the kids could have as many as eight to ten "parents" doting on them and paying for their college and sneaking them $50 bills in their Pierre Cardin coat pockets. And there would be all of the grandparents! What kid could hate that?

No one ever knows for sure that they've made a good decision regarding their choice of marriage partner at the time of the wedding. Usually the wedding is nothing more than a lavishly orchestrated event to display to the world a white taffeta fluff-blob that is the bride. (Eileen's own ceremony had been a tasteful, cozy affair at a small wedding chapel in Lancaster, officiated by a kindly cleric who was missing both thumbs and kept dropping the paperwork. She was more intent on watching him fiddle about—how did he lose his thumbs?—than on the words she'd repeated.)

After her divorce from Glenn, she was very happy, although she never doubted she would hook up with another man someday. Maybe even get married again; men usually insisted upon it at some point. But for the time being, she enjoyed having lots of men friends who served a variety of purposes. That way, she got the best out of all of them and didn't have to suffer any of the undesirable stuff. After a few hours of entertainment: "Oops, look at the time, I have to go home [to my precious solitude]. It's been great seeing you. We'll have to do it again real soon." That was so much more favorable to being forever linked to only one person. ("Shopping alone? Where's Glenn? How's Glenn doing? I heard Glenn speak last weekend, and it's only a matter of time before Glenn is discovered!") As if her own life was spent lurking under rock beds.

No, it was her experience that as soon as you allow one man to be *the* one, then not only were you limited to his sparse good qualities, but you also had to endure all of the bad stuff. Griping, nagging, belching, farting, and, most dreary of all, having to listen to his interminably boring conversations and foggy attempts at humor: "Gosh, honey, the sun's been out for two whole days now. Pretty soon you'll have to water the lawn. Hahahaha hahahahahaha. Hey, what's the matter with you? Where's your sense of humor?"

Well, dear, I think I left it on the rope hanging around my neck. Now, where's the nearest rafter I can pitch this puppy over?

However, Eileen loved a tender man. Seldom seen, seldom experienced.

Men seemed to hone their lovemaking skills with what they saw in porno movies. That rough jabbing and stabbing might make women scream on the screen, but not in pleasure. She's an actress; that's what she's paid to do. The only thing that truly distinguishes a man above all other men these days is his lovemaking ability. If he can't do that, *blaaaat*, time's up, give 'em the hook, it's time to move on. If he's a lover, lure him in and hold on. That's a relationship worth nurturing. There's a whole lot you can put up with from a man if he steams your peas just so. Yessiree.

"OK, so is this the one about men or breasts or life or dot, dot, dot? Sorry, didn't mean to make you jump." Daniel stood with two hot dogs slathered with chili, onions, and mustard.

Eileen brightened. "Well, well. Showing up with a treat like that, you can scare the bejeebers out of me anytime you like. No, I'm just silently railing about the usual, as usual."

"Maybe you should chit-chat a bit more with your neighbor artists—it might keep you from turning into a burbling bag lady when you're fifty."

"And thwart my ultimate destiny? I wouldn't think of it. Here, let me hold those while you get us drinks. Need any money?"

"Nah, I'm good."

Daniel dodged the crowd and returned shortly with two lemonades. Eileen sank her teeth into the hot dog. "Mmm, boy. Not exactly health food, but sometimes, you know, you just have to have one."

"Absolutely."

Suddenly her eyes brimmed with tears. "What is the matter with me?"

Daniel didn't know but patted her arm.

CHAPTER 5

At work on Monday morning, the hospital alarm went off. Everyone glanced at each other—what now? Usually, there was advance notice of fire alarm drills. Eileen peeked out into the hall as if actually seeing the red bell ringing would somehow clear things up. She smelled smoke.

"Hey, uh, there's smoke out here, Winston."

She grabbed an extinguisher and ran out. A quick thought to her fire prevention training last year led to brief panic. Was this an A or B or C fire or all three? She glanced at the extinguisher. Where in the heck was the lettering? Oh, there it was. It was labeled A, B, C. What do you know. But wasn't there also a D extinguisher? What did that mean? Maybe this was a D fire. Oh dear Lord almighty, just get to the fire.

Luckily, Benjamin from radiology came along and freed her from her alphabetic quandary. He grabbed the extinguisher from her and ran through the computer room to the switchboard office. Smoke and sparks flew from the wall heater. Eliza, the operator, clung to the wall, her face twisted in a silent scream. Eight switchboard lights were blinking like a crazed tic tac toe game. Benjamin quickly sprayed and smothered the sparks. Outside, the fire engines screamed their way to the hospital. Fire fighters weighed down with equipment clomped their way to the computer room, evaluated the damage, announced that the threat was over, and clomped their way back outside.

Eileen trudged to her office, wondering when the next calamity would strike. Nerves were on edge, and just in time for another board meeting. The board generally met once a month, unless there was something urgent to handle. Then they might meet several times a week until the situation was sorted out. Eileen didn't go to all of the meetings, but Winston usually wanted her there to be his second pair of ears and eyes. She dreaded today's noon meeting.

Several months ago, it was announced that there were five lawsuits filed against the hospital. It was unheard of. This was a small town; no one was litigious-minded, as nearly every business was owned or run by a neighbor or family member. If you had a problem, you just talked it out over coffee and whoopie pies. If something really went wrong, well, sometimes things just happened. It was sad and unfortunate, but it was also just life. Eileen noticed the law firm's name at the bottom of all the pleadings: Gordon, Larson & Kammerer.

She reread the report on her desk for the sixth time, her eyes unfocussed, her brain scrambled, and decided to head early into the board room. Lunch would have to wait for probably dinnertime. Slowly and uncharacteristically quiet, the rest of the group filed in, including Winston, who sat next to Eileen.

Otto Feldstein, one of the senior members, started the meeting by mentioning the possibility of an out-of-state corporation buying out the hospital, if, *harrumph*, (there it was!) Sunrise could stay out of trouble. The harrumph signaled his doubt loud and clear.

Eileen's eyes had widened, and she jabbed Winston.

"Uh, what? Stop that," he hissed. "He's just kidding."

"No, he's not. You always say that, and then whatever it is happens."

"We'll talk about this later."

Eileen glanced at him, frowning. She noticed Neil hunkered on the windowsill and mouthed, "What the...?" He just nodded.

She decided then to doze through the rest of the meeting. Staying awake was painful. However, sometimes dozing was more painful. Her mind was still digesting the world of Virgil and its acid-reflux-inducing humiliation. Luckily, he wasn't at today's meeting.

Back in those early post-treatment days, Eileen would find herself walking home with Virgil. after she got off work. Usually the board meetings ended around the same time that she got off work, and he would catch up with her on the sidewalk. He lived on Spruce Street in a wonderful old mansion surrounded by oak trees and high, neatly-trimmed shrubbery. At first sight of the grounds, Eileen was certain that the Ellingworths' monthly landscaping bill could feed a large cluster of World Wrestling champs. There was a pool. The first few times Virgil walked with her as far as his house, and she would walk the rest of the way to hers. Outside the gated driveway, he would say, "Here's where I get off," always with a wink and a grin. When the time came to advance the strategy, he offered to walk her clear to her house, truly an act of charity since it was another seventeen blocks.

"Let me just drop off my things at my place and I'll walk you home."

"Are you kidding? It's nearly another mile. You don't have to do that."

"I don't feel like going inside just yet. Besides, I didn't make it to my workout today and I still feel a little cramped up. Need to get those endorphins flowing. Before I get home. Where there's no chance of endorphin activity. Ha, ha, ha."

Eileen knew better than to rise to that dangerous bait. Well, maybe not. "Is your wife gone for the evening?"

He just laughed harder, as if she had said something hysterically funny.

"I'm sorry, is your wife gone permanently? Like, dead?"

"No, no, nothing like that. Just—never mind. How 'bout we toss for it?"

"Huh?"

"Got my lucky dime here. Quick, heads or tails?" He tossed the object in the air.

She blurted, "Tails!"

He caught it and flipped it over. "Tails it is. I get to walk you home."

"Now, wait a minute."

He was impossible; he just laughed and took her hand and she melted.

"You can keep the dime," he said.

She looked down at it. "Whoa, this is one of the old ones—1942."

"Yes, it's my lucky Mercury dime. I started collecting them when I was a kid. Got a drawerful of em."

"This one's so shiny. I've seen a few of these, and they're usually caked with black gunk."

"I keep one with me all the time. Spend it only on something special."

His eyes glimmered and danced. Her heart went to her throat. She knew she shouldn't be doing this, whatever *this* might be. But darn it, she'd just finished a tedious year of cancer treatment and was so thrilled it was over and here was this my-oh-my handsome and gracious man flirting with her. She felt like the heavens had opened up and rained down upon her waves of sunshine to clear away her misery. She pocketed the dime.

They walked in pleasant silence.

He played serious, saying, "It's just that, uh, the thought of my wife being a source of endorphin production is very amusing. I had never conceived of that possibility. We have sort of a business relationship—cordial, but that's about it."

Eileen did a double take then remembered, *Oh yes, the wife thing. Here we go.* She took the plunge.

"Sounds dreadful." What was the matter with her?

He laughed again, a little more naturally this time, and they stopped at the intersection. It was a busy intersection with no light. As she peered down the street for oncoming traffic, he held her back a little with his arm in front of her body. Oh, she was a sucker for that. It was such a gentle, involuntary gesture. Gallant yet understated. Then he took her hand and they scampered across. Her heart heaved to her throat. There was a bit of activity southward as well. This guy was her dream. She couldn't believe this was happening. He was married. But he would get a divorce. How could he not? She already had it figured out.

At her door, he didn't linger. He grinned and said, "Hey, I really enjoyed this. You are great company." He winked and quickly turned to go home.

Occasionally, he offered to drive her home, when he had a huge briefcase to haul around or it was raining or snowing. Then he suggested they stop and get a bite to eat on the way home. Nothing fancy, pizza or stromboli. Then the cozy French café. They were all little drops of honey-soaked temptation he would trickle her way, dainty morsels luring her in. All of it could be considered innocent, but she knew she was being seduced, and she loved every tantalizing moment. She wondered what he would do next. She knew she was being manipulated, but she loved it.

By this time she'd started to fall big time. She was ready to do him. She had a funny feeling about it. She knew something was up, something she should deal with, but she just didn't care. She didn't even want to hear what it was. This guy was it. She had never felt like this before. Having just recovered from cancer treatments, it seemed to her that her first priority was herself. Virgil's attentions made her feel fabulous, gave her something to hope for, made her feel like a queen. A far cry from the cobwebby, droopy, leaden feeling that had been a fixture of her body for so long. This smoothed out everything. It felt so right.

This is how it would always go.

"Same time next week?" Virgil touched Eileen's flushed cheek.

"Well, I don't know. I guess so, unless something better comes along."

And she would burst into giggles and wrap her arms around her beautiful Virgil and shower kisses all over his face.

He would grin and kiss her back. Then he would take her arms and gently lock them around the back of her neck, and they would kiss deeply and passionately until they became woozy with it. He would press his body hard against hers, and she would press back, and soon it became a bit of a wrestling match and they would both burst into laughter again and fall down on the bed.

"I really must get going," he would say. "I've got to get the car to the mechanic before he closes or I'm never going to get out of here at all. My bewitching one, I will return."

They would share one more brief kiss, and he would dash out.

He was the love of her life.

Too bad he was married.

The following week, he'd come again.

"You just go in there and lie down, and I'll be with you in a minute." Eileen heart couldn't thump any harder.

He removed his clothing and lay on the bed. He had to hand it to her, there was a nice cross breeze in her apartment. It had been a while since he'd spent so much time in an apartment. (Or was it a condo? He couldn't remember.) He'd lived at home with his parents until he'd married Jenaveev.

His family home had been a cavernous place; there really wasn't any point in him living anywhere else. Paying to live anywhere else.

The cool air tickled the little hairs on his body, stimulated and relaxed him. He felt at peace here. Apartment living wasn't so bad. Or was it a condo? He glanced up at the mirror above the dresser.

"Hey, is that my dime?"

It hung down from the mirror on a delicate silver chain. He had almost forgotten about it.

He wondered if she ever wore it around her neck. The dime would land somewhere between those lovely breasts. Even the right one, the one that was a little tipsy.

She came out wearing nothing but a long, baby-blue silk scarf draped loosely in strategic places. "Yes, sir, indeed it is."

He forgot the question.

She slunk toward the bed and murmured, "I've done some very important research…and intend to…dazzle…and amaze…you with the facts."

She dangled the scarf above his body and lightly touched him here and there. He was clearly aroused but played it cool.

"Oh, is that so? Do tell."

He put his hands behind his neck and lay back, utterly vulnerable.

She threaded the scarf down and under his leg, his arm, one foot then the other. Other parts. *Slip, swish. Slip, swish.* Slowly.

"This is crucial information. I must swear you into strictest confidence." She bent over and whispered slowly, "Do you think you can keep a secret?"

A tiny lick on his earlobe. A little bitty one. Then she backed off.

He adopted his official tone. "My dear, you must be aware that confidentiality is the hallmark of any business. And I am, above all, a businessman. A very successful one at that." He blinked in emphasis.

She whispered, "Well, you almost have me…convinced. But…I…might…need…mmmm…a little more…proof."

He'd had enough. He rolled over, grabbed her, and kissed her hard. Their limbs intertwined. The passion tumbled over and around them, and they got caught up in it for several moments.

Then she broke away in laughter and blurted out, "If you must know, the Mercury dime is a symbol of liberty. It's actually a winged liberty dime, not really Mercury the Roman god. The thing on her head is a Phrygian—say *frij-ian*—cap, worn by freed slaves in Roman times. It was first minted in 1916 and continued until 1945. Now I must kill you."

"You've got to catch me first."

They rolled over and over one another in frenzied abandon, shutting down the realization that neither of them was completely free.

———

It was a miracle. As tired as she was most of the time, Eileen always had plenty of energy for this. However, this time she was distracted. What was that twittering orb reflecting along the wall? It moved in time with their love making—or did it? No, it moved a bit more rapidly, quite jazzed.

Usually Eileen was transfixed in the act, absorbing the beauty of commingled souls. But this time she wondered if the light was a reflection from his watch. She felt along his arms. No, he wasn't wearing one. Certainly no wedding ring. Heaven forbid. She almost started giggling. He was usually very patient with her often misplaced giggles, but this time, during—*oooh*—that moment, no, it wasn't a very good time. Then he hit *the* spot. My oh my, no, she would have to think about this later.

She lay back. What was she worried about before? Oh yes. The small, round beam was still there, fluttering, but slowly now. She tried to follow it back to its source. The Mercury dime was ablaze in sunshine. For sure, the glittering orb was a reflection from that little coin hanging from her mirror.

"Penny for your thoughts?"

Oh yes, there was a man in her bed. A very good place for him to be.

"How 'bout a dime? Look over there." She pointed.

"Oh, do I have to? Work, work, work." He struggled to lift himself on his elbow and was nearly blinded by the sight. "Hey, I told you it was lucky."

After he left, she sauntered over to her mirror and picked up the dime to get a closer look at it. It felt warm in her palm. Her fingers traced the word LIBERTY.

After the first few months of seeing Virgil and making love, he'd actually told her he loved her. What a shocker. She'd never expected that. That seemed to change the dynamics of this whole arrangement. *I love you.* What the heck was that supposed to mean? What about the wife thing? It didn't make sense.

But he'd seemed so good-natured, almost giddy, about it, that she went along with it and indulged in the sun-kissed feeling that goes with being loved by someone you adore. The logistics would work out later. She reveled in reciprocating the sentiment every chance she could. But as the months passed, she could never recreate that moment. As it turned out, he never said it again. At first, she thought he had just gotten shy, or in a man-like way had decided that since he'd said it once, he was covered for all time. That it would be redundant. That it would sound desperate. She had all sorts of explanations. But as the relationship wore on, she began to get crankier and crankier with the arrangement.

She tested him and said, "I love you." And waited. He said nothing. She looked at him coldly and said, "You can go home now."

"What's the matter, honey? You sound a little upset."

"I believe I've had quite enough of you for right now."

Virgil didn't press his luck by pursuing this line of conversation further, and he quietly gathered his things and left, no doubt thinking, *I can get this crap at home.*

Still, she became smitten again when he talked about his kids, Nick and Noelle. Their mother had this Christmas thing, he said. They were twins, should be about twelve years old now. Eileen was amused at the "about." A truly dedicated dad.

Her eyes brightened when Virgil talked about his children. She and Glenn never had kids, and she would have loved to. He'd always growled that she was too much of a kid herself; how could she expect to raise kids of her own? They were a *huge* responsibility. What he really meant was that he needed her to take care of him. There could be no diversions from that. He really needed that more than anything. Who would pick up his socks? Who could he bemoan his unfulfilled potential to? So with the last soul-wrenching jolt of his withdrawal method, she'd had to skedaddle. *See ya, honey, you big overgrown kid, you.*

From Virgil, she couldn't hear enough about Nick and Noelle. She imagined that she was the mother and Virgil the father and they had this very normal, traditional family like a '50s sitcom. She experienced their entire childhood vicariously through Virgil. She grew to love the little suckers. She even began to think, *The heck with him, it's the kids I want.*

Occasionally, a teeny little discrepancy would rear its ugly head. She would never get the endearment she wanted from the kids if she were the cause of the marital breakup. They must love the mother, no matter what she was like. Virgil was getting more and more reckless about where they were seen and what they did in public. She loved it; they seemed like a bona fide couple. But the kids? No way could she let them see something like that. That would be too hurtful and humiliating.

The tricky part was letting him know. She was sure she was right, but she had a sneaking suspicion that he wouldn't be as charmed by the idea. But by God, there were plenty of good, valid reasons for him to leave the wife, none of which had anything to do with her. The woman was a walking loser, apparently. Why should Eileen be the fall guy for that situation? He's the one who'd gotten himself into the mess; let him extract himself. Not that she wasn't willing to help him out, but this was something he had to do himself. She would not be the reason. The other woman. The woman the kids would deplore for splitting up their parents.

So she just had to say no more. Forget about it. The wife has got to go. Sorry. And that would be the end of it.

She didn't want to do it on her turf. If she didn't get the response she desired, she wanted to be able to make a quick getaway. If they were at her house, she would never be able to get rid of him. His eyes would glisten with tears, and he would cajole her to rethink, all the while trying to wrap his body around hers. She was always a sucker for the physicality of a relationship.

But she knew he would agree with her. They were meant to be together. None of this made sense with the wife thing, even he had to see that.

It would be at the steak restaurant. She would dress modestly. This was not to be a coquettish plot.

She had offered to meet him there. She couldn't trust herself to be alone with him at her place for even a moment. Even if he picked her up in his car, she might be tempted to pull him inside her apartment. One thing she could always count on was her own hopelessness.

One thing she didn't count on was her out-of-control nerves. She was shaking and sweating. Maybe it was the flu and she would pass out and choke on her tongue and writhe uncontrollably or… no, no those weren't flu symptoms, she had to keep walking toward him. Ugh. He was sitting in their usual spot, smiling broadly, then stood up to greet her. A small smile started to creep along her lips but she bit down to keep her control. This was so hard for her, unnatural, really, why couldn't he just do the right thing on his own? She shouldn't have to be this demanding.

He could read her stern expression. They'd been through this before.

She sat down without saying a word and unfolded the napkin on her lap. Point blank, he had asked her, "What do you want?"

When Eileen told him, he said, "It'll never happen. I will never leave my wife. I've told you that." He laughed slightly, thinking she must be kidding, that this was still on her mind.

Eileen's insides churned into knots. Her brain, seemingly shaken to its limits during her chemo treatments, found a new atomic bomb going off inside. More mental convulsions. But she couldn't let on that she was affected. Not just yet. She would hold it together for one last precious minute.

She shook her head. She would show him her most civil comportment. "Well, then, if you can say with complete confidence, as you seem to be doing, that you will never leave your wife, even in light of all that we have together, then you can bet that I can say with just as complete confidence that it's over. We have nowhere to go under the current circumstances." She bit her quivering lip to keep from bursting into tears, or at least from adding, "And you can kiss my ass."

She stepped away from the table, her head held high by pure will. Her filet mignon medium-rare *avec truffes broules* stayed behind.

He was visibly shaken. He had no idea that she had the power to truly resist him this way. He had money, damn it.

On the other hand, she did like meat a little too much to be classy.

She had kept walking, determined not to show emotion until she was in a safe haven. Home. She nodded hello to the neighbor, opened her door, put her keys in the little basket on the counter, took off her watch and shoes, and checked her answering machine. No blinking light. Then she collapsed.

The cellular structure of her brain nearly burst with the unfairness of it. *It is the reality, but—oh no, no—it is so, so wrong.* She sobbed and writhed until she was worn out. Then suddenly she mused, *This is good exercise.* With that offhand thought, she knew she would be fine. Eventually. She looked at herself in the mirror, the same mirror where she once claimed to see in her eyes their happy future together, and swore silently to Virgil, *Your life will be utter crap from now on.*

It wasn't a threat. She had no power to do anything directly to him. She wasn't going to turn this into a *Fatal Attraction* thing. He simply wasn't worth it. Nothing really was, and she couldn't lose her own dignity that way. No, she just simply knew that if he was capable of living such a duplicitous life, he deserved to suffer the depths of hell. She would muster together the powers of all of her guardian angels, gods, ghosts, muses, moons, and ascending planets and incur their collective wrath toward messing up his life. Forever.

For starters, she knew she had that picture of him from the hospital board pamphlet. One can do a lot of damage to a person through a picture. Or maybe it was just superstition. Yes, that was it. Just superstition. She took the picture out, looked at it briefly, but as soon as tears started welling up, she sprang into action. She didn't want to get waylaid by a bunch of stupid sentimentality.

She took a hammer and pounded his image into oblivion. *Bam, bam, bam.* Then she took a Phillips screwdriver and gouged out his eyes. Poke, poke. And his mouth. The picture was shredding quite well at this point. Then she took the ragged remains and threw them in the sink, lit a match, and watched the remnants shrivel and burn into black ash. She loved the way the sizzling embers along the edges curled into a perverted grin.

Since she was in the bathroom, it was only convenient to throw the whole thing in the toilet. And all that activity caused her a particular urgency, so she sat on the toilet, did her business, and with much relief flushed the whole mess.

It's over. His fate is in his own hands.

What a feeling of redemption. She was cleansed. She went outside for a walk and a soft ice cream cone.

When she got home, she showered. On the way back to the bedroom, she stepped on something that stuck to her bare foot—the Mercury dime. It had fallen on the floor, and she reached down to peel it off her foot. The chain had slipped off. She felt like throwing the coin down the toilet too. Virgil had used it as a ruse to charm himself into her life. Then she remembered. It was a symbol of liberty. His careless use of it to encroach on her life wasn't the dime's fault. He was an opportunistic idiot. She found the chain under her bureau, laced the dime back through, and carefully hung it back on her mirror.

She immersed herself in her miniatures. For her own amusement, she painted little frogs with huge erect penises hopping toward hatchet-wielding rabbits ready to slice them off. She realized that she had some issues, but she knew it was just temporary. She painted over the frogs with bouquets of roses and baby's breath, planning to sell the canvases to elderly ladies.

Despite assuring herself that this was indeed the best, and only, way to end things, it hit her again, and she collapsed in a weeping heap on the bed. The phone rang and she jumped up, thinking, *Virgil? He's getting the divorce!* Then she kicked herself for thinking the stupid thing.

"Hello?"

"Hey, beautiful!"

Daniel always knew what to say.

"Hi, sweetheart, how are you?"

The sobbing undertones to her voice must have come through loud and clear.

"Now, wait a minute. What's going on? Your dog die—again?"

She laughed in spite of herself. He could be so goofy. "No, I finally read the riot act to Virgil. Now, don't sniff like that. I know you never liked him."

"Like him, shmike him. I don't know the man from dirt. I only knew that he treated you like crap. That's the only part I care about."

She teared up again, loving the fact that her friends were so fiercely loyal to her. She didn't know how she ever inspired that kind of loyalty, but she was always grateful for it. Even if she didn't particularly think that they were right.

"He actually treated me quite well. The only problem we had was that pesky little sleeping-with-another-woman-every-night thing."

"You mean the wife. He slept with his wife."

"If you want to call her that."

"I don't want to call her anything. She was his wife, *non*?"

"All right, all right, the stupid wife. She was more the other woman than I ever was, though."

"Yeah, yeah. We all know you had the purest, most beautiful love ever imagined in the history of mankind since Tristan and Isolde, but frankly your playing the tragic heroine just doesn't become you. The guy was simply a creep. And an opportunist. He wasn't doing you or his wife any favors."

"I know, I know. I'll see that for myself eventually. Can't I just hurt now? Indulge me, please. I feel so drained. I really thought he was baiting me to make him leave his wife."

"He probably was, but he's too stupid to realize it. Eileen? Oh, come on now, honey. Hey, Lukey was asking about you again. If you don't relieve that poor guy's misery, I'm liable to do it for you."

Daniel had always had a little crush on Luke in Housekeeping at the hospital.

"And, hey, I gotta show you the latest look in business cards. We came up with a design that's a real doozy. How about if I come over and pick you up and we go to that little Mexican place on the corner? Nothing like drowning your sorrows in some cheese-slathered pork burritos, rice, and beans. Mmmmmmm, grease."

Good old Daniel.

"I'm not really hungry," Eileen said. "Well, on second thought, maybe I am. Let's go."

She quickly slipped into her comfiest pair of leggings; actually, they were a sort of underskiing garment with cushy, warm fabric against the skin. She lived in them all winter, which sometimes lasted eight months in southeastern Pennsylvania.

As they swung around the corner to El Burro, they passed the familiar faces, bloated with alcoholism and self-abuse, of the street people who hung around the area. As usual, they passed them without a glance, but suddenly Daniel halted in his tracks and looked back at them.

"Someone you know?"

"No, no. I just thought of something. No, never mind." Then he glanced down at her. "You know, leggings aren't supposed to be baggy."

"Well, sheesh, I know they're a little old, but I don't want to be one of those women who wear screaming Lycra." "Yeah, some people are pretty presumptuous about one size fits all."

They headed into the restaurant. Eileen now felt quite hungry at the thought of the hot, comfort-food meal facing her. And the good company. Plus she had those baggy leggings to fill.

They ordered and Daniel got up, to use the restroom, she supposed, although he usually left with some sort of twisted euphemism, such as "drain the main vein." This time he simply left. *Oh well, maybe even he gets tired of listening to himself,* she thought.

She looked around the room for a while and made her usual conclusions about the nature of the relationships of the other diners. First date, second date, tonight's-the-night sexual tension, long-term partners. It was always fairly easy to tell by the couple's demeanor the stage of their relationship

There was first date over in the corner. First and last date. Their faces practically cracked under their forced smiles and nervous clutching at their wine stems.

Second date was a little harder to identify. She often confused them with the long-married. Polite conversation, a bit less laughter, more introspection. Do we want to go for the third date? Is this worth leaving my dog/cat/kids/TV for?

And the long-married: God, I can't wait till we get home to see the dog/cat/kids/TV. Very similar.

The most intriguing, of course, were the tonight's-the-night couples. Over there, in the other corner, of course. Their sexual energy vibrated the room. The girl positively shone with the assurance of having chosen, and the guy was so nervous with anticipation that he dropped the salt shaker. *Splaat* and little salt piles spread all over the table. They bent over and knocked heads, now nearly hyperventilating from glee.

The foursome across the aisle obviously consisted of a long-term couple and another couple who were just thrown together, maybe a blind date. The long-term couple barely touched their food as they talked loudly, laughed, and made big arm gestures to drive home the point of the discussion. The other two laughed politely and appropriately and glanced at each other, as if trying to feed off the exuberance of the lively couple to lend strength to their own budding relationship. My goodness, if we both are enjoying ourselves with this couple, then *we* must be a good couple too!

Eileen hoped they were planning to go to a long movie afterward, as opposed to a hockey game or a party where they would be expected to interact. The long-term couple would be exhausted once they got home, probably would undress carelessly, he in his boxer shorts and 1987 state fair T-shirt and she in her Virginia is for Lovers T-shirt, and they would collapse in bed without saying a word to one another. In a few years, they would probably divorce.

She was distracted by an annoying conversation from the table next to her. Two women, one yammering on and on like a jackhammer. "And then he said… and then I said…and then I go…and then he went…and then I was like…"

She never came up for air. Her friend sat next to her, cobwebs forming on her eyeballs, wishing, oh, please, if the cloth napkin were only long enough to twist into a noose or maybe catch fire in a heavenly act of spontaneous combustion…

"OK, so tell me the life stories of our fellow diners." Daniel had finally returned to the table, looking smug.

"What? Oh, hi. Success once again prevails in the bathroom? What took you so long?"

"Uh. Oh, everything's fine. Since I had some extra money from my last raise, I thought I'd share some with those guys outside."

Eileen narrowed her eyes at him. She had never heard anything so ridiculous. He never gave money to those guys. Why hadn't he handed it to them when they'd passed earlier? She chose to ignore it. *He'll 'fess up when he's good and ready.* He wore a slanted half smile and avoided her eyes.

They ordered their usual heap of meat, rice, and beans smothered with cheese and dived into the mess. Mexican was the ultimate comfort food.

"Take a gander at some of our new card stock designs for business cards. Beveled edges."

He fanned them out on the table

"What is it exactly you do again? I know you've told me—"

"Dozens and dozens of times?" He took a deep breath, mocking anger. "OK. I create and systemize composite graphics symposiums for sales collateral and multidisciplinary functions." Daniel chuckled.

"You really are a pain."

"Thank you, dear. I love you too."

When they left the restaurant, the block was surprisingly cleared of the colorful gentlemen who usually congregated there. Eileen narrowed her eyes again at Daniel, who again avoided her glance.

"Let's check out the thrift shop down on First." He wanted to get out of there quickly, she could tell.

She was always looking for cheap frames for her miniatures, so she was all for it and didn't care what his ulterior motive was.

They stepped into the shop and were hit by a draft of musty air. Eileen loved browsing the thrift stores. She wrapped herself in the loneliness of the discarded items and wondered what their stories were. Why would anyone want to get rid of framed photos? Or books with inscriptions? Or handcrafted items? Once she'd found a framed embroidery that read LOVE IS PATIENT, LOVE IS KIND, LOVE IS YOU, MOTHER.

The prices were great, however. She saved all the photos taken from the used frames she bought. Maybe some day she could throw them away. Every time she started to pitch them in the garbage, a huge wave of nostalgia would hit her and she'd think about all those people being rejected yet another time. She couldn't see how anyone could chuck old photos. Were they found in an attic belonging to the former owner? Photos should always be identified so they can always be useful to someone finding them, she thought, whether it be a historical society or a family member. There was always a story behind a photo.

Meanwhile, across town that same evening, the Ellingsworth family was spending a usual Friday night scattered about the house, Virgil in his den (slightly perplexed; he thought he and Eileen were doing so well), Noelle up in her room, Nick downstairs in the basement watching TV, and Jenaveev talking on the phone. At the first knock on the door, no one paid attention, each expecting someone else to get up and answer it. More knocking and Jenaveev, who was closest, sitting on the barstool at the kitchen counter, sighed, scrambled off the chair, and said into the receiver, "Mona, gotta answer the door. No, no, you don't have to go. Just hang on here a minute. Yes?"

The gentleman was old and ragged and smelled of sour apples. Jenaveev peered suspiciously at him. "Yes?" she repeated.

"Is this the place?" He handed her a card with their address scribbled on it and the words PLENTY OF JOBS AVAILABLE. WORK WITH YOUR HANDS. FREE COFFEE.

Jenaveev gaped and gave a weak smile. "Um, just a minute. *Virgil!*"

A creak of the floor. Silence.

"Yes, dear? Virgil said softly.

She headed toward the den. "Do…you…know anything…about this?" She handed him the card. She was hyperventilating.

He said, puzzled, "No."

He looked out the window and the heavens broke loose with them. Scrambling over their bushes, peeing on their rhododendrons, straddling their fences. Like cockroaches, there seemed to be hundreds of them. There were about thirteen.

Virgil went to the door, tried to keep his composure. "What can I do for you?"

Four of the men staggered over and huddled around the front steps.

"How ya doin'?" one said. "There's this guy downtown; he's handing out these cards."

A grubby hand showed Virgil the card.

Virgil seethed. "Well, um, I'm so sorry, there's been a mistake. We don't need any work done around here right now. A guy, you say? What did he look like?"

"I dunno. Tallish. He had a nice wallet. Brown hair."

"You're full of crap, Oscar," said another of the men. "He was bald."

"Both of you are blind," said another. "He was wearing a hat."

It was clear that these guys wouldn't clear up the mystery.

"Again, I apologize," Virgil said, reaching in his pocket and handing out bills. Five ones, a ten, a twenty. "Here, take this and, uh, share it with your friends. This should be enough to get you all home and help pay for your, uh, time."

"Sheesh, what a gyp," one of the men groused.

"Hush, Oscar, we got some money."

Virgil closed the door. Immediately, his quiet neighborhood was punctured with drunken yelling, bottles crashing, and boisterous laughter that went on and on as the men trudged down the street. The din bounced off the swimming pools, ricocheted off the granite walls and sturdy oak trees (carefully cropped at the top to save precious views), and gradually faded into the distance, returning the neighborhood to its original gracious solitude.

Virgil was jealous of their simple camaraderie. He looked down again at the card, turned it over in his hand. *Hmm*, he thought, *nice stock*.

Ancient history, all of it. It was ages ago, yet the details of their affair continued to percolate in Eileen's mind over the subsequent months, black and sticky, like bubbling tar.

The board members filed out of the conference room. Eileen glanced up and happened to catch Virgil outside in the hallway, peeking in. He'd finally showed up for the meeting but hadn't noticed her. She started shuffling her papers, intent on checking her notes and making sure she'd captured the essence of the meeting. Still, she felt it, and she despised the heat that radiated from her that seemed to waft toward the heat from Virgil. She wouldn't look up.

He caught up with Otto, who grasped Virgil by the shoulder and boomed, "Good of you to join us. Up for a drink? I'll fill you in."

As they headed up the hall, Eileen let out a breath.

CHAPTER 6

The next day Eileen realized how hard it was to be optimistic about the hospital's future. Workers were being laid off in record numbers. That morning it hit Jerry. He had worked in maintenance for thirty-five years and by today's standards would have been fired long ago for sexual harassment or never hired to begin with. His friendly dirty jokes and comments, delivered with a toothless smile, were always a breath of fresh air for Eileen. But no, management of all businesses in this country had suddenly dictated that we must all address each other with carefully orchestrated artificial language and behaviors, with no deviations for any purpose whatsoever.

While Jerry's giggly and ever-present "How ya hangin?" always made Eileen smile and retort, "Not as far as you'd like," he'd had to be fired because someone felt she was offended by such leering comments. Women in other countries struggled to avoid landmines in their neighborhoods, endured forced genital mutilations, weekly gang rapes, and lived off eighty cents a day rolling bidi cigarettes, and here in the good old US of A women were paralyzed with humiliation because of a little rude humor. And the rest sanctioned it by paying them thousands of dollars settling lawsuits to ease their "pain."

Eileen seethed. In the time it took to say "inappropriate touching," you could tell the guy to knock it off and, *boom*, it's over. Throw in a good swift kick to the groin if you like, and there would still be time to spare.

Meanwhile, poor Jerry, who wouldn't hurt a flea, had to lose his job because his behavior was no longer socially and politically correct in this country. Eileen wasn't sure how Jerry would cope. He had a three-hundred-fifty-pound wife and ten children. Or maybe it was six children. All undoubtedly needing to eat at some point or another. Luckily, Jerry was resourceful. With his carpentry skills, he would find something.

The thirteenth step of cancer recovery: uncontrollable crankiness. Yes, it *was* all about her. And she would miss Jerry.

The firings hit all levels: nurses, vice presidents, accountants, and practically everyone in the business department. Eileen wondered how the suits expected to get the bills out. She figured they were acting out of their usual short-sightedness—they'd let everyone go to make more money for the people at the top, not thinking that if the billers were gone, no one would be bringing money into the place at all:

"Heya, George, I got rid of all the billers, nurses, and registration staff. Think of all the extra money left for us now."

"Good work, Jenkins. There will be a nice bonus in your next paycheck. Oh, wait a minute. Do you know anything about billing third-party providers? Hmm, well, I take that back about the bonus. Without the receivables from that source, we just won't have enough money for your bonus and my requisite five-hundred-ten-percent bonus. Sorry, Jenkins, but I'm sure you understand."

Winston was largely oblivious and impervious to it all. Most of the greed was generated from the hospital's financial managers, who seemed to come and go like cars on a carnival ride.

It's all just a game with these people, Eileen thought. The winners in life have the most stuff, which they care about as much as plastic pieces tossed across a board game. They have to make enough to keep their wives happy and not too suspicious about all those late nights with their irritable metastatic patients. So many dying of cancer, so little time to boink the nurses. Or the secretaries. Or whomever will sit still long enough.

A dark cloud hung over each coworker she passed in the hallway. Supposedly, the department meetings were confidential, but everyone seemed to sense what was going on. Dravis, the orderly from the ER, rushed past Eileen in the hallway with a quick, sidelong glance—no smile, no sign of recognition. Sue from the lab kept her head down, focused on her typewriter, twiddling her fingers on the keys.

Eileen usually loved mornings when the administration crew started work. There was always lots of mingling, laughing, and coffee drinking as they shared events of their family's evening or discussed a surprising development on a favorite TV show. The shared camaraderie brought warmth and clarity and was a great start to often stressful days.

Most of these folks were not the type that Eileen would necessarily choose as her friends. Most couldn't embrace any lifestyle that excluded football, high school sports, cookware parties, lingerie catalogues, tidy meat-starch-vegetable dinners, and American-made cars. But they all approached the work relationship with open hearts and a spirit of cooperation. We're all in this together.

Eileen hated thinking that should the hospital fail, these wonderful employees would become in their next job a little meaner and more cynical. Their future employers would be enemies first, the necessary evil, another negative entity to contend with in their never-ending, soul-sucking slog through life. Future coworkers would be potential combatants, not to be trusted. These people would become less effective workers, skittish and fidgety, until finally, through a generous and friendly boss, a pinprick of security would poke through their guard.

Already it had started. Each worker was closing in on himself or herself, shuttering away from the uncertainty that seemed to permeate the halls. At the next job interview, he or she would ask, "So, how long have you been in business? Do you have any reason to believe that your company will take a dive shortly? How about turnover? Why is the predecessor leaving this job? How is your bottom line?" He or she would peer at the interviewer carefully, check those eyes for sudden nervous blinking, the hands for erratic fluttering. He or she would accept the job offer, much gratified but holding his or her stomach tight and jaw set. It would be years and years before he or she could relax and enjoy coworkers. Maybe go out for a drink now and then. Then, perhaps, he or she could let go.

Eileen could almost imagine stalactites and stalagmites hanging from the ceilings and jutting from the floor, dripping with oozy doom.

She headed back down the hallway to the lab. Celia was a rough-and-tumble phlebotomist. She loved black and submerged herself in it from head to toe. Somehow, she'd gotten permission to wear a black lab coat. She wore heavy eyeliner and mascara that made her eyes look like little leggy insects. Every finger of her left hand had two sterling silver rings each. She had a pierced nose and ten piercings along her right earlobe. To look at her, you wouldn't dare entrust her with your veins, but she was a master. She managed to lightly tap into the least visible vein, leaving nary a drop of stray blood. Her "just a little poke" was truly that. She never missed and never bruised. In this small town, everyone knew her and trusted her and was rarely freaked out by her.

Celia could get a job anywhere and perhaps would end up in her dream home of Buffalo, New York. She loved the snow, she'd often told Eileen. Said she could get lost in its depths. Life could truly shut down after three feet of snow. She'd shut the doors and windows, curl up with goose-down blankets, and sink into a book. Or build a snow cave and hide in it, hunkering in the fresh, patted-down snow and breathing in its cold. She couldn't stand the excitement of Maple Leaf after a couple of inches of snow, she'd told Eileen. Ooh, shut down the schools, the college, the shopping mall. And the throngs rushing into the grocery stores, stripping the shelves bare, as if this might be the last chance to purchase food ever. And Celia loved that Buffalo was so close to Canada, as she strongly suspected she was destined to end up there.

Celia had expertly administered Eileen's chemotherapy infusions into her deadening veins.

After discovering the lump, the bottom line from Eileen's research was to wait a cycle or two to see if there was any change in it—whether it got bigger or smaller, moved around, or even disappeared entirely. She'd been happy to wait. Oh, she did make an appointment the following month for her yearly gynecological exam with dear Dr. Laske, but she didn't mention anything about a lump.

She'd sashayed into the office in August, and after her initial evaluation, the nurse asked if she was having any special problems. Eileen said, "Well, I have a sort of lump in my breast that I thought maybe I should have checked."

The nurse bit her lip and stammered. "Uh, yyess, I, uh, believe that would be a serious thing."

She raced off for the doctor, leaving Eileen humming to herself and marveling at the mating hippopotami on the wall calendar. Luckily, Dr. Laske didn't share Eileen's lackadaisical approach. She hustled her off to mammography and an appointment with a surgeon for an evaluation.

During all of these preliminary examinations, Eileen nonchalantly read Arthur Ashe's autobiography. She was interested in him because he'd played tennis in Byrd Park in Richmond, where she'd lived as a child, and it was such a shame when he'd contracted AIDS from a blood transfusion. She knew you weren't supposed to imply that it's more of a shame when someone contracts AIDS that way as opposed to the other—snicker, snicker—way. Ashe had seemed like a nice guy.

She never finished his book.

Her surgeon was great also. Dr. Jaax was young, cute, and very personable. They could give each other a hard time without either of them getting into a sensitive snit. Eileen was embarrassed to have to ask someone to drive her to this little surgery. The preadmission office had insisted on it. But why, though? It was nothing, really, a minor boo-boo, a tiny confusion of waylaid cells. She didn't want to ask her parents because she didn't want to worry them. It was such a little thing. Their worrying would make it worse for her. Daniel was a perfect companion—he doted on her—and the obvious choice for the task. They also shared similar tastes in men.

Daniel picked her up and shoved some hot, fragrant tea and a cream-cheese bagel toward her.

"Are you comfortable? Did you eat breakfast?"

"Honey, you're a sweetheart, but I'm not supposed to eat anything. I think."

"Have some tea; there's no sweetener in it."

She sipped the tea—mango and spice, very yummy. Comforting.

He unwrapped the bagel for her.

"No, no, I couldn't eat anything even if I was allowed. Which I don't think I am. Thanks, though."

She reached over and gave him a peck on the cheek. Gay men were so wonderful for little displays of affection. There was never the pressure of inadvertent—and inevitably, unrequited—male sexual tension and expectation that made casual heterosexual relationships so tedious. No worries about misconstruing behavior, having to listen to the whining "But you led me on!" Stuff that made a girl want to pulverize a guy's face. In a nice way, of course. She must be dainty.

"Are you OK?" Daniel asked. "I'm sure everything will be fine. Don't worry."

Of course, it would be fine. "Thanks, I'm just glad you're here with me."

Daniel parked the car and rushed around to open Eileen's door.

"You're so sweet, Danny-bear."

Arm in arm, they marched toward the admissions office.

At the hospital, Daniel waited outside and Eileen was prepped. She was given a local anesthesia and Valium. Neither worked too well. She could feel the scraping of the scalpel or whatever the hell it was, steel on flesh against her rib cage. It wasn't really painful, or was it? She was aware of the pressure—and that awful scraping. She shouldn't be feeling anything, should she? Bleary-eyed, she raised her hand to indicate she needed more anesthesia. Darn, she always had the same problem with Novocain at the dentist's office. She always needed double or triple doses. Her nerves must be hot-wired.

They took their frozen-tissue biopsy from her. The next thing she knew, she was propped up on pillows in the recovery room. Geez, this wasn't bad at all. Especially now that it was over. Dr. Jaax scurried over to her; he was such a nice man. She was embarrassed to have put him through all of this effort for some dumb, useless lump. She was sure it was nothing serious. He must have compound fractures to set, maybe even some with bones poking out of the skin, or festering kidneys to cut out, tons of diseased body parts to remove that were more critical than this. She looked up at him a little apologetically. *Yeah, you and I are the healthy ones. We're a cozy pair amid all this sickness.*

"Yes, well, it's cancer." He nodded, and added, "But *na, na, na, na...*"

She didn't hear the rest of it. Shock seared shut the part of her brain that evaluated what her ears heard.

Cancer? How can this be? But, no, now was not the time for theorizing why, when, how, where. Why her, when did it happen, where was she when it started, and what was she doing at the time? No, no, there would be plenty of time to fret over that later.

It's cancer. Every nerve cell in her body screamed at the words.

But the doctor was still talking. Bless him, he knew that the best way to deal with it was to keep moving forward. Keep telling the patients what would happen next, let their fear get lost in the mundane, day-to-day procedures of treatment and therapy. There were tons of things to happen next: surgery for lymph node removal and recovery from that, X rays, body scans, blood tests, blood tests, and more blood tests, then chemo, radiation, hold the pickles.

What had assaulted her body to such an extent that it had reacted with cancer?

CHAPTER 7

In a tiny cottage on Georgetown Street in Maple Leaf, Sammy was crying again and wriggling around. He grabbed his ears and wrung them and yowled.

"Mommmmm!"

His mother came running. "What's the matter, sweetheart?"

"Hurts!"

Ruth Crenshaw cradled him in her arms. He wriggled harder and almost fell on the floor.

"I know, I know, honey. You're going in for surgery tomorrow and then it will be all better."

He continued to wail. She laid him gently on the sofa and went to get a Tylenol. She hoped the surgery would take care of this; Sammy was in agony like this at least four times a year. She couldn't take it anymore. Obviously, it wasn't much of a picnic for Sammy either. She hesitated to give him the medicine the doctor prescribed to help him sleep. He was so young. She didn't want to make him a druggie.

But she had to get some sleep tonight. Lewis, her husband, was out of town, and she had to fend for herself this week. She was so tired. Sammy would keep her up all night unless she could make his pain go away. She reached up into the medicine cabinet and checked the bottle carefully. It seemed to be OK. It wasn't midnight yet; he wasn't supposed to take anything after midnight because of his surgery tomorrow morning. What the heck. She was going to do it.

"Come here, Sammy, honey. This will make you feel better."

It was just a little bit of codeine.

Ruth Crenshaw awoke with a start. A second later her alarm went off, and she felt relief that, first, she had gotten some sleep and, second, that she'd woken up in time. She went over to Sammy's room and peeked in. He was sleeping, his face pale and his lips chapped, and his breath came in short little spurts. She whispered, "OK, honey, it's time to get up."

No response but a slight jerky movement of his head.

She sighed. He looked so comfortable; she knew once he awoke, he would be in pain again. His respite was also hers. She sat down on his bed and brushed her hand gently along his cheek. His eyes opened and he looked clearly at her.

"How're you feeling? Didja sleep OK?"

"I feel OK." A very little voice.

"Let's get up now. C'mon, honey, I'll help you get dressed."

He felt so limp and sleepy; Ruth hoped that she could get him to the hospital before he woke up completely. Poor little guy.

"Has he taken any medications since six p.m. last night?" Lydia, the admissions clerk looked at her.

Ruth got a sick feeling in her stomach.

"I thought it was after midnight. I mean, I thought he couldn't have anything after midnight. I gave him a little codeine and a Tylenol at around ten last night. He was in such pain and screaming…"

"Well, that might be OK. I'll check with the anesthesiologist."

"Oh, I hope we can still have the surgery. I can't bear to see him suffering like this anymore. I haven't slept in days, and I have to work, and my daughter is staying with my mom, and I want to get her back and—"

"Just relax, Mrs. Crenshaw. I'll see what we can do."

Ruth crumpled in a heap on the chair. Sammy had had these ear infections every year from the minute the calendar hit November until April. Just like standard time. Nearly one a month. Otitis media. Finally, the doctor had suggested a bilateral myringotomy, tubes in the ears, which would be a more permanent solution. The tubes would allow for drainage in the middle ear canal and help prevent more infections. Ruth was all for it. Most of the neighbor kids had had them done, and it was a normal procedure. You never had to have the tubes removed; they just eventually disintegrated as the kid got older.

She kept trying to think about how great it would be once Sammy had the surgery. She would no longer have to leap over furniture to drag him away at the first sign of a sniffling friend. Not that it ever helped anyway. He would catch a cold even if he heard of a friend having a cold. Sympathetic infection. She wouldn't have to be a fanatic about keeping him away from his sniffling friends. She still had this last hurdle to get through, and her son's pain would be over.

She held his hand as he lay on the litter. Right now, they were just waiting for the anesthesiologist. It was really just a little bit of codeine. It couldn't possibly hurt. Oh, and the Tylenol.

Dr. Ritchey approached them. He was already wearing green scrubs.

"Hey, there, scamp, how ya doin' today?" he said.

Sammy looked up at him. "Are you the one who's gonna cut into me?" His arms were stretched out along his sides, and he clenched the sheet in his little fists.

Dr. Ritchey placed one hand on Sammy's arm and another on Ruth's shoulder. "No, Sammy, I'm the anesthesiologist. I'm here to give you medicine that will make you go to sleep, and when you wake up, your pain will be gone. But first I want to get to know you a little. Have you had anything to eat today, Sammy?"

"I wasn't hungry."

Ruth shook her head. "All he had was a little water. Did they tell you about the codeine? I gave him a little codeine syrup and a Tylenol last night."

"Anything since midnight?"

"No, this was at ten or so."

"Well, that should be no problem. Do you feel drowsy, Sammy?"

"No."

"Scared?"

Sammy's lips tightened.

"Don't worry, little guy. You won't feel a thing."

Another doctor approached. Ruth recognized Dr. Casterelli, who would perform the surgery.

"Everything looks in order," the doctor said. "Are we ready to head to the OR?"

The OR was freezing. Dr. Casterelli asked Ruth if Sammy liked any particular kind of music. Classical was usually preferred during surgeries, the doctor said, but they were open to suggestions. The nurse covered Sammy with a blue wool blanket, nicely warmed.

"The patients are asleep, for the most part," the doctor explained, "but they are still conscious and slightly aware of what they hear. We've had to turn down requests for Screeching Hot Nails, or whatever they're called, but we try to accommodate other more reasonable requests to the extent we can."

Ruth thought a moment. "We sing along together sometimes to Harry Belafonte. Do you have any of that?"

Dr. Casterelli exchanged a glance with one of the OR nurses who gleamed at him and said, "Told you so."

"All right, I'm outvoted. I'll put away the Mozart this time."

The rubber mouthpiece went over Sammy's trembling lips. The gentle calypso and Harry's smooth voice carried in waves over Sammy's brain and he fell asleep.

The next day the name Sammy Crenshaw was on the OR list of problems.

Ruth sat in the waiting room fiddling with her opal earrings and called a lawyer.

Eileen stood under the hot shower for twenty minutes. Sometimes this was better than sex. One advantage of renting was not worrying about water use. It was a sweaty walk home from work, even without Virgil these days.

Toweled off, she headed for the kitchen when she noticed a message on the answering machine. With a big sigh, she wondered who it was this time—that lady who hollered in her circus-announcer voice that Eileen had won yet another all-expense paid vacation to Las Vegas or Reno; or dear Miles, who prattled on so; or AP East, the local telephone company, with another ruse to make her buy their useless stuff. AP East saw Eileen as their ultimate capture. If they could get the elusive Eileen to buy their crap, boy, they'd really arrived. For instance:

Ring ring.
"Hello?"
Click.
Fifteen minutes later:
Ring ring.
"Hello?"
Click.
And on and on in fifteen-minute increments for two hours. Then:
Ring ring.
"Hello?"
"Hi, I'm calling from AP East Telephone Systems. How are you this evening? We are offering a special deal to you tonight for Caller ID."
"Glenn, is that you?"
Click.
Their audacity was wearying. This time she sighed and pressed the message playback.

"Eileen, it's Maria. I'm sorry to bother you at home. We've got a big problem; our telephones are going crazy with complaints. Eliza burst into tears and left the switchboard with the lights still blinking. You know how frazzled she gets under even the best circumstances. Please call me."

So much for semihibernation tonight. Maria was the tough-as-nails office manager and not one to ask for help.

She called Maria. "Do you want me to come in? Did Eliza come back? What are all the complaints about?"

"We wheeled her down to the emergency room. She's OK, just stressed. Julia came in and took over the phones. I think we're all right now. I'm going home."

"See you tomorrow?"

"Maybe yes, maybe no."

The next morning Eileen went into work bearing homemade donuts to soften with sugar and fat everyone's distress. She nearly dropped the box when she saw Maria's ashen face.

"Look at this," Maria said.

It was the OR report for yesterday's surgeries. It was pages and pages long. Usually the report was a simple list of names and a few notations. This one included paragraphs of complaints and disturbances. Crenshaw, Sammy, infection.

Lockhart, Amy, acute infection. Wilson, James, bilateral infection. All bilateral otitis media; all infections. On and on it went for ten surgeries.

"What the heck was going on in there?" Eileen said. "Are they sterilizing the equipment in the toilet, for chrissakes?"

"I have no idea. But you will. The parents are lined up outside Winston's office."

Eileen marched toward his office. There they were, hissing and gesturing to one another.

"If I had known my son would get butchered here, I would have headed to Philadelphia."

"Yes, I know. Hasn't this place entered the twentieth century of medicine?"

"Maybe we'd better look around more carefully; they probably use leeches for bloodletting."

"I think I'd rather have leeches instead of those crackpot doctors."

It was a nightmare. She was glad no doctors were congregating in the hallway. The main nurses' station was right around the corner; surely they had their ears plastered against the crack in the door.

Winston cowered in his office. "What am I supposed to tell those poor people?" he whispered.

"You have to at least tell them that we are sorry, we understand their concern, that it's our concern, that we are doing everything we can to get to the bottom of this situation. Haven't you learned anything?"

Eileen was shocked at her candor, but she couldn't help it. He was the boss, but he was acting like an idiot.

He looked at her.

Eileen nodded, "Go ahead and say it. 'I'm such an idiot.' I know you can do it. C'mon, c'mon."

He shrugged and laughed a bit.

Boss's way of admitting he's an idiot, Eileen thought. She felt validated and smiled back.

"Go on, tiger," she said. "You can do it."

PART TWO

CHAPTER 8

"*Dad!* Where's the tire pump?" Noelle wanted to get an early start on her bike ride, but her tires were flat. "*Dad?*"

Nothing but silence from the bedroom. Normally, that would be good, but she really needed that tire pump. She sighed and decided to take a walk instead.

Virgil had heard her. Damn, what timing. He was a tad indisposed at the moment in an attempt at carnal knowledge of his wife.

Sure, sure, honey just a minute; I'm making love to your mother, or would be if only I could get it up. See, we're trying to show affection for one another so that you view us as a devoted couple and loving parents. The shrink said that it was important we act as if we adore each other, even if we can't stand the sight of each other. Shrinks are so wise; I would never have thought that was a good idea on my own. I'm learning so much about being a better person from this shrink. She has shown us how evil it is to have any thoughts that undermine the stability of our family.

I've learned that I really don't dislike my wife, Jenaveev, that I really love her unconditionally because you kids need to see that. I've learned that since I was a spoiled little rich kid, I don't have any right to my own happiness now, that the suffering Jenaveev bore in her life needs to be appeased on a daily basis. Everything I do must be an effort to make her life more pleasurable. I understand now so much that was always unclear before. I'm not entitled to anything because I'm a man and Jenaveev was mistreated by her father, who was also a man, and he left because *her* mother was a worthless, slatternly drunk, so I have to do everything in my power to make her life as wonderful as possible. Because she's a woman, and women are entitled to everything special. I'm still so worthless and weak, although I'm trying to do better. Ugh! Oh well, I tried. What did I do with that tire pump?

"What's going on?" Jenaveev cackled.

The shrink would love this scenario. Oops, he had to stop thinking of her as a shrink when he was trying to make love. Ol' Mighty Moe took offense to that terminology, and he had enough trouble getting him to respond on demand. Poor Jenaveev was starting to think it might be her, and he couldn't undermine the stability of the family by allowing her to feel any insecurity whatsoever. There should be a drug for this. In order to maintain the stability of the family.

Jenaveev was certainly no slouch when it came to bedtime calisthenics. Virgil cupped her breast while he lay next to her, and after a brief flinch, she rolled over on him and ground against him. He could do worse. Then again, it had taken her years to take the initiative even to that minor extent, and sometimes he got a little resentful that she seemed to feel she'd made such tremendous strides. She thought she was a regular hot mama. But Virgil couldn't have any regrets; again, it was that family stability thing.

He wistfully thought back to a few years ago and wished he could still walk around naked in front of sweet Noelle. It was so cute when she would make some remark about his penis. "Daddy, can I touch it?" At fourteen, she was a little old for that now, although occasionally he'd "accidentally" leave the bathroom door open, in hopes that she'd walk by and peek. It lent a sort of innocent sexuality to the family that poor Jenaveev, despite her dry attempts, could never provide.

"Sorry, honey, I must be tired." Virgil rolled over onto his back

"Sheesh. Again." Jenaveev slumped over to the side of the bed.

"Was that Noelle calling? I think she needs something." Virgil got up, stretched, and headed to the bathroom.

Jenaveev's Christmas pregnancy had been an inspiration for her. When the twins were born during her sweat-soaked frenzy on December 24, she'd wanted to give them bold, holiday-inspired names. She'd carefully looked up the correct spellings and proclaimed them Nick and Noelle. Virgil thought it was cute at the time. Maybe—well, once that newborn blood-gook was cleaned up—just maybe, there might be hope for all of them, he'd thought. He hadn't really wanted to participate in the birth process, but it had seemed the thing to do.

He'd hoped he would be called out of town. "Gee, honey, your water broke? I'd love to hear all about it, but my plane's leaving for Cairo right now. Save all those memories to share when I get back. Every last minute of them." Yeah, right. No, he'd been there, wincing and biting his lip to keep from passing out. Yes, a lot of help he'd been. He would never be able to look at that yawning cavity with romantic notions ever again. It had made it all so clinical and yucky.

No woman with true consideration for her husband would demand that he join her during the process. Yeah, yeah, all that blah-blah talk about how hard it is for the woman to carry and deliver a baby, the least the man can do is participate at that level. But even *she* doesn't have to see things from that vantage point. She might as well be having an exceptionally painful gynecological exam, for all she knows. Even *she* would pass out if she saw things from the other end. No doubt about it. Better to wait till everyone's sponged off and smelling of baby powder; that's the only way for mothers and babies to present themselves for the first time.

Virgil loved his children; he really did. Unfortunately, like all men, he was not blessed with the hormonal activity of birth/postbirth, which gracefully allowed a woman to forget most of what went on during childbirth. It was as if a huge cymbal clanged over the memories, making them disappear forever, he thought. It was lucky too, otherwise no child would ever have brothers or sisters. Men were not graced with this ability. They never forgot those first moments. Even now, whenever Virgil looked at Noelle or Nick, his first, very fleeting thought was *However did that pustulant mess ever turn into such a beautiful, coherent child as you?*

Nick and Noelle often noticed their father's bewilderment, but they thought he was wondering how he ever got stuck with kids. They felt shame. And then they got gypped every year having their birthday so close to Christmas. If they never had to hear "This is your Christmas present *and* your birthday present!" again, it would be a miracle. And not to have to murmur through gritted teeth, "Oh yes, that means that I'll love it *doubly* well [you crummy cheapskate, you]!" would be a miracle too.

That was one of the few sentiments that both Nick and Noelle shared. They would exchange glances and almost feel in sync with each other. There would be a teeny seed of recognition and camaraderie, and it felt good. But they still mistrusted each other, and that soon overrode any good feelings. God, they were twins, shouldn't they be completing each other's sentences, exchanging knowing glances, telepathically communicating with one another? That's what all other twins did, those they'd heard about anyway. They could barely stand to be in one another's company most of the time.

Maybe they were twins, but just not to each other. Maybe each of their real twins was living out a separate existence in Arizona or Oregon. Maybe they were switched in the hospital nursery. Maybe their parents stole them from the nursery, and they weren't really related at all.

Wishful thinking, all dashed by a look in the mirror. Their auburn hair and aristrocratic noses were dead ringers for Mom and Dad respectively.

CHAPTER 9

Jenaveev loved the sun. There was no better way to follow up a hot round of golf in the sun than coming home for a quick dip in the pool, lying on her specially made chair, and soaking in yet more rays as she lazed the day away. As a fair-skinned redhead, however, this had its risks. Consequently, Jenaveev had contracted an unusual condition, an ulcerated lesion of the uvula, that dangling tissue toward the back of the throat. She was told that in another year or two it might turn into malignant melanoma of the uvula and become award-winning alliteration. It seemed that her little habit of falling asleep in the sun, her head lolling on the back of the chair, her mouth wide open, had left her prey to this rather unusual incidence.

She was scheduled to meet with her oncologist on Wednesday. Her first thought was *Oh, it's so chic to have an oncologist these days.* And she didn't even have to contract cancer to be able to show off for her friends. "My oncologist. It's so much more vogue than saying my dermatologist. Or my plastic surgeon. Or even my shrink. It's so *de nouveau.*" Only Jenaveev said it "duh *noo*-vu." But, of course, one could not correct her. She had a purulent uvula.

The doctor decided, just to be safe, to give her a few rounds of radiation.

There was a moment early in their marriage when Virgil and Jenaveev had daintily broached the topic of divorce. They were naïve. They knew they were unhappy, they just weren't sure if it was because of an individual problem with one or the other of them or if their entire entity together was wrong. It happens when two mismatched people marry; the first few times there's a disagreement, they find it a little sexy—alluring, even—and another reason to get caught up in passion. Their minds are electrified at the idea of looking at a different point of view.

"Eat green beans with fried fish? That's crazy; it undermines the whole concept of 'fish 'n' chips.' It simply isn't done."

"Who says one must have 'fish with chips'? It's so greasy, and green beans are much healthier."

You know she's crazy, yet the idea tickles the mind. It's a combination you've never entertained, and you must admit you are secretly intrigued and you must kiss her madly and immediately.

But after the fifteen years of fish and green beans, you finally realize that she's just crazy. That charming yet dissident point of view of hers has evolved into an abnormal obsession, and you think she should be banned from society.

They were both a little surprised when they realized that their marriage was not meant to be. Still they tried and tried to hold on, covering each strained misunderstanding with polite murmuring, hoping that that tiny remnant of civil behavior would be enough to hold the marriage together.

Finally one evening Virgil came home from work, Jenaveev had the dining room table covered with flotation tank brochures, and she was prancing in front of the mirror, practicing her lines.

"The flotation tank. When you *really* want to get away from it all. Experience nothing."

She grinned in the mirror, stepped back, and held her arms up, hands outward, game-show hostess style. Virgil's eyebrows arched, and there he was in the mirror with her; they looked at each other and saw two perfect strangers. Worse, they saw two perfect strangers who seemed to intuitively loathe one another. Neither one said a word, but their eyes said it all.

But now, after years and years of shrinks and tiptoeing around the topic and not doing anything about it, they'd become comfortable in their misery. Now Jenaveev became ballistic at even the thought of divorce. It was impossible.

"You can't possibly leave me! What will I do? I know I'll just commit suicide. Nobody cares; you never cared about me. I've tried so hard to play golf for you. No, wait a minute. I've tried so hard to…to…. Well, OK then, my father left me when I was nine, and I've tried so hard to not be left again. I'll commit suicide; you know I will. *I need you!*"

It did bother Jenaveev a bit that it didn't seem as if Virgil was seeing anyone else right now. His horrible perkiness was gone. She couldn't lord that over him. She even saw a little look of misery on his face that she didn't believe she was the source of. Could he possibly miss someone? And not indulge the feeling by sleeping with that person? Why wouldn't he? If she's just a passing fling, why not get it out of his system to better pretend he could stand being around her, his wife? It almost made her feel something for him when she could see he was miserable and there was nothing she could do to make him more miserable. She couldn't accuse him of anything; he was obviously not doing anything. Had they reached an impasse? Could she not make him endure more pain? If anything, he seemed to enjoy her current infirmity; not enough for her to accuse him, but just a subtle lessening of his constant misery. She was at her wits' end trying to figure the boy out.

Virgil was afraid it would happen. After a couple of treatments, Jenaveev lost all of her hair. He marveled, *The way she clenches so, I'm surprised she let any of it go.* One day she got up to go to the bathroom, and her hair simply stayed behind. On the pillow. Virgil did a double take; he wasn't even quite sure at first that she had left the bed, but then he heard her familiar coughs and snorts in the bathroom. *Please, please, please*; he hoped she wouldn't turn on the light and look in the mirror.

But soon there was a scream. "Oh my God!" She came tearing out of the bathroom. "Look at me! Will this never end?" She started wailing.

He tried to comfort her. "Yes, honey, you've lost your hair. They explained that with your mysterious sympathetic symptoms you might make yourself…um, you might lose your hair. Remember, we bought that lovely wig and those scarves. And just look at what a finely shaped head you have. Not everyone can say that."

"Do you really think so?"

"Oh my goodness, yes, the very best."

Looking at her tear-streaked face, crinkled in fear and horror, Virgil was reminded of their wedding day. Only it was his face that had suffered the torment that day.

He scratched his head. He'd been so naïve to think that he could "save" her and through his goodness make her a better person whom he could learn to love. She'd clamped on and never let go. Since he couldn't get rid of her any other way nicely, because he was not an asshole, he'd figured he might as well make the best of it. She was his project. By gum, he was going to be a corporate head; what did it matter whom he married anyway? Weren't all women basically the same? He'd needed all his energies to forward his career; he didn't have the extra time or energy to disentangle himself. She would do well under his tutelage, he'd thought. He could be a sugar daddy with the best of them.

So now he was left to deal with her hair all over the bed sheets. She didn't want to touch it. She couldn't bear to even look at it. He scooped it up in his hands and was about to chuck it in the trash but asked, "Do you want me to do anything special with this?" *Perhaps create a shrine for it, complete with a plaque engraved with loopy cursive writing, waxing poetic of all of your virtues*, he thought.

"No, just get rid of it," she said. She was pouting, so he knew she wanted some sort of reverent word.

He couldn't do it. Into Mr. Hefty it went.

"Well, I suppose now I have to learn to do the scarf thing. It'll make me feel like a peasant."

He wasn't sure if she meant because she had to learn something or because she had to wear a scarf. He wanted to say, "Well, at least you have a rich, good-looking husband driving you to the doctor's office and anywhere else your heart desires." Eileen had taken the bus to her treatments.

Heavens, why was he thinking about that woman? It was over a year ago. After all, she r-r-r-r—wait, he'd get it—she r-e-j-e-c-t-e-d him. That's right. How humiliating.

———

With a loud clang, the quoit hit the pin and settled comfortably against it. Nick sighed. The game of quoits was a lost art these days. With the emergence of computer games, with their manic activity, flashing lights, piercing sounds, and quick results, very few people appreciated the quiet dignity and precision of a perfectly executed quoits game.

Nick loved the physicality of it as well. He couldn't imagine how his friends enjoyed the cramped, closed-in, hunched-over posture of computer hacking. They reminded him of the illustrations of wizened old goblins in his old *Children's Garden of Verses*. At this rate, humans truly would evolve into pale, lumpen, warty things teeming with sunlight-hating fungus. Come to think of it, he'd recently noticed a proliferation of antifungal ointments advertised on TV. If you want to crouch cooped up in your computer den, here are the medicated tools to combat into submission those pesky body temptations to run free outside. What's the good of outside? You can't download any of it, so what's the point?

Anyway. Then there was the rivalry with horseshoes. Those poor misinformed horseshoe freaks. Quoits operated on a completely different set of physics. You couldn't just fling the thing willy-nilly like you were some drunken horseshoe player at a family reunion or employee picnic. You had to consider the physics of tossing a circular ring through the air at a small target. Unlike horseshoes, it took much more precision and skill to place them just so at the other end.

Nick knew quoits was the superior game. People didn't play them much because there was no violence, no sex, and no virtual reality. It was an actual reality, a foreign concept these days. Nick felt that he was part of a very special group, a feeling he certainly didn't get from his family. He was well aware of the irony of his favorite pastime being some sort of metaphor for his father's work, with the circular grommets. Was it really a desperate maneuver for his dad's attention? No. If he'd wanted that, he would have just brought home a gun.

He strongly suspected that he and his twin sister Noelle were an accident and, as such, were a constant source of guilt and suppressed rage between their parents. And the rage wasn't always so well suppressed. He could feel it in the core of his being; he cringed every time he heard his parents screaming at each other. If they weren't screaming, then it was their cold sarcasm, with icy edges dripping freezing pricklies all over the house. Like a leaky roof during the thaw after a blustery winter snowstorm. He'd fallen asleep many times feeling those freezing drops of sarcasm falling on his eyelids.

Their mother had been downright hostile toward them as kids. He couldn't bring himself to call her "Mom." She used to give them little sips of bourbon to shut them up when they were babies. He'd overheard her telling her friends while they were playing cards. He'd imagined he could remember the awful stuff burning down his little baby throat.

"Well, what could I do?" Jenaveev had cried. "They were bawling like banshees. My God, they have a life of leisure; what could they possibly have to cry about? It was embarrassing." The girls had all nodded and murmured and rearranged their cards.

She had thought he was outside playing basketball. She'd bragged to her friends that thereafter her kids never gave her an ounce of trouble.

Nick thought his dad caught her a couple of times, but then she simply stopped doing it in the evening. When they'd gotten old enough to tell, she'd abruptly quit, which of course caused Noelle and Nick to fall headlong into severe alcohol withdrawal.

They'd been in and out of the hospital emergency room; it was called UFI, unidentified febrile illness, complete with DTs and everything. People said they were difficult children, never to their faces, but Nick could see their remonstrance in their expression when they cooed over them. There was always a sarcastic edge to it. They might as well have just said aloud, "Oh, you awful bratty children, you."

It was inevitable that they would get hooked on "mother's milk." She was hooked on it herself. She never ventured too far from her own bottle. Nick knew his dad had nearly divorced her several times because of it, but she'd begged and pleaded and wailed, so he'd relented. "Shh, you'll upset the kids. Fine. I promise I'll never leave you."

Nick knew. The old guy should have shown some gonads. He'd never shown any gonads for anything important. He could hold his own on really stupid things, like the precise size, shape, and calibrated pressure required of the garage door opener, but when it came to important stuff, he crumbled like feta cheese. He didn't realize that his weakness was so transparent, that what he was trying to portray as family strength was nothing but a pathetic lie.

It might have been difficult if they had divorced, but at least his mom would have learned to be somewhat self-sufficient. Yes, they had done Nick and Noelle a load of favors by staying together. Now Nick knew that lies, manipulation, and incessant whining would get you anything you want in this world.

Playing quoits tilted his life to the honest and true. He didn't like his parents coming to his competitions. If they wanted to persist in the phony, teeth-clenching family togetherness stuff when they happened to be together, fine. He supposed he could suck up the rumbling pain in his stomach for the duration. But when he was alone with his quoits, he wanted total freedom to indulge his passion.

With each throw he flung aside all the fakery building inside him—out through his fingertips into the smooth steel quoit so it flew magically through the air, caught the peg in a quick grab, and rolled around and around and around in a dizzying fit of passion till it gently settled on the ground. Perfection.

CHAPTER 10

Passing the lab, Eileen waved at Celia, who nodded and motioned her over. "So, what's the deal, hey?" From Celia, that was practically a soliloquy.

Eileen shook her head. "It's not good," she whispered. "We're having some issues in the operating room."

"Like, no kidding? I left Centralia for this?"

"You lived in Centralia? I had no idea." Underneath Centralia, Pennsylvania, was a perpetual fire due to leaky underground carbon monoxide from abandoned mine operations. Most of its residents had fled, with scant governmental assistance, certainly none from the mining company. "I thought we had problems."

"At least you could smell the gassy fumes. Here, we're dying without notice."

That got Eileen's dander up. "Well, don't abandon us too." When Celia shot her a black-eyed look, Eileen backed down. "So sorry. I'm taking this a little too personally."

Celia remembered and placed a hand on Eileen's arm.

"But bottom line, am I out of here?"

Eileen looked down and shrugged. "What's Love Canal up to these days?"

Eileen remembered vaguely the weekly trek to the hospital for her chemo treatments issued by Celia's very capable hands. After the very first treatment, she'd gone to a hockey game with Miles, as just friends, of course. He had VIP seats as a legislative aide in Harrisburg—and felt great, if not a little stoned. She had bought a little set of wristbands, recommended to curb nausea, and was totally convinced that they worked. She was determined she could get through treatment with as few drugs as possible. They were little cloth stretchy bands with a sort of button sewn inside that pressed against a key antinausea pressure point inside the wrist. They were ingeniously designed to offset little twinges of queasiness brought on by, oh, say, car rides, or maybe a few too many black olives on your pizza. They were, however, no match for this.

After the second week, her head in the toilet bowl at 3:00 a.m., she sprinted to the hospital saying, "Drugs, drugs, drugs. Whatever you have to give me, I want them all." So she was armed with lorazepam and Compazine to help with nausea and to help her sleep. She kept a constant flow in her bloodstream.

Her chemo regimen was relatively mild by chemo standards but still oppressive. By the time she was halfway through the treatment, at three months, she knew it was the end for her. Hair falling out in big clumps in the shower, total drain of creative impulses, mental capacity of a turtle lying upside down in the middle of a busy intersection. A constant feeling of crisis mode in the midst of crippling fatigue. A constant sense of urgency that her whole life was going to fall apart, she had no control, and she was going to end up lying cold, useless, and pathetic on a sidewalk grate but she had absolutely no strength to do anything about it. And that only exacerbated the anxiety. She felt a sickening mixture of fear, helplessness, and hopelessness. Freezing cold one minute and superhot flashes the next. At one point she likened it to an atom bomb going off in her head. Total cellular confusion. Nothing felt right, nothing felt safe; she was living totally off the cuff and just hoping she didn't do anything irreparably stupid.

The stupidest things she did, thankfully, she probably didn't remember. But she did remember leaving her clothes in the two dryers in the vault-like cellar of her apartment building for over a week because she simply forgot about them. Doing laundry in a facility shared by a hundred or so others, including sometimes mean and vindictive types, you wanted to be sure to own up to your clothes as quickly as possible, lest you find them strewn about the laundry room, dangling from rafters, stuffed in door jambs to keep them open—if the clothes were still there at all. Suddenly, in one horrifying moment (everything was exaggerated in a negative way on chemo), she realized that *Oh my God, my clothes are still downstairs*, she had left them down there for a whole week, and *Oh my God, what if they're stolen?* She could barely afford meat that week; she couldn't afford to buy a bunch of jeans and underwear and tops. *Oh, life is just so miserable I can't stand it anymore.* She crumpled in a heap of tearful, exhaustive misery, but she dragged herself up because, after all, she still had to go down and get the damn clothes. And so she did. And they were there in a wrinkly pile on a corner of the table. Wrinkly, but they were there.

Another time she forgot to replace the gas cap on her car. She went to fill her tank one day, and after she'd opened the little gas tank door with her key, there was nothing there. No gas cap. Just the gaping hole where the gas nozzle went. At first she thought that someone had swiped the cap, but why would he or she obediently lock the little door back up? Too much to ponder; just buy a new one. Add another key to the key chain. Now she needed a key for the little door and a key for the gas cap. A key for the ignition, a key for the Club steering wheel lock, and a key for the car door. It was a heavy price to pay for relentless paranoia, but it was worth it for a twenty-year-old junker car. No, no, erase that; the little car can hear you. It might take offense.

But she always worried about the inevitable stupid things that she would do. Here was a whopper: She thought she had met the man of her dreams when Virgil came into her life.

CHAPTER 11

"Are you listening to me? You don't care about me at all, do you?"

Every day of his life. Day in, day out. "Now why would you say that, honey?" Virgil sighed.

"How do you think you would feel if you lost all of your hair? You might as well lose it; it's almost all gray now."

Yes, and has been for the past fifteen years. Prematurely gray in his mid-twenties. Virgil wondered how that could have happened. Probably at some point his follicles had all blanched in terror at his life. Eileen had loved his hair, loved playing with it and running her fingers lightly through it. She had such a soft and tender touch that expressed so much feeling. *Oh, for heaven's sake, stop.*

Virgil slept in his bed next to Jenaveev. He knew he should make some effort to hold her, touch her, make her feel like a woman. But he couldn't.

The usual sour thoughts pinched his brain. In good health, Jenaveev was as useless as a person could be and still stand upright. Luckily for her, her bone structure was solid. Virgil marveled at the physics of her. No house cleaning for her. A maid came in once a week, and Jenaveev refused to lift a finger to maintain the house between those times. Cooking? Ha! Why should she cook when they could afford to buy out every day? Rich people don't cook. She was horrified when that Boston Kitchen place closed down. It threw her equilibrium totally off. That was probably when her uvula began to putrefy. She did do a little of her own and the kids' laundry because he refused to do hers, especially when it was accompanied by her explicit instructions. He wasn't sure how she even knew enough about doing laundry to give such explicit instructions. She must have seen it on a soap opera. "Now, Clara, please don't mix the silks with the rayon. You know how they don't get along, and I can't stand to wear peevish fabric."

She was antimatter, the only living being who did not impart an energy field. Instead, she sucked up all available quarks, protons, and atoms wherever she went, leaving little pockets of vacuum-filled air behind. A true physics anomaly. He imagined there was a whole chapter in scientific journals dedicated to her, called the Jenaveev Corollary to the Principle of Life Forces aka Big Bang in Reverse.

Virgil bounded up, making the bed shake and Jenaveev's body lurch soundlessly, like a deep ocean-bottom dweller. He smiled and got ready for work.

It was another treatment day for Virgil and Jenaveev, the last one. And what a treat it would be! Sitting at his expansive desk, looking out at the muddy Susquehanna, Virgil fiddled with a sample of the new computer table grommet, grumbling.

He left work at half past twelve to pick her up for her one o'clock appointment. He drove up the driveway and trudged inside. She was on the phone.

"Oh, here he is right now. Yes, he takes me to every treatment; he is such a sweetheart, I know." She scowled at Virgil. "Bye, now." She hung up the phone.

What's the matter, honey? he thought. *Are you bothered by worldwide starvation, pestilence, disease, ozone depletion? Man's inhumanity to man? The spiraling costs of real estate? What, what?*

"I just don't want to go today. Can't I stay home?" Her face crinkled in mock pain and fear. She cast a sidelong look at Virgil just to make sure he was watching her.

"Absolutely not. You know you have to go. This is the last one. C'mon, honey, let's go."

"Sometimes I think that these treatments are worse than if I simply died from cancer."

Oh, honey, don't go there. Just don't go there.

"And I bet you agree, don't you?"

Nope, none of that fake "sweetheart" stuff to his face. That was just a show for her friends. And she didn't want any of them getting any ideas to swipe him out from under her feet while she was still breathing.

"No, of course not. How can you even say that? You don't have cancer; this is just a precaution."

A heavy silence hung in the air, and Virgil decided to take advantage of it. He thought about Eileen. She had said that her breast had "grown back."

No point going there.

Suddenly, his wife broke the reverie. "I'm sorry I've been such a crab. This is all very hard for me."

Virgil stared at her. "Oh sure, honey, I know it is." He woke up to reality. "Oh yes, I'm sure it is. I'm sure you'll do just fine and it will all be over before you know it. That's what the doctor said, and that you could continue on as if nothing ever happened."

"I wish you could quit work and care for me all day long. I think that would make a big difference, and I wouldn't be so crabby in the little time we do spend together. Don't you think?"

Virgil knew this would come. His work was his only respite, and she knew it. She would love to crush that out of him too.

"Well, someone has to keep you in golf balls, don't they?" He laughed. Virgil had to say it even if he knew that it might not pass as a harmless joke. He cringed at the inevitable onslaught.

But no, she was contemplative. "Well, I suppose you are right. I don't feel like playing golf much these days, but I'm sure I'll come back to it."

Gee, taking it seriously. He would never have called that one.

Virgil's work was becoming less of a respite. The hospital board reports indicated an unusual number of infections associated with certain surgeries, especially with the bilateral myringotomies, the tubes-in-the-ears surgeries for kids. For some darn reason, five of the operations this past month had ended up with infections, and the poor kids had needed to stay in the hospital an extra two weeks. That was nearly unheard of these days, unless you were practically dying. The hospital lost so much money when patients stayed that long.

Virgil got a cold feeling in his stomach when he reviewed the list of supplies used in these procedures. One glaring factor they all shared: use of the metal AGAF ventilating tubes, a grommet his company manufactured.

And then there was that dratted little switchboard operator, Eliza, who always complained about the cold ventilation drafts from the nearby computer room. She'd insisted on having her own space heater under her desk, even though it was plainly against hospital policy. On his personal recommendation, they'd decided to install an electric wall heater instead. It worked on the same principle as the portable space heater, but it passed inspection, or at least it used to. The in-house fire marshal goon must have gone out for donuts when he was supposed to check her worksite. That electric heater had caught fire, due to—thank you very much— another of AGAF's grommets that was supposed to connect a fan and reduce overheating.

What next? The cafeteria food was bad; that must be another grommet failure. The emergency doors didn't close automatically when the fire alarms go off; that must be his fault too.

CHAPTER 12

Eileen wandered over to the radiology department. The department had been hit with fewer layoffs as the technicians tended to manage their own high turnover. Benjamin, the lead technician, was always a joy, all smiles and thumbs up to her; she secretly suspected a hyperactive thyroid from all that radiation.

Ugh, radiation, that was the worst of her treatments.

The fish tank caught her eye. Exotic, colorful fish, silently flitting through the water, meant to soothe edgy nerves. She stepped up to the reception desk and asked for Benjamin, but the receptionist motioned off into one of the curtained rooms.

———

The fish tank. One very active fish. Always around feeding time.

The gowns, finally getting the hang, literally, of them. Tie in front, tie in back, and what the heck is that little string in the middle for?

The nakedness, not caring who's poking and probing now. Her metabolism going crazy. Hot, sore, sweaty, raw skin—even a T-shirt feels like sandpaper. The ointments proffered to soothe, either sticky aloe gel or gooey, industrial-strength moisturizer, as heavy as kindergarten paste. Then cornstarch. She felt like she was being basted and floured for a fine gourmet meal, except there was nothing fine about it, more like a biker barbecue. Hot and red and burnt, plus she had those tattoos to direct the radiation.

She tried to think of the radiation as powerful superheroes swooping down to her aid. Those books encouraged you to think like that. But toward the end of the treatments, mostly she just felt fried. They said to keep your protein intake high. *Keep it very high! Calories, calories, calories—you can't consume too many!*

At the same time, she read first-person accounts in countless books and magazines that encouraged eschewing any and all meat. Like Gretchen (in one of the immuno-cancer-quackery-tell-alls) had done. Gretchen was going to die. Dr. One said she was going to die; Dr. Two said she was going to die, maybe in one month, maybe three, but you betcha it was going to happen soon. So she went to Mexico, communed with magis, and learned to cleanse her system using specially formulated herbs and chelated minerals and was importuned to never, never, oh, never let the flesh of mammal ever pass her lips again. Once again, nothing beat the it's-all-your-fault approach to shame a cancer patient into adopting ridiculously restrictive diets and other habits. Eileen couldn't recall, but figured Gretchen had probably died anyway.

Eileen had agreed. After cleansing her system with chemo, she didn't dare infiltrate it with the poisons that had inevitably caused her plight to begin with. Macrobiotics, that was the way to go. Rice and oatmeal. Oatmeal and rice, maybe a bit of kale. Clean as a whistle, her body would be. But of course, the restriction only exacerbated her misery. After a few excruciating weeks, after which she felt like her body was eating itself raw from the inside out (and her doctor chastised her for losing weight), she crawled her haggard, threadlike self quickly to the closest carnivore house and gulped with impunity sirloin, fried chicken, mashed potatoes drenched in gravy, even veal parmigiana, poor little baby calves. And thick, thick milkshakes.

"Eileen, how in the world are you doing? Great to see you!" Benjamin held out his arms and grasped her tightly. "Oh, my goodness, I almost forgot," and he suddenly released her. "You OK, now, you know around there?" His eyes flickered to her chest.

"Ow ow ow ow ow! Sorry, no, just kidding. I'm all patched up, thanks."

He grinned and waggled a finger at her. "You, always the same."

"How's it going, Benny?"

"Well, if you're asking purely rhetorically, I'll give the pat answer, 'Fine, and you?' But if you're asking thoughtfully…"

Eileen nodded. "I guess we're all about the same."

He hugged her again, gently. She could feel his rapid heartbeat and once again suspected the thyroid.

CHAPTER 13

Jenaveev was not much of a worker, but she really took to selling flotation tanks. She truly believed in their therapeutic magic and that every home should have one. Virgil encouraged her to work as much as possible, so, of course, that meant she worked as little as possible. He suspected that deep down she really believed in the business. It was just her own orneriness against anything he wanted that kept her from working more.

Every so often, a couple of times a week, she would go to a school or a physical therapy clinic and talk about the wonders of flotation. The tanks were different from hot tubs, designed for the user to stretch out flat with just the head barely above the water level. They were more for meditation than socializing purposes. She worked for a friend of hers, so she didn't have to put in too many hours. Poor, sappy old Julian was thrilled to have someone of her family name and prestige selling his product. She'd tried it once and was sold on it. She called it the "ultimate form of nonexistence."

Virgil thought the experience actually allowed one to be more sensitive to one's environment, not less. It wasn't really a nonexistence experience. But he didn't try to correct her. As long as she was enthusiastic during her presentations, she didn't have to be completely accurate, or even articulate, on all of the particulars. He was not really sure she grasped the sensual stream that was heightened during the flotation session. The "cosmic" concept of it. But again, it didn't really matter, and maybe she could bring in some of the common-man market, those who would turn up their noses at such New Age type experiences but would be quite impressed with a corporate wife expounding about something.

Her activities did highlight the Ellingsworth name and the AGAF corporation, though, and that was good enough for him. The Ellingsworth home didn't have a tank; Virgil had said they spent enough on maid service and they already had a pool, so he wasn't getting another thing to attract dirt and mold that they would have to pay someone to clean.

―

Noelle wanted her mother to get involved with the preparations for the daddy-daughter dance, but she was too tired and grouchy. Jenaveev instead hoarded herself in the back room with murder mysteries and romance novels and watched videos.

Noelle pirouetted around the room in the new dress that Virgil had bought for her, but her mother just growled at her. A sudden flash hit Noelle: *She's jealous of me.* A vision of her mother came to her as a haggard old crone who never took pleasure in anything that didn't provide immediate satisfaction for her. It horrified Noelle. She remembered that bouncy, pretty woman who'd waved at her father when they'd come out of the movies that one time. Who was she?

Virgil carefully pinned an orchid to her white chiffon georgette dress and gallantly extended his arm to his daughter, who snickered as she held on. This was still their special day of the year, the father-daughter dance at her school. She sat in the car feeling, despite herself, like a princess. The quarrels and pettiness of recent days disappeared and Noelle felt a glimmer of the goodness that life could bring. She looked up at her dad with gentle eyes, and he looked down at her and smiled.

In the car, they were mostly quiet. Noelle looked out the window. "Is Mom going to be OK?"

"Oh sure, brand spanking new soon."

They both laughed.

Red flashing lights met them when they reached the school gymnasium. The town fire truck blocked the parking lot and blasted its horn as Virgil approached. An officer waved her arms at them and shouted, "No dance tonight! Broken water main!"

Water pooled along the parking lot. Groups of tuxedoed boys splashed and hooted in the water and tried to pull in a shrieking girl or two.

Noelle sighed. Virgil patted her hand and said, "We'll have our own night out, honey."

He turned the car around in a crush of gravel, which prompted another horn blast from the fire truck, and headed back to town. "How's about we go to Philly? I'm up for it. Your mom's not expecting us until late."

Noelle shrugged. "No, let's just go to the steak place."

Virgil hesitated then shrugged too. "Sure, it's perfect."

CHAPTER 14

The hospital continued to buzz about its future, or lack thereof as it would seem. The OR secretary stopped to see Eileen and pass along the latest buzz about the ear infections.

One poor boy moaned and was in tears all night since his parents belonged to some sort of religious group that didn't allow pain killers—well, narcotics—for youngsters. The nurses on the floor couldn't stand to listen to him anymore. They moved him to a room with a nearly deaf elderly woman who'd just had cataract surgery, so she couldn't hear or see much. Last week, they had three such moaners. They had better get the situation figured out, the secretary said; everyone was scared to death of doing the myringotomies. And worse, they were starting to get the nervous giggles any time one was scheduled. Humor as coping mechanism.

Eileen read on the outpatient admission list that Virgil's wife was getting treatment. There was a sort of unspoken rank among cancer victims. Once you've had cancer and you hear that someone else has had it, you immediately make comparisons. Who had it worse, who had to endure more treatment, who has the better chance. The ho-hum cases were those that had simply required surgery: many skin types, breast cancer where just the lump was removed. Those hardly even counted as cancer.

The worst cases were those with stem cell transplants. Eileen was awed by those people who'd essentially had their blood completely removed, were blasted with ultrakiller chemo, and then were hopefully revived with their blood transfused back into them. Eileen herself had had two surgeries, one for the lump and one for the lymph nodes, chemo for six months and radiation, followed by what was supposed to be a five-year course of tamoxifen, which she cut back to three and a half years after feeling her pelvis erupt, likely from endometrial changes caused by the tamoxifen. Neverending. That had been enough for her. So much for piquing her curiosity. She figured on the cancer panache scale, she deserved a pretty strong intermediate category.

Huh, Jenaveev was just a cancer wannabe. She didn't even rate on the scale.

CHAPTER 15

Virgil had worked at AGAF so long he couldn't imagine working anywhere else. It was an important job, as the world revolved around grommets. Ubiquitously used in all areas of modern life, from space heaters and surgical supplies to keeping unruly electric cords in line, controlling lines on boats, and keeping your shoes tied. He'd started working at AGAF right after college, figuring that it would be just a temporary situation until he sorted out what he really wanted to do. It was temporary for twenty years, and counting.

His father was good friends with the chief financial officer and insisted his son was a brilliant match for the company. Despite the glowing review, Virgil still had to go through the interview process. He never quite forgave his father for subjecting him to the humiliation, having to answer those simpleton questions: "Where do you see yourself in five years?" "Are you a feeler or a perceiver?" "If you could be any animal, what would you be and why?" Really, what sort of psychological torture did he have to endure to get a job? Answers: "I see myself outstanding in my field (planning the new golf course)." "I like to perceive something then feel it. Don't you?" "I would be an elephant, so I could sit on you and hopefully make you shut up."

At that early age, he hadn't yet developed the skills to dazzle and charm. Now he had learned that the best way to success is not to take anything seriously. Always act unapologetic and as if you have nothing to lose.

His father, Claudius Ellingsworth, was a lawyer. Occasionally, young Virgil would tag along to work, excited by the dark brown smells of success and expensive woodwork. He loved watching the pretty ladies in their short skirts and pressed blouses bustling back and forth through the hallways, leaving behind wafts of flowery scents. He loved marching into the bejeweled and mirrored elevator, surrounded by men in dark suits and hues-of-red ties. They all smiled and said hello to his father and to him. He felt sure this was going to be the life for him.

His dreams, however, did not coincide with his actual drive. He cheated throughout college. It was a dare, a thrill, and provided the extreme self-satisfaction of not getting caught. It was also a little out of desperation, because he wasn't inclined to study. Studying was too boring, and not at all fun. There was more thrill and skill, he thought, in cheating. From his huge social circle, he learned who'd had certain teachers in previous years and would buy past tests. He would openly look at his neighbor's paper, the student who willingly leaned back to please the rich kid.

He was a very successful cheater until ratchety old Prof. Silas T. Wren, his poli-sci instructor, caught him. Wren was furious. Virgil had never had such vituperation leveled toward him. Not that he never deserved it; everyone was usually so in awe of his money that they didn't dare try. But intimidated, Professor Wren was certainly not. He was merciless in his condemnation. Even when the administrators tried to explain to him how important it was to have the Ellingsworth support and not rock the boat, he refused to cave. Finally, the school board had to intervene and overrode Prof. Wren's recommendation to expel Virgil permanently from the program. Virgil graduated, but law school was not in his future.

Ellingsworth Sr. undoubtedly was grateful to distance his lad from the more traditional Ellingsworths of Baltimore.

Virgil had hated leaving the comfort and family prestige of Baltimore for the rustic Maple Leaf. Not only did no one know him there, they didn't even know his family. He had to make it on his own, without the silky hoist to the top.

He discovered that he rather liked the competitive world of commerce. It was a bit like drugs—the inner workings could be dirty and vile but the end result fancy and ecstatic. And most profitable. He wasn't confined by the pressure of keeping the business afloat, as he could always live quite well on the family trust fund. He could run the business into the ground and sigh to his father that he'd tried, but, phooey, it didn't work out. He took risks that a state college graduate would never take and led the company toward its most profitable years ever. He scoured the country looking for the best designers, engineers, researchers, and craftsmen. Also the prettiest receptionists.

Maple Leaf was no Big Apple—or even Baltimore, for that matter—but he was determined to turn it into something more than a black speck on the map and a turnpike rest stop. His company would turn heads. As drivers sped along the turnpike and saw the flashy billboards for American Grommets and Fasteners, they would point and exclaim. He would do for grommets what Ford did for cars.

The company had been founded on grommets for surgical procedures and electrical work, all very serious and mechanically engineered. Virgil wanted to drive the company's products for other uses. He thought that with the proliferation of computers and computer-connected devices, there was a need for something to tame the electrical cords going from ports to sockets. Some of his clients complained about getting their legs or knees or elbows caught in the unruly cords. Looking under their desks at the masses of wiring, Virgil knew there was a solution. Of course, he wouldn't think of it himself, but he knew there had to be one and he would probably find it and pass it off as his own idea.

As the days of portable typewriters and shorthand had led to electrics, Dictaphones, and eventually desktop computers, speakers, keyboards, and mouse pads, the morass of wires under one's desk had become unmanageable. With work-site cubicles, it was impossible to organize and connect the wires without unsightly extension cords. One of the AGAF supervisors had drilled out a hole in the back corner of his own desk. He'd covered it with an upside-down paper cereal bowl with a notch cut out of the side for the cords and to hide his handiwork from the boss. When Virgil had noticed the bowl—not ugly, really, but somewhat out of place—he'd lifted it and—eureka!—the desktop grommet idea was born.

Eventually, Virgil became president of the company.

CHAPTER 16

Like a dying couple's last copulation during a disaster, sexual tension in the hospital was high. One of the revolving-door financial managers, Bryan, heavily married, asked Eileen out for a drink after work.

"We can discuss your, um, future. How's about it?"

She looked at Bryan. His small, darting eyes and damp forehead told the whole story. He had performed dutifully for his wife, the lovely Miriam, and together they produced two children who were the precious delight of their lives. Now Miriam spent her days gazing wistfully out the window and dreaming of romantic encounters with tall, dark, gentle strangers on pastoral pathways while her love-starved husband craned his neck for a peek at his secretary's cleavage.

Eileen's silence encouraged him, and he raised his eyebrows at her and nodded. She was tempted to do him just to shut him up. But he had an overbite that she wanted nowhere near her petunia.

"Oh, Bryan, go home to your wife."

Bryan shuffled off, smiling broadly.

CHAPTER 17

To escape Jenaveev's disturbing mood swings, compose himself, and air out his brain, Virgil planned a trip. GLK had invited him to their annual client convention in the Poconos, but it was hardly a hot spot. He decided to slip away to Ocean City, Maryland, instead to see the sights. Beautiful, silk-toned ladies in thong bikinis would soothe him. He didn't have the energy to consider any clandestine activity. He just wanted some peace and quiet in the midst of nubile nakedness. Nick was taking care of his mother, and Noelle, well, since the dance (or, non-dance) he hadn't seen her for a while. Clara, the maid, was always around too. It would only be for a couple of days. He just had to get away.

He started driving south, through congested Baltimore and over the Bay Bridge, where the expansive waterway below him beckoned. At the end of the bridge, he pulled the car over and got out. The tossing waves seemed to lure him, and he was transfixed watching the water. A fisherman limped past, holding his rod across his shoulder and a bucket of fish in his other hand.

"What're you catching?" Virgil asked. People were friendly out here.

"Oh, little of this and that. A little bass."

"Nice."

"Also have some crab pots I gotta go check on now. Nice chattin'."

"Sure, see ya. Good luck."

Virgil was disappointed. He had never had a discussion with anyone about fish before in his life, except for the restaurant kind, of course, but for some reason he wanted to engage this man further. He sighed and slipped back into the driver's seat.

Then it was on to the scenic Eastern Shore and finally Ocean City. It was early in the season, and few folks were out and about. He chose a nice little motel in nearby Bethany Beach, checked into the room and dived onto the bed. He lay there quietly, waiting for his head to stop spinning. Now that he was here, he had no interest in women of any kind. Even scantily dressed ones, although if one happened to stumble into his room, he would react appropriately. However, he preferred to simply pass out.

He woke up at nine thirty, and it was dark. He called the front desk to order a salad and a grilled cheese and tomato sandwich. The clerk just laughed at him and referred him to the nearby all-night diner. He decided the salt air and humid breezes would do him good and headed for the only neon light in this dud of a town.

Helene, his waitress, suggested the blue plate special—sliced turkey, filling, mashers, and green beans. The idea churned Virgil's stomach, and he ordered his original meal. She shrugged, jotted down his order, and headed back to the kitchen. The place was empty except for a few large-butted folks hunkered down at the counter.

One man turned when he heard Virgil's unknown voice and hailed him. "So, how's it going, my man? What brings you to our lovely burg?"

Virgil grunted, "Oh, this and that. Any sort of night life around here?" He was just being friendly, but maybe if they offered up a good idea, he could take them up on it.

Both men turned around on their stools and erupted in laughter.

"Here? Man, this here's the definition of a family town. Hottest night is Friday, when there's bingo at the senior center." He peered at Virgil with eyes nearly hidden by bushy eyebrows. He wore a baseball cap emblazoned with a big F. "But you know, though, there is one thing."

Virgil looked over at the man. "What's that?"

The man pushed off the stool and slid in Virgil's booth. "Name's Jimbo. Good to meet you." Virgil mumbled a response. "So, during certain rainy nights, just before summer, some claim to see Davy Jones."

Virgil was puzzled. "Of the Monkees?"

Jimbo grimaced. "Of who? No, no, this goes way back over a hundred years. Davy Jones's locker—don't ya know?"

Virgil had some vague recollection of the term in relation to the open sea or pirates, maybe from a book or movie. "Uh, I guess so."

"Aw, man, you don't have to pretend. Just say you don't know."

Impatient, Virgil said, "So what of him?"

"So, anyways, during nights like this, some folks can see him on the beach. He's the devil, like, of the ocean? People don't usually see him until they're drowning."

Virgil held back a yawn, which Jimbo mistook for an intake of breath. "Oh, it's OK, my friend. It's just a dumb local legend."

"Hey, Jimbo, ya eatin' your pie?" his companion asked.

Jimbo squeezed out of Virgil's booth and headed back to the counter. "Sorry, bud. There's really not much going on around here, to answer your question."

Virgil nodded as Helene placed his food on the table. He tried not to display his disappointment at the gray tomato and white iceberg lettuce. At least the cheese was melted and the bread unburned.

Afterward, he checked out the pool hours and saw that it had closed at ten. A swim would have felt really nice right now. He looked out at the beach and thought he saw a dark hulking object in the sand. "Nah." He decided to take a long, hot shower instead and watch a little TV. He should write a book, *Surviving Lesionous Uvula Presquamous Cell Carcinoma of Your Spouse for Dummies*. Hmm, probably wouldn't have much of a following. He fell asleep thinking of red ants crawling all over his body.

He awoke at eight the next morning, feeling refreshed and vital, a surprise considering his vile thoughts upon retiring. Now he would take that swim. Afterward, he would have a leisurely breakfast and maybe call home to see if there had been any life-threatening developments. He should have given his family the phone number of this place, but then they might have called him.

At the front desk, Virgil pulled out his card to pay for the room and something fell out of his wallet. Irritated, he looked down as the Mercury dime—a shinier, newer replacement for, well, that *other* Mercury Dime—rolled under the counter. He bent over, picked up the dime, and suddenly felt a tightness behind his eyes. He would just go home.

CHAPTER 18

With the sudden rash of problems in the operating room, Neil from Salto Duthie needed to spend more time in Winston's office, helping with various internal mishaps and spin control and offering general advice. The board meeting that afternoon was solemn, as they all were, with Eileen's reading of the minutes from the last meeting. The door opened and in came Neil.

Although she had seen him hundreds of times, for some reason he really perked her attention now. Previously, he was just another married man, although she allowed that he was cute and funny and attentive to her. He had mentioned a while ago, to her great surprise, that he was divorcing his wife, and it suddenly occurred to her that the divorce should just about be final by now. She had known him for so long as good old Neil, someone she could count on to make her smile with a joke, a flirtatious remark, or self-deprecating comment. But now, not only could he make her smile, maybe he could make her sing, for he was available! Available in that hot-eyed, "I'm looking for a rebound girl" kind of way, sure, but available nonetheless. They'd always had fun together, but Eileen had never thought to consider him as a potential dating partner. Now that he was available, she thought, *Hmm, definite possibilities there.* She had talked to him a bit about Virgil, so he might just see her as a neurotic loser or a "friend" with no other possibilities. It was worth exploring anyway.

It could have been her imagination, but he was looking at her differently too, it seemed. Had those eyes always beckoned hers to travel into his soul like that? She didn't think so. Maybe he was myopic. No, he seemed to search her eyes for any faraway look that might be attributed to missing Virgil. She searched his eyes for a misty loneliness from his departed Kerry Ann. They greeted each other as they always did, but there was a definite difference—a heightened awareness, a sense of sexual tension, a skittishness that was never there before. Butterflies fluttered in her stomach. He lightly touched her shoulder and electricity coursed down her arm and past her chest before settling into a slow, steady burn in the nether regions. Whoa. This would definitely make the board meetings more interesting.

Then the board president, old Sol Heckman, mumbled, "Any corrections to the minutes? Fine, then. Let the minutes be approved. Have you had a chance to read the packet of materials also sent to you? We are quite chagrined to note there has been an alarming amount of mishaps in the operating room."

There was a shuffling of papers as the members rooted for the report.

"The surgeries have all been performed by the otolaryngology group," Sol continued. "Is there any significance to this? I thought they made it through the credentialing process with exceptionally high marks. Do they need to repeat their certification? What's going on here?"

Sol was a bit of a curmudgeon and usually said what he pleased. Since he'd been around for two hundred years, everyone let him.

"No, I don't believe that's it," the chief resident, Dr. Zirkle, was quick to interject. "The physicians themselves seem genuinely perplexed by this development."

Eileen had heard personally from one of the scrubs that Dr. Champlain shouted out after the most recent reported postsurgery infection, "Goddamn it, hasn't anyone cleaned this equipment? What's the matter with you people?" She kept that little tidbit to herself. She wasn't expected to participate at these meetings.

"Yes, the doctors were becoming a bit agitated about these ongoing infections. We have to isolate the circumstances and figure out what is the precipitating event. The doctors are in danger of becoming knife-shy."

Knife-shy? That was a new one. Eileen assumed it meant that the doctors were threatening to take their knives elsewhere. She didn't believe it meant that they were in danger of putting down their knives permanently and joining a Buddhist cult. *All righty, here comes the committee thing.*

Dr. Zirkle continued, "We have decided to form a committee to evaluate the incident reports connected with these events. Gentlemen, upon reviewing these materials, we greatly anticipate your recommendations and expect to concede to same."

Neil suddenly gave her a cross-eyed look. She nearly burst out laughing but caught herself by bearing down very hard on her bottom lip. She rearranged herself in her chair so that she wasn't facing him. But she did catch Virgil's eye. He was staring at them. *Get over it, you sad-sack petard.*

After the meeting, Eileen headed down the hall to her office.

"Eileen, my dear, don't turn away from me like that. I might get a complex."

Eileen looked back and glowed. "Neil! You could use a little complex to ratchet down that ego of yours."

They hugged briefly. "It's good to see you," they both said, then laughed nervously.

"Where are you going now?" he asked. "I'm just going to grab a sandwich across the street. Wanna join me?"

Eileen said, "Sure, why not?" He was not wearing that ring.

They did this all the time, but today it felt different. Why did her heart quicken and suddenly spread warmth throughout her chest? Not a hot flash; this wasn't like someone suddenly tossing a hot blanket on her. This was like someone coaxing her into a down comforter. She was self-conscious and loved it.

As soon as she stepped through the hospital's front door with Neil, she regretted agreeing to lunch. She was hungry and needed food, but already she felt warm and giddy, and her appetite seeped away. *Calm, calm, calm, calm,* she thought.

He smiled at her. "So, in the mood for anything in particular?"

Lordy, any simple comment could be misconstrued. She decided to take the very high road. "Well, I'm in the mood for a guarantee that the hospital will make it. But barring that, the café has great salads."

No, no, no—she wasn't in the mood for a stinkin' salad; she'd be starving again in an hour. Why did she...?

"Salad? Well, there is some lettuce-like substance at the pork barbeque place. Will that do?"

Neil to the rescue. Ah yes, that would do quite nicely. She smiled and nodded.

They settled in the booth and ordered mile-high pork sandwiches, with cole slaw for Eileen and potato salad for Neil.

Eileen, dying to ask him about the details of his divorce, settled on, "So, how are you doing these days?"

His eyes shaded for a moment, but then he brightened. "Well, your hospital is certainly keeping me in neckties lately. It's been one thing after another."

That's not what she was talking about. She could tell he knew it, but he just shrugged.

This might take a while.

CHAPTER 19

Despite himself, Virgil liked his wife's new pale and wan look. It's what had struck him when they first met.

They'd gone to high school in Baltimore together. He was in the slightly-bad-boys-who-had-money group and she was in the very-bad-girls-who-had-no-money group. Two groups destined to share the same path, at least for a little while. A bunch of them used to hang out at the Green Mount Cemetery, an old-time celebrity graveyard of sorts, and smoke pot. It was pretty easy to do; they would hide behind the gigantic monuments when they saw the cops or graveyard patrol drive by. John Wilkes Booth was purportedly buried there in an unmarked grave, and, in their more lucid moments, they would search and squeal and argue that they'd found the spot.

Jenaveev, who called herself Grace then, joined the group soon after her father left her mother when he found out she was enjoying more than advice from her psychiatrist. And from the librarian. And from the grocery clerk. It seemed Grace's mom had left no stone unturned when it came to satisfying her libido. Her dad had even hesitated before leaving because he was getting it too.

But finally he took off for Nevada, and no one ever heard from him again. They would get an envelope from time to time with enough money to keep Grace's mother from chasing him down. The mom had much better taste these days; now she made love to a bottle of rum like nobody's business.

Virgil hadn't been particularly attracted to Grace at first, but she immediately recognized him as a lifeline, grasped onto him, and held tight. Virgil was somewhat flattered because she was unusual-looking—very thin and pale with that wild, bushy mane of red hair cascading all over her face and shoulders. Her green eyes peered out, wide and innocent. She didn't have the usual popular-girl look—tasteful hair, just-so blonde; perfect makeup and clothing; and contrived behavior. Yes, Grace was captivating in those days.

She would go to any lengths with drugs; she wouldn't turn anything down. LSD, mescaline, uppers, downers, smack—all of it. She wasn't timid about it, or giggly or reluctant. She wasn't holding off for someone to talk her into it. Many of the girls just followed along to be part of the group. Not Grace. She aggressively joined in without any hesitation. She never had her own dope, but she was quick to offer payment, which was usually turned down because they all knew she had no money.

Amazingly, she didn't seem jaded, always gazing at Virgil with those hollow, big green eyes. She didn't have much to offer in terms of humor, personality, or insight; she was just a true drug groupie. In their shared haze, she seemed like the one loyal thing. The others would get into spats about some sort of democratic nonsense, and there would be shunning and cussing and throwing things. She never joined in, for any side; she would just sit there nodding. They all thought she was wise and deep. Later Virgil realized it was just the drugs. She had no opinion about anything, except that which impacted one of her physical senses: I'm hurt, I'm cold, I'm hot, I'm hungry, I need money. That was the extent of her perception.

He'd hated to admit it later, but she was much more interesting as a junkie than she was sober. At least her drug-induced stupor shut her up once in a while. She was never more agreeable than when the drugs were flowing freely

In spite of her oddity, or maybe because of it, Virgil remained intrigued with her. She seemed ladylike and dainty, her pale face always shrouded in that wild mane of red hair. When they'd started seeing one another, she felt that the name Grace was too ordinary, even unseemly, so she changed it to Jenaveev. More elegant, she'd said.

Too late did he realize that she was merely strung out and once she overcame her addictions, she would become an uncensored shrew. Her opinions, once stifled by insecurity and drug haze, now tumbled from her like avalanche boulders, and were enthusiastically encouraged by her therapist. Spoiled by therapy, she'd learned that each and every one of her minute thoughts was legitimate and needed to be expressed, explored, and condoned.

Virgil's parents had hated her from the beginning. Yet he was close enough to his rebellious years that that only added to her appeal. He thought they were being snobbish and uppity. Their aversion indicated their lack of depth, and he was embarrassed for them. He had plucked a delicate flower, and he intended to nurture it into a blossoming orchid.

In those earlier days, Jenaveev had a dog that obediently followed here wherever she went. He wasn't much of a dog, just a plain-looking white-and-black part-terrier. Part lots of other things. A bit on the pudgy side. He wasn't particularly affectionate or particularly mean. He was just there. A friend would walk up to him to pat its head, hoping to elicit some dog-like glee, and he would sit patiently and allow himself to be petted. He wouldn't look up or wag his tail or grin. Sometimes he would look around, get up midpat, and simply walk away. He didn't seem to be particularly devoted to Jenaveev either but always managed to be there, trailing behind her. She never talked about him or to him when she was around the rest of the group. She didn't talk much to anyone. They all just expected the dog to always be there with her. She called him Max.

One day, Max wasn't with her.

Virgil asked, "Where's Max?"

Jenaveev said, "Dead." She hummed it.

"Oh."

She said nothing more about it, and no one asked. They were all more interested in getting high for their own morose reasons; they didn't need to hear another pathetic story to undermine their own.

Weeks passed and Jenaveev became crankier. She'd never had much of a personality, was always very quiet, but after Max's death she blossomed into a nagging shrew.

"Let's go get pizza. I want mine with artichokes and *no cheese*! And after that I want to go to the park and play on the swings!"

Virgil was intrigued even more. He thought it showed depth. He asked her to marry him that night.

"Wheee, Virgil, higher, higher! What did you say?"

"Marry me."

"Yesssssssss!"

Her mane of red hair flew freely behind her. She seemed more thrilled with the height of the swing than the proposal. That intrigued Virgil even more. He was used to women fawning all over him. He had money. Rather, his family had money, ergo it was inevitable that he would also have money. This girl, Jenaveev—what a wonderful name!—his money had no impact on her. Or, at least, it seemed not to. He must have made a good choice. And he just had to have that red hair. Wanted to bury his face in it forever. He could be happy with that. Couldn't he?

His mother had warned him, "Honey, you can take the trash out of the trailer, but...well, you know the rest."

The comment confirmed to him that they were being elitist. At the time he would do almost anything to piss off his parents, smug, self-satisfied old goats that they were. They just couldn't bear the thought of their precious son marrying down. They had their hearts set on several other girls in their group. Daughter of a railroad man, a banker, or a lawyer. The usual stuff. But this—this choice would reflect badly on them. He was more determined than ever to have this red-haired goddess. He would show them.

The luster soon died from Jenaveev's hair and from the relationship with Virgil. She had been quite comfortable as a nothing; now she was supposed to be something, and the thought was excruciating to her. She had no idea how to be something. She figured it didn't really matter; she would flaunt her money instead. That was easy to do.

She started slowly, casually piling on her Personal Shopper 12 identical sweaters, different colors. The shopper had learned never to question her hirer's judgment. This woman was a spending rhino; the personal shopper was proud to be the main contributor to the most colorful creature in town, Mrs. Virgil Ellingsworth. Her combinations were shudder-worthy. Dainty, intricately laced blouses paired with heavy woolen pants. Gauzy Indian skirts with corduroy blazers. Her choice of fabric colors consisted of purples coupled with oranges and olive greens.

At Virgil's urging, she finally did get that job as the flotation tank representative. It was just a bit part, a teeny bit of nothing to amuse her for a few hours a week. She secretly loved the idea of immersing oneself into nothingness. She hated the actual flotation tank, however. She thought it felt like drowning in a coffin. It reminded her a little too much of her childhood. Those tiny dark closets, harboring bat's nests and mice droppings. That freezing cold room, dark as pitch at night, the murky silence broken four or five times a night by the clacketing train passing nearby.

She was afraid if she crept into the floatation tank, someone would lock it and she'd never get out. They would know she was an imposter and would be cast back into the dusty, moldy world of the screeching bats and skittering mice. Forever.

But the floatation tank—she rhapsodized on and on to her clients about it. She felt it would be good for others, others who weren't flooded with money to help them forget their problems. And if they didn't have money, then of course they had problems.

Now Virgil, recently returned from Ocean City, watched his wife—her hair long gone in that Hefty trash bag—spread out on the hammock, idly reading the weekly tabloid and absorbing the latest stink on the stars. On the ground next to her was a can of beer. Still reading, she reached down, inserted her middle finger into the opening of the can, and pulled it up to her mouth, gulping its contents as most of it dribbled over her chin and pooled in the little divot at the base of her throat, all the while not taking her eyes off the page. Charming.

Yes, he had penetrated the depths of her soul and revealed the void therein. Damn, how he hated that his parents were always right.

Many years earlier, Virgil had driven home feeling a silly anticipation. How would Jenaveev greet him on this first routine day after their wedding (and honeymoon in Mexico, where Jenaveev had always wanted to go)?

He fiddled with the key in the lock and opened the door. Jenaveev stood there totally in the buff with a long-stemmed rose between her teeth. As he gaped, she took the rose and began to caress the petals against her skin, dancing it lightly across her breasts until her nipples crinkled with excitement. Then she dangled it down gently against her sweet triangle, lifted her arms and ran it down one and up underneath one of her voluptuous breasts then over across the other, and began to slink seductively toward him. He felt a hard tightness that strained against his pants. She lightly ran the rose between his legs, dropped it on the end table, draped her legs around his waist, wrapped her arms around his neck, and kissed him deeply as she ground against him. Then she put her hand down there, and before he knew it he was lying on his back with her toes in his mouth and…

No no, no. That was not Jenaveev. That was how Eileen had met him at the door for his fantasy come true a while back. On the contrary, on his first day home from work after his wedding, he was greeted by Jenaveev with her foot up on the kitchen table—on his placemat, of course—painting her toenails. Merlot red, cotton balls between her surprisingly large toes. She barely looked up as Virgil entered.

"Oh, you scared me. Now I have to do this toe all over again." She gave him a slightly annoyed, slightly coquettish expression that was supposed to pass for charm but came across as awkward disinterest. Still, it was their first night of a lifetime of routine nights, so he tried to make something of a sensual moment of it and reached around to kiss her on the back of her neck. She jumped sky high, spilled the nail polish, giggled nervously, and looked up at him with what passed for sensuality for her, but for him already started to make him gag. He knew that was his cue to go over and squeeze her breast or something, but the mood was over for him and he just glowered and started upstairs. She called Clara, the maid, to clean up the mess.

His life could have taken a different path. He'd tried his hand at being a counselor of sorts as part of his psychology credit in college, but found himself always titillated by his patients' problems. Women especially loved to come to him, sometimes with just the slightest pretext of having a problem, but by the time they finished their tearful lamentations, Virgil just wanted sex.

Emma was one of the first. She fretted that her mechanic husband never seemed to be able to get his hands clean. No matter how hard he scrubbed, and she could attest to his attempts, his fingers had caked-on black, gooky, oily stuff, especially embedded in the nails. It really grossed her out. She couldn't stand for him to touch her in a personal fashion. She feared that little black tarry microbes were penetrating her mucous membranes and slowly poisoning her. She feared that her husband was planning to kill her in this slow, torturous way.

Virgil gazed soberly at her, imagining her pert, naked ass trembling in his face. He wanted to tell her, "Hey, baby, have you ever done it with a clean man?" He carelessly flashed his immaculately manicured fingers as he reassured her. He wondered if she noticed.

It was these past peccadilloes that would make it very hard for him to get a divorce, even if that was a possibility, which, of course, it wasn't. Jenaveev was faintly aware that Virgil's behavior was less than exemplary, even if she didn't know specifics. Anyway, she was ready with lots of fodder—unexplained absences, strange smells on his person, and remember that crazy reaction of the cat, Torpid, when it sprayed on his clothes? It must have smelled some strange substance. Cats, vengeful creatures that they are, can sense unfamilial sex and express their disapproval accordingly. Of course, it's not so much protection of their turf; they just have a faint nudge of recognition in their pea brains of how great it was to have sex in their prespayed days and can't stand for anyone else to enjoy it, even a human-like creature who seems to have an incredibly dreary life otherwise.

Clearly, there were enough signs that would lead a judge or jury to sympathize with Jenaveev over Virgil. A woman can act distraught and no one questions it. Especially mothers. Just being a mother sanctioned any thoughts or behaviors a woman might have in the eyes of society. Oh, the poor woman! Left to take care of those two poor children all by herself! He would have to pay and pay and pay.

Subsequently, Virgil saw their family as the ramshackle jalopy backfiring down the road, spewing smoke out the exhaust pipe, wheels wobbling, muffler dragging on the asphalt, sparks flying, the whole thing rattling and rocking back and forth—yet still the owners clung on. They were "maintaining the stability of the family." That's what their shrink said was most important. Virgil paid big money for their weekly family sessions—the repetitions, the games, the drills. The shrinks had to be right.

After she married Virgil, a cold, steel wall crashed down to separate her new life from her poor past. No longer Grace, she was now Jenaveev.

Jenaveev had spent most of her days playing golf, even when the kids were babies. She had convinced the country club to provide a day care. "How can you expect us to be all we can be in golf if we have to be responsible for our own kids too? It's inconjugal." Everyone nodded in agreement. No one ever corrected her, especially not at the country club because she might have taken her money away. They shouldn't have worried; they were the only game in town, and Jenaveev would never quit the country club. It was much too prestigious. She could never tell her friends that she played golf at the public course. And all of her friends were members of the club. She could never make friends with people who didn't have money. She wouldn't even know where to begin.

She had ridden the city bus once, six years ago, the Number 139, a traumatic experience that had sent her to bed for a week, muttering, "Those horrible, horrible people."

CHAPTER 20

Eileen opened her eyes, feeling that thin film between early morning consciousness and *ahh, sleep*. She reached over to pat down the pillow and heft herself up to see the clock (she kept the clock as far away from her as possible because its glowing digital face annoyed her, the numbers ticking past an endless torture during sleepless nights) and abruptly felt all the nerves in her body on fire. Today would be a sick day. A pair of mourning doves cooed outside her window in agreement. She would sleep and hopefully keep maudlin thoughts at bay.

She left a message for Winston; she only said she was having one of "those" days. She hated going into detail.

She settled into her bed, loving the feel of the heavy, puffy quilts cuddling her like a comforting sigh. Luckily, that day she would have six hours of delectable unconsciousness and easy dreams. Tomorrow would be her deposition, and this was the best way to prepare.

CHAPTER 21

First thing in the morning, Eileen dropped by the hospital boiler room to see if there were any wannabe paramours left now that Jerry was gone. She loved the warmth of the place. The heat surged into her edgy, predeposition nerves, calming her.

There didn't seem to be anyone there. As she turned to leave, she heard a low humming and thought it was the furnace, until it evolved to singing:

"At night we dance under black skies and watch for the drinkin' gourd…"

She felt a chill despite the heat but was pleased to see Milton, another hospital old-timer.

"Oh my," she said. "I didn't think anyone was here. How are you, Milton?"

"Doing rightly well, miss. I guess the hospital got tired of waitin' for me to retire and decided to close under my feet."

"What was that song you were singing?"

"Uh, well, nuthin', miss. Just a little or another of a ditty I heard." He smiled tightly and added, "Time to head to the cafeteria now."

"But…"

Milton liked Eileen, but deep in the corpuscles of his blood and his DNA clung the ancestral memory of himself as another chained black man standing on a wooden viewing platform.

CHAPTER 22

Virgil was a little worried. He suspected that the fire in the switchboard and the postsurgery infections were caused by faulty grommets manufactured by his company. He conceded the conflict of interest, but why should he tell anyone? It wasn't up to him to identify the problem; that's what the hospital's team of lawyers was supposed to do. Maybe they wouldn't find out. The hospital was doomed to failure anyway. If it would just close down before the investigation finished... He would paint a dire picture to the board at the next meeting.

He could claim that no one knew what the surgeons were doing. Everyone ass supposed to fill out their respective forms: the nurses completed their daily notes, the surgeons completed their operating reports, the laboratories completed their biopsy reports, utilization review completed their it-looks-like-everyone-did-what-they're-supposed-to-do reports, and medical records transcribed the whole mess. But we couldn't possibly know if the doctors were doing what they said they were doing. They could be having yo-yo matches with the innards. "Oooh, the large intestines really wind up nice and tight so you can do a Rock the Cradle" and "No, no, let me try; you always get to do Rock the Cradle." If a bunch of blood spurted up and nailed the nurses, it was highly suspicious that something wrong had happened. But nothing really "wrong" ever happened in the operating room; "unexpected" was the correct term. Perhaps "unforeseeable." "No sir, counselor, we had no clue that his large intestine would suddenly start flailing around the room like an urgently expelled balloon. According to his preadmission blood tests, his intestines were not unruly. Very obedient intestines."

The board always liked to gang up on the doctors—they were overeducated upstarts who knew nothing about how to run a business. That the doctors even dared to influence policy was ludicrous. GLK had helped Virgil see things clearly.

GLK was the kind of law firm surrounded by a cloud of gloom and doom and dripping with power and prestige. It was so big and impenetrable, no one really knew what went on behind those hallowed, heavy mahogany doors. The staff were forced to sign pages and pages of nondisclosure documents. They were barely even allowed to admit that they worked there. However, there was plenty of speculation, and, bit by bit, little crumbs of information slipped out. There was always someone who knew someone who knew someone who had a slim connection with something going on at the firm. Even the most innocuous tidbits of information took on a lively interpretation. The guy at Pizza Bomb mentioned once that a belabored, overtime-working group ordered ten pizzas one evening: two sausage, two pepperoni, two cheese, two vegetarian, and two super deluxe. What kind of work could inspire that artery-clogging appetite?

It was whispered that that was the evening they were working on the seamy sex scandal between the hooker and the city councilman and everyone was suffering from oral fixation, which could only be relieved by food. "Oh, read this: 'And then she slipped her hand down between his legs, and he grunted and grabbed her from behind her neck and pushed her down…' Oh man, hand me another slice of sausage, will ya?" And they salivated and read to each other, the pizza grease dripped down on their chins, and they lapped it up with their tongues.

If any of the gossip reached the ears of the almighty GLK management, they just laughed nervously and shrugged it off as a rumor. If a rumor had the misfortune of being attributed to a staff member, a stealthy investigation would ensue and one day the staff member would find his ID card mysteriously inoperable. The elevator wouldn't stop at his floor, none of the office doors would open for him, no one would look him in the eye. He didn't exist, didn't work there, never did. You little minion, just go home, will you?

CHAPTER 23

Eileen reluctantly left the warmth of the boiler room and then checked out the operating schedule for the day. Two more myringotomy surgeries were listed. She couldn't stand it. One was at 7:00 a.m., the other at 9:00 a.m. She checked her watch. It was 10:45 a.m. They should both be done and the patients resting comfortably, she hoped, in recovery. Better yet, the 7:00 might have already been discharged. No, they were checking all surgery patients very carefully for infection before they were discharged.

It was irregular, but she decided to go up and check on them. The staff knew her well enough to know that she wasn't spying on them. She was too jittery to get any work done right now anyway.

She headed to the elevator. She passed Neil, who winked at her and flashed a thumbs up. She wasn't sure if that was for their date this Friday or if he already knew the operations were a success. *No, there's no way he would know that.* She smiled back at him but hurried on her way.

Neil looked back at her as she entered the elevator. *On some mission, no doubt,* he thought. He hefted his heavy, black lawyer's bag to his other hand. He wanted to tell her about what they'd found in the documents. They were able to subpoena other hospitals in the country that had reported failures or infections using the grommets from Virgil's company. The reports coincided with the procedures at Sunrise Hospital. The problem wasn't with the hospital; it was with those dratted grommets. Unfortunately, it wasn't going to be enough to save the hospital. It was still up for a vote by the board. The hospital still had to pay for its defense in more than fifteen lawsuits filed against it. And it wasn't just that; the hospital was losing too much money on its charity care program. Sunrise was the last hospital that treated without questions asked up front. No one sneered when a patient flashed a Medicaid card or declared they were self-pay. Nearly every week there was a grateful patient who wrote to the newspaper praising the hospital for its heroic medical care "even though I have no insurance." But public accolades didn't pay the bills. Government money was dwindling. The benefactors were leaving town; healthy people were going elsewhere, leaving the sick and disabled. The economics didn't make sense anymore; anyone could see it.

As soon as the elevator doors opened on the third floor, the recovery room level, she recoiled at the strong smell, a sickly sweet mixture of something bleach-y and something else, no doubt related to raw infections and the various agents poured into patients to slow down the same. Eileen gagged, then cleared her throat and stepped out of the elevator.

Georgia from the nurse's desk looked up. Her hair, usually in a curly bob, strung about her face, doing no favors for her complexion, which had faded from pasty pale to a damp gray.

Georgia put her finger to her lips then whispered, "Careful. We just got two screamers to pass out. No, no, that's a good thing. Promise."

Eileen nodded as she came around the counter and squeezed Georgia's shoulder.

Georgia spun around in the chair, stood up, and hugged Eileen tightly. "It's never been like this."

Eileen had spent time at Georgia's home, eating generous meals of roast beef, mac 'n' cheese, and stewed tomatoes; playing Uno with her kids; and joking around with her husband, Drew. Now Eileen could hardly recognize her.

"We're working on this, you know." It sounded weak, even to Eileen's own ears, but it was all she had. "You take good care. I'll keep you posted."

Ugh. Not a good beginning for her lunch with Paige, from the ER. She had no appetite. She took the stairs back down and headed to the emergency room. She motioned to Paige that she would wait outside. After a few minutes, Paige ran out the door, jumped up and down a few times, did a few jumping jacks and touch-the-toes, then saluted Eileen.

"Whew, I've been dying to do that. I'm so hunched over all day I'm afraid I'm going to freeze up."

Eileen smiled. "Great idea," she said and burst into jumping jacks herself. "I've just come from the recovery room and poor Georgia and need to blow it all out somehow."

They did jumping jacks for a full minute and a half, Paige checking her watch, and then headed over to the Chinese place around the block.

As they nibbled through their crunchy Happy Bird's Nests, Paige asked, "So what's going on? You must have the scoop." Paige was too focused on ER life-and-death scenarios to keep up with the latest hospital news.

"Honestly, I don't know," Eileen said. "No one will know for sure until after the board meeting next week."

"Well, let me tell you. If I lose this job, I'm moving to Philly. You try to stay here and support this dump, and this is how you're rewarded. I'm sure there are lots of jobs in Philly. Maybe I'll turn paralegal."

"Excellent choice. You can stir up trouble for people all day long and get paid for it. And then when you get really good at the legal stuff, you can come back here and explain to us what the hell happened."

"No, I think you'd need a team of Harvard prelaws to squeeze that one out. The best I could do is show you how to set up a deposition."

"I think we will all be experts in that after this is over. Did I tell you that I'm being deposed this afternoon? I guess they want me to rat out Winston. Winston is too generally befuddled to do anything dastardly. I don't think he has it in him. Maybe I can swing it around to talk about, oh, those Phillies or something."

"From what I hear, lawyers don't have much of a sense of humor."

"Then that will be my challenge. To make 'em crack a smile. Probably sound like splitting china."

Back at the hospital, Eileen reached for her deposition outfit hanging behind her office door. It was an exquisitely tailored, cream-colored, light woolen-weave suit, beautifully belying its origins from the clearance sale rack.

She hadn't wanted to jinx it by wearing it all day and risk spattering coffee, ink, or Happy Bird's Nest on the pretty pearly buttons. She couldn't look wrinkled and bedraggled for her legal debut. Not caring to put her near-naked self on display for the entire hospital—her office door held a long, rectangular pane of glass—she headed for the handicapped restroom outside the lab to change and primp in private.

She closed the door and locked it, wincing at the smell of faded bleach. Clearly, this would be cleaner than her office, but she was careful not to let her bare feet touch the floor as she removed her clothing. She felt awkward, stepping on her shoes, hiking up her pantyhose while balancing on one shoe like a spooked heron.

Suddenly, someone rattled the doorknob and she froze. Then a knock. Really? What was the proper etiquette response to a knock on a locked restroom door?

She said nothing; the knock continued. She said, "Uh, sorry?" and was relieved to hear footsteps heading away.

She resumed grappling with her pantyhose, and there was another knock. "*Taken*," she hollered, deciding that the situation fell out of bounds of normal courtesy.

Her pantyhose now secure, she pulled up her skirt and reached to fasten the back hook when someone pounded on the door, yelling, "*Get out, get out! I gotta use the can now!*"

That seemed to leave little room for discussion, so Eileen grabbed the rest of her clothes and pushed open the door, crying, "Geez Louise!" hospital-speak for "What the hell?" which was wasted on the green-faced lab technician who barreled into the bathroom, locked the door, and from the sound within, proceeded to lose her hospital lunch special, chicken parmigiana with spaghetti and peas. Eileen cringed.

Celia looked over and shrugged. "Nerves are shot, guts are exploding. What can you do?"

Eileen hobbled down the hallway, clutching her clothes. Christ she hadn't even had a chance to button up. Hopefully she could make it to her office, window in the door or no, and finish up. If she kept her head down, she figured she could pass for a patient's family member bringing in a change of clothes. *Quick, only one more hallway to go. Twenty feet; so far, so good.* But then, *Crap*.

A familiar figure turned the corner. It was none other than Virgil.

Eileen frowned and tried to look small, but then she just had to glance up and caught his eye. He lifted an eyebrow, she pursed her lips, and in that split moment the months vanished, the shared skin memory electrified the air, and the heartache was forgotten. A strangled chuckle erupted from each of them. But Eileen hurried along, hoping that toilet tissue didn't drag behind her.

She smoothed her skirt and checked herself out in Winston's mirror. The length hit just below the knee. She wasn't sure if her legs would show during the deposition, and she wanted to make sure she could not be taken as being provocative. There was a time and place for that. She sat in Winston's office chair in front of the mirror striking different poses to make sure that no one would catch a cootch shot. She wished the skirt was a little more drapey, but it was such a fabulous suit that she willed it to be just perfect for the job.

She met with Neil first. His blue eyes went slightly out of focus when he saw her. She thought maybe she *was* trailing toilet paper, but then he said, "Mmm, nice. OK, then. They're going to ask you a lot of questions that you might think are stupid or irrelevant or irreverent or irredeemable or... Sorry."

"Or irreproachable or irresponsible?" Eileen smiled.

"This is serious."

"You're not helping matters any."

"I think we should bring in a third person."

"A chaperone." Eileen nodded.

"See if Virgil is available," Neil said.

"Ahem. Very funny." She said nothing about the brief encounter in the hallway.

"OK. Let's start over. Have you been deposed before? They're actually going to ask you that."

"No. I've been a good girl."

"Basically, just answer the question as succinctly as you can. Without embellishment. Don't do their work for them; make them specifically ask whatever it is they're trying to get at."

"What *are* they trying to get at with me?"

"Simply, they're trying to make the hospital look bad. They're going to try to get anything from you that might indicate that the administration is poorly run, poorly managed, that the hospital was an accident waiting to happen."

"Heavens, no. Accidents are waiting for a hospital to happen."

"You know what I mean."

Neil continued to prepare Eileen for her deposition. He said that Kammerer would act like the nicest guy in the world, be her best bud, but it was all just a ruse. Their only goal was to beguile her into saying something that would hurt the hospital.

"The only thing he cares about is that you're a female, and he expects you to perform like a stereotypical female and let your vanity and insecurity get the best of you and turn you into a befuddled hysterical mess."

"Oh, how lovely." She paused. "Do you suppose they know…"

"My guess is they don't. Virgil strikes me as the kind of guy who likes to play Mr. Personal Man with the ladies—"Oh baby, let me emote with you"—but it's just his little dream world and they all know it. In real life these women aren't contenders, so to speak. Does this bother you?"

"Yeah, a little, but I wouldn't have asked if I couldn't take getting slapped with it."

"So I really doubt that any of your, say, history has been deemed significant enough to be brought to the attention of his lawyers."

She looked stricken. "Not a factor, I know." She suddenly thought of the flushed photo and wished she had another.

"Oh, honey, I'm speaking lawyer-ese. Don't be crushed. I'll bet he'll be much more uncomfortable than you will."

"Yeah. Don't worry, I'll be cool as a cucumber."

They both grinned.

The table dwarfed the rest of the conference room and every seat was filled. Eileen quickly glanced around, her keenly honed dining-observation technique allowing her to rapidly identify each participant: Sam Sleaze, who probably day traded during work hours; Prim Patsy, whose face shellac required an hour of prep every morning; some old guy who showed up at all the office doings just so they couldn't make him retire; Nervous Nanette, who couldn't sit still, flipping through papers, jotting down notes with noisy scratching; Sullen Stephen, a black shock of hair drooping in one eye as he hunched over his notebook thinking, *I should've been a cowboy.* Eileen also saw a woman who, from the glinty intensity in her eyes, had to be Renee Finkster.

The deposition was quick. Her name, position, years at the hospital. She suspected they must have dug up a little too much background information, because they were excessively polite. She stuck to yes/no answers.

"Do you typically attend the board meetings?" Sam Sleaze started out.

"Yes."

"When was the first time you were aware of the hospital's problems?"

"Objection! Hearsay," Neil announced.

"Are you asking her not to answer?"

"No, my client may answer. I just want the objection noted for the record."

"What problems specifically?" Eileen said.

"The surgical complications, lawsuits, etcetera."

"Well, yes, I learned about the surgical problems around the time the lawsuits were filed."

"And not before?"

"Correct."

"As the president's assistant, isn't it unusual that you wouldn't be aware of any surgical problems until a lawsuit was filed?"

"No."

"Could you explain why not?"

"Typically, I don't see the reports until after they have been routed to several other departments—the OR staff, nursing supervisors, utilization review, loss prevention, materials management…I think that's it."

"Dietary?"

"Pardon?"

"Never mind. They're prepared as computer printouts, aren't they?"

"Yes."

"Then why can't they be distributed to all appropriate departments at the same time?"

"Each department must complete and sign its section of the form. And they must be distributed in a specific order. Once the forms are completed by everyone, then they send them to us." Eileen sat up straighter.

And on and on about forms and procedures until all eyes fogged over and the shuffling of papers drowned out the yawns.

Neil had no questions for her and winked when she was done.

CHAPTER 24

Eileen was disappointed. She had no sense that her testimony would, as she had hoped, save the hospital. During breakfast the next morning, it was no help to read in the newspaper about the day's run/walk benefit for breast cancer. It felt like she was being mocked. "See we're doing this great stuff for cancer, and you're doing *nothing*!" She suspected they got so much press because of the innate underlying titillation factor, visions of ardent, boob-flopping women running for a cause.

Cancer was so rampant these days, one could hardly read a newspaper or a magazine or watch TV without hearing some reference to it. It had become almost mundane. Those who hadn't suffered it didn't want to hear any more about it. And those who had resented the trivialization of the disease by its constant overexposure in the press. The near-monthly parades of pink annoyed Eileen. No one held benefit runs for rape victims. She felt it was the same thing. Of course, when she wrote to the *Chronicle* op-ed page voicing her opinion, the anonymous comments ran the gamut of "What do you have against pink?" to "You should be killed."

Even worse was the "Can you top this?" approach where cancer survivors were shown performing all manner of circus tricks and feats of endurance. Those stories especially irritated Eileen. Those people were in severe denial. Their stories never offered Eileen hope; they made her feel even worse about not being able to get out of bed some mornings. But, hey, look at Shirley Slash-Me-to-the-Bone who runs twenty miles a day then climbs Mt. Kilimanjaro all by herself while playing the piano with her toes. All that and a cancer survivor too!

If a woman had survived the hell of cancer and still had that much energy, she should be spending it in activities that were more valuable to humankind, Eileen thought. Now, *that* would be real news. Eileen could empathize with Shirley's need to show the world that she had conquered this disease, and that having endured it, she was able to do whatever asinine thing she wanted to with her life. But to hold that up as some sort of model to the world was insulting to the rest of the survivors. *So Shirley Slash, keep it to yourself, will ya?*

Real cancer survival was making it through your first day of work without feeling crippling fatigue. Or making it through any day without that afternoon nap. It was making love to an attentive soul who says, "I love you." You don't even care how he means it. It might just be the biblical, charitable love or the "I love what you're doing to my John Henry" love, but it doesn't matter; it just makes your mind and soul soar with pure glee.

Survival was those many precious moments of smiles and teasing and laughter with your really good friends. It was being able to leave the house without suffering a paralyzing fear that you were forgetting something crucial. It was taking a long walk and feeling each muscle flex and extend. It was feeling that first glimmer of an original thought inching its way through your mental fog. It was eating really good food. It was cooking really good food.

Those little everyday accomplishments were extraordinary to a cancer survivor. Scaling mountains just seemed ridiculous to Eileen. Every single minute of life was precious and something to savor, from just listening to your breath. "That's me. I'm alive. Here's proof." And think of how absurd it would be if you went through the battle with cancer and then blew it all by careening off the side of an icy cliff in a failed attempt to scale it. It would hardly make the costs of hospitalization, medication, counseling, and your own struggle for survival seem worthwhile, would it?

No, scaling mountain cliffs was not Eileen's idea of searching for validation after recovering from cancer. Saving the hospital—now, that would be real validation. Even though she'd have a better chance of success rappelling up a mountain.

In her next painting, she sketched the sentence "Cancer's a wake-up call, but some people keep hitting the snooze button." On the tiny canvas, of course, it only looked like a big smudge. She ended up painting a scene of moose over it, but left a tiny smudge on the left corner as the work's trademark. With moose, she figured, no one would question the smudge.

Time to stretch and relieve the hunched-over-artwork kinks. A long walk would free up her knotted joints. She wandered toward the lake, carefully dodging the little piles of goose goo that made it a little tough to clear her mind. *Daniel must have been here,* she thought. *And why does my life seem to revolve around poo?* Suddenly, she saw the bobbing horde of pink. *Oh, nuts, that's right. The stinkin' breast walk.* She decided to hang out at the end of the lake until they had all shuffled past.

She often wondered about her own possible cancer-causing scenarios. Once she'd gotten over the initial paranoia of it, it became kind of fun creating her own. Let's see, it could have been from using the microwave oven at chest level while wearing antiperspirant/deodorant containing aluminum zirconium during full moon cycles. Or maybe wearing rayon clothing over underwire bras while taking birth control pills under skies burnt out by global warming. Maybe it was all due to daylight savings time and the stress it causes the body to artificially change its life cycle twice each year. Lose an hour, gain an hour—what a pain. Maybe it was the Three Mile Island fallout from over a decade ago. Maybe it was Glenn.

Eileen had been excited that day she was notified by a research group that wanted to ask questions about her history for a cancer study. She thought it would be her chance to help find out what arbitrary mix of dastardly ingredients caused the disease. She hoped her memory would serve her well; could she remember all the weird new products she'd tried, those oddball artificial fats/sugars/salts that she'd consumed? What kinds of toothpastes, deodorants, and shampoos she'd used throughout her life? What about hair color or bleaches? Soaps? The microwave oven? Years of smearing lip gloss tainted with hydrogenated oils? What deadly combination was it? She knew she'd have to remain calm and let her memory work for her, not worry about remembering every little thing she had consumed. *What about eating tar? I think I nibbled on a piece of hot tar from an asphalt bubble on the road in front of my house when I was a kid. Maybe that was it.*

She'd driven herself crazy until the magical day arrived. Eileen opened her door to the researcher and coughed at the reek of tobacco. She stepped aside to let the heavyset woman enter her apartment, and they settled at the kitchen table. Eileen had set a plate of oatmeal raisin cookies on the table with a pitcher of iced tea. The researcher promptly grabbed two cookies and a napkin, which she kept dabbing at her face, working her mouth in a remotely lewd manner that made Eileen suspect she was spitting out the raisins, a suspicion borne out afterward when she tilted the plate toward the trash can and the little black morsels tumbled free from the napkin, making little plinking sounds into the trash.

So what did the researcher ask her? Only about her periods. How many did she have a year, how many days apart, how many days did they last—for this year, for that year, on and on and on from age twelve to thirty-two, when she was diagnosed. Intrusive questions to badger the cancer victim, all in the name of science. A few weeks later, a grandiose article appeared in the newspaper stating, "Studies show that women who have irregular periods are .0042784 percent more likely to develop breast cancer." The study had been sponsored by none other than the same company that did their research on her. A company that also, coincidentally, was soon having an initial public offering on a product that—surprise!—helped to regulate women's periods without hormones.

She had hoped her cancer would make a difference. After all, this was her, Eileen Hanley, who had cancer, not just any schmuck, so she wanted someone to look very carefully at the signs and indications and really come up with the cause of this nasty disease. Instead, it was just one more company taking opportunistic advantage of a sick person for their own profit and recognition. So much for her dream about finding the source of cancer in some widely used household or environmental product. There was no funding out there for that. There was only funding if the theory/hypothesis consisted of blaming the woman for some action or inaction on her part.

Several weeks later the research group recanted the finding: "The control groups were calibrated to a covariant unequal to the cosine of the derivative." Oh, were they now?

She never believed anything she heard about cancer anymore. Statistics were always skewed. How one or another race of people rarely get cancer, however; neither did they often live past age fifty. There might be a cancer advantage to eating seaweed and boiled turnips, but you probably wouldn't live long enough to know for sure.

The medical establishment, via various corporate strangleholds, was apparently continuing to evoke its wrath against Rachel Carson and her femaleness for daring to impugn the chemical industry for its apparent blatant contributions to human cancers. Not only was she an upstart, but a girl upstart! We will make all females suffer for the most female of cancers, breast cancer, and blame it all on gross female habits. Not exercising enough, not having babies, having too many babies, eating too much fat, not eating enough fat, not drinking whole milk, not, not, not. We will have women so confused and helpless that they will become slaves to our drugs and our invasive procedures and whatever miracles we say they will bring. Because even though the cancer was all your fault, girls, we will do our best to rescue you. Now give us a pretty smile. Ooh, looks like you need a little whitener too. Which may also cause cancer, tee-hee. The ghost of Rachel Carson will fade into oblivion. The miracle of corporate marketing will prevail.

Eileen desperately needed to rescue the hospital, to leave something important behind.

Eileen looked for organic fruits and veggies now every time she had the chance. She hated to admit it, but they did taste better, more like vegetables used to taste when she was a kid. Regular vegetables, lately, tasted like chemical byproduct. Yes, she hated anything smacking of trendiness, and she wasn't about to belt herself to a redwood tree, but she was a true convert to organic now, when she could afford it.

The excited murmurings and laughter of the sea of pink had finally passed and headed toward town. Eileen was blissfully alone at the lake, with only the muted sounds of bubbling water coming up from the springs and spreading over the rocks.

She noticed one lonely-looking fisherman out in a rowboat, hunched over, his fishing rod hanging motionless. It was nearly the end of fishing season; most of the puzzled, frantic, hatchery-bred trout had been snapped up long ago. On the season's opening day, the lake had been crowded boat-to-boat with eager fishermen, each proud to show off his unique fishing acumen. It was the periwinkle grubs or the special imported worms that did the magic; no, it was simple Weis brand canned corn; no, it was the special rabbit-food bait, crushed and smeared with peanut butter. They all had special tricks of the trade that lured the fish in, and no man was willing to admit that the stocks of hundreds of fish dumped fin-to-fin into the lake helped their odds a teeny bit.

But this lone fisherman didn't seem intent on catching a fish. Eileen saw that it was Milton from the hospital. In a deep, rumbling tone, he was humming the same tune, that carried easily over the calm water, that she'd heard earlier in the boiler room. Eileen waved at him, and he nodded. Slowly, he packed up his gear and then paddled to shore. Eileen decided to wait for him but didn't want to seem obvious, so she hopped over to one of the dry rocks and kneeled down to dangle her hand in the cool bubbling water.

"That haunting song, Milton, what is it?" she asked when he came ashore.

"Well, miss, I don't know if it has an official title. We always just called it 'Watch for the Drinkin' Gourd.'"

"The drinkin' gourd? I don't think I know what that is."

Milton hesitated. "It's, uh, the Big Dipper."

Now she knew.

"That's an old slave song, isn't it, Milton? I heard that escaping slaves used the Big Dipper to guide them."

"I guess there was a little of that."

This clearly would take some coaxing. Eileen said, "Let me help you" and reached down for an armful of his fishing gear.

"Oh, miss, you don't have to do that."

"Call me Eileen. And I insist." She lugged the gear over to Milton's truck and dumped it in. Milton locked up his rowboat, frowning at her clumsiness.

"Say, Milton, did you hear about the hospital supposedly being part of the Underground Railroad?"

He paused. He carefully rearranged his fishing gear. "I'd heard a story or another about it."

"Can I take you to dinner? I'd love to hear what you know." She hesitated. "It might help the hospital…"

Milton darted a glance at her and shook his head. "When rich folks have a mind to do something, ain't nothin' anybody else can do." His face softened. "But you want to hear a story, I'd be glad to tell you one."

They settled in at the café, Eileen with her chicken salad sandwich (with Romaine lettuce and sprouts, *ick*, that she promptly plucked off) and iced tea and Milton with his roasted open-faced turkey with gravy, mashers, and black coffee. He dug into the food with zest, and Eileen waited patiently.

Finally, he wiped his mouth and said, "It's been a while since I've talked to anyone about the history. I haven't even told my kids." He shook his head. "I guess we're just trying to move on…" His voice trailed off.

Eileen reached over and took his hand. "I understand, Milton—some memories you'd rather not pass along."

"I hate to say it's embarrassing, 'cause it's just history, it's just what my folks talked about. But it still feels wrong."

"Everyone knows that slavery is wrong," Eileen said.

"No, miss. Well, yes, miss. But what I meant was that escaping was wrong. Against the law anyway."

Eileen smiled. She didn't think there was an unlimited statute of limitations on the heads of fugitive slaves—or more particularly, their descendents—but she could understand his paranoia. "I think even the stupid people realize slavery is wrong."

Milton gave a short laugh. "Ha, yeah, you'd think. Anyhows, we're just glad things worked out the way they did."

"Tell me." Eileen's eyes blazed.

Milton stared vacantly at the floor. "This would be easier if we had a far."

Eileen waited. *Afar?*

"See, we'd get a far going in back—you could do that in those days—and we would sit around, roastin' doggies or marshmallows or whatnot, and the words just flooded out."

Oh, a fire. "I can see that. I think there's something about darkness and crackling embers that opens people up." Eileen hoped she hadn't broken the mood. She bit her lip and was determined to stay quiet.

"That's sorta like it was. You get all dreamy-like; your thinkin' shuts off, and it's free-fall memory talk."

He sipped his coffee and winced. "So, my granpappy would start singing," he murmured, "'We splits de oak logs and gather the beans. And at night we dance under black skies and watch for the drinkin' gourd.' And we would all join in: 'And we're headed for the riverbank, watch for the drinkin' gourd' and so on. And then my daddy would start off, telling about Jonathan, his great-great-uncle who lit out from Atlanta, and I can't rightly recall all the details now. I think we all made it up as we went along. But I do remember this part."

He took another sip of his coffee, winced again, and called out to the waitress, "Ma'm can I have a glass of water? Much obliged."

He went on. "My daddy always told me, 'Son, don't ever talk bad against the hospital, always be respectful.' And we'd look snarky-like, we were just kids then, but he would give us a look, and we'd hush up. He'd say, 'The hospital saved your uncle's life; you'd a-probably never been born without that place.' Course he meant my great-great-great-uncle or something. Then he would talk about 'him' and 'he,' and we knew who daddy meant.

"Uncle Jonathan came from around Richmond, Virginia, and lived on a tobacco plantation. His story must have been awful, 'cause daddy would just shake his head and grunt and wouldn't give up too many details of what he'd been told. One time he slipped and said that Jonathan was whipped eighty-six times with a cat-o'-nine-tails until the blood ran in little streams down his back. Left scars that crisscrossed his back like he was a tic-tac-toe board. The only thing he had done was go to the neighbor's farm to see his girlfriend.

"Finally, he lit out one night. All he knew was to head north, follow the North Star and people would help him. He ran and stumbled across unfamiliar railroad bridges, not knowing when the trains ran, and hoped he could make it across without getting run over. Once, he heard the train whistle when he was in the middle of the bridge—they usually had little alcoves about midway where you could duck into— but thought he could outrun it. He ran and ran and slipped and fell, and he knew he couldn't make it to the end and just crawled over to the edge of the bridge, threw his body over, and hung on for dear life. The train went on forever, and finally his hands slipped and all he knew was blackness until he fell into the water."

Eileen gasped.

"But it was OK for Jonathan, 'cause the water was deep enough and the fall wasn't too far. He swam to the bank, and there was a hand there waiting to pull him up. He didn't care if it was the paterollers; he just wanted out of the water. Lucky for him, it was another colored man, a freedman, who plucked him out of the water. Jonathan stayed with his family a couple of days, and they told him how to get to other sympathetic folks' homes who would take care of him. He jumped a train, too, that took him clear to Pennsylvania."

"And the hospital helped out?"

"That's what I was getting to. It was better here, in Pennsylvania, safer, but there was still a threat that southerners could come after their slaves, their property. That's what the paterollers did. Patrollers, you know.

"So, when he got to the hospital, they took him in, hid him in the tunnel, cleaned up his wounds from the fall and from clamberin' over thorns from every such plant you can think of. He was fainty-sick and his feet were a mess, as you could imagine."

"Who were 'they'"?

"The names never made their way down to us. Or me anyway. It was all secretive."

Eileen pressed, "So there is a tunnel in the hospital?"

"Of some sort or another. It's a fact."

CHAPTER 25

She went to work the next day feeling both apprehensive and excited. While on the one hand it seemed inevitable what the workers would be told eventually, on the other hand it was exciting to be part of what would probably be a historical event.

The rest of Milton's story gripped her. After "they" had cleaned up Jonathan and allowed him to rest for a few days, Milton had told her, Jonathan eventually made it to Canada through the Underground Railroad network. Afterward, he helped other family members escape, including Milton's great-great-great-grandfather.

Eileen already knew that the hospital was founded in 1840 and treated soldiers injured in six wars: the Civil War, WWI and WWII, Korea, Vietnam, and the Persian Gulf. And now this rumor, confirmed by Milton, about its part in the Underground Railroad. How could all of it disappear in a puff of history?

Eileen walked the halls as if in a trance. Clusters of folks gathered together, whispering and shaking their heads. Everyone seemed to have clay in their mouths. It was probably worse up on the patient floors. The hospital census report indicated a full bed count this week. Where would all these people go if and when Sunrise closed? Sure, there were plenty of hospitals in the big city, but that was thirty miles away, and the doctors probably wouldn't all go there. Some of the doctors would inevitably move away to more secure places. Or any place where there was a job. They'd invested time and talent to build a loyal clientele here only to have their future snatched out from under their feet. If only she could find some evidence of the tunnel.

It was hard to concentrate that day. Winston was nowhere to be found. Eileen had plenty of work on her desk, but she wanted to join the clusters of people, even if their gossip was unproductive.

Neil poked his head in the door of her office, "Ready for lunch?"

Eileen waved and nodded.

Neil had loved his wife; he really did. What was not to love? Kerry Ann cooked award-winning ravioli, tender pillows of pasta that nearly melted in your mouth, lovingly mixed, pounded, and shaped by hand and filled with delicate crab meat. He used to love sneaking up on her when she was immersed in the sticky flour and put his hands around her waist and pull her toward him. She would giggle and struggle against him, squealing, "What are you doing, honey?" He loved the little white, powdery patch of flour that always found its way to her nose.

She also baked the most luscious cakes for the kids in any animal shape you could think of; he often wondered how she got the design for the giraffe she made one summer after Hayley saw them for the first time at the zoo. Hayley went crazy in love for the sweet, misshapen things, and for three weeks—that seemed to be the length of crushes with her three-year-old attention span—everything had to be giraffes. Giraffe T-shirts, giraffe coloring books, giraffe books to read, giraffe stickers. Kerry Ann even sewed a giraffe Halloween costume for her. Hayley was so cute when she held a stick up through the neck hole, and she insisted on doing it herself. Neil had offered to hold the head up for her during the trick or treating, but she would have nothing of the sort. Her eyes were hidden in one of the spots on the giraffe's neck.

Kerry Ann was a dear, sweet, homespun woman, always quick with a word of encouragement for the downtrodden, a warm smile for the sick of heart, and a gooey chocolate brownie for a cranky kid. She was adored by all.

Neil almost felt like the luckiest man alive, and would have been had he been born without specific reproductive parts. Kerry Ann would participate if Neil initiated lovemaking in a nice way. But she really rather preferred to remain a virgin at heart. Neil was going crazy. He didn't know what to do.

He longed to reach out to her, to feel that tickle that built up into something more urgent, an urgent and exciting pressure, feeling the mutual electricity between the two of them grow warmer until they gasped and stumbled toward the bed. However, he never felt anything from her, just a polite compliance. She was probably planning the weekday menus.

The last time they made love, he was hoping for a son. She never expressed a preference; she thought doing so was lewd and might precipitate more attempts. But this last time, he felt her yield, or at least he thought that's what it was. She sighed a little, and his tadpoles raced off, each searching—oh yes, searching—for that perfect, sassy little follicle that would embrace it and love it forever.

Neil imagined that one particularly enterprising fellow, Rusty, beat out all the others, bullying his way through, pounding the little guy next to him, and running neck and neck with another until the loser panted and struggled and drifted off into the uterine wall. Finally, Rusty was there! Lots of pretty little things, but he wanted something with a little extra, with passion, dammit! Then he saw her. A perfect little thing, a definite wiggle to her, a little dodgy. Their eyes locked. She flirted with him. He was going to make it; he saw that she wanted him. He got closer and closer, but at the final moment when he thought he was really going to do it, she suddenly veered away and he careened into the side of the fallopian tube. He heard a cackle as he melted into nothingness.

Neil was very tender—he knew he was—but dear Kerry Ann never gave in to the passion that he wanted to inspire in a woman. It was like those jokes about the guy who's granted three wishes. Kerry Ann had all the qualities he thought most important in a woman: she was a warm person, a great mother, a caring individual. He never thought to require passion. He thought that would come naturally. When two people love each other, that always comes along, doesn't it? Well, he knew then that it didn't. His insides had burned with the desperation of it all. He'd figured that he couldn't put up with it forever, but it had crushed him to think of leaving her because of it. She was such a good person. There were plenty of neurotic and creepy women out there. He could do *so* much worse.

But it had soon became a moot point. Kerry Ann started spending more and more time at the church; he had never heard of so many church-related activities. The choir, the stewardship committee, the bazaar for the homeless, the bake sale for the battered women, the Sunday school preparation committee, the youth group—on and on until finally she'd just stammer, "I have to go to the church, for, you know."

And then he knew she was having an affair. She was never a good liar. In a way, he felt happy for her, that she was at least able to enjoy sex with someone. He was a little amazed at this discovery about himself. He was, of course, a bit angry – or maybe it was disappointment, an urge to prove his skill, or maybe just good old jealousy – that it wasn't him she was having sex with. But, all in all, the connection between the two of them just wasn't there; technique had nothing to do with it. He wasn't at home all that much himself.

When she came home that evening, she was shaking and nervous and he knew that this was it. Throughout the evening he had wondered how this scene would play out.

She looked at him, eyes dark and veiled, and said simply, "You know, don't you?"

"I think I do. Do you want to talk about it? Is it serious?"

She looked away, her eyes brimming with tears. "Yes, I think so."

"What should we do about it?"

"I really love him. He captured my heart before I even knew it was trying to escape."

Neil gazed deeply at her. She was capable of passion. He'd never guessed it. "Well, that's the end of this, then." He tried not to say it with a question, but the inflection of his voice lifted at the end, out of his control.

She gazed back. "Yes," she whispered.

―

Neil reached for Eileen's hand and held it warmly in his own. They walked across the street to the deli. The silken feeling swirled up her arm, circled her heart, and settled comfy-like below her navel.

CHAPTER 26

Virgil wished someone would tell the hospital staff not to take this personally, that the decision would be made purely for business reasons. If it no longer made business sense to continue operations, the conclusion should be obvious.

Why, at his factory, he had installed little green and red lights above the restrooms, carefully timed. When someone went in and shut the door, the green light turned red for exactly seven and a half minutes, which was plenty of time for anyone to take care of business, after which the light would blink green and the door would automatically open. Good business practice. But these hospital people would wither under such discipline.

The staff always got so emotionally involved. Why couldn't they just see it as an incompatibility of numbers, like he did? All this moaning and groaning about "the history of the hospital," "it's been around forever," "I've made so many friends," "this is such a good group of people," "I'm going to miss you" just didn't make any sense to him at all. The hospital wasn't making money. That's all there was to it. Would *they* continue to keep money in a bank that kept erratically deducting hundreds of dollars from their accounts every month? No! They would hightail it out of there and take their money elsewhere. That's exactly the kind of decision this was. Staff always made things more difficult for themselves.

But of course, Virgil, the rest of the board, and most of administration had to put on at least a minimal show of grief. They had to put into practice some of those techniques they'd learned at their myriad of personal growth seminars. The ones held at the place with the golf course, the scantily clad babes clustered around the pool, and the drinking at the bar until tongues were cotton and brains were mush. All that coloring and charting and personality revealing could be put to the test during this trying time.

Some of the managers were thrilled to death that they could put into effect that emotion allegedly called compassion. They'd been told that it might come in handy some day, but they'd really had no idea.

CHAPTER 27

Jenaveev was so proud that the radiation had kept her so thin, Noelle knew. She could even eat potato chips again, her mom had told her. She was thinner than Noelle now and never neglected to make a snide comment about it. When Noelle was thinking about going to the junior prom, her mom suggested that she wear one of her own dresses, except, she pointed out, "Oh, I don't think you can get in them. You are the growing girl, aren't you?"

Noelle sighed and mentally noted yet another thing never, ever to say to her daughter, if she ever had the chance. Yes, she had learned so much from her mother. So much not to do—her list would fill the Philadelphia phone book. She would be a stellar parent someday. One of her friends once said that parents should die when a kid reached the age of fourteen. They pretty much lose their usefulness after that. Noelle had thought at the time, *That's cold.* Now she was beginning to understand.

It made her uncomfortable to think that her mother competed with her. Her mother! If only she would act like a mother instead of an old crone trying to shoulder her way to some imaginary finish line. Noelle's own smooth skin was tanned and muscular. Her blue eyes were crystal-clear, wide with wonder and innocence, whereas Jenaveev's rheumy, bloodshot eyes reflected fatigue and boredom.

Noelle often wished she had a mother like Tawnya's, Nora, chubby and cheerful, yet very active. She was always ready to take the girls to the movies or show them cool stuff on the Internet or ride bikes with them. She was the perfect mother. Noelle's mother always derided Nora (certainly not to her face!) with comments about cottage-cheese thighs, but it was really only a little cellulite, and Nora had more muscle in her legs than most of the boys Noelle knew. Noelle's mother couldn't bicycle around the block without an oxygen tank. Unless there was a sale at Pomeroy's.

But of course, her mother was too weak to even take Noelle shopping now, or at least that's what she said. Noelle thought it was because she couldn't stand to see her daughter all dressed up and pampered and looking so pretty. Her dad never treated her mother like that. Her dad and mom never talked to each other like they loved each other. They talked about mundane things, just like Tawnya's mom and dad, but never with the same smiles and winks and caresses. Once when Tawnya's dad said he was going to the store, her mom flew over to him, jumped into his arms, and said, "Please don't leave me!" And they kissed and giggled, and Tawnya gagged and shrugged. Noelle rolled her eyes but felt a tickle that this was the right way.

That tickle was unlike the sick feeling in her stomach when she was around her parents. Once she asked Tawnya if her parents made her sick, and Noelle would never forget the baffled look on Tawnya's face.

Tawnya said, "Oh, you mean, like, because they're old? They listen to stupid bands like the Turtles and the Beatles? Yeah, I know exactly what you mean. But it's OK, really. Our kids will probably say the same thing about us and the Backstreet Boys."

But Noelle didn't mean that at all. Her parents never listened to music together.

And then there were boys. Noelle was thoroughly confused about boys. From a hormone standpoint, she had lots of desires and cravings, but emotionally she knew she was simply not equipped to deal with it. She was afraid to trust her cravings because they weren't accompanied by any gauge of good sense. She made the mistake of asking her mother about it. She'd looked puzzled and asked, "Love? What do you want love for? You want someone you need."

Noelle had stared at her for a moment.

When she'd posed the question separately to her dad, he'd sputtered and shook his head. "You're too young to worry about love. It's really a superfluous emotion that does no one any good." But he seemed choked up, and Noelle wondered why.

Noelle had no idea what it should feel like to fall in love. She felt very confused and cranky and horny all the time and couldn't seem to get any relief. Her dad irritated her, and she wished he would get a life. She should be fretting about her mother, she knew, but frankly, she wished she would get over it too. This should be her, Noelle's, time. Her mother couldn't even grant her daughter a little shining spot while she was becoming a teenager. She hogged the limelight for herself. Her mother's impending death thing was tiresome.

Nick had to get out of the house, or at least away from the living room where his parents were engaged in their usual nonsensical banter, attempting to outdo one another in the emoting department.

"But Jenaveev, honey, what do you feel like doing now? Are you tired? Hungry? Would you like to go for a little drive?"

"Knock it off, Virgil, you've always been such a horse's tail."

Noticing Nick peering at them from the hallway, his mom chuckled with hollow glee, as if it was all just a little lovers' quarrel.

Nick cringed and headed outside.

His dad had built him a quoits pit in an old barn on the property, so he could escape to where no one would bother him.

He scuffed at the clay, the good, dense Pennsylvania clay he imagined was the remnant of the Appalachian Mountains as they'd melted from their once mighty height and settled into the earth to form the gentle, rolling mounds of today. Apparently, he picked up *something* from earth science class.

As he picked up quoit after quoit, he almost forgot the insanity of his family.

Then he heard footsteps and his father's voice. "So, are we going to win the tournament?"

He didn't mean to, but Nick sighed loudly.

"What's wrong, Nick?"

"You and Mom. Why are you together? I know you hate each other, and I feel awful pretending that we have this glorious family. Why are you so afraid of everything?"

"I can't leave your mother now. She's so sick and weak, and she needs me. And, no, we don't hate each other." He glared at Nick.

"She doesn't need you that badly. She just pretends because she thinks that's what you want."

"That's not true."

Nick shrugged and walked away.

Virgil couldn't stand it. Here he was, continually telling himself he was suffering for the sake of the kids, and his son thought he was an idiot.

He sat on a hay bale and felt the ends prick into his butt. He didn't move. He felt the hay, became the hay. If he were a real man, he would go over to the makeshift closet his son had put together in the barn and grab a blanket to sit on so he wouldn't feel the prickles. But then someone might miss the blanket. What if someone needed the blanket for a spontaneous picnic and he had removed it from its familiar spot? That person would be devastated. It would be his fault.

No, he must sit there and endure the prickles of the hay. It was his destiny.

The next morning Virgil trudged down to the kitchen where Noelle was already seated at the table reading the paper and eating her puffed wheat cereal.

He sat down next to her, and without looking up she said, "Dad, what tortuous game are you planning to subject yourself to today?"

His kids had no respect for him. He was a joke. When did all of this happen?

"Where's your brother? Where's your mother?"

Now Noelle looked up but ignored the questions. "Dad, did you sleep with pirates last night?"

He wearily got up, stepped over to the foyer mirror, and saw a crease line in his face in the shape of an X. X marked the spot: this was a loser. Not buried treasure, as he had once believed, but just a big, fat loser. When treasure stays buried for too long, it turns to dust. And he'd made no attempt whatsoever to dig it out. He had thought it would always be there and as long as he just waited until everything was just right, then he could fish it out. But no.

It was gone, and he was left with an ugly wrinkle. He must have had quite a battle with the sheets last night.

He headed upstairs. Funny things had been happening. Not just losing keys, but weird things. Once, he was in the bathroom, doing his business, and suddenly he didn't know where he was. He'd wandered out of the bathroom into the hall and wondered where the picture was that used to be on the wall. No, that was at his parents' house, or, no, it was his grandparents' old row home. It had been confusing.

He'd read that Alzheimer's was a nondiscriminatory disease. Maybe his brain was turning against him. He was so young, though. And still so handsome.

Nick had gotten an early start on the day and was already in his quoits practice area. He groaned as he saw his dad approach. Two days in a row. He thought his dad was too busy these days to check on him. Virgil smiled a vacant smile that Nick noticed without his usual sneer. This expression of his father was unnerving.

Virgil blurted out, "Son, to be a hero, you have face the gauntlet."

Nick looked at his dad. What was he talking about? Usually Nick just snarled to himself and forced himself to be congenial, all the while hating himself for it. But this time he was genuinely puzzled.

Suddenly Virgil picked up one of the quoits and hurled it over the edge of the cliff and into the woods below.

"Hey, Dad, what the—?"

Virgil shot him a look, and they watched the spinning oval disappear and fall with a soft thud.

"I'll buy you another," Virgil grunted and left.

Nick had to make his final preparations for the upcoming tournament in Atlantic City. He wished he could go alone, but knew that he had to humor his parents' wish to make this some sort of family holiday. It was a charade, but he couldn't let himself worry about it; he had to concentrate on his game.

None of his friends' parents seemed to be particularly crazy about each other either, so maybe that was the norm.

He thought about a couple of kids in school who had such a glow about them; not the specious, toothy smiles of the football players or cheerleaders, but an inner glow and confidence and cheerful manner that made him stop and wonder. When a wrong snack fell down from the vending machine, one of the kids would laugh and shrug, not kick and yell and shake the machine like Nick would.

Nick watched those others and felt empty. There was a secret other life he wanted to be part of and wasn't sure how.

CHAPTER 28

Winston had suggested to Eileen that she take a few employees from various departments to lunch to get a more personal idea whether any of them might plan lawsuits if the hospital closed. The department heads were supposed to gauge that sort of thing, but sometimes employees were more reluctant to talk to their immediate supervisor about such things than Eileen.

Eileen left Winston's office grumbling. She was busy enough without having to shake down her coworkers. She thought she heard a fly buzzing past her ear then realized it was Mandy from the preadmission testing office. There was no time to duck into the restroom. She would not ask Mandy to lunch.

"S'cuse," Mandy peeped.

Mandy tended to be troubled and unable to build declarative sentences unpeppered by excruciating pauses. Her "well" and "you know" and hesitations clogged your ears until you got so frustrated having to listen to the interminable nonstatements that you finished her sentences, thoughts, and philosophy on life just so you could finally go about with yours. Eileen suspected that was Mandy's intention all along, that she could look smart without any effort. It was an excruciating wait for her to try to express a complete thought, meanwhile slowing your own thought process to a crawl. Your own mind needed to take a couple Valium or shut down completely for a time until she could finish a thought. You'd try not to be rude, so you'd stop what you were doing while she eked along. It was worse than trying to bike down the Atlantic City boardwalk through noon crowds on a hot summer day.

Eileen noticed Mandy was reading the latest best-selling novel, *The Baleen Chronicles*. "What did you think of the book, Mandy?"

"Well…I thought…yeah…well…you know…"

"It's pretty long, isn't it?"

"Yeah, well…but…I think…and…the author…tried…I think."

"I liked the part about the whales breaching on the beach possibly being connected to the intrusive whale-watching tours. It was clever the way they snuck in that idea."

"Yeah…I really thought…you know…whales are good…"

And on it went.

"So, how are you doing these days? Any particular plans after the implosion?"

"I'm sorry, are they going to explode the building?"

"No, hon. Never mind."

Mandy would be fine. Eileen was sure Parnell in HR would find a spot for her, if need be. She would be a perfect HR assistant.

During a soul-soaring lunch with Neil, she determined through deep probing and intense physical analysis that without hesitation he had no plans to sue the hospital. There, she'd done her part for Winston. Afterward, Eileen wanted to get naked. She wished she could go to a nude beach, just to lie in the sun—slather on lots of sun block— and feel the rapture and her body, as it seemed to have come full circle in its recuperation. Southeastern Pennsylvania, aka Amish territory, however, wasn't particularly "clothing optional" territory.

Virginia Beach had been her special place when she was a child. She'd loved the big, wide, white sandy beaches that seemed to last forever. She'd loved renting one of their sturdy rafts and running out into the surf with it and jumping on, then paddling out as far as she dared, looking back to catch a wave just so. If you were a little too soon, it would simply float under you, making you go up and down like a buoy. Sometimes it was relaxing to just stay at that level, catching the beginnings of the waves and rolling gently along with them.

Sometimes, even then, one would catch you by surprise, crest earlier than the others, and crash down on top of you. You'd notice people pointing and shouting, and you'd look back, scream, and either paddle furiously backward to avoid it or swim ahead to miss the worst of it. Sometimes you couldn't avoid it, and it would crash right down on top of you, turning you topsy-turvy. You'd hit your head on something—the raft? The sand? And you'd think, even at that young age, that, oooh, this was it, this was what death was like.

But then you'd bob to the top, your swimsuit all askew, shake yourself like a dog, and all would be right with the world again. Except you'd be a mile away from where you started. So you had to trudge back up the current to where your parents were sitting, oblivious to your little drama, your mom reading a *Smithsonian*, your dad sleeping under a beach umbrella. You'd wonder if anyone noticed your valiant fight with the elements and how bravely you survived. No one noticed the cool stuff. However, if she'd missed a shirt button, everyone would be all over her.

Virginia would be great for a nude beach, but she doubted there was such a thing. Plus, it was too far away now.

The nude-beach thing wasn't something that Fodor typically wrote about. Eileen had heard of a gay nude beach, but didn't feel like invading their sexual frolics, which is really what that entailed. She decided to get a massage instead and checked the yellow pages. She loved those listings in the phone book: Zulu's Sponge and Wipe Massage, LMT or Fanny's Afterglow Clinic, LMT. She chose Healing Garden, LMT.

A cancer survivor, above all, should be entitled to this glorious treat. But no, there were forms to fill out and questionnaires to complete, and you couldn't just run a line down the no column. Urrsch, stop—cancer, that's a yes. The only X in the left column, staring out at her in two ugly slashes. And then the chirpy practitioner—she's only doing her job, she has to ask these questions, the state board is always looking over her shoulder and could rescind her license if she failed to accurately complete the questionnaire with the prospective client, and then she'd have to return to her cashier's job at the Herbal 'n 'Cense shop.

So Eileen checked yes. Cancer, yes. And the practitioner's reaction? She pored over Eileen's answers, obviously looking for the yesses that had been hammered into her brain, not ever expecting to see any, never being told exactly what to do when there was one, particularly from a person who looked so obviously healthy, shining, and rosy. The practitioner had probably been about to ask her for tips on how she got that glow.

When the practitioner saw Eileen's yes, a little wrinkle formed above her eyebrow. Eileen could tell that her helpful, hands-on, empathetic mind was searching for the right response to this dilemma.

The practitioner swallowed. "Um, you have cancer?"

"Had, really. It's been a couple of years now."

"Oh. I don't think I'm supposed to work on someone with cancer."

"It's history. I have a cancer history. It doesn't define who I am at the present moment."

"I understand. Oh, I'm sorry, I'm sure this sounds really rude. I don't think I'm supposed to do this. Gosh."

"I've been treated systemically and surgically; I'm sure there's no danger."

The practitioner's mouth formed words that she didn't pronounce. Her eyes failed to meet Eileen's. Eileen guessed she was thinking, *Wow, one of those.*

The practitioner checked a well-thumbed manual of some sort. There was a dirty splotch on the side where oil-stained fingers had rested.

"It's not catching," Eileen added hopefully.

"Well, I guess I could do a light massage."

CHAPTER 29

Virgil's doctor had said it was just stress, ran some tests, and suggested an antidepressant. "Don't worry, champ, you're still with us. Try to get a little more exercise. And rest. Sleep strengthens brain cells more than anything else."

Dark clouds, billowing and gray, hovered over the valley. The sky seemed to have dropped twenty thousand feet and covered the county in a sticky gloom of gray-green. The weather this time of year changed from bright sun to drenching downpour within minutes.

Virgil had to leave that morning for Newport News, Virginia, for the annual products convention but wasn't particularly thrilled at the prospect of driving in whatever sort of storm was brewing. He usually loved these trips, loved any excuse to get out of the house. And this gave him a legitimate excuse. He usually didn't even mind driving in storms, even though the company would pay him to fly, because the extra concentration kept his mind off his troubles. But this storm had a menacing quality that Virgil hesitated to challenge.

Jenaveev was already at the breakfast table. Virgil's stomach sank even more. The sick feeling in his stomach had become so familiar it was almost comforting. Ah yes, that good old nausea—things must be normal in the Ellingsworth household.

His wife didn't even look up as he approached. She was immersed in a movie tabloid and chewing idly on a breakfast stick, the kind with intertwining fruit and cream. A little glob of the cream had dribbled below her lip. Virgil had a fleeting memory of a porno flick he had seen and chuckled. No, any globs on his wife's face had to come from food: prepackaged, premixed, prefrozen. Jenaveev's eyes darted up at her husband's chortling but she said nothing. She really didn't care what he found amusing, he knew. What was more important was why Meg Ryan was leaving her husband. That was real news.

The best part of the day was always when he opened the door to his BMW and crawled into the driver's seat. He would sit there silently for a minute or two, alone in the garage with the garage door open. He'd press the button to his window and lower it four inches. And then just sit there. It was the only time during his day that he felt peace. The cool breeze and fresh air wafted in, clearing his brain fog. The pins and needles that pricked him endlessly throughout his body were motionless. This was the only time he felt that anything was possible. His life could be perfect.

He picked up his car phone and made an appointment with his lawyer. No, this was a personal matter.

The interstate was too hectic for his mood. His thoughts were rushing and chaotic, and he didn't want to mirror that in his driving. He turned off on Route 15, which in Virginia soon became a two-lane highway through rolling pastures with well-groomed horses nibbling tender grass behind miles of white rail fences. Undoubtedly, during plantation days this was prime territory. Those darkies probably did OK on a place like this.

A bicyclist caught his eye, lurching him from his antebellum reverie. Like deer, one bicyclist was usually followed by a herd of them, and he braked in anticipation. A parade of cyclists crossed the intersection, completely unmindful of oncoming fifty-five-mile-per-hour traffic. Virgil suddenly wished he was one of them. He could pull over, grab his bike from the trunk (had he owned one), and pedal to catch up with them. They probably wouldn't even notice that he was a new participant.

He could ride along for a while, join them for lunch at a cute rustic café in Warrenton, laugh and meet new friends, make a pass at a beautiful blonde.

He would be surprised that she was so beautiful. Under a bicycle helmet and gear, she was rather plain, but when she shook her hair out at the restaurant it would cascade down her back in golden waves. He would tell jokes, and everyone would be mesmerized by his wit and wisdom. The blonde would gaze at him shyly and smile. Her blue eyes glistened with desire. She would sleep with him eventually.

On the other hand, the skies were still stormy, and he would no doubt be caught in a torrent, which would rust out his bike (had he owned one) and cause him to slip on wet leaves and tumble to the ground in a bone-crushing heap. The others wouldn't notice him, as they would have ridden ahead. He would hear their laughter fading as they rode away. The blonde would not look back.

His car phone tootled. Ah yes, this was much better. Temperature-controlled, clean-smelling, stereo with woofers and tweeters.

"Hello," he said into the phone.

"Oh, I'm sorry, dear, I dialed you by mistake."

Jenaveev.

He hung up without further comment. He believed she did the same.

CHAPTER 30

Jenaveev also felt renewed vigor after her husband's departure, for at least fifteen minutes. He left for work every morning, but it was always different when he drove out of town. She felt scandalous, independent, and brazen. But after fifteen minutes or so, the feeling died, leaving her anxious and desperate. What if he never returned? She didn't know how to pay the bills, call for a repairman, get the car a tune-up. She did change a light bulb once.

It was all so pedestrian; it didn't equate to her self-perception. She should really have a personal assistant. They did have Clara, their maid, but Jenaveev needed someone to attend to her every personal need. Someone to vouch for her, kowtow to her, and anticipate her every move. She should be waited upon; people loved to wait on people like her.

Virgil *had* to come home. She couldn't and wouldn't handle these demeaning household chores. She drummed her fingers on their smooth granite countertop.

Meanwhile, in Virgil's BMW, Screamersville, Virginia, popped out at him on the map. Virgil's metaphorical namesake—he must drive by. Maybe it was populated by those Munch-like characters. He could imagine everyone with a ghastly drop-down face, head in hands, mouth open in horror. If he stopped to get gas, a screamer would trudge out holding an ALL EMPTY sign and claim there was no gas for miles around. If he stopped by the diner, they would be out of food and the water would be contaminated. Rats would swarm the grocery store aisles stocked only with dry bars of soap. Tourists would flee, screaming. His kind of place.

Screamersville turned out to be a typical Southern byway town, just a four-lane divided highway surrounded by gas stations, billboards, and a stray loping hound. Perhaps Virgil would return later to explore its underbelly.

Absently, he dialed a familiar number. Since Eileen hated phone calls, they had had a phone code. Two rings, hang up, and then call right back. Often Virgil would leave for work before her, big manufacturer prez that he was, and he would call as soon as he got to work. She would still be languishing on the bed, fresh from the heated, sticky love. She would race to the phone, and they would try to relive one or two particularly memorable moments. *Oh, when you did that, I thought I would go out of my mind* and *When you did this, I felt the same way.* The sort of conversation that no one would ever want to overhear.

Now Neil answered. Virgil nearly dropped the phone but managed to disconnect. Hopefully she still didn't have caller ID. In the depths of his gonads he knew he had been replaced. The phone code had been violated.

He wanted that. He'd always wanted her to move on. He knew this would make things easier for him, make him feel less guilty, make it easier to get over her, make it easier to throw himself into his own life. He didn't really want it for her sake, however.

CHAPTER 31

Today was the second Saturday of the month, the day Eileen volunteered at the animal shelter. It was very convenient, only two blocks away. She had started there as part of her own self-therapy after cancer treatment.

She'd tried a regular support group for a while, and that was very helpful, but eventually she realized she wasn't as bad off as the rest of the women and knew it was time to move on. Around the room, each woman would confess her fears, hopelessness, and trials of the previous week. Eileen's main problem was that she was tired, so she'd get more sleep; it was all rather simple.

Other women would voice problems with husbands, daughters, reconstruction gone awry, postchemo pneumonia, near-death stem cell therapy, dastardly things. Dora was suffering her third relapse and was scheduled for a stem cell transplant in a couple of weeks. Lannie had had a recurrence after a twelve-year period of being cancer-free. "The Baroness," just diagnosed, who wore gaudy gowns and heavy makeup, hoped for a reconciliation with her estranged daughter. Tess expressed the endless problems with her reconstruction.

Eileen had begun to feel that she was taking a nosy interest in everyone else's problems, and that wasn't really the goal of the support group. It was not for titillation or observation. So she'd left.

The animal shelter was better therapy for Eileen. Cats made her sneeze and cough, so she was limited to working with the dogs. She bathed them, played with them, talked to them. She loved sudsing them up in the huge bathtub they had for such things. She would work their little furry bodies into a lather and then gently massage their backs, legs, muscles, necks. The dogs were delirious with joy. She didn't have to participate in the euthanizing, so, as far as she was concerned, every dog that wasn't there when she came in the next time was adopted into a new family. The workers there understood, and none of them went into detail about the euthanization or the fate of those missing from her previous visit. That fit her nervous system just fine.

There was no denying the therapeutic elements involved in babbling nonsense to a nonjudgmental being who happily waggled his butt at every brilliant word leaving your lips. You are so smart! You are without doubt the most perspicacious person on the entire planet! And, oh, how loved you are!

Wynkin was a sweet miniature collie. He must have just been brushed this morning, Eileen thought, because the static electricity made his fur stand out like a huge doggie halo.

"How are you doing, baby? How's my sweet thing?"

Wynkin wagged his tail and crouched down with his little butt arched in the air as she approached the cage. He nearly danced out of his skin with joy.

"God, how can anyone let these little guys go?" Eileen shook her head. Humans did not deserve the loyalty of dogs. We were showered with it and should be much humbled by it, she thought.

As much as Eileen loved her little stint at the shelter, she could never work there full-time. If her heart throbbed any harder, it would explode from her chest. She couldn't face the direct reality that most of the animals would not find a home beyond these walls.

―

Jenaveev sat naked on her veranda, wrapped in a mink coat, sipping a Tom Collins. It was her third. She wasn't supposed to drink much because of that little problem she used to have, and because of the medications she took. Virgil was expected home tomorrow. She felt like splurging.

It was a perfect mink day, the air damp with rain fizz, cool and fresh. She didn't wear the mink much anymore because of that time the city kids drenched her with fake blood outside Nordstrom's, stupid urchins. But by golly, she really did like the coat and couldn't quite understand why she should be deprived of her pursuit of happiness. The blood had been a cheap, diluted red dye and cleaned out quite well from the mink, leaving it even more lustrous than before.

With a half gurgle, half giggle, she thought, "What—there's a word for it—ironing. Ugh, I can't iron now. I could never iron. Clara should be around here somewhere; let her iron. She's...what was I talking about?"

She threw off the mink coat and straddled the veranda railing. Clara rushed out and helped her down and into bed.

―

Nick tiptoed up to the house, hoping to sneak past any family member there, but tripped on the top step. His equipment clattered to the ground.

Clara rushed over, shaking her head and hissing, "Shhhh, your mom," a phrase that had become a declaratory sentence in their household. Noelle was already at the table. When she turned to face him, he jumped; she wore a mud mask of thick, green goop. She sat reading the paper as little globs of avocado-clay-whatever dripped down on her plate of tuna salad. She was hopelessly gross.

He said, "I like the new look. Should ward off wild beasts well."

"So there's more adoring fans for you. You're welcome." She licked off a piece of avocado and spit it toward Nick.

"Hey," Nick said, but he laughed.

He grabbed an energy bar and headed outside. He needed to go... somewhere.

The tiny, budding metropolis of his neighborhood would have to do. Maybe he could find a new pair of quoits gloves or biscuits for the dog or a new book on how to win the stupid game, how to psyche out your opponents, because it was a game of mental strategy. You had to have a measure of brute strength to toss the five-and-a-half-pound object with some accuracy for that distance. But there was also, like poker, a strong mental component. Maybe he could find some psycho-type book that could provide tips for mentally undermining the other team.

As he meandered under a row of sycamore trees along the sidewalk, he heard a crow shriek and felt the flutter of wings as the black bird dive-bombed toward his head. He waved it away, but two more crows darted above him, their wings flapping furiously, and another three perched on a branch, squawking their displeasure. He could almost smell their french-fry-fueled rage. He ran toward the end of the block.

Later, he saw Noelle riding her bike on the other side of the street. Without the green gunk on her face, she looked all right. She didn't notice him, and he stood there watching her pedaling furiously up the hill away from their home. For some reason he had a flashback to when she was about seven years old and had this ridiculous pink bike with plastic flowers stuck all over it and pink streamers flying out of the handlebars. Suddenly he thought about how cute that was, although at the time he'd thought it was incredibly dumb. He'd been embarrassed that she was related; she'd looked so stupid and juvenile with those idiotic plastic streamers. But now, watching her determination in pedaling up that hill—most girls he knew would gave gotten off their bikes and walked them up the steep hill; she was pushing and pushing—he could practically see the steam coming from her brain. She was determined to make it; he admired her.

He thought of that image of her when she was seven and just how cute and precious she really was, and he suddenly felt very sorry for himself and for her and for all the anger and hostility they'd had toward one another for practically their entire lives. They had missed out on so much. They'd had so much more than many of their friends— more toys, more sporting equipment, more money, more cool places to go—but now he wished his parents hadn't plied them with so much crap. He wished they could have simply been a happy family. It would have been so nice to spend a simple evening together once in a while as a family, just playing cards and laughing and gently teasing one another instead of being hustled around to one party or sporting event or another.

Nick wandered around, gazing at each store window but not really seeing anything and not really looking for anything. He couldn't bear to think about buying yet another plaything. He could buy anything he wanted in that store right now, come home loaded down with junk, and his parents would look at him and exchange that little glance that they hoped would say, "See, our boy is happy. He buys stuff."

He almost shoved his fist through the gift shop window. The teddy bears looked so silly with their manufactured grins. He couldn't wait for the quoits championship in Atlantic City.

Noelle wanted to be the best bicyclist in the world. Or at least on her block. She didn't go for speed, but endurance. She could ride all the way over to the river, up along the river to the city bridge, along the main road to the railroad bridge, then back along the farm fields to home. It was a ten-mile ride. Not too bad for a fourteen-year-old.

Her dad told her not to go by herself, but her friends lollygagged. Tawnya talked too much. And Noelle liked to have some time to herself to think, or maybe not to think; sometimes she thought too much.

There was a strip club sort of place she knew, along the main road part of her trip. Sometimes she would get off her bike and stroll past because she was curious about what went on inside. She hated seeing any men going in or coming out because they always looked so gross and she was a little afraid of them. But she wondered what the women were like and what exactly they did in there.

She had lots of sexy thoughts for herself but didn't want to do it with Richard-down-the-road, or, God forbid, Nick's friend Randy, or anyone else just yet. She'd listen to Madonna, a slow, hip-grinding number, and sway seductively to the beat, wondering where that was coming from. She liked looking at pictures and touching herself. Brenda was doing it; she snuck her boyfriend Marc into her bedroom at night.

Noelle pedaled slowly toward town and wondered what was going on in her neighbors' homes. She often saw the neighbor kids yelling and screaming and playing hide-and-go-seek or something, and they seemed to be having a blast. She couldn't remember ever playing anything like that. She had many friends, and she'd always had the parties that everyone wanted to be invited to, but they were always highly orchestrated. The first hour would be clown time (or magician or trapeze artist or whatever). The next hour would be swim-in-the-pool time, with a coached game of Marco Polo with prepicked teams of boy-girl, boy-girl, calculated ahead of time from the RSVPs received. The following hour would consist of food, carefully catered by Boston Kitchen and including carved roast and cheeses, decorated radishes and other vegetables, and fruit salad, no pears, of course.

Once everyone had pigged out sufficiently, they would all mill around until the cake and ice cream showed up. Like at a wedding reception, Noelle would never open her presents during the party; her mother insisted it was more tasteful to open them in the privacy of her home after everyone had left. Then her mother could openly ridicule everything in the packages without worrying about hurting anyone's feelings. See, her mother did care.

And then, the thank you notes. Noelle never neglected the thank you notes. Her mother always ordered them, preprinted with the same message for everyone, including Noelle's name. Noelle was free to add a little heart or star or some tidbit or another to personalize each one, but her mother did not insist upon it. Again, she said that that was what all the classy people did. Usually the message read something like, "We're so happy you could join us to celebrate this joyful time; please accept our thanks for your gift with this quick rhyme."

Her mother was so proud of her own cleverness. Noelle wasn't so sure, but she didn't think it seemed all that classy or clever. It seemed pretty dumb. But she never said anything. She wished she never had to have another party. Sometimes they tried so hard, it made her tired. Life shouldn't be such a struggle at her age.

The place was right up ahead. It almost looked like a boarded-up, condemned building, but the neon light outlining a couple of shapely legs was brightly lit. One leg was crossed over the other, set in a constant rocking motion. No matter what time, day or night, like a beacon those legs penetrated the vista. If a man had any doubt about entering, those legs hypnotized him—back and forth and back and forth, beckoning him forward. They were just legs, after all. What could be so wrong in that?

―

Nick wanted to be the best. During practice today, he threw a leaner and then deliberately knocked it away with his next shot. That's what he could do to any opponent who dared to try to top him. His next two shots were both leaners, one on top of the pin and the next topping both. He just shook his head. He knew he was good. But it wasn't enough. He knew he had it in him; he just needed to think of a way to test his abilities to the max.

He went into the garage and pulled out a clean tank T-shirt from the dryer and wrapped it around his head like a blindfold. He jerked his head around a bit to test its tightness. No, it was on good. He lifted it up a bit to see where he was going, then said, "No, no, if I want to do this, I have to do it all the way." So he made his way from the garage to the backyard where the quoits were set up, the blindfold firmly in place covering his eyes.

What a great feeling! Darkness, yet he could sense things in ways he never imagined. He figured he would have to peek again when he got close, but, no, he knew exactly where his quoits were set up. They were…right… here. He bent over and was astonished to feel the little round stack of iron beneath his fingers.

Now, where was the pin? The little hob was hard enough to find sometimes even when he looked for it. Let's see, what direction was he facing? He could hear a dog barking. That was Dierdre, the neighbor Maxwells' corgi; he'd recognize that bark anywhere. That was to the left of his starting point. He could feel the dent in the dirt that his feet had worn through. A little dirty divot in the ground. And just to be safe, he could hear the Smiths' laundry flapping in the wind. Their clothesline was directly adjacent to the right of the pin, about thirty feet away. Oh, man, this was easy!

He reached down and picked up one of the quoits. He swung it back and forth a few times to get the feel and to imagine just how much thrust it would take to make it to the peg. He tuned in to the memory of the perfect coordination of muscles and mental power that had enabled him to hit the peg in the past. The eyes were a tiny part of it; it was all a joint effort of the body and the mind. OK, OK, he was ready; now go!

He threw the quoit toward the peg and heard it fall with a soft thud. No *clang* from the peg. He wasn't going to look yet. He tried the next one, went through the same drill. This time, *clang*! Success!

CHAPTER 32

Eileen idly tapped her fingers on the keyboard as she finished the report for Winston. When the hospital closed, she would have to find something else. She reached up to touch the Mercury dime that hung from the necklace next to her skin. Oddly, it was still a talisman. She felt better.

She picked up a pen to write notes from her last phone conversation with Neil—they did actually get some real work done before the more pleasurable fieldwork—and nearly started chewing on the tip out of habit, till she remembered the germ thing. Chemo had ruined her forever for spontaneous pen chewing. She remembered hollering at Virgil once. (Her new intimacy with Neil unfortunately triggered vivid memories of Virgil.) After an evening of lovemaking and cozying up under the covers, Virgil had just happened to mention, "Oh, I feel like I'm coming down with something. My throat is kind of scratchy. I might not be able to see you for a few days."

She'd looked at him. "What? You know how sick I get from even the slightest cold!"

He'd tried to laugh it off. "Oh, come on, now, you probably won't get it. I don't even have symptoms yet."

"That's exactly when you're the most contagious. Haven't you learned anything from your work at the hospital?" She'd tried to soften it with a smile, but she really was pissed and felt she was compromising herself by going easy on him.

"Well, I've learned to stay away from sick people if I can help it."

"Charming. OK, you can go now."

Two days afterward, sure enough, Eileen had felt like she'd been hit by a freight train. The world was heavy, her senses dulled, except for severe crankiness. After a couple of days of that, she got the sore throat and physical aches and pains and lastly the never-ending cough. Since she fought every day just to have enough energy to get through the simplest tasks, this extra load was too much of a burden. She needed to stay home and sleep, sleep, sleep. Virgil. He had always been oblivious. When she had confronted him, he responded, "I thought you were kidding. Don't get upset at me." He'd turned it around to make her look like the bad guy. Yes, here's good old Virgil, trying to be the fun guy, the happy guy, and you dampen his spirit by acting like he was intentionally cruel.

No, she didn't think he was cruel. He was too stupid to be cruel. "You're thoughtless and selfish," she'd told him.

"Selfish? Why, if you knew the things I did for my…"

He'd almost said "wife." Even Virgil in his most careless and self-absorbed way had to recognize that as a no-no.

But Eileen knew. She narrowed her eyes at him and grinned slightly. She couldn't help it; it was so asinine it was almost funny.

"For your what, darling? For your homeless shelter? For your local Red Cross? For your American Foreign Legion, I suppose?"

"Why, yes, that's it exactly," Virgil had laughed, always ready to laugh at his foibles, he really had thought the world of himself. "You know how committed I am to supporting the charities of my community. Honor, justice, the American way—it's *my* way, you know."

She'd had to join in the laughter. Their situation was so ridiculous, you just had to laugh.

CHAPTER 33

As Noelle rode along, she passed the public golf course, recently built. Her mom had long wanted her to take up golf. Originally, Noelle thought it would be a good thing to share something with her mother, but she just didn't like golf at all. It seemed so stupid. Fourteen-plus clubs needed to hit one small ball five hundred yards or so? You could probably kick it in quicker. And it was such a waste of valuable land. All the pesticides and wasteful use of water.

Noelle remembered when this area was a nice little forest. She used to have one of her secret places there. Once when she was following one of the paths through the woods, she came upon a little lake all by itself. She never knew it was there before. She never heard anyone talk about it. She got goose bumps when she saw it; it was so beautiful, and she thought it was put there just for her. She would sit on a big old log there and think. She'd write poetry there, which she never showed anyone. There was also an old building farther up the hill that housed crazy people. At least that's what everyone said. She'd felt a little creepy sitting there on her log all by herself, thinking about all those crazy people who could be on the loose.

But she didn't have to worry about it now. They'd cut down all the trees and covered everything with fake grass, and the lake was shaped and landscaped into an "obstacle." What a waste. The crazy house was still there. It was just on the outskirts of the fifteenth green. Sometimes the people would come out and peer at the golfers. There was a fence around the house so the people couldn't interfere with the players, but they would just stand there watching and sometimes shout out some garbled words.

Of course, her mother never played on that course. Just the thought of playing on less-than-immaculate greens made her cringe in embarrassment. And all those scruffy-looking people in cut-off jean shorts and long, scraggily hair, lugging their own golf bags. To her mom, that was an image completely contrary to the entire golf experience. How dare they sacrilege the game that way?

Noelle had continued to make up excuses not to play golf with her mother until she'd finally quit asking her.

Her mom enjoyed playing at the club. Most of the players knew each other—if not by name, then by sight—awarding each other polite little nods and a raised pinky in greeting as they passed one another. The gentility of the sport seemed to calm her mother. And she finally got the hang of the raised pinky thing.

CHAPTER 34

For a law firm, Salto Duthie was different. They always had picnics during the summer, and they would invite all of their clients as well as employees *and* spouses and children. A rare treat at law firms. Most lawyers generally didn't want to be anywhere near their own wives, ever, and especially didn't want to socialize in public with them around coworkers, and they frankly didn't care to engage in carefree conversation with Susie-in-Records' husband who trapped muskrats for a living. Not to mention the fact the lawyers were always looking for an excuse to make a play for Susie-in-Records herself and hoped that the bountiful spirits would be enough to make her forget that the lawyer was an arrogant son-of-a-bitch and would she please suck him off just a little? Wouldn't she like that? Of course, he couldn't have his wife around for that.

Eileen learned that every summer around July, Salto Duthie would send out this announcement to all its clients:

Let the good times roll! Salto Duthie wants y'all to loosen your ties, pull on those elastic waistbands, and join us in an old-fashioned BAR-B-Q. Pony rides for the kids, horseshoes, country rock music, dancing, and much more. Open to our clients and their families. Located at the Dandy Dude Ranch, RD 1, Hollybrook Road. Follow

Route 649 to Rabbit Warren Way, turn left and travel 2.5 miles to Hollybrook. Watch for the signs. RSVP and specify the number of adults and children in your party. Hee-haw, see ya there!

Eileen was so happy that the firm represented the hospital now. GLK had invited hospital staff to their client events, but those were completely different. That's where she'd had her first experience with law firms, and it was a grim one. GLK's client get-togethers were held in a huge ballroom in the city and always ended up a free-for-all love fest. Men sprawled all over the sofas, grabbing at women who were more than willing to wind themselves around their laps. Spouses and children were never invited. Eileen had only gone once; it was too sordid for her taste. She'd prefer to keep that stuff private.

On her bike, Noelle doubled back past Racy Ta-Ta's and heard a familiar chant. She stopped short. It wasn't the sort of place that would generally invoke a flash of memory in a fourteen-year-old. Suddenly, she thought, she'd look for a job. Not as a stripper; even she wouldn't go to that extreme to vex her mother.

Most of her friends worked, either baby-sitting or dog-sitting or even bussing tables. This would surely be more interesting than that. She was so curious about this place and so sick of obsessing about her mother that she decided to go in; she knew she looked older than fourteen.

Her heart raced as she marched past the beefy-necked thug at the door and peered into the dark hall until her eyes got used to it.

"May I help you, darlin'?"

A friendly face. A rather large blonde woman in heavy makeup, with pink nail polish and huge breasts barely draped with gold lame, came over to her with a grin. "Can we put you to work?"

Noelle fixated on the large breasts. Her mother often pranced around the house in the nude, or nearly nude, but she didn't look anything like this. Jenaveev's body was raw-boned angles jutting out under flaps of wrinkled, leathery brown skin. This was wonderful. Very pink and fleshy and voluptuous. Sexy. Noelle felt very warm. She wondered if she would ever look like this. She really hoped so.

She heard the familiar song again, the one that had made her stop here today.

        Two lips together, twilight forever,

        Bring back my love to me...

Two of the dancers lightly clapped their hands together. The men were in raptures, watching.

"Yes, I am looking for a job. Of course, I can't do...that." She flicked her head over at the dancers as they shimmied and swayed on the dance floor. "Well, I've done the patty-cake before, but not...you know."

Blondie looked her over. "Well, hon, you are a bit too young for Racy's patty-cake, for sure, but you can help us out, if you'd like. Run simple errands, get us drinks, food, toilet paper, sweep a bit, that sort of thing. Do you think you'd be interested?"

Noelle glanced over at the men; a few of them peered at her.

"We'll keep you far away from our patrons. Don't want to give our hard-working girls any unfair competition. Or make our men uncomfortable." She winked. "And it will keep you safe too. Name's Gina. Good to meet ya." She held out a hand.

Surprisingly dainty, Noelle thought. She grasped it; it was such a warm hand.

Noelle flashed a thought of her mother, screeching at her to play golf with her at the club so she could meet the "right" people. Noelle hated golf; it was a stupid and wasteful game. She remembered her special little lake spot that had been razed for the public course and thought how nice it would have been to lounge around naked, in the woods, surrounded by women like this and their male admirers. That would have been a much nicer use of her favorite spot instead of the stupid golf course that was there now. Now her precious lake was smack in the middle of the ninth hole, a driver's nightmare, and was filled with Titleists and Pinnacles.

It might not be the smartest move she would ever make in her life, but right now, at this very minute, she wanted nothing more than to join these women and support them in any way she could.

She felt a wave of relief, like a leaden weight lifted from her soul, as she grinned at this beautiful, sexy lady.

"I'm Noey, and, yes, I'd be happy to work for you."

Of course, Noelle couldn't tell her mother where she was working; she would have a fit.

But her mother never paid much attention where she went on her bike rides anyway, so she just pretended she was going on extended rides. It was only for a couple of hours after school a couple of days during the week and a couple of hours on Saturday. She could really go in any time she wanted. The folks at Racy's paid her under the table, so to speak, not to be confused with the other things they did under the table.

They tried to shelter her from some of the seediness. She only worked in the dressing rooms and backstage. She could only see the dancing from the sidelines and couldn't see the more tawdry behavior going on at the tables. And, Noelle thought, she really didn't want to see any of that stuff. Plus she might be embarrassed to see someone she knew—maybe one of her friends' fathers, maybe even her own dad. She wasn't that curious; it seemed a little icky. Besides, she could hear enough from the sidelines. She liked being a part of the production but didn't care to reap these particular rewards. Backstage was just fine for her.

But she did peek once or twice. Through the gray tendrils of cigarette smoke, she saw expressions on the men that at first she found repulsive, but then, curiously, her attitude changed a little. They looked…grateful. She doubted that her mom did anything like this for her dad, so these men must have the same sort of situation at home. She couldn't imagine any of her friends' mothers shimmying like that. It would be fun to learn, though.

Gina kept a close eye on Noelle. Clearly this young one was a sheltered girl from the top of the hill. Her own girlhood was a bit different. Yet, here they both were.

The spotlights made it difficult to see the audience. It also helped the individual dancers fantasize about who was out in the audience, instead of actually seeing the sweaty, desperate, bloated faces.

When the dancer starts out, she's always kind of excited. She wouldn't get into this business unless she was at least a little bit proud of her body and felt sexy in it. So the first couple of times she goes out there, she fantasizes that there's a special guy, probably one she'd seen on the street or one she knows, one who's really cute, one she has a crush on. And she dances for him, secretly, seductively.

And she can get away with that for a very long time. It's only when she starts to get a little tired and looks at the crowd and sees who's really out there—oily, hungry-eyed men—that a seed of disillusionment is planted. And soon the disillusionment grows into a full-blown depression. That's when she must get out, before she's sucked in and loses herself completely. This business could be a real ego-booster, while she's feeding off the fantasy she has created for herself. When the fantasy gets harder to maintain, when she starts seeing it as only his fantasy, then it's time to quit.

Gina sighed and motioned to Noelle that she needed more soda.

CHAPTER 35

On Sunday morning Eileen got up early to start packing up her miniatures to show at the flea market. They were tiny enough to load the whole batch in a big tote box. She was lucky; she felt sorry for the artists who had to lug around huge copper sculptures or 24x36-inch canvases or who had elaborate displays.

Like Kitchen Katie, who made refrigerator magnets, mugs, and oven mitts and displayed them all in an elaborate kitchen setup, complete with stove, refrigerator, sink, table, and cabinets. Even lacy curtains over two faux windows (which, of course, were illuminated by a hidden incandescent nightlight). Kitchen Katie, always very rosy-cheeked and panting, would bustle about her little pretend kitchen, wiping down the counters and rearranging her wares. She'd even set the timer, and when the buzzer went off, she'd look for the ever-bubbly cherry pie that was painted on the fake oven. She would even spray the area with cherry scent. Eileen suspected KK was an egg short of a baker's dozen, but all artists had to stick together no matter what. Most people thought all artists were crazy anyway, so it was important that they supported one another.

Eileen could fit twenty of her works in a box, and that was plenty for a show. She only did the show about once a month; that gave her enough time to replenish her stock and keep pace with her energy level. She would love to do the juried weekend art show in Mount Gretna held in August every year, but just the thought frenzied her, and she knew she wouldn't have the stamina to last a whole weekend.

Sometimes, in a hurry, she would buy the little frames outright, but she preferred to make her own. There was something about slicing through the mats and foam core that soothed her soul. She could tell a clean slice from the sound. She got lots of inquiries from people wanting her to frame their stuff, but she'd heard too many horror stories of artists finding that framing had become their full-time work, leaving little or no time for their art. That was not for her; she didn't need the extra money that badly.

At least not now. If she was booted out of the hospital, then she might rethink it. She could see how someone could get caught up in the framing end. Framing didn't require getting bogged down in creative thought or compositions. Someone brings in a work of art and you instantly see the perfect frame and mat for it. There was a certain deep sense of satisfaction taking the raw art form and turning it into a full-fledged masterpiece. Framing was really an art in itself. The frame could make or break a piece.

Since Eileen's pieces were so tiny, she could get by on scraps of molding, which she purchased fairly inexpensively at the lumberyard. Joe the lumberman was always helpful.

"Hey, Eileen, we've got some good stuff for you today. All the art shops are stocking up for the big Save the Trout benefit next week," he'd said with a nod the last time she was there.

"God, how many pictures of trout can one stand to display?" she'd reply. "It's not like fish are masters of pose. Let's see, this one is, uh, swimming up a stream, and this one is lapping up a creek, and, oh, this is really exciting, this one is wriggling down a river."

"Have you ever seen a salmon run?"

"No, but I helped it buy pantyhose."

"No, no, I mean like in Alaska?"

"Oh, I know. Fish in the raw are fabulous creatures, fighting immense obstacles to reach their spawning ground. Panting, jumping, scraping by, breaching dams and dodging sea lions to reach their birth home. Hell, if man had to fight such odds, we'd be extinct in no time. It's just a bit harder trying to capture that magnificent fish spirit on paper. Always that blank expression."

"Boy, you're tough, sister," Joe grinned.

"No, I'm a honey. Really," she shot back, beaming.

She continued packing up her pieces, grabbed a couple of muffins and some yogurt and cashews, and headed out the door. The shows were fun, but sometimes they felt like a grind. It was an all-day thing, and you had to time your bathroom/meal breaks just perfectly so you didn't miss any big sales. Miles joined her sometimes or showed up later to watch her stuff so she could take a few breaks. He didn't quite understand the whimsy of her pieces, but he was a good soul and humored her. Miles and Eileen had been friends forever. They'd tried the relationship thing many years ago but realized that they drove each other too crazy so could only be best friends. Funny how things turn out.

She loved the people watching. She tried to imagine what sorts of lives or jobs the patrons had. No doubt wonderful, fulfilling things that allowed them to while away their Sundays at the flea market. Without working. One thing she never did was count on a sale from someone who commented, "I'll be back." They never came back. No one knew why browsers felt obligated to say that; it wasn't like they were hawking long-distance phone carriers or anything. Eileen personally didn't mind not selling everything; it meant that she had fewer items to prepare for the next show. She suspected that was not the best profit-management strategy, but, hey, she had a job and never expected this to ever be a full-time gig.

It was a lovely day. The sun's rays bathed the dreary stalls and cheered exhibitors and browsers alike. Eileen heard Bruce Springsteen on a nearby radio. She usually thought it was rude for exhibitors to play music, but that was only if it was whining country. Springsteen was fine.

After the Bruce Springsteen concert long ago in Philly with Virgil, she had said, "Oooh, now there's a guy who can eat crackers in my bed anytime." Later, she was in bed and Virgil was fiddling about in the kitchen. He approached the bed, crackers in hand.

Her face lit up. "Oh, you think you rate, do you?"

He said nothing, just grinned. "Oh, I believe I've made my point."

He set the crackers down on the nightstand and dived into bed next to her. She wound her legs and arms around him and they smiled and smiled…

"Born in the USA, I was… Wake up, snookums!"

Her blue eyes flashed around to the face of Richard Nixon. Miles had found a rubber mask.

"Scare me half to death, will you? Wasn't there a Julia Roberts or something for sale?"

"And ruin my mock-o image? No way."

"Oh, I doubt such a minor thing could ever dampen the rugged machismo that is the core of your being. Do you have a tissue?"

"Of course. Hey, wait a minute…"

"Oh, get over it, real men carry tissues."

"Boy, do they ever. The double-blow kind."

CHAPTER 36

Eileen felt guilty heading into the hospital on Monday, tanned (despite the sun block), rested, and ego-stroked after another successful weekend of sales. At lunchtime, she saw Tanesha, one of the ICU unit secretaries, eating by herself in the cafeteria and peering idly out the window. It was rare for any of the nursing staff to eat alone; they usually clustered together murmuring shared tales of physician insolence and keeping up with increasingly convoluted administrative procedures and patient woes.

Eileen missed the starched white uniforms and caps that had been replaced by casual wear. Some of the nursing staff could pass for grocery clerks.

Tanesha was usually vibrant and full of fun. She called her patients Rip Van Winkle when they regained consciousness. It was irreverent, but no one ever complained because it was usually such a tense and awkward moment that one welcomed the slight comic relief. None of the family members ever really knew what to say, so they just let her babble on. She acted out of love and compassion for her patients and their grieving relatives. But now her brow was furrowed, her deep brown eyes welled with tears, and an occasional tear would dribble down her fine copper skin. Her expression was dead.

Eileen grabbed a salad and a chicken breast from the counter and slid into the booth across from Tanesha. She put her hand over Tanesha's. "Are you OK?"

Tanesha glanced at Eileen, her eyes empty. "I really can't believe this place might close. It's been here since the Civil War. What's going to happen to it? And to us?"

"Tanesha, you're the best unit secretary we have; you'll have no trouble finding another job. As far as the building goes, we'll try to sell it first, just as it is. If that doesn't work, I don't know what will happen."

Tanesha shook her head slowly and squinted slightly. "I just don't get it. Did I ever tell you that my ancestors, my great-great-grandmother and -grandfather, met here?"

"No, I never knew that. Was it a doctor/patient thing or a doctor/nurse thing?"

"No, they met as slaves, on their way on the Underground Railroad. There's a tunnel passageway underneath the hospital. Did you know about that?"

Eileen blinked. "Funny, I just had a talk with Milton about it. Did you ever hear his story? I had always heard things but was never sure if it was just a rumor or what."

Tanesha perked up. "No, I've heard about it too. The traditional thought in my family is that they carved their initials in the walls of the tunnel. I've always wanted to see if I could find that."

Eileen said, "You'd think their first concern would be protecting themselves and finding a safe haven. They were really putting their identities at risk by exposing themselves like that."

"They adored each other and they were dead-set on making it through and becoming productive members of society. But they could only do that if they were free."

"They must have trusted that the tunnel was a secret too. I think it's time to find it."

"If it was a secret hideout back then, then it's got to be… I can't imagine anyone taking the effort to maintain something like that through the years. You remember the flood we had five years ago from Hurricane Francis, Francine—what was it?"

"Yeah, something like that. What a mess," Eileen said. "The main level of the hospital was closed for a few days because all of the seepage. The hospital *never* closes down. I understand it was that grommet guy's fault." Throw in a little humor at Virgil's expense.

Tanesha looked puzzled. "What? Who? Oh, you're talking about that board member from American Grommets. Has he fled for the hills yet?"

"Not that I'm aware of." Everyone at the hospital was vaguely aware of "that board member" whose company was causing so many problems.

Since speaking with Tanesha, Eileen felt better than she had in a long time. She now had a goal. Excited about the Underground Railroad, she went home and flicked on her laptop to do some research. Just as her computer sprang to life with flashing lights, a beacon shone in her brain. After the familiar hissing and humming of the modem kicked in, she typed "Underground Railroad" in the search engine. And got 121,000 hits. Lots of references to Harriet Tubman, John Brown, and Frederick Douglass. She read about Harriet Tubman, an escapee herself, and her successful journeys helping slaves run from the Eastern Shore of Maryland to Canada.

Secrecy was paramount. Just like Milton had said. Slaves and escapees communicated with each other through songs and symbols. It seemed as if most of the religious references prevalent in their music were metaphors for freedom from slavery. In fact, the earliest slaves weren't particularly keen on Christianity, but once they got the gist of the symbolism, they figured they could use it for their own purposes.

Go down, Moses, way down in Egypt land
Tell old Pharaoh, let my people go…
No more shall they in bondage toil
Let my people go.

Eileen wondered at the arrogance of the white massas who were blind to this obvious metaphor. Slave owners were just happy that religion made the darkies submissive. Whites were charmed that the slaves would take to heart the simple Bible stories and legends (and lessons!) perpetrated by the white ruling classes.

Slaves' escapes were not achieved haphazardly. There was a highly effective network of communication through people, symbols, codes, constellations, and possibly quilts. And they headed straight for Canada—none of this messing around in the northern abolitionist states because after the expansive Fugitive Slave Act of 1850, no black anywhere was safe. This act required the immediate return of any black to his or her master and called it a crime not only to help slaves escape but to avoid returning them to their masters. Blacks who were previously freed found themselves having to offer real proof or else return to slavery.

Eileen wanted to soak up all of this information. All week long she studied the issue. She couldn't believe that a mere one hundred forty years ago, in the same land on which she currently frolicked, flirted, and frittered about, in the same dirt, the same air, with the same insects and animals and plants, human beings were actually owned by other human beings. The concept was as foreign to her as the idea that dinosaurs once ambled the earth.

She marveled that it was an ingrained part of history, that students recited dates learned by rote: Civil War, 1861–1865; Gettysburg, 1863; Harpers Ferry, 1859. Give that girl an A+. But, Eileen thought, we rarely associate those dates with the actual horror of the events.

The Civil War was a fight between the grays, who wanted to continue the practice of owning people and to recede from the union to preserve that freedom, versus the blues, who probably didn't care too strongly one way or another about the slaves but had an inkling that it wasn't such a grand idea, and besides, they needed above all to preserve the union and lasso those rapscallion Confederates into submission. The Battle of Gettysburg was a very bloody, ghastly skirmish that first tipped the scale to the Union favor. Harpers Ferry was where an impassioned, slightly insane white guy, John Brown, was willing to risk everything, including his life, to save those otherworldly dark-skinned people by raiding a federal arsenal.

A human being owning another. Eileen knew that slavery had persevered since the moment the curved spines of Homo sapiens twanged erect, allowing them to stand on two feet and lord over others. But this wasn't dinosaur times; this wasn't even one hundred fifty years ago. There were undoubtedly people alive today who had word-of-mouth personal knowledge of that episode in history. People who knew people who knew people. Like Milton.

She read until her eyelids drooped and she barely had enough energy to log out of all the programs and turn off her computer. She closed her laptop and lay down on her bed. Her sleep was interrupted by fitful dreams of Wynkin, the miniature collie from the animal shelter, being chased by a saber-toothed tiger. She awakened with a gasp, scrunched the covers up around her chin, sighed, and fell back to sleep.

The next weekend she opened her eyes with the same split-second Saturday thought: *Oh God, I gotta get up. No, wait, it's Saturday! Yessssss.* It was no use preparing for the flea market; she was pulled by a different inspiration. She would drive to Philadelphia to research and buy some books about the Underground Railroad at the US Government Bookstore. She had seen quite a few titles that looked helpful on the Internet. Maybe she would discover the role her hospital had played.

She ate a quick breakfast of pumpkin muffin, half a grapefruit, and coffee (with foamed milk, natch). Days like this, she relished her freedom.

Once she was on the turnpike, she noticed a billboard for a recreational equipment and supply store. The billboard was plastered with fresh-faced, smiling people performing all types of activities, impeccably dressed in the latest waterproof and insulated (yet lightweight!) duds and using the newest state-of-the-art equipment. She thought about what she'd read about the slaves and how their passion and energy were directed toward real-life drama and survival. It was ironic that nowadays one must artificially manufacture one's own "adventure" in often bizarre forms—scaling fake rock walls, parachuting out of planes, bungee jumping, etc. She suspected that if one simply spent more time learning about one's children, why, that would supply most of the adventure anyone would need. She noticed a crowd of kids on the corner, African Americans, slouched in baggy pants and flicking their gang symbols to one another and bouncing to rap music.

She loved Philly. She breezed right into one of the parking garages, didn't blink at the $10 weekend parking special, and parked. The federal bookstore was in the historic district, ten blocks or so away, but she thrilled at the thought of walking. The smells of the city were sublime. Better than NYC, she'd been told. Even the street vendors were better; these roach coaches were worth the stop. You could grab a quick bite—anything from tuna sub sandwiches, pizza, or Chinese food, to name a very few—for a cheap couple of bucks.

She studied the handwritten menu at the coach on the corner of Walnut and Sixteenth. She peered at the words "Boccoli & Beep" and barely suppressed a giggle, but the wonderful smell wafted through the air, and she knew she had found lunch. The man inside the cart smiled at her as he spooned out into the deep, round aluminum container a thick layer of seasoned rice followed by a generous pile of broccoli and beef, all slathered with brown sauce. The sauce was not thick or gooey or press-your-fingers-to-your-temples salty like teriyaki. It was milder, and the blend was perfect.

Rittenhouse Square wasn't too far away, so she headed there to sit and enjoy her lunch, even though it was in the opposite direction from the bookstore. She sat on the park bench and wondered if anyone realized that she was from out of town. An old man in an olive beret and a tan corduroy jacket grimaced at her and sat on her bench.

"Damn dogs."

She glanced sideways. Did she want to entertain this?

"The way they traipse them around with their little doily sweaters and jangly bells, they're not dogs at all."

A passing poodle drifted over and sniffed at his foot.

"Little priss-pots."

She looked over; the man's eye was moist.

"Now, Zachary— ol' Zach—now, he was a dog. He was a duck dog."

Eileen imagined a blond lab with floppy feathered ears and an orange beak. Hmm, would the horny ducks on her lake sidle up to Zach? But the man was obviously moved by the memory.

"Best huntin' dog a man could want."

The boccoli was gone; just a few more bites of beep and she could be on her way. But she got a vision of Wynkin's little eager, fuzzy face and she asked, "What happened to Zach?"

"What's that?"

She wished she had kept her mouth shut, but now imaginary Wynkin was nibbling on the edge of her lunch tin.

"Excuse me, but it sounded like you were talking about your dog. Did something happen to him? Zach, is it?"

The man examined her with his milky eyes. Yep, she looked all right, not too loony.

"He was a rascal, always would gallop around and around the sofa when I got home. Round and around in circles, couldn't catch up with him. He was so excited, I guess, to see me. Couldn't figure it out. Got rheumatism and up and died. Buried him out back, under the dogwood tree. Ha, what do you think about that?"

"I'm so sorry. I have a dog friend at the shelter where I do volunteer work and…"

"You're not a real person, 'less'n you have a dog."

He groaned and struggled to his feet and shuffled slowly down the walkway. She had been dismissed. He walked off to the side a bit, as if allowing for a trotting dog beside him.

She really must try to adopt Wynkin, she thought, even if she had to move out of her apartment, buy a farmstead with acreage, and incur crushing financial debt.

She walked tearfully; even now, the slightest thing morphed into melodrama. She wondered when it would stop. She was glad to be surrounded by all the anonymous humanity. No one looked at her, cared about her, or was even remotely interested in her, and that was just fine. Everyone had his or her own problems, taut family dramas, and rushing thoughts, and that her own were of no special importance to them was oddly comforting to her.

Blocks later, she entered the federal building. She was unnerved by the hordes of uniformed police. It didn't occur to her until now that this place might be a target or threatened by anyone. The guards looked her up and down with grim expressions and reluctantly pointed the way to the bookstore. Guilty until proven innocent seemed to be their creed.

Eileen was amazed by the quantity and quality of reference materials in the bookstore. She thought the materials would be cheaply made, hand-typed, loosely stapled with upside-down pages. But no, everything was professionally prepared—sleek and inviting. Even Daniel would have been impressed, whatever it was he did. But she once again felt uncomfortable by all the armed presence and a little overwhelmed by the amount of literature, so she grabbed several books and catalogs and headed for the cashier. It was clearly not a place to linger and browse.

She stopped for a final bite to eat at Latimer's, the deli of champions and ballet dancers, and admired the autographed photos on the wall. She had forgotten that a bite at Latimer's could feed a small country, so she had the leftover turkey and cheese sandwich boxed up to take home and made sure the pickle was not forgotten. She smiled at the thought of savoring a bit of Philly later back in her kitchen in Maple Leaf. She probably wouldn't even eat the sandwich—she tended to neglect leftovers until they nearly crept from the refrigerator as a new life form—but she would enjoy the idea of having a bit of Philly at home with her. Better than a shot glass, coffee mug, or refrigerator magnet.

On the way home, fog smothered her car. She felt lost in the sameness of it, unable to see billboards, the trees along the side of the road, nothing more than five feet beyond her headlights' glare. Occasionally another car passed in the opposite direction. Bright lights on, bright lights off. *Click-click. Click-click.* They say that brights aren't supposed to work in the fog, but they always helped her. She marveled at her ability to continue to drive fifty-five through the heavy blanket of vapor. She hoped a big pothole or rock didn't suddenly appear on the roadway; there was no way she could stop for it in time.

A dim red light ahead broke into the cloud. It appeared to be flashing. Yes, four-way flashers of a car pulled to the side of the road. Whew, she was glad she was female. There was no way she would stop, and no one would really expect her to. This dense fog could swallow a girl whole. Thankfully, the owner didn't try to flag her down. She wouldn't have stopped anyway, but at least she didn't have to feel guilty.

When she finally made it home, she crawled into bed and slept for twelve hours.

CHAPTER 37

Eileen really wanted to go to the Salto Duthie picnic but felt a little uneasy with Neil being there. His divorce had been final for months, but she didn't want to shove their relationship down everyone's throat just yet. Including herself. He thrilled her, but she was still a little gun-shy and wasn't ready to take the plunge with Neil on a legitimate level. However, he was still welcome in her bed—oh, lordy, me—anytime. Like now.

"So, uh, are you planning to go to the picnic?" Eileen asked Neil when they came up for air.

"I think so. Hayley wants to go because she'll see her friends there."

"Oh. I don't know if I should go, then. It's too soon, don't you think?"

"Well, I don't know. What were you planning to wear, black leather and whips as usual?"

"No, I thought I'd save that for the office Christmas party. But really, you know I'm more of a pastel person. Baby blue and feather pink. And I don't like to be dominant in bed."

"Is that so, my dear Madame? Then, pray tell, what do you call it when you slink over to me and drape your legs around my waist and grind your you-know-what into my you-know-what?"

"No, no, no, that's being sultrily servile. Don't you know the difference?"

"I'm not sure that I do. Perhaps you should show me again sometime."

They ended up wrapped in the sheets again. She couldn't help it. She always had enough energy for this.

She agreed to go to the picnic. And meet Hayley, finally.

CHAPTER 38

On Sunday Eileen dabbed on the finishing touches to her latest piece, a herd of cows being milked by one little boy. He sat hunched over his little stool, shoulders rigid, as line after line of cows' backs reached to infinity. The cow he was milking chewed green hay nonchalantly, eyes half-closed. Into this work of art went a little scribble of a Mercury dime, or the hint of one anyway. The true image was really quite intricate, and she wasn't sure she could capture it. *Ta-da, finished.* She headed out for food. A satisfying resolution; painting was hungry work.

And there, at Chino's Harbor Seafood Restaurant, she saw Virgil and a woman— whom she supposed was his wife, Jenaveev—together. She had picked up some more books at the library on the Underground Railroad and was ready to do some heavy-duty research over a plate of lobster linguini. It was inevitable that she would run into them sometime, since the town was so small. He didn't see her at first, and Eileen took advantage of that to just observe them.

Jenaveev teetered on high heels, her red hair bushy and unruly. Or was it a wig? It was the first time Eileen had ever seen her. She wore heavy makeup, smeared on like a thick coat of varnish, bright green eye shadow, and brighter red lipstick. Subtlety was obviously not her goal. At first glance, they looked awkward together; he seemed faintly embarrassed to be accompanying her, and she seemed plainly provoked. She alternated so quickly from grimacing at her husband to giggly hand-waving at the waiter or someone at a corner table that Eileen wasn't positive the woman wasn't having seizures. She half expected to see horns sprout on one half of her head and a halo on the other. If she suddenly started spewing vomit, Eileen was definitely leaving, lobster linguini or no.

Then there was the moment. The host called them to their table. Virgil looked across the room, probably at the buxom, blue-eyed blonde. Jenaveev nudged him with her elbow and nodded over to the waiter who was indicating their table. It was a simple but telling gesture, proprietary even, between longtime partners. There was an aura about them, a bond there. Eileen was surprised to see it. Her stomach lurched a bit.

Some people are drawn to one another from a deep-down need that no one else can articulate. Sometimes you have to delve into the far reaches of the subconscious to realize that he wants her because she fills that little divot in his heart that was looking for a soul to save. She wants him because, well, his money, of course. Not too much delving to come up with that one. But it's not just a superficial greed for money that attracts her to him. Her desire for money becomes a kind of sensuousness toward him because he can provide it for her. And he, in turn, doesn't seem to mind that she's only interested in him for his money. Since he doesn't judge her for her money-lust, she becomes validated. In their own peculiar way, they looked like they belonged together.

Eileen was surprised at her reaction. She thought she would be jolted pell-mell into a downward spiral after seeing her former passion partner with his wife for the first time.

Eileen caught a quick glimpse of his eyes trying to meet her own. She wanted to avoid any melodramatic scene, so she briefly nodded and quickly looked away. She could go eat somewhere else tonight. She was more in the mood for steak anyway. Better brain food.

———

Later, over her medium-rare filet, she noticed another couple in the dark corner. He was alarmingly attractive. Perfect symmetrical features, blue eyes shining like tender buttons, slight sloping nose, firm mouth with full but not too full lips. Maybe this was one she could learn to draw.

She grabbed a pencil from her purse and sketched a quick outline. The young woman with him had perky, curly blonde hair, no doubt fragrant with Pert. Her eyes were open a little too wide, as if any moment, as swift as a blink, her handsome partner would disappear. It would turn out that her fears were well-founded, as eighteen months after the birth of their second child he would glide out of the closet and into the arms of the sous-chef of this restaurant. And he claimed he came here for the frogs' legs.

CHAPTER 39

Monday again. Eileen saw Maribeth out of the corner of her eye and groaned. Was it enough of a glance that Maribeth would know that Eileen saw her and was deliberately avoiding her if she didn't stop? Or was it fleeting enough of a glance that could be taken for not really noticing her at all because she had her mind on other things?

Maribeth answered the question for her. "Oh, Eileen, I need to talk to you." Tears welled up in her eyes. "I had my mammogram, and they think they saw something. I'm so worried."

She went though this every year. Every year the technician fumbled with the image, giving Maribeth a teasing hint that the validation might finally come her way. Oh, if it were only so, Maribeth would then seek out Eileen and be initiated as a bona fide member of the club, the breast cancer sisterhood. She desperately wanted to be a member. She would give anything to have that camaraderie. To really *suffer*. She knew she deserved it. She had high hopes.

Eileen was tired. She was in no mood this time to flame Maribeth's anguish. Any time there was a hair-like imperfection on the X-ray film, Maribeth was frantic. Eileen wanted to say, "Honey, talk to me after you've had a chunk of your chest removed and a pus bag dangling from your waist. Then maybe we'll have something to talk about."

Instead Eileen sighed softly and said, "Oh, Maribeth, I'm sure it's nothing. Try not to worry about it. I'm sure you're fine." She smiled and patted Maribeth's shoulder.

Maribeth knew she should be relieved. But no, she felt herself fading away into the crevice. Another face blending in with all the others. She was just that nothing-person again. That evening she went out to her car, smiled slightly at the jiggling flower and hula-girl bobbleheads that covered her dash and drove home to her scrapbooking, where she placed an acid-free teardrop next to a photograph of her family.

The lab was completely dark. Eileen did a quick double take and checked her watch, fretting briefly that she must have missed daylight saving time again and woken up an hour early. Usually the lab was awhirl with activity in the mornings—preadmission testing, preoutpatient surgery testing, patients from the emergency room, and patients looking hung over and miserable and not being able to wait for their doctor's office to open. To see the place totally dark was mystifying.

She stopped at the admissions desk. "Lydia, what's going on? There's no one in the laboratory."

"Hiya, Eileen. I know. Isn't it scary? Someone said they're all at a meeting."

In her office, Eileen dodged calls from both Virgil's and Neil's law firms, GLK and SD, and from the press about documents related to those dratted grommets. The records department was used to requests, a process that had become quite a lucrative side business for the hospital. But these were beyond simple requests for emergency room or operating room records. Eileen coordinated these requests because they involved documents from many of the hospital's departments.

She had to locate all the documents related to the questionable surgeries, tracking their circuitous route from the moment supplies had been ordered to each person touching the supplies and personnel working the OR during the mishaps—every single person who'd laid a hand on the patient or anything that was used on the patient before, during, and after surgery. Every department, from Materials Management, which ordered the supplies, to Pharmacy to Housekeeping was involved.

Eileen cleared the requests through Neil, then sent each request to its corresponding department then waited for them to compile the records and send them back to her office to make arrangements for numbering and organizing. Winston asked Eileen to do all the organizing, to save money. The hospital wasn't too keen on having all sorts of people from all over the town looking at private patient records and preferred to keep as much of it in-house as possible. Confidentiality was a relative term to some, and the hospital couldn't risk loose tongues in a copy center. Then the documents were off to SD for final review. Eileen liked the idea of helping Neil out and maybe impressing him a bit from a professional standpoint. *See, I'm not just cute.*

GLK, as attorneys for Virgil's company, AGAF, would also scour through the information, seeking any means to thwart the hospital's reputation. With its review, SD hoped to scope out in the documents any possible threat to the hospital and do damage control before GLK clawed over it.

Neil had sent over one of his paralegals to help with the documents. Lucinda, impeccably dressed in a navy suit with a lacy pink cami peeking out, beamed at Eileen then quickly went back to poring over a pile of documents while her fingers tapped impossibly fast on a laptop. Eileen smiled back and felt like asking her, "Do you know that your boss has a tongue that would shame a South Street whore?" But she refrained. Lucinda looked like she was no stranger to tawdry, should the situation warrant it. And Eileen didn't want to give her any ideas.

CHAPTER 40

Virgil had to stop by the law firm to review some of the documents. He wasn't crazy about Gordon, Larson & Kammerer, loquacious and pretentious louts that they were. He knew, however, that they were the best defense firm in the area. He steeled himself for the stop at Renee Finkster's office.

Renee clearly had the hots for him, and she didn't do the hots well. She was relatively attractive, forty-ish, with thick, brown hair cut in a short bob. She was never married, or if so, it was such a long time ago it hardly counted, and no one knew her history. She was outwardly comfortable with her childless state and inwardly glad she'd never had to make the choice. Now she felt she was entering her prime. After all, she was a woman lawyer who had Made It Big. Shouldn't that be a babe magnet?

Unfortunately for her, it was not. Her all-business demeanor clashed horribly with the pinched, kittenish expression she shot at Virgil at every opportunity. He felt embarrassed for her. He thought maybe she had had plastic surgery gone awry, but she did not seem to be a plastic surgery type.

Virgil cringed as he knocked on her door. Perched pertly on her ergonomic chair, she looked up, crossed her legs, and motioned him to enter.

"Our folks are looking through the documents now," she said. "Don't worry, we'll get to the bottom of this."

Her words were all business, but she darted a come-hither look to him that unfortunately smothered itself in her tight skin and big teeth. And the eyes. Her eyes were spooky: too intense, too focused, unable to impart any of the subtlety of sex. He wondered at the fact that she had many features that singularly were attractive but in the aggregate didn't work at all. She exuded an air of efficient brittleness, like the praying mantis that bites her mate's head off after sex. Or was it before sex to get that extra oomph of manic reflexes? Either way, he shuddered at the thought.

Her crossed leg swung gently against the other leg. In one last chance, Virgil briefly thought about wrapping those legs around his head in a lewd sexual act but knew for sure those brittle gams would snap like twigs. Might give him whiplash; he'd better not even consider it.

"Do you want to get a drink later, to discuss it further?" she asked.

He shrugged. "Sure. If you don't have time now, later would be fine."

He could do her, sure he could. He wasn't attracted to her, but just knowing how grateful she would be might make it worth it. Charity was a good motive, wasn't it? But no, he couldn't consider it. Better to wallow in the miserable bedroom ministrations of his wife. At least he didn't have any expectations. Plus, he had to work with Renee; he couldn't stand seeing her regularly after having carnal knowledge of her. She was definitely a six-drink, love-her-and-leave-her type. A business-trip fluke, where you don't have to worry about ever seeing the person again. "Well, hey, the next time I'm in Fort Worth, I'll definitely look you up. I promise."

They made arrangements to meet in a half hour, at eight o'clock, and he headed toward the elevator. He passed the other attorneys' offices on his way out. He saw Jed, the workaholic who always looked up at him with the same bleary-eyed expression. No recognition, no human contact, just a wordless "Oh, you, that client-person again."

Virgil heard another lawyer swearing at the top of his lungs on the phone. In the next office, two lawyers hovered over documents, their heads bent together, fingers pointing at highlighted sections.

What a joyless profession. He felt lucky. At least he was in the business of creating things, not just unraveling others' problems. And he was paid a lot more too.

"So look at this."

They met at the bar across from the firm. Renee pointed a bony finger at the report prepared by her staff.

The grommets used in the myringotomies were Virgil's. All of them had caused infections, just as he suspected. Virgil shook his head and grimaced. AGAF hadn't been sued yet, but it was only a matter of time. If he was sued, he'd have to seek outside counsel due to GLK's conflict of interest with the patients' families.

"How much does it cost the hospital for these infections?" he asked.

Renee explained that the hospital was losing thousands of dollars. The DRG, or Diagnostic-Related Groups, a patient classification system, only allowed a certain amount of payment for the surgeries. When the costs went beyond that, the hospital lost money.

"Why don't they just bill the patients for the balance?"

"They try to, but some of them are Medicaid, some are indigent, some are just middle-class people who fully expected their insurance to cover their inpatient stay. Most people can't absorb a sudden five-thousand-dollar hospital bill on their own, so they set up a payment plan. Meanwhile, the hospital has its own exorbitant costs it must pay out monthly: staff payroll, insurance, equipment, etcetera."

"What about collections? They know how to get results."

She chuckled. "I know that's what you or I would do. But you're talking about a hospital. This is a nonprofit entity. The nature of the business is not to strong-arm people to pay for their treatment of sometimes life-threatening illnesses. Think about it."

"How much does this affect my company? I mean, how much would it cost me to keep the grommets in place and pay out the damages? Just for a little while. Some of the doctors really prefer to use them. We haven't come far enough in our product development of the polymers to set in motion a full-scale replacement."

"Again, that's how you or I would do it, but that kind of mentality is frowned upon these days."

Corporations were renowned for carefully measuring their potential losses against removing a profitable, yet problematic, item from the market. Most companies balked against the removal until the very last minute, until the losses started to reach the level of costs to change the item. That's when the CFO would finally and reluctantly recommend taking the item off the market. It was always such a chore. The company had spent countless amounts of time, money, effort, and manpower to develop and manufacture an item just so. Creating the perfect assembly line to work in perfect synchronicity to create the item to exact specifications. It was brutal. And then when you get it all down and the product starts to become profitable, it's infuriating to have to make all the changes again and start all over from scratch. Simply infuriating.

"Can we just put this under wraps for a little while until I figure out what to do?" Virgil asked.

"The hospital is probably already leaning toward changing its grommet supplier for these types of operations. Do you really think you could make the recommendation to continue with these grommets and pull it off?"

Virgil paused. Deep down, he knew that the hospital recommendation should be to eliminate the usage of the metal grommets. But doing away with them would remove a very lucrative resource for his company. The medical grommets were his bread and butter. If only they could just wait a little longer, until he completed the trials of the desktop grommets and pursued the polymer medical grommets.

"Are we absolutely sure that it's the product's fault? Maybe the kids all had the bad habit of poking things in their ears after the surgery. Cotton swabs, fork tines—you know how kids are. Have we included that issue in our questionnaire? And what about that kid with the codeine? That couldn't possibly be a good thing."

Despite her hots for him, even Renee was tiring of his line of avoidance. "I think you have to come to terms with this." She was surprised that he had read the cases.

He almost relented. Suddenly he thought about the heated gaze exchanged between Neil and Eileen in the boardroom, in full view of everyone, most of whom probably suspected his own little dalliance with Eileen. *Cuckold!*

He felt cuckolded. And that snotty little offhand smile of hers, as if to say, "You look vaguely familiar, thanks for joining us today." Suddenly he didn't feel so charitable toward the hospital.

Let's crush them like bugs, he thought. *The board is having its vote next week.* Aloud, to Renee, he said, "Go ahead and agree to remove them, the grommets. But keep this under wraps. No announcement to the media. We'll just quit supplying them to the hospital. We'll say we have a temporary supply deficit, nothing about it being a precaution. After next week there will be so much chaos surrounding the hospital, no one will care about the stinkin' grommets."

Renee smiled just slightly. She almost looked attractive. "Atta boy," she said with a nod. She had heard the gossip about his affair with that girl, but she really didn't believe it. "Good to wrap this one up. The Amber Fuel situation is requiring everyone to be on board, Larson being Larson."

"The disbar rumor? Really?"

Renee perked up an eyebrow at him. "No rumor."

After their third drink, Renee shot him a lazy look, still with that staring penetration, but, heck, at least she was trying. "So, what are you going to do with the excess product that won't be used by Sunrise?"

He looked away. "Actually, there's a hospital in Florida that's been sniffing around for a cheaper substitute for their surgeries. I'll sell a big supply of the grommets to them."

Virgil had hoped the furor about the surgeries would die down, that they would discover the infections were caused by lack of hand washing or some such thing. He wasn't crazy about dealing with the goobers in Florida. They already had enough problems with cutting off wrong limbs and such. But it was clear that any more probing here would cause more harm to him and his company's reputation. Time to cut his losses, offer a settlement. The hospital would cease to exist and wouldn't be able to sue him personally. His company probably wouldn't even have to make good on the settlement.

The vote was next week; he knew exactly what he would do.

Suddenly he noticed that Renee had sidled up quite close to him. He shot her what he hoped was not too serious a look of irritation—she was his attorney, after all—and said clearly, "I have a big day tomorrow. Let's call it a night."

She stiffened. "Oh, yes, by all means."

Marching off with a sharp *click-click* of clunky shoes, she left behind a whiff of rangy perfume—musky, resplendent. It was her favorite; it reminded her of her horses. In another five years, her hair would be long and gray and hang in dry clumps and she would wear Birkenstocks out in her garden.

CHAPTER 41

With time running out, Tanesha and Eileen tried to think up a ruse to gain access to the basement of the hospital in search of the alleged network of tunnels. Eileen decided to chum up with Ralph from the morgue, a pasty, fleshy young man who made her skin crawl, but since he did the grunt work—cleaning up after autopsies, labeling the bodies, putting them away in their respective little drawers—she figured he was the link.

Eileen could have just asked the pathologist—no one would question her authority to go anywhere she wanted in the hospital—but she felt that Ralph would keep it confidential without making a big deal of it. He probably couldn't care less what was going on. But the pathologist—indeed, any of the professionals at the hospital—were all on pins and needles and wanted to be top of the gossip chain. If Eileen, the president's assistant, wished to seek out the basement of the hospital, there must be something really important to gain there, something that would affect the very essence of the hospital, something that the pathologist would want to know about first. Whereas good old Ralph was only looking for his next opportunity to get high.

Eileen stopped at the lab's main desk and spoke to Trina. "Is Ralph in today?"

Her look showed that no one had ever asked that before, certainly not anyone associated with the president. "Gee," she said, "I think so. Do you want me to page him?"

"No, that's all right," Eileen answered. "What time does he usually go home?"

"He usually leaves at three thirty. Say, is he in trouble or something?" She said it in a tone that revealed everyone knew he was in trouble and why but was sure no one would ever do anything about it.

Eileen didn't give her the satisfaction. "No, no, not at all. I just want to ask him something. I'll come back at three thirty."

"Well, sometimes he leaves a little early."

Trina seemed determined to get the guy in trouble. The lab staff punched a time clock, so Eileen couldn't imagine that he left that much early.

"I'll keep that in mind."

Eileen went back to her office, where there were two large piles of documents on her desk. Winston stood by with his hands in his pockets, staring off into space.

"What do we have here?" Eileen said.

Winston shook his head and sighed deeply. "This is all the paperwork related to the botched surgeries."

"They weren't botched. The kids just got a little sick afterward."

"Eileen, we had to pump those kids with drugs; they were on antibiotic drips for a week."

"So you have a little reading material. Weren't you complaining about insomnia? Actually, isn't this for Neil's office to take care of? Why are you messing with it?"

"It's my hospital, dammit. I should have a bit of an idea of what's going on here."

"Suit yourself. But it makes me wonder why you hire all these other people if you expect to do everything yourself."

"I know, I know. I'm never going to be able to read all of this. It's just so damn frustrating. The hospital is in a dive, and there's nothing I can do to save it."

Eileen looked at Winston. "These incidents alone aren't the cause of our problems, are they?"

"No, but we've been battling a lot of things, just barely keeping above board. We needed a nice windfall, a spectacular bequest, an endowment."

"Sort of like winning the lottery, you mean."

"No, I'd like to think the odds were a little better. People die all the time. Generally, the local hospital is the first place people think about to leave their money when they don't have heirs."

"We don't have too many people like that around here with that sort of money. Here, the survivors are fighting over the Florida timeshare, the SUV, the copycat house in the subdivision."

"I suppose you're right." He massaged his temples. "I really liked this job and this hospital. I expected to retire here."

"How do you know you won't? We've weathered worse things than this. What about that time we had the severe ice storm and lost electricity for over a week until the crews could get to us? We worked off generators, postponed a few surgeries, and did just fine."

"That was an emergency. That's exactly what we're equipped to deal with. This is completely different. This is a long, ongoing drain of our resources without any relief in sight. I suppose I'll have to move to Philadelphia; they're always looking for administrators."

She had to think of something to cheer him up. Outrageous usually did it.

"Hey, I saw old lady Grimshaw at the Weis market the other day, and she was looking mighty pale. Doesn't she volunteer here a dozen times a week? From the looks of her, she could pass any day now."

"Don't count on it. She'll probably give it all to her cats."

———

Ralph Waters was the man. He was the first in town to have a CD Walkman, back when everyone was struggling with cassettes. When you needed dope, he was happy to oblige. He was best friends with all those who bought his dope.

Ralph's great-great-grandfather, Ezekiel Waters, was born in slavery in 1848 to Sadie Thompson and Earnest Collinswood, the great magnate of South Carolina at the time. Earnest also had three other children with his wife, Gloria. Their plantation, Hearth's Wood Haven, was the finest in Jasper County. Zeke could work tobacco fields like no one's business and would have made his daddy proud, had Dad, or Mr. Collinswood, wished to acknowledge his existence. Unfortunately, Gloria had her hands full with her other three shining white children and, with social mores being what they were at the time, was not so inclined to lavish much attention on her stepchild and slave, Ezekiel. Zeke didn't expect as much, however. His own mother, Sadie, sang to him in rich, brown tones, even did the harmony parts, and he would fall asleep at night feeling almost cozy.

As it happened, after the War between the States, Zeke's son, Lucas, in a fit of blood nationalism, was encouraged to travel to Africa, to Sierra Leone where he understood freed slaves of British colonies congregated in large numbers. Failing to attain either fame or fortune—the first diamond wasn't discovered there until a year later—Lucas returned to the United States in 1929 and married Anna, daughter of the white Methodist preacher, but, unbeknownst to him, not before he'd impregnated Willow, back in Africa. The unclaimed family he left in Africa would eventually include his great-granddaughter Mindah, a precious little girl with twinkly dark eyes whose left arm would be chopped off at the elbow by rebels in 1994.

Ralph was unaware of his illustrious history, or of his faraway half cousin. He thought he was the cool white guy in this sour little berg of hicks and wannabes.

Eileen checked her watch. It was a quarter past three. She figured she would head back down to the lab and head off Ralph on his way out. While she doubted that he actually left early every day, as Trina accused him, she figured he wouldn't want to hang around much later than his punch-out time.

She waited at the lab reception desk. The reception area was packed, standing room only, all chairs occupied. Unless the lab was suddenly giving away a new car with every new stick, this was a much-needed service. Where would all these people go once the place closed? The hospital was so convenient to so many elderly. How would they make their way clear across town when the town had little public transportation? Eileen couldn't figure it out.

"Are you Eileen?" Ralph, confined to the underbelly of the hospital, didn't know any of the admin people.

"Yes, I am. Hi, uh, Ralph? I really appreciate your talking with me. Is this an OK time?"

He checked his watch. "Yeah, I'm pretty much finished for the day, but I have to leave at three thirty. I have to stop and, uh, get groceries for my grandma."

Oh, pish-posh, Ralph, I don't plan to keep you a minute past that magic punch-out time, Eileen thought. "Oh, certainly, I understand," she said. "I just have a few questions."

They started walking toward the back and down the metal stairway. Each step echoed through the empty chamber.

"You know, I've never been down here. Ralph, have you ever heard the rumors about the hospital being some sort of safe haven for runaway slaves? You know, a long time ago?"

He grinned a bit and shrugged. "I think we've all heard about that. I don't really know what the big deal is."

There was no real love lost in Maple Leaf for the historical struggles of African Americans.

"So you're not curious at all, Ralph? No romance in your soul? Doesn't it move you to think of desperate men and women crouched in fear of being discovered by ridiculous white people who felt that they owned them?"

She was losing Ralph. He idly ran his finger along the wall as they walked. "Um, I guess I never really thought about it."

"OK, Ralph. Do you have any idea what they're talking about? Tunnels and secret passageways and such?"

"Oh, I don't think there's anything like that here. But feel free to check it out if you'd like."

Eileen sighed and continued to follow Ralph to the morgue. He shuffled down the hallway, and they passed through the metal double doors to a very sterile-looking white room. Should be sterile, it was too darn freezing cold for any germs to stake a claim. It looked just like an operating room but was much larger and had unmistakable metal drawers all along the far wall.

Eileen wasn't at all clear about what she was supposed to be looking for. She supposed that if Ralph said there were no secret passageways, he would know; for that matter, if anyone knew of any secret passageways, it would be no secret. Small towns thrived on that sort of gossip.

"This here's the morgue."

"The what?" Eileen imagined stray bits of blood, dead tissue, maggots.

"You know, where they do the autopsies." Ralph was clearly taken with Eileen's expression of horror. Slyly he added, "I don't *think* we have one scheduled for today."

She hadn't really thought about it before; she vaguely thought that autopsies happened at the police precinct or in the funeral home or in some other impartial place. On the other hand, a morgue wasn't exactly the sort of place one could set up like a bookmobile. Pitch a tent, call your next body, please. So the hospital was in both businesses—saving lives and handling dead people. So much depended upon what happened in this little room. She could just imagine it:

"Oh, so *that's* what his problem was! Who'd a thunk?" Smack the forehead.

"I told you, Doc, we shoulda used 10 ccs of phenytoin, not 50, like—see this here proof?"

"Damn it all, I shoulda believed you. Thought you were jerkin' me around."

"Ha, ha, ha, ha!"

No, no, Eileen was sure that didn't happen. But maybe it did, and maybe that was why Dr. Healy, the pathologist, suffered such awful breakouts of hives.

—

The two men, Virgil and Winston were meeting in Winston's office. The door was closed.

"See here, Virgil," Winston said, "We seem to have a problem. It appears that your grommets were used in all the surgeries."

He stared at Virgil.

"Are you sure?" But Virgil already knew it was the truth. It was just a moment of idiocy to buy himself a bit of time to come up with an acceptable response. Which was, "We'll certainly have to explore the issue."

"Yes, it's most unfortunate. Could it be a coincidence? Has your company heard of any problems from any other hospitals?"

"I'll have to check the history on that. We've had no reason to statisticize the issue before these incidents."

"You're talking crap. Statisticize? These are my patients, in my hospital. I don't—"

"It's my hospital too. I'm a board member, don't forget."

Winston rolled his eyes. "Yes, and that's a most interesting aspect of this whole debacle."

"What do you mean?" Virgil couldn't believe that Winston would do this face-to-face.

"C'mon now, Virgil, hasn't it occurred to you that conflict of interest seems to be rearing its ugly head here?"

"Sir, I have never been anything but professional in my dealings with the hospital. If one of my products appears to be causing problems, then of course we will withdraw it for further study. Notify Materials Management immediately to put a halt to the distribution. I'll take it upon myself to figure out what to do with the remaining stock."

"Don't you think we've done that already? After those first several kids were hurt, we suspected the grommets. The physicians suspected them, and we stopped using them. There's a company using a polymer grommet that seems to work miracles. Some physicians even use a simple three-day antibiotic therapy, which seems to work instead of any surgery at all. We will be looking closely at all of these and other alternative options. I just wanted to tell you so you wouldn't find out about it at the next board meeting in front of everyone."

"This sounds like a decision that the board should have made."

"It did. We had a special committee set up to look into these things."

"I see."

"Now, excuse me, I have another appointment." Winston nodded toward the door.

Virgil felt arrested, tried, and convicted, all at once. Sure, it was his product that had caused the illnesses, but certainly he deserved more respect. They should be dancing circles around him, afraid of offending him or, at least, hurting his feelings. He commanded respect in this town; why was this little $125-thou-a-year pipsqueak casting aspersions on him?

All of this diversion, and he was almost ready to make his big breakthrough with his paisley computer-desktop grommets. Maybe it was time to get out of the scientific business with these things. Of course, there were the funny looks from his management group when he'd mentioned his idea.

"Yes, I said paisley grommets. What exactly do you not understand about that? Don't you realize that this is the day and age where it's all in the look, the style, the hook? Computers aren't just for boring offices anymore; people want them to fit in their décor. Living room, den, family room—we have grommets to fit each mood, each personality. Desktop wire management. Keep those nasty wires under control with a fashionable motif. Maybe even fabric-coated grommets to really add that homey look. Have your entire desk covered in upholstery to match the rest of the room."

His staff had looked at him like he was crazy.

Just as Winston was looking at him now.

"Oh, and by the way." Winston had resolved never to say anything. But so much had changed. "You really lucked out with Eileen. That could have been nasty. You know very well."

Virgil stared back with dark eyes, then turned and walked away. At least he had that.

Maybe he was going out of his mind. He hated to admit it, but he was actually looking forward to the trip with his family. Maybe he would pick up some pointers from Nick and begin his own quoits practice. Maybe he should think about designing his own quoits too. That would give him something to do to keep him out of legal trouble. Nick said that there was no decent workmanship of the quoits here in the States; he had to import them from England. Maybe Jenaveev would want to have dinner with him. They could spend a nice romantic dinner together and maybe try to ignite a spark. If Jenaveev wouldn't, maybe he and Noelle could spend some time together and get to know each other. Virgil had no idea what his daughter was up to these days.

The clock struck four and he sauntered home. Neil drove by in his blue Honda, and Virgil could have sworn that Eileen was in the seat next to him.

His house was dark. So much for a joyful homecoming. He wondered if any man ever really got that anymore. Men were just doofuses. *We aren't even the sole breadwinners anymore, and even when we are, like me, we're still treated like doofuses. We're just a minor spurt; really, what good are we?*

He looked at the matches sitting next to the fireplace. They were the long, plank-like matches that could fire up from a foot away. Maybe he should just torch the place, take off, lay low for a while, and collect the insurance money.

Nah, that's been done ad nauseum. He couldn't go out in a cliché. Jenaveev would never forgive him. And if he disappeared, how would he collect the money? People were already suspicious of him; he didn't need to add to it.

Where was everybody? He chuckled and said to himself, "Maybe they're hiding in the rec room waiting to jump out and yell surprise for husband/father appreciation day or something. Sure, and maybe monkeys will fly out of my you know what."

He turned the knob. Everything was dark. No smells of residual cooking, or in Jenaveev's case, familiar TV dinners or Grocer-Quik Fixins. There was a slight odor of a candle that had recently burned out.

He plunked down on the sofa. A teddy bear sat on the mantle. One of Noelle's. She was fourteen now; it has been sitting there probably since she was eight. He was so used to seeing it there, and it really was in an odd little spot. The living room was no place for teddy bears. But it seemed to fit in now. Or disappear.

He didn't even see the point of pouring himself a bourbon.

CHAPTER 42

LOVIE

Lovie sprang up from his cot. He thought it was the clamor of birds that waked him but realized it was the singing and yelling of his neighbors, the field hands. It was time to get up. No pokey sleeping in was allowed for slaves.

Breakfast was corn puddin' soaked in a little milk—always the same, 'cept on Sundays they'd get a little piece of salt pork. The big meals were saved for special occasions such as Easter, Christmas, and a few others. Sometimes on the chid'rens' birthday, the marster's chid'rens, they would be invited to a feast. Ooh-whee, those were the days. Pheasant, chicken, ham hocks, pumpkin, biscuits, creamed corn, taters, peas—tears came to his eyes at the glorious thought of it all.

But this morning, the usual would have to be enough. Lovie gobbled his corn mush, stretched, and headed outside to join his mother.

"Lovie, you up yet, you lazy bag of bones?" His mama, Esther, had already been out working the fields and returned to join the kitchen folk in preparing the main meal for the field hands.

Lovie's work didn't begin until the marster's family got up. He was still too young for the heavy fieldwork, so's he mostly just fetched things, like water, kindlin', and feed for the animals.

He looked up at his mother. She looked oh so tired. Her dark face was puffy and glowed with sweat. Her bloodshot eyes peered down at him, and she smiled. She reached out and tousled his hair and smooched his forehead. He loved her so much. He wished she didn't have to work so hard.

Perplexed, Eileen perched on a stool next to Ralph in the morgue. Her thoughts were interrupted by the squeaking whistle of his nose as he breathed. So far, nothing but dead ends, so to speak. There didn't seem to be any hidden cellar, basement, or passageway below the hospital. The ground floor was just that, the ground floor. No secrets, no romance.

Why, then, the rumor about the hospital? About the Underground Railroad? This was a socially conservative area; nobody really cared about blacks one way or another around here. Why would they simply make up this wonderful story about the heroes of Sunrise who put their lives and reputations at risk by assisting escaping slaves? It didn't make any sense. She knew there had to something to the rumor. She scanned the room and noticed, at the back, a door with a curtained window.

"Where does that lead?" Eileen asked.

Ralph looked down at his shoes.

"C'mon, show me," she said.

Ralph walked Eileen over to the door and pushed it open. The unmistakable smell of weed permeated the air, but there was nothing but shrub brush out there. It looked like old Ralph had himself a little hideaway.

"The garbage is out here," he said, as if the great outdoors always smelled like this.

She just shook her head. Another false lead. "Where does this go?" She'd lost her bearings a bit in relation to the front of the hospital.

"You follow the little path around, and it leads to the side parking lot and then to the emergency room entrance."

Now she remembered. This was the back of the hospital, which abutted a high bank of trees, bushes, brambles, vines, and bamboo. Probably a bit of poison ivy too. While it was nice to have this little bit of nature in the hospital's backyard, it was a tad unruly. There were no windows on this side of the building, so it was easy to forget about it. But every so often the brush would scrape against the building, clog up the roof gutters, and generally make a mess, so that an arborist had to be called to rein it in. The hospital probably should have cleared it all out, but Eileen believed there was some question about who owned the land. Now that she had a chance to look at it, there was a nice little nature oasis back here.

As she wandered along the bushes, her frustration soon led to glee. They weren't just any bushes, they were blackberry bushes. With big, juicy berries. She knew that wild blackberry bushes had somehow become politically incorrect due to their tendency to run rampant over all other local flora and stifle any chance for native plant species to thrive. But my goodness, they were scrumptious. How could that be a bad thing? And why was everyone so bent on restoring the horticulture to what it used to be? If they were that passionate, better they should protest housing developments, road mazes, and industrial complexes. In fact, everything was pointing to the fact that there were more people, and what did people need but food? Blackberries, to be exact.

She returned home after work and armed herself with long sleeves and pants and tough gloves and set out again to gather a big bowl for canning, freezing, and maybe a big black raspberry pie. Neil was coming over later that evening. Back at the blackberries, she picked as many as she could, trying to keep her personal sampling to a minimum.

She noticed a section where there was a heavy cluster of shrubbery underneath the blackberry bushes. It seemed to follow in a winding line of low-growing shrubbery. She lifted some of the vine-like branches and noticed a dirt path. It was curious. Finally, as she scrambled around, it suddenly dawned on her. Of course!

She continued to work through the blackberry brambles until she noticed a slight clearing in the brush. Although clearly overgrown, it was unmistakably a path. Maybe this led to the tunnel! She bent over and peered inside the bushes, scouring the area for any concrete evidence. She crawled through the brambles, glad she had decided to clothe herself from head to toe. She saw nothing there. But she knew, she just knew, that this was the spot.

She decided that, though it needed some work, she would bring this place back to life to recreate some of the history of those folks fleeing desperately for their lives. She would fix the place up a bit, find out exactly how far the trail went and where it led (probably to the river), and then bring Tanesha back here.

She worked through the brambles. At least she could make one last effort to present something worthwhile to Tanesha anyway. Through the maze she saw little alcoves off to the sides here and there, which might have been the runaway slaves' places of refuge for the night. She figured that once the slaves had reached the river, a boat would pick them up and take them to the next safe haven.

She marveled at the precise communication that must have been necessary to make these risky connections safely. It was ironic that in this day and age of telephones, pagers, fax machines, e-mail, cell phones, car phones, and PalmPilots, none were used for anything nearly as important as the communications that must have occurred during those desperate times. Now that technology had enabled lightning-fast communications, Eileen noticed that people rarely used it for anything more crucial than "Hi, I'm on my way" and "It's your turn to stop for pizza on the way home from work, dear."

Eileen spent the entire next day cleaning up the place. At first, she delicately tugged a branch or grasped a weed. She peered closely at every inch and was reluctant to touch anything; who knew what leaf or twig might have some sort of historical significance? But no, that was silly. Leaves don't last forever, and there was no chance that the loose brambles covering the path might be over one hundred years old. The older stuff was probably underneath, if it was there at all.

So she cleaned out the path and enlisted Daniel and Miles to help out, and soon there was a neat, clean pathway straight to the river. Daniel and Miles weren't the best of friends, but in this worthy endeavor, they seemed almost jovial.

"Hey, Miles, ever had poison ivy in your privates?"

"Sure. Hey, how did you know about Ivy?"

Eileen rolled her eyes.

Eileen only got one small batch of poison ivy, itchy, miserable stuff. She was pleased with the results of their efforts. She'd never even realized that the river was so close to the hospital. To get there by road, it took about fifteen minutes. The pathway followed along the bank, sometimes climbing up higher on the hill when the edge closed in on a property line.

She didn't know the neighbors well along there. She saw people come and go while she busied herself with her workday. The lady on the corner in the ivy-covered Craftsman always pushed another lady in a wheelchair along the sidewalk. The Bartholomews lived in the grand old house in the middle of the block, the three-story brick Colonial built in the 1800s. Lucinda Bartholomew was a homemaker and overall do-gooder who dreamed that every Junior Club meeting she attended was another step toward heaven. Eileen wondered if any of them were blood descendants of "conductors" along the Underground Railroad.

Eileen had been to Gettysburg when she was in school and had taken a yawning interest in the battlefield activity that had occurred there. At the time, the fields seemed, well, just like fields, and what's the big deal? She and her friends, when they were kids, also looked for arrowheads in the fields and woods. It seemed as if the history of the country had been rammed down her throat from the time she could read. Pennsylvania had been the hub of activity from the beginning of significant civil society. She had been to Philadelphia plenty of times, gazed at the crack in the Liberty Bell, sat in the room where Patrick Henry wrote or read his speech, whichever it was.

But nothing had affected her quite like walking through this clear, wooded pathway for the first time. This was history without pretension, without a sense of heavy posterity attached to it. No powdered wigs here, no siree. These people were desperate for their lives and not thinking of what material things or philosophical ideas they would leave behind for their children. They were only thinking of freedom for their children. This was just as important; the words "Give me liberty or give me death" probably rang true more for them than for the wimpy, wigged sots in Philadelphia a hundred years earlier.

It was so cozy and hidden and green-fragrant, Eileen had to lie down for a minute. She wanted to embrace the earth that had lent itself as the escape route for these people. She felt overcome with the history of it. She was also tired. It was nice to immerse her mind in something completely different for a change. She wanted to feel the runaways' collective suffering, to experience the tragic history through this woodsy aura.

All poppycock. She was a privileged white gal. Her situation was far removed from anything even remotely resembling the state of slavery. It was audacious for her to assume that she could ever feel even a fraction of that experience, even vicariously. But, heck, she was here now, here in these same woods they'd huddled in one hundred fifty years ago. In the quiet rustlings and whispers and chirps that made up this world, she bet there was a common link here somewhere. There had to be some plant, some sound, some smell, or maybe a combination of them all, that was the same during that time.

She instinctively touched the Mercury dime she had placed in her front shirt pocket. Maybe it really was lucky. She started to nod off and let the combination of sensations fill her dreams and award her wisdom of the period, but then, damn it, she got pricked big-time from the blackberry thorns, and the bugs buzzing in her face were driving her crazy. So much for tenacity. If white people had been slaves, none of them would have ever escaped successfully.

LOVIE

Lovie Williams crouched in the dirt. A twig snapped and he halted. Waves of fear seared through his body. But dammit, he knew in his heart he was right. People weren't meant to live this way. A human owning another. Just ain't right, his mama tole him. He would miss his mama. But Esther had gazed at him from her bedside, her kerchief askew and dusty, her cheeks wet. Her rough hand had squeezed his so tightly he nearly cried out. But she said, "You go now, son. It's time."

If he held still, so still, whatever it was would pass and he could continue on his way. He was headed up to that place where he would feel the dirt of freedom under his feet. He wondered if it would feel any different. He had heard that your feet started to tingle once you landed in freedom territory, but tingle in a good way, not like after you been workin' the fields all day barefoot, tramplin' over briers and such.

His situation wasn't as bad as some. His marster was all right; he beat Lovie only once when Lovie had stirred the ashes under the kitchen pot all sloppy-like and spread soot all over the floor. He knew it was a bad thing, but he didn't do it purposeful, and he cleaned it right up after. No matter—when ol' Marster Gavin seen the mess he waited till after Lovie cleaned it up and set the switch to his back. Happened all the time to others. For Lovie, that was the only onest.

Lovie halted and listened. Nothing. Must have been a squirrel.

Eileen was startled awake. A little squirrel was peering at her, shaking its tail in jerky movements. Relieved, she laughed at it, and it scampered up the tree. *Oh, little squirrel, tell me what you know.*

As she stretched her neck to peer upward, something pulled at her hair. She reached back and felt that her hair had caught on something on the tree. Rough bark, or maybe another squirrel playing tricks on her. She disentangled the strands and looked at the trunk. Her eyes grew wide and she felt a prickly chill.

Eileen raced back to tell Tanesha. She wanted to do it just perfectly, not raise any suspicion about what she was up to. But how to casually get someone to follow you to the morgue? You had to take the elevator down to the basement floor, and there was nothing else there—no latté stand, no snack bar, nothing. The only purpose you have to go down there is to resolve some business with dead people. She decided to play it straight.

"Tanesha, could you come with me? I have something to show you." Eileen flashed her best dazzling smile tinted with a little mischief, and Tanesha couldn't resist. She smiled back and instantly became a part of the secret.

"What's going on?"

"You'll see."

They walked along the hallway and stopped at the elevator that led downstairs.

"Why are we stopping here? Doesn't this go to the morgue?"

"Just c'mon."

They stepped into the elevator and Eileen hit the B button.

"Now, wait a minute." Suddenly Tanesha's eyes grew wide, and she looked at Eileen again with amazement. "No way. You found it?" Tanesha jumped up and down and grabbed the collar of Eileen's dress.

The elevator bounced. Eileen imagined it plummeting them to their cement-crashing deaths.

"You are awesome!" Tanesha gushed.

"Hold on there, sweetheart, before they call the cops on us."

Tanesha continued to jump up and down and grinned broadly. "I've got to see it." She dropped her voice to a whisper as the elevator door opened. "Oh my God, I can't believe it."

"Just wait. I don't know for absolute sure, but I think this is the place. Come here and take a look at this."

She led Tanesha to the tree that had assaulted her hair and pointed. Tanesha bent over and peered at the bark.

"Oh my God," she repeated.

The object was a small, metal tag that had been nailed to the base of the trunk. On the tag was carved CHARLESTON, BLACKSMITH, 307, 1825.

Tanesha shook, her eyes wide comprehending the enormity of it. Eileen shared Tanesha's chills and felt, too, that she was discovering the place for the first time. Between them, their chills vibrated up and down the entire length of the escape route, from the greasy swamps of South Carolina and beyond to the crisp coolness of Canada.

"Our ancestors were from Charleston," Tanesha said. "We heard that the slaves had to wear ID badges like this to identify them as skilled workers. This is the real deal. This could have been a family member of mine."

She reached out and gently touched the tag. Traced the letters with her fingers. "Proof. There's been so little documentation of anything that happened during that era. The blacks make it sound like some sort of grim fairy tale, that's if they speak of it at all, and the whites are too ashamed to admit anything. There's a weird sort of unspoken agreement among both sides to keep it hush-hush. So except for historians, not many people really know what happened, other than the fact that slavery went on, it's gone now, and everyone, please go about your lives."

Eileen hugged Tanesha.

Tanesha continued, "The conflicts still haven't been addressed and resolved, even now. Whites still want to gloss over it, still ashamed to admit it. 'Oh, that was another people in another time.' And blacks want to dwell on it obsessively. 'See how badly you treated us then? And you're still treating us that way now.'"

Eileen said, "We have to do something with this. We can't let this become an anomaly, a quirk of the bushes. Someone's bound to hear of it and chop the tree down or do some sort of nonsense."

Eileen and Tanesha swore to each other, gal-pal style, never to tell a soul until they came up with a plan to officially memorialize the site. They intertwined pinkies in their secret pact.

LOVIE

Lovie remembered the whispered words at the last stop: *Crossroads, then ten miles later, house with lantern, then water and freedom.*

He peered into the black water. He could barely see across it to the bank. He couldn't believe that he was so close, but there was still danger. He was in safe territory, Pennsylvania. But he was from farther south, and the only thing he knew is that slaves weren't completely safe anywhere, except Canada. He'd heard that it was safe here, in the land of the Quakers, but he still felt on edge. Then he realized he'd always felt on edge. Would he even know how to feel otherwise? He imagined "safe" would be a bright blue color, kind of like the sky on a bright, sunny, cloudless day.

Suddenly the clouds drifted, and the fields to his left were bathed in glorious moonlight. It was a full-moon night. The tips of the wheat waved at him in the light breeze. Suddenly, Lovie decided to run. So much pent-up nervous energy, and now that his trip was nearing the end, he had to expel it.

He ran and ran until his legs lost all feeling and didn't even seem to touch the ground anymore. He loved the feeling. He never got to run much back at Marster's place. They didn't look too kindly on it. Not that they didn't work him and the other'n to the bone, everything from lifting and bending to pulling and pushing. Sacks of taters, bushels of strawberries and cabbages, the horse-drawn plow. The heavy labor never ceased. But he never ever ran just for pleasure.

Now his senses were alive, no longer shoveled beneath the repression lorded over him for so long. It was a pleasure to feel the cool air whip about his head. He never noticed before the soft muffled puffs of air against his ears as he ran hard. What was that? He would find out. Someday soon, he vowed, he would learn to read and he would pick out some science-type books and find out exactly what caused that feeling. Once he learned to read he would find out all kinds of stuff. He would become the wise old uncle that everyone looked up to. People would clamor for his advice.

He ran back to the bank and squatted along the water. He could see the other side now, and he saw a dim, flickering glow from a lantern.

"Lovie? Is that you?"

He froze. He hadn't heard his name in so long, he thought he was dreaming. Could he trust this? He waited.

"Moses is here, waiting for you."

Yes, that was the code!

He splashed into the water, crying, "Here, I'm here!"

CHAPTER 43

"Well, it's all over. We're shutting up shop." Winston greeted Eileen at the door of her office.

"What? How? Who?" Eileen's stomach dropped to her knees. "How come I missed the meeting?"

"The board was tired of prevaricating, as they put it. Called an emergency meeting last night."

"Sounds like Otto."

"Yes, well." Winston bent his face down and massaged his forehead. "GMK offered a settlement to the hospital on behalf of Virgil's company, and the board promptly voted to shut down. It'll take years for the lawyers and insurance companies to figure it all out."

Eileen stepped backward and reached for a chair. And missed. "So do I pack up my desk ASAP, or what?" She hated the quiver in her voice. And she forgot all about the delight of her recent discovery.

"Well, not quite," Winston said. "But you can start looking around for free empty boxes. I hear that Weis has good banana boxes."

"God, Winston."

Eileen's eyes brimmed. He reached over and hugged her. They held each other for several moments. Winston was being callow to spare her, she knew, but it was too soon. Some feelings were too strong to express, and too strong not to.

———

Nick was alone a lot but didn't feel lonely. He brushed off most of the other guys who wanted to hang around with him. Randy would occasionally join him in a quoits game but would hear distant girls' screams and shortly head off in that direction, sometimes with a vague lewd comment about "pinning a real hole." Luckily, for the girls' sakes, Nick knew that Randy was most definitely still a virgin. As was Nick. Nick wasn't interested in girls. His sister was a silly dolt, mostly, and that was enough for him.

He wanted to win that tournament and then start his own club. He wanted to become a master teacher and have kids from all over come and take classes. He wanted quoits to become the new fad.

Computers were dumb, he thought. You had to sit too still to play on the computer. And he had to be home to play on the computer. He would rather lose himself outside. Once he won the tournament, he would design his club to be within one acre. There would be four pits within the acre. In the middle there would be a crisscross pattern of trees and shrubbery. He'd seen the pattern on one of his grandmother's old quilts, and he loved the symmetry of the design. Four squares of quoits pits with the points of the squares touching like diamonds. In the middle would be another square of trees and a gazebo for refreshments and restrooms. He read the magazines; he knew there was a fledgling group of quoits players who needed a place to go. He would provide that place.

But goddamn it, his parents were sniping at each other again. It filled his head and squeezed out the good, fresh feeling of his plans. Their arguing hit his brain like little pinpricks, constantly battering him into exhaustion. He had to get out of the house. He ran outside, tripped over his mother's golf cart, and sprawled on the sidewalk.

Scraped his elbow and knee. *Ouch.* He sighed and peeked inside to see if it was worth it to tell his parents. Nah. He couldn't hear their voices, but he could tell by his mother's bobbing head and his father's protruding neck veins that they weren't particularly approachable right now. The emergency room was within walking distance, and the staff there knew him. He trekked the several blocks to the hospital. When the double doors slid open, there were Paige and Mary Jo, respectively ER receptionist and physician's assistant, leaning up against the counter, shaking their heads as he hobbled up.

"Tut-tut, little man," Paige smiled at him, "What have you done now? Come, now, let us show you to your room. No chocolates on the pillows, but I believe you will find it to your satisfaction."

"Have you not been sick? We haven't seen you for, what, three weeks?" Mary Jo walked around the ER counter, her white shoes squeaking against the floor.

Jokesters. No sympathy around here.

His chart was a foot thick. Nothing too serious, but nearly every inch of his body had been injured at some point or another. Mild head trauma, contusions, lacerations with stitches, abrasions, sprains, strains, and dislocations. He wondered why they never asked more pointed questions or dragged his parents in. They never brought in the child protection people, and he was glad because he wouldn't know what to tell them. He could play it out with puppets. Anatomically correct Mom puppet jawing it out with Pop puppet with baby puppet cowering in a corner, its little plush arms covering its head.

Instead, the nurses joked that he must read the Red Cross first aid manual and check off each thing as he gets it. "Hey, you'll have to check out page one hundred twenty—poisonous snakes! Haven't had that yet!" It was a kind of reverse Boy Scout achievement program. Only he got his merit badges in the form of stitches, splints, and gauze bandages.

"I know why you like coming here, Nick," grinned Mary Jo. "It's to impress the girls with your war wounds."

Nick blushed a bit. "Why would I want to do that?"

"Oh, you have quite a female fan club, don't you?"

"Um, I don't think so."

Nick wished there was another hospital he could go to. The next closest one was thirty miles away, a little beyond limping distance. He was stuck with this one.

"You guys are nuts," he said. "Can you fix me up, or am I gonna have to walk clear to Englewood?"

"Take it easy, Nick. We're just trying to lighten our load today. If we can't make fun of our patients, why bother working here? We love you, guy, you know that."

"Hmph."

"Should we call your parents?"

"No, they're not home. Just get Dad to sign the forms the next time he stops in."

He wanted to say they were home badgering each other, their favorite activity, you know. But that would hardly accomplish anything.

"What happened this time?"

"Tripped over Mom's golf cart."

Paige and Mary Jo exchanged looks.

"It's dark out. What's she...oh, never mind."

Nick shrugged.

"It's OK, OK," Mary Jo said. We'll get you fixed up real quick. You had your tetanus shot the last time you were here, didn't you? So we can spare you that."

Which was good, Nick thought, because the shot had made his arm hurt like hell, and he didn't need that misery when he was practicing for the big tournament.

Mary Jo peered at the wounds. "Oh, I don't think you're going to need stitches, but it's close. We'll get by with Steri-Strips. Just be sure to keep it clean and change the bandage every day."

"Yeah, yeah, I know."

"And use that antibiotic ointment we gave you."

"I think I still have some left."

Nick trudged out, patched up. He wandered slowly toward home and looked at his watch. Well, that only used up an hour and a half. The parents were probably only getting warmed up. They were probably either screaming full-bore at each other or had settled into a hissy-fit of silence. *Oh, joy.* He just couldn't wait to get home. Next time, he thought, he should aim for a broken leg or concussion; that would allow him to stay overnight or longer in the hospital. He knew that was crazy, and he didn't really mean to hurt himself, but it sure was a tempting thought. *Mmmm, home-cooked meals brought to you in bed. How bad could that be?*

Where could he go now? It was too dark to practice. Nope, no more stalling. He had to get home; he had some homework. He wondered where Noelle was. He hadn't seen her since her bike ride.

He stopped in at the pizza place and ordered a ham-and-cheese stromboli. He asked them to throw some mushrooms in there too, for veggies. There was probably nothing for dinner at home. Generally, after their fights his mother locked herself in her den, gazing at her golf trophies and sobbing, and his father sped off to who-knows-where in his BMW. Mention anything about food and they just looked at you like, "Who the heck are you?"

Hoo-boy, what a day. He dragged his mother's golf cart into the garage. If he slipped into the house through the garage door, he could head upstairs the back way and bypass the family goings-on. The stairway was mostly used for storage and was cluttered with canned goods and dirty laundry flung down for the next person who did the wash, which was usually Clara, the maid, who stopped in three times a week. The stairs creaked loudly, but he knew they all would pretend not to notice.

He lay down on his bed in the dark and stared at the shadows on his wall as the streetlights reflected the edges of his curtains. The shadows looked like daggers. That seemed appropriate, and he fell asleep.

—

The next morning, out of habit, Eileen checked over the OR report. Thank God, no myringotomies, not that it mattered anymore. She also glanced at the ER admissions for yesterday and noticed that little Nick Ellingsworth had been admitted again. Contusion left knee, laceration left elbow. Nothing serious, but still. Her heart plummeted a bit. She couldn't help but feel sorry for those kids.

She tried to shake it off. It was none of her concern. Still, it bugged her.

At the end of the day, Eileen wandered along the emptying halls. She noticed Evelyn, from the social work department, looking down at the latest ER admission list and groaning. Everything took on such exaggerated meaning these days; Eileen had to ask her what was up. Everyone was afraid that someone else might have an inside line to something more important.

"It's that poor Ellingsworth kid again."

Eileen stopped. Were they mind reading now? Was levitating far behind? "Oh?"

"He must be in here twice a month. Funny, if he were a few years younger, the authorities would be after the parents for child abuse. But once the kid hits double digits—ten, eleven, twelve—no one cares anymore. Not to mention that his father is one muckety-muck here."

Eileen had often wondered how his kids were faring, and now she saw her chance to pry. Evelyn had always seemed in her own world, so she most likely wouldn't have been privy to Eileen's history with Virgil. She played dumb. "So, uh, what do you think is going on? Do you really think there's abuse in that home?"

"No, not abuse. Heavens, no. His parents are bastions of the community, whatever that's worth, but, well, we've found something funny with those types of home situations. Heck, I shouldn't be telling you this, but what does it matter now? You know that their family have been seeing us for some time for counseling."

Eileen shrugged in an offhand manner. "Yes, I've seen their names on the weekly printouts for your department." She was stepping very lightly, but she was sure she was on to something juicy. "I mean, you know, don't tell me anything confidential." All the while, she hoped with every breath that Evelyn would. The hospital was on the skids; soon the whole world would know anything it wanted, wouldn't it?

"Oh, sure. We're all about generalities now, aren't we?"

"So, Evelyn, do you drink? Wanna stop at Mandolin's for a glass or two? Tonight is hummus and pita night at happy hour. I think they throw in some cucumber slices too."

"Great, a real health fest. Sure, why not? I'd love to. Everyone is slinking around here like the living dead. Let's go have a little fun. I'll meet you there."

"Why don't we walk up? It's only a few blocks, then we could burn off any alcohol before driving home."

"Well, isn't that socially responsible of you. Great idea—it'll be good to get these old bones moving a bit too.

Eileen grabbed her tote bag and Evelyn her designer purse, and they headed out the door.

Evelyn shrugged and said, "I'll just say bad marriages and kids don't mix. People stay in a bad marriage and their kids secretly plot to rub them out or they're decapitating small animals in the basement. But that's OK, it's a 'transitional period' as the parents work out their problems in therapy."

Eileen saw an image of Wynkin and shuddered. She pulled open the door of Mandolin's to a wave of cigarette smoke and boisterous voices. They pushed through the crowd and found a small table on the upper level.

Evelyn continued, "After years in this business, I've seen so much. It's hard to even believe in marriage anymore. So many bad choices with long-ranging effects. Some permanent. We do our best with our little games and drills, but..." Evelyn clutched her drink, and the ice rattled in the glass.

After a couple of Purple Hooters, Eileen was tempted to unload her own story on Evelyn, and her own history with a certain Ellingsworth. Evelyn was now her closest, bestest friend, and Eileen should reward her for her confidences.

"Wow, I've often suspected a connection," Eileen drawled. "But you know, I have a funny coincidence—"

Suddenly, a gent in a suit and tie sprawled on Eileen, spilling his drink on the floor.

"I've lost my drink. Can you find it for me, beautiful?"

"Sorry, sir, you're on your own."

"Where have I heard that before? Hey, that's why I'm here. Ha, ha, ha. May I join you?"

"No, I'm sorry, we're having a private conversation. Maybe next time."

"I'll hold you to that, sweetheart."

He stumbled toward another table, his empty glass aloft.

Evelyn rolled her eyes and continued without missing a beat. "If that guy, for instance, has kids, they'll probably spend a lot of time in the emergency room."

"We should probably get going," Eileen said, reaching for the check.

"Yes, I'm too old anymore to stay out late on a school night." Evelyn tossed a few bills on the table.

They walked back to their cars.

"Let's not be strangers." Evelyn brushed a hand across her cheek. They hugged.

Eileen unlocked her car door and again thanked Evelyn. After she got in her car, she peeked back at Evelyn who was muttering to herself and shaking her head.

CHAPTER 44

Eileen glowed. Neil had just left her again. That is, left her relaxed and sexually sated. They both needed the release; the postclimactic tragedy of the hospital's fate could only be fully absorbed through total skin-on-skin contact. The other stuff would have to be put on hold.

She knew one of these days they would have to venture out in public with their relationship, but she frankly wasn't looking forward to it too much with its inevitable tempests—the kid thing, the ex-wife thing, the job thing. She had agreed to the Salto picnic but wished it was over. Reality could really ruin a good sex life.

Well, she wasn't going to let it ruin the wonderful feeling she had right now. How could women ever claim to be satisfied with 'just cuddling'? Why didn't they just get a dog or a stuffed animal? The rewards of a richly textured sexual tryst were beyond peer. The blood vessels of her skin were alive and tingling. Her private area was a little messy and achy right now, but a good kind of ache, like after any good workout. He was a master.

She splayed out on the bed and luxuriated in the feeling.

She knew she was lucky to have such freedom. She blamed it on her grandmother, Lily. Lily led the legendary hard life, married a rascal of a man who beat her and left her with four kids. Of course, he didn't work to any significant degree, and drank or gambled anything he did earn. But at least he had the decency to die young, so Gram was rid of that burden fairly early. She still did everything she could to raise her two girls and two boys to be good, caring, hard-working people. And she did a great job.

But she always wanted to do other things. She wanted to play golf, basketball, tennis; she wanted to ride a bike. She wanted to see the world and experience everything she could. After she recovered from her first bout with breast cancer, she gleefully took up bowling. However, cancer would take its revenge and ended her life, with her experiencing the worst pain and debilitation of body imaginable. Even on her deathbed, she whispered that she wanted to play tennis and that she planned to take up bike riding. Eileen hoped that she was now doing all of those things and more. But there were undoubtedly other things that as a good, Christian woman Gram couldn't bring herself to crave, even in heaven, so that's where Eileen came in.

Eileen couldn't imagine her grandmother experiencing the pleasure and serenity of a really good lay. She often wondered if Gram had ever been in the tender arms of a skilled and attentive lover, a man who could bring her to the edges of ecstasy time and time again. Somehow, Eileen doubted that she ever had. She probably wouldn't have been quite so high-strung if that had been the case. Eileen felt sure that Gram was up there, secretly egging her on, joyful to tears that she hadn't fallen into the same life trap that Gram, and so many other women, had fallen. Setting themselves up to become victims, even though some were very strong women. Marrying bad men, letting themselves become too financially dependent on men, choosing a career they hate, having kids without a husband or reasonable means of support.

And then there were the women who supposedly "had it all." A home, a job, a husband, the 2.3 kids, and a life of total exhaustion and confusion about what their role in the world should be. How proud can a woman be of her job if her personal or family life is a mess? How proud can a woman be if she's at home but her kids are still a mess? Or her husband is spraying his sperm all around town? A woman has to be constantly vigilant, can never relax and let her guard down. If she does, she'll end up losing everything.

Eileen thought again of her grandmother. She had married a bad man, Harold, but back then, it seemed like all women married bad men. There didn't seem to be any other kind of man. But Gram had learned her lesson. Once Harold's pancreas shriveled into a walnut and self-destructed along with the rest of him, Gram refused to take up with another—invariably bad—man and did everything she could to raise her kids by herself in the best manner she knew how. She was independent, and there were lots of hard times. But she was the most innovative woman Eileen had ever known; she could come up with a cheap, homegrown version of about anything. When she could no longer reach the top cabinets in the kitchen and couldn't risk balancing on a wobbly footstool, she rigged a dangling wire hanger to open the doors.

So Eileen's blissful evenings with Neil were in homage to her dear, sweet grandmother, who would have loved the freedom to enjoy the sensual aspects of life that she was able to enjoy. Just as Eileen's body deserved these moments of skilled tenderness, so did her grandmother's. It was Eileen's pleasure to have her vicariously participate. As Neil caressed Eileen's skin, he was reaching generations of women of her ancestry, women who had no doubt ached with unrequited desire for the gentle pleasures of the flesh.

Neil headed out the door, shaking his head. Eileen was a bit wilder than his ex-wife. Kerry Ann truly was a wonderful mother in the best sense of the word. Eileen would be entertaining and lively—now, wait a minute, he wasn't thinking of Eileen as wife material, was he? Already? Catch a breath, man; what's the hurry?

He couldn't help it. He liked being married. He liked to come home after work and hear about the silly, homey things that went on while he was at the office. Marybeth in the carpool ran into a fire hydrant on the way to school while she veered away from a pigeon in the street. Hayley spewed ketchup all over the table when it came out with a gasp. He loved to hear about the little mundane daily things that happened to these people he loved so much it ached.

His own job was sometimes so intense, so filled with cutthroat deadlines that always seemed so crucial during the day, but this family chatter really helped him find perspective on what was really important. Was it really necessary to dog his secretary about getting that motion out today? She seemed pretty busy with other things. She barely let out a sigh when he plunked the pleadings down on her desk, but he knew she was pissed.

He hadn't talked too much about his own job at home because much of it was confidential, but also because he didn't want to stress out the others. Once he left the office, his work stayed behind. He'd always prided himself in being able to do that. He knew it would take the hospital personnel a long time to reassemble after the break-up, but he felt good about the future. They could all work this out together. He shook his head again at his luck at picking a wonderful wife, who would also become a wonderful ex-wife. And picking a girlfriend who would help bring them all together again.

―

Eileen looked through the paperwork she'd bought at the US Government Bookstore in Philadelphia and realized she had all the information she needed to complete an application for National Historic Landmark designation. The discovery of the slave tag, she felt, had to seal the deal. Still, the proposal had to be cleared by the secretary of the interior. She nearly suffered hand cramps writing out the application so quickly. She neatly addressed the envelope, directed to Mr. Silas T. Wren. She reached for her Mercury dime, still dangling on a chain around her neck, held it tightly in her fist, and said a little prayer.

Neil picked Eileen up for dinner later that night.

She had a gleam in her eye. "Hi ya, tiger. Let's start with appetizers at your place?"

"Madam, pray tell, what exactly do you have in mind?"

"Something very tasty that involves compromising your virtue, natch. You got a problem with that?"

She was bright-eyed and rosy. He loved her to death. Or could learn to, he was sure of it.

He laughed. "Lucky for you, I have the bail bondsman in my pocket."

"Fine. Bring him along. The more the merrier."

"You are truly a cad."

"Cad-ess, to you, my dear."

They sped off to his condo. Her eyes were all mischief. And, ooh, a touch of heat there too. At his place, she sidled up to him and kissed him delicately on his neck, his nose, and fully on the mouth. Her hands wandered all over his body. His hands had to dance along. They tumbled into bed and were much too late for their dinner reservation.

He was dazed but awake. He could feel her trembling slightly beside him. He looked over at her and could tell she was weeping silently. He weighed it in a split second and decided not to bother her with questions. He knew that her fears for her health and her future sometimes got the better of her, in spite of her bright nature. Forcing her to articulate something that burned into her soul would not do it justice.

"I love you," he whispered.

Sometimes that was all she needed, he knew. Eileen sighed and scootched her butt against him. Those words were an especially good boost for meeting his daughter tomorrow, he thought.

Eileen woke with a start, experiencing that split second of "Where am I?" It was followed by a "Why is there light in my closet?" and the slow, puzzled realization that she was asleep somewhere other than her own bed. Neil's bedroom window, with the sunlight streaming through it, was located directly to the left of the bed, the closet's location in her own bedroom.

She felt the extra warmth around her. *Oh, but there's a man in my bed; how nice!* She nuzzled against his muscled back and legs. Mmmmm. She was so lucky. Suddenly she remembered. He'd said he loved her. She had felt that old familiar depression last night—about her health in decline, her finances in ruin, fears about everything. She remembered all over again the silly things that had upset her.

She recalled when she hadn't been able to afford something as basic as soft lotion soap, though it didn't matter. She couldn't use it anyway because it gave her a rash. Her hair had fallen out in clumps, which had actually been kind of interesting. She always lost a little hair whenever she washed her hair, but during chemo the hair would wrap around her hands and stay there. She would have to untwine it from her fingers and stick it in the garbage. She probably should have saved some of it. She never actually went bald, but she did lose nearly two-thirds of her hair. Since the basic texture of her hair was thick, most people didn't even notice too much. But when it got wet, it felt like a tiny sliver of hair. That thin, aristocratic-hair look. She was proud of it. But that soon lost its charm as her skin itched, her fatigue built, and her brain burned with the cumulative effects of the chemo. The thin hair only signified more weakness.

And then there was Virgil. Now that she felt so much stronger, she squirmed thinking of him. She felt relief now for breaking free relatively unscathed.

Ah, but Neil! She could feel his rhythmic breathing next to her. Even though her thoughts seemed so loud to her, he still slept sweetly next to her, with no clue of the whirlwind in her brain. He was the master of her anatomy. Had she mentioned that?

CHAPTER 45

Nick never quite fit in with the other kids. For one thing, he hated the baggy trousers all the guys wore. He knew that the parents hated them too, which should have meant that he automatically embraced them, but he couldn't quite make them fit into his philosophy of life. He had no interest in shoplifting, hated the chafing of the loose fabric against his skin and the weight of it, and just plain thought they looked stupid. He figured that anyone with any sense of taste would naturally hate them.

Once, he was out with his buddy Randy and walked past Kong and his gang, who were doing their usual flashing jack. Kong whistled and yelled, "Woo-hoo, look at those pretty string bean legs!"

Nick strode comfortably by in regular jeans, maybe boot cut. Nick just smiled and walked on.

"Oh, boys, running late for your clarinet class?"

Randy had looked over at him, ready to put up a fight if Nick said the word. Nick could tell that his smile puzzled Randy.

"You're just gonna let 'em get away with that?" Randy had asked.

"Hell, yes," Nick said with a smirk. "Their fashion started because guys in prison always wear baggy pants."

"So it's prison chic."

"I suppose. What I heard, though, is that the prisoners like them because it makes it easier to put the bone on. You know, no struggle, just let it fly."

Randy burst out laughing.

Nick continued, "I have no idea why they're so popular now."

The young black men approached them. "What'chu laughin' at?" one of them taunted.

Randy sputtered, "You guys are nothing but bitches in those pants."

Randy's laughing got Nick laughing, and their laughter was so clear and honest and unafraid that Kong's natural inclination to cut them melted away, and instead he joined in, not having a clue what they were laughing at.

When they regained their composure, one of the Kong-ites asked, "What'chu mean?"

When Randy told them, the laughter immediately stopped and Kong said, "You full a shit, man." And they shuffled away but were careful not to touch one another.

CHAPTER 46

Sunday morning. Oh yes, it was Sunday. But it was dead quiet—no twittering from the birds outside, no sunbeam bursting through the blinds. Eileen listened a little more closely, and, nuts, yes, it was raining.

Her bones ached; she dreaded the thought of displaying today. The rain didn't keep the crowds away, but it didn't invite them much either. She hated these days. She woke pumped up with excitement about spending the day sitting in the sun, chatting with people, and selling. Rain wasn't in the plan. That meant she would have to dig around for her rain gear for herself and her display. It meant wearing some hideous jeans and sweatshirt, covered up with an even more hideous coat to keep warm and dry. No cute ballerina T-shirt and calico skirt today. It was mukluks-and-puffy-down weather. Naturally, the past work week had been Tahiti-like.

Yesterday had been the Salto picnic and the official introduction of Eileen to Neil's daughter, Hayley, as her dad's special friend and not just this person who always seemed in close proximity lately for some reason. They had decided that Eileen would drive separately and meet them there. Hayley had eyed her with daggers at first, but Eileen smiled and gave her a hug. It was hard to resist a happy hug. Then when the music started, Eileen grasped Hayley and whirled her in a country dance. Hayley was too stunned to be upset. When the dance was over, Eileen spun Hayley around in a final twirl, let go of her hand, and abruptly headed toward the wine bar. Playing hard to get was a good ploy for little girls' attention too.

So, motherhood was a possibility.

But on that morning, Eileen lay there deciding whether to die or get up. She felt nostalgic for her fertile days when every morning she would wake up and, while still groggy, put the thermometer in her mouth. It usually felt cool against her tongue. She would glance at the digital clock and mumble, "OK, it's six fifty-five a.m. By seven I have to take out the thermometer." And then she'd try to remember before she fell back asleep. She'd also try not to think about going to the bathroom, which was usually what she had to do first thing. But the instructor had stressed that it was important to stay in bed to get the very first reading, before your body moves, before the systems start chugging into action.

She'd manage to stay in a sort of suspended consciousness for five minutes. She feared she would accidentally fall back to sleep and crunch down on the thermometer with her teeth, releasing a killing dose of mercury into her bloodstream. Little had she known then that there was already a killing dose of something in her bloodstream.

The cancer treatments had plunged her into temporary menopause. So at least she didn't have to take her infernal temperature every morning anymore.

She could always not exhibit today, but she feared easing up would lend itself to happening again and again, and soon she would be sprawled in a fetal position on her bed until the entire weekend was over. She only displayed once or twice a month and was determined to keep to that minimal schedule. Doing more would make her sick and anxious. There was always a threshold to maintain, and it seemed stuck at this bare minimum. But displaying at these shows was the only time her heart soared. It always annoyed her that the best part of her life had to be sacrificed to her day job, ongoing and obligatory. On days that made it tough to go to shows, she really resented the hospital job. She could have called in sick more often, but she hated doing that; she would lose all those days.

But now, being flung into involuntary early retirement, she'd lost her lofty feelings about her job. She would miss it: the predictability, the routine, and the money.

Today, when she trudged out in the sloppy wet and wind and set up the plastic cover-up, it seemed her life was on an endless loop.

She'd been on a roll with her little paintings during high school. Every evening after school, she couldn't wait to eat a quick dinner, do her homework, and then, finally, start painting. She drew little pictures as birthday gifts for her friends and family. Everyone was thrilled to get one, even if they really wanted that new Fleetwood Mac album. She loved painting. One day she brought her miniatures to a local gift shop, and Donna, the owner, purchased them all on the spot. Eileen knew her future was bright, but when she got home, her parents, not particularly delighted with the money made from her art, asked her, "So which college do you plan to go to?"

College was an absolute necessity. All young girls of breeding went to college. How else was one to meet an appropriate man to marry? Lolling around here in this dump, hawking pictures—she would never find a suitable man that way.

So of course she went to college (BA in art history, Penn State). And then to justify the cost of and her parents' sacrifice for her college education, she had to get a job that would make good use of the skills she had learned. On and on for years, she had to put on the back burner the thing she really wanted to do with her life. She would doodle in the evenings, but there was always dinner to make, a husband to keep amused, house and family needs to take care of. To keep from going crazy from the frustration, she told herself she was gaining crucial life experiences she could draw upon to make her paintings even better when that day finally came—and hopefully it would, wouldn't it?— when she could finally do what she really wanted.

Eileen now knew that at the moment she'd had to squelch her dreams in favor of an outside-relegated plan of what her life should become—the blueprint all plotted for her without any of her input, with no consideration for her talent, her creativity, her soul—the tiny micron of matter stirred that would become her cancer. At college, she'd huddled in a heap, weeping on her fresh new textbooks, their words beckoning her to pursue the worlds within. And if the naggy beckoning didn't work, well, little missy, you have a big fat quiz tomorrow and better get your lazy ass in gear, now. She'd shaken off her dream and sighed. She knew the angst would allow her to connect in her painting someday. Grief was good; it was the ultimate inspiration.

Well, she had accumulated enough grief to create a veritable masterpiece someday. Michelangelo, watch out, your little fat naked cherubs will have nothing on Eileen's creations, once she has the opportunity to express herself. Eileen shook her head as she carefully hung up her work. That's a laugh. She'd be lucky if her art made it onto the walls of the local bowling alley someday, where unsteady, smoky bowlers would careen over and peer shakily at her work and shout out to the hot dog seller, "Hey, are these for sale?" and nod drunkenly at the response, their sole participation in art appreciation acknowledged and complete.

Still, she looked forward to her show. Maybe someone special would attend, someone with money, someone with connections, someone to whom her art would speak so intimately that the person's heart would burst out of her body with the soul-on-soul connection of it. Yes, little naked doggie peckers could have that effect on people. She might have to change her subject matter, she thought.

Eileen brightened suddenly, seeing Miles walking toward her. He held a circus-sized umbrella adorned with leaping dolphins. He forged a wide path toward her.

"So, it's that fear of intimacy thing, huh?" Eileen said as she hugged him.

"You can never be too careful in flu season. Hungry?"

"Somehow, I'm in the mood for a tuna salad sandwich."

"All righty, I'll be right back."

Miles always enjoyed his share of female attention, but he really, truly wanted a redhead. Named Erin. No, there wasn't such a person, not that he had met. Not yet. He'd never even known any redheads, ever, but just knew in his heart that she would come along, and that she would be *the* one. Eileen had pointed out Jenaveev to him once when they were at a hospital festival, but Miles scoffed. No, no, no. He had no wish to break up that happy couple. And there was a bit of weirdness with the idea of having sex with someone who had sex with someone Eileen had sex with. They'd talked about it. It was just too incestuous. Might as well do it with a dog or something. Not that Jenaveev wasn't attractive in her own minimalist way, but Miles wanted his own babe.

"Oh, Miles, you could have her any way you want her," Eileen had advised. "She's prime. She needs it bad."

Miles had cocked his head. "No doubt. Doesn't do it for me, honey. Sorry. Desperation smells, don't you know?"

"No, can't say that I do."

Miles continued, "Even if I did dip into that red-haired quagmire, where would that leave hubby?"

"Oh, please. His type can get it anywhere he wants it. I'm sure he has plenty on the side. There's no accounting for taste."

"Spoken like a true ex."

"Ew. I left him, if you would be kind enough to remember correctly."

This was easier than trying to deal with things on a deeper level. Some things she would rather keep to herself.

Miles scoffed. "Are you sure he realizes you're gone? These married types compartmentalize their lives so that they can completely forget what's going in one of the parts. Maybe he's hoping that you're pining away for him. 'Oh, is she ever going to be hot for me when we finally meet again.'"

"I don't think even he's *that* dumb."

Miles returned with two sandwiches in a bag and two birch beers in large cups. Eileen squealed. The guy in the next row had brought a keg of the real thing. This was so much better than the strange red stuff sold in stores.

"Hey," Miles said, "Why don't you take a walk around? I'll mind the store here and keep prospective buyers riveted with my scintillating banter until you return."

"Miles, that's so kind of you, what gives?"

He bowed deeply and hoisted the umbrella with a flourish. "Call it the new me. Now, go."

Eileen didn't puzzle over Miles' uncustomary thoughtfulness, she'd been through it before with him and wouldn't be swept up in it again. She did have a fleeting sense that graciousness was his wedge against getting close to anyone. The two of them would likely have made it as a couple if not for that. Now she welcomed his friendship without having any expectations. She'd have to introduce him to Paige sometime. Paige wasn't a redhead, but, in a certain light, there was a distinct auburn glint to her hair.

But for now, it was time to check out her competition at the show.

She wandered along the makeshift aisles, hopping over the puddles forming in the gravel pathways. She rarely had the chance to look around at her shows, so this was a welcome escape. She waved at the old guy who sold hubcaps, bumpers, hood ornaments and other car supplies. She nodded to the lady who sold old vacuum cleaner parts. She smiled at the couple displaying used farm equipment. On and on it went, old bicycles, handyman's tools, 70's furniture. Eileen's heart sank. This was nothing but a junk show. How could she expect to be "discovered" by people clearly interested only in redecorating the double-wide? Oh, what a snotty thought, she knew. She took a deep breath and looked up. The clouds were barreling through the sky as if in angry haste to get somewhere else. She knew the feeling. It'll happen, it would, it had to. Her loyalty to her art would reward her, some day.

She shuffled back to Miles, her head down. He took one look at her and said, "Well, if I knew it would put you in such a chipper mood, I'd volunteer to man the deck more often."

Eileen shrugged and sighed. "Thanks. I was probably better off not knowing about the scruff I'm in company with."

"Scruff?! Scruff?!" Miles declared in faux outrage. "Have you not seen the champ around the corner selling old radios? Great, old, tube radios, made from Bakelite, classic stuff. Babe, you're in good company around here, fer sur."

Eileen rolled her eyes, "OK, OK, perhaps I was a bit hasty. Bakelite radios, you say? The teeming crowd around his booth must have blocked my view."

"Well, now you're just being mean." Miles stuck out his lower lip and Eileen had to smile.

Then, a distinguished-looking man dressed in a Tin Cloth jacket over a peek-a-boo boiled wool sweater stopped in front of Eileen.

"Hello, Ms. Hanley, I was hoping to catch you." He glared at Miles who quickly looked away.

"Yes, sir, what can I do for you?" Eileen sprang into marketer-mode. She'd deal with Miles later.

"Your work is so intricate and unique."

She immediately thought, Ah yes, compliments were wonderful, but moolah makes the world go 'round. And keeps her in hot fudge sundaes.

"Why thank you, it's so kind of you to notice."

"I'd love to buy these two, if they are still available." He pointed out two pieces displaying matching cavorting pigs

Yes, baby, come to mama.

"I believe they are still available," Eileen said. "Thank you, I'll get them ready for you."

Yes, yes, yes, yes.

After Tin Cloth man left, Miles asked, "OK, what little doody-dinky thing did you draw on those?"

"Why Miles," Eileen exclaimed, "I didn't think you paid any attention to my work. So, hey, what did you say to that guy while I was away?"

Miles' face clouded over. "Why, I know not of what you speak." But his eyes sparkled. "Well, he may have gotten the mistaken impression that you had to meet with your financial advisor about your stock portfolio. Pork bellies and such, you know?

"Sheesh, it's a miracle the guy came back."

"So, is it my fault I'm not right in the head?"

"That excuse would be more believable if you didn't count on it a little too much. To answer your question, I drew little dimes on both of them. Or, tried to anyway. The little suckers are hard to capture. But I keep thinking about them."

At the end of the show, she decided, she deserved to treat herself to dinner. Miles had to leave to work on his computer at home—he was building his own from scratch—so she looked forward to an evening alone at the Chili Bowl.

She often feared that the reason miniatures were her preferred medium was because she couldn't actually draw. Or, more specifically, she couldn't draw people. OK, OK, she couldn't draw faces. She knew that other artists who specialized in landscapes, still lifes, pets, and wildlife had difficulty with portraits. Often they zeroed in on one particular person—an ex-husband, a mother, even themselves—and every person in every drawing was a mirror image of that one ideal person. Or, rather, the only kind of person they could draw.

She decided to incorporate into her dining routine that night a relentless search for facial features—what made each face unique, what conglomerate of features magically incorporated into a beautiful face, pretty face, nice face, friendly face. At the mere mention of each category, she could automatically imagine a face as an illustrious example. So how come she couldn't describe it or draw it?

At the table at one o'clock, catercorner from hers, she saw the perfect male face. She fixated on it. He was in profile, the ring-finger side of his face toward her. And, no, there was no ring on the finger. She marveled at his perfectly formed little features; they all melded together into a neat, tidy face. Nicely filled-out skin along the cheekbones—not too fat, not gaunt. A fine nose. Good symmetrical ears, fairly small but not precious. Nothing stuck out to shock the observer. She could draw him right then and there. It would be a magical face.

Suddenly, he turned toward her. She flinched at the big bug-eyes peering down at her. Were they…? Yes, they were slightly, so help me, cross-eyed. Had he reached over and slapped her soundly across her nicely formed teeth, she would not have felt more discomfited. Such a tragedy of nature should not be possible. How could individual characteristics, so perfect in themselves, cause such a horror in the aggregate? She was convinced she would never learn to draw faces. Faces were impossible.

CHAPTER 47

Ah, Neil, Neil. Eyes nearly transparent blue, but vivid, so vivid, and intense. His eyes were truly the passageway to his soul, and she could get lost in the silky journey. Eileen looked in his eyes and saw everything that was right and good with the world. They were kind and innocent and wise. Not a touch of guardedness. Except when someone asked him a question or interjected a remark that was rude and invasive and clearly none of his or her business. Then his eyes would shade over ever so slightly with a razor-thin shield of distrust. His gaze would never waver; it would remain clear and focused. Only a true expert of Neil's face could notice the difference. You hated to get that look—because you would know that you had disappointed him. There wasn't a worse feeling in the world than to have deeply disappointed this man who could tame the world and bring it to your feet, if only you trusted him.

Eileen had seen the look once, and it had nearly crushed her. Luckily, she wasn't the recipient. It was Neil's daughter. They were at Hayley's softball game, and Neil was supposed to take her home. His home. He had fixed her room up and was excited about having her stay with him. But Hayley suddenly said that she was spending the night at her friend, Tara's instead.

Neil got the look. It wasn't hurt or anger; it was sheer disappointment in his daughter.

From the expression on Hayley's face, it was clear she had expected something completely different, the typical whining, cajoling, and begging that her friends had all told her were the benefits of divorce. She'd been told that her parents would be playing up to her for the rest of her life to try to make up for the tragedy they'd caused by getting divorced. They'd all told her she would have it made in the shade from here on out. She could do nothing wrong. Every bit of bad behavior would be excused out of the guilt and misery of the parents.

She was normally a good kid; she never thought she would want to try any of the stuff out on her parents. But it was so tempting. She was angry that they got divorced. She'd hoped to get a reaction from her father, but this was not what she'd expected. She felt horrible. She felt that she had tried to manipulate her dad and he knew it with his razor-sharp vision. He had enough problems trying to deal with his life without her playing this stupid mind game with him. She was ashamed and knew she would never try it again.

At the very least, she'd expected him to sigh, resigned to his fate, and mutter, "Well, OK, honey, that's fine, maybe next time." She'd really expected him to say that. Her friends had insisted that that would be the way things would be from now on.

Not "We had agreed that the plan for this weekend was for you to stay with me."

That's what he said. A statement of fact. No timidity at all, no room for misunderstanding.

And that look. His normally twinkling blue eyes were cold and stern. "This had better be good," they seemed to say. "Don't push me," the eyes added.

Suddenly, a lump came to her throat and tears flooded her eyes. She couldn't stand to make her dad angry. She had to cave; she couldn't help it.

"I'm sorry, Daddy, I really do want to spend the weekend with you. They all said I should play it. To punish you," she stammered.

"Punish me for what?"

He wasn't going to give her a break, not at all.

"Oh, I don't know." And she burst into tears. "I want to go home with you, Dad."

Then he softened. "It's OK, honey, let's go home." He held her tight and stroked her still baby-soft hair. She was still his princess, but he would never spoil her. Nothing was worth that.

He also looked over at her friend, Tara, who stared back and then quickly looked away. Hayley was about to call out to her, but Tara waved and said, "See ya in school on Monday?"

Friends were great that way. Sometimes you never had to explain things. Adults would have simpered and moaned and engaged in the silent treatment or poked and prodded and asked tons and tons of intrusive questions to get to the bottom of everything that was going on. They would pick apart every minute detail and analyze its aggregate parts and strip it of its dignity and its essence. There would be endless intrusive cell phone calls at all hours of the day and night. Then they would tire of the process, get angry in their weariness, get frustrated at failing to come to resolution and thereby conclude they had "nothing to talk about," and part as mortal enemies.

Twelve-year-old Hayley hoped she would never grow up like that.

Eileen, observing this interlude, happily added a couple of mental checkmarks, one for Neil and one for his daughter.

CHAPTER 48

Yes, that was ratchety old Mr. Silas Wren, formerly Professor Wren, who'd received Eileen's application. Apparently, he'd been neither ratchety nor old, after all, while Virgil was at college, because Silas now held a vital position with the secretary of the interior. He looked over the application of the Sunrise Hospital in Maple Leaf, Pennsylvania. Maple Leaf. What a pleasant-sounding town. Reminded him of his old alma mater, just across the border near Baltimore, where he'd taught political science for four years. Interesting.

The soon-to-be-defunct Sunrise Hospital was requesting that the property be designated a National Historic Landmark. Part of the Underground Railroad, according to Ms. Eileen Hanley, who wanted to construct a museum. This was a great time to apply; the country was slowly removing its blinders concerning that era, Silas mused. The younger people seemed ready to embrace all of the country's history, good and bad. Many were curious about that crucial time and pored over any available information. During the past five years, he'd seen more requests for information concerning the Underground Railroad than in the previous twenty.

Silas peered through his glasses as he reviewed the hospital's application. He glanced over the section listing potential conflicts to historic designation.

He sighed. Always the same problems—neighbors wanting to rezone the property for residential subdivisions, likely to improve their property values. And they were no doubt tickled pink about not being bothered by those pesky ambulance sirens anymore, although they surely hadn't minded the fact that the hospital's proximity had already increased their property values. A fast-food franchise also wanted the site. Hmm, fat chance, folks, Silas thought. And there were others: the county parks department wanted to build a recreation center and soccer field, and the city wanted to turn it into a memorial for a local philanthropist, subject to a referendum, of course. Doesn't anyone get along over there? Silas wondered. Oh, and then there was this. A local business owner wanted to buy the property to enlarge his company. Some guy by the name of Virgil Ellingsworth.

Silas shook with laughter. Such sweeter irony simply did not exist. So, dapper Mr. Ellingsworth wanted to shush away the gnatty good-deeders so he could have his big business playground expanded. The same Virgil Ellingsworth who'd bought copies of exam papers and tried to pass off the answers as his own in Prof. Wren's own poli-sci class. The kid hadn't even tried to change the idiomatic language of the essay answers. Supreme arrogance.

Silas could still recall the bratty expression of self-satisfaction on that snippy little chiseled face when the college review board denied Silas's request for expulsion of young Ellingsworth for cheating. Silas had been reprimanded, of course. Privately. The board members had tried to convince him that the Ellingsworth money was much too important to their school. Did he realize how much they donated? They could operate for twenty-five years without tuition raises—"not that we ever would, ha, ha"—on the amounts the Ellingsworth family had endowed to the college. They would simply have to put up with the irrepressible lad for another year.

Silas couldn't sign the approval fast enough. Ms. Eileen Hanley's hospital was going to get its historic designation.

———

Virgil stood on the sidewalk outside the hospital and assessed its potential. Yes, he believed the building would work out just fine. Once this silly hospital closed, he could get on with real life, which was starting a new paisley desktop-grommet branch office of his company. He brightened thinking of the pending success of his venture. Of course, the building would have to be substantially renovated once all of the hospital's appurtenances were removed. No doubt it would take a while to get rid of the smell. Maybe he could move all the business offices over here in the front section and the manufacturing operations could take over the patient rooms. Perfect feng shui, as they called it, wasn't that right? Remove the nastiness of illness and disease and replace it with a vibrant, successful new business. One that creates something, doesn't just process a succession of ill people.

He felt sharp. He checked himself out in the mirrored windows at the hospital's entrance. Yes, he looked pretty damn good too.

CHAPTER 49

A dreary gray filled the skies. No identifiable clouds to make things interesting, just a thick mat of gray turning the whole world dull and listless. One was compelled to walk in this weather, if only to lift the spirit and prevent the soul from descending into the deep gray void that was often southeastern Pennsylvania.

The weather didn't matter to Eileen; she was intent on walking anyway. She had found walking to be especially helpful in chasing the blues during her illness, and she managed to maintain the habit even afterward. Now she walked to chase another cancer, the cancer that was destroying her hospital, her home for the past twelve years. It wasn't that it was such a tragedy for leaving behind thousands with no access to medical care. Everyone would be taken care of; they would probably go to Englewood, twenty miles to the west. There were also plenty of outpatient facilities nearby, satellite clinics of Englewood, to treat minor emergencies.

The real tragedy was the loss of her work home, a common meeting ground for all those employees who had become her friends. These friends were the kind of people she would never seek out intentionally because on the surface they seemed to have so little in common. Most of them had not gone to college. They'd lived in the same town for their entire lives and for their parents' entire lives and had families and children. Eileen was a bit of a wild woman and an eccentric, in their estimation, she was sure. But they'd found a common ground in trying together to create some meaning in this nutty world.

Eileen wondered, as she often did, if maybe she should turn this miserable situation into an opportunity to move to Philadelphia or New York. Those cities were so alive; the people were so unstrangled. She was a little weary, though. Her fire to keep trying new things was dimming, and she really did want to settle down. She wasn't sure how her artwork would sell in a big city. Here, the locals thought it was cute and quaint. She worried that her creativity might be crushed by the intense analysis from highbrow critics trying to outdo one another in recognizing and articulating the latest obscure trends in artistic expression. She drew little critters doing people stuff. That was it. Except for the naughty scenes she slipped in once in a while, her art was fairly straightforward, almost cartoonish. She was quite sure it wouldn't meet the requisite sophistication (and obfuscation) to make a big splash in the big city.

Winston was going to relocate to the Midwest, in Illinois. He'd already lined up a job at a big private hospital conglomeration there. His family seemed excited to leave and try something new. He'd asked Eileen if she wanted to join him, said he'd be thrilled to have her. But there was no way she could travel there. She had all she needed here. Except a job.

The hospital had offered Eileen a small severance package that would help tide her over until she could figure out what she wanted to do next. Of course, she had to keep up the payments on her health insurance. No scrimping allowed there. She could manage for a couple of months paying all her expenses without a job if she had to. The thought was delicious: *Ummm, not having to work for two whole months, time I can spend refining my art.* But she knew it was unreasonable; she couldn't support herself on her art right now.

She could always do temp work, and she knew that was the sensible thing to do. However, there was something in her that was tired of always being sensible. She had a sense that being sensible kept her out of critical danger, but hadn't really allowed her to accomplish anything terrific either. She was old enough, and wise enough, to realize that being sensible would not shoot her to the stars. She could be content lounging among the rest of the sheeplike drones of the world, exchanging gossip, poring over the TV guide for no-miss shows, paging through celebrity rags, searching cookbooks for the ultimate potato salad recipe. But was that really enough? She didn't think it was. She loved immersing herself in her art, but it turned her a little too inward sometimes. She needed an outlet that was socially significant, that could allow her to make a difference in her little community. Something that would put a smile on a stranger's face. Then, she knew, her inspiration would flow unimpaired.

When would she hear back from the Department of the Interior?

CHAPTER 50

"What's the matter, honey? You look like you're carrying the world on your shoulders today."

Gina could always tell when Noelle was upset. Noelle never said a whole lot while she puttered around doing her chores, but she was usually quick with a smile when someone said something to her. Today she was in her own world, miles away. Her face drooped and her eyes brimmed with tears.

"My parents had another fight last night. I was trying to get to sleep, and I was just about to nod off and woke up hearing someone screaming. Then they realized they were getting loud, and they lowered their voices to hisses. I couldn't hear anything but their hateful, penetrating Ss, which seared my eardrums. It was mumble, mumble, mumble, mumble, *sssssssssssssss*, mumble, mumble, *sssssss*, mumble, mumble, mumble, *sssssss*. Why don't they just get divorced? Why do people stay together and make themselves and everyone else around them miserable? Why can't they get along?"

"Aw, honey, I'm so sorry. I'm sure they think they're doing the right thing for you and your brother by staying together. It's hard for parents to leave one another when there are children."

"I think they're just too lazy to do it. I'm sick to my stomach all the time. Then I wonder if it's my fault. I would love to get a shot at another set of parents. I guess I couldn't really tell them that, though, could I?"

"No, then they might turn on you too. Better they direct their anger at each other. I'm so sorry you have to hear all of that. Look at the bright side, honey. Soon you'll be going off to college, and that's what they made the West Coast for."

"I guess. The worst thing is, I don't have a clue what to look for in a guy. Parents are supposed to be a model for their kids. All I know is I don't want anything like what my parents have together."

"That's a shame. Noelle, I don't know your parents, and, honey, you're way too young to even think about settling down with a boy, but just try not to make the same mistakes they made. Get to know the guy really well. Check out his behavior in different situations, and get a good gauge on his character. See how he acts in the grocery store, check out how he returns merchandise, see how he treats the waiter, his doctor, his mother, his boss. A guy can act like Mr. Perfect Date Man forever; you've got to catch him off guard in day-to-day circumstances and annoyances to see what he's really like.

"Best of all, pick someone you feel comfortable with, in your gut. I've learned that the gut is the best barometer of a relationship. It's such a simple thing, but a lot of women ignore their gut, or maybe they're happy they have someone who makes them lose their appetite because they figure maybe they'll finally lose some weight."

"The gut test might be difficult for me," Noelle said, "because my stomach is in knots all the time now. Have you ever had a boyfriend? You know, from the guys who come here?"

"It's funny. I think of this as a job, just like anyone going into those high-rise office buildings in Philadelphia. My personal life stays personal, and I don't bring it in this place. We are actresses, more than anything else. Sure, there are guys who try to pick us up, wait for us after the show, try to get together with us. But I've found that if I act polite but firm, they leave me alone.

"It's the girls who refuse to separate their personal life from this dancing business who really get in trouble. Once they start to believe their own fantasy, they're lost. I probably wouldn't want as a boyfriend a guy who would come here. He would never be able to take me seriously."

Noelle was thoughtful. "Do you think you'll be here forever?"

"For heaven's sakes, no, girl. I make incredibly good money, but I can already tell that my enthusiasm is starting to fade. You can pretend to be hot for these losers for only so long. I'm only twenty-four, and I've saved up enough to go to college and be a vet. You know, veterinary medicine."

"Really? That's great."

"I love animals; they're so honest. Not like people."

"Cats are a little strange."

"True, but they're still precious little fuzzy creatures."

"I suppose." Noelle let out a big sigh. "Gina, you'd make a great mother."

"Aw, thanks, sweetheart. Lots of folks wouldn't quite agree with you. I've got to get out of these sweats now and get back to work. Just hang in there for a couple more years. You're a teenager. Your parents probably don't expect you to be around the house too much, so take advantage of it and stay the heck away as much as you can. When you do have to be home, stay in your room with the door shut. Listen to CDs. Read. Do homework. If they're good do-be parents, they've read the latest psychodrivel in child development and know that as long as you don't engage in murdering sprees or have your face smothered in coke powder, they should just leave you alone in this crucial stage of your life."

Gina was the single most significant influence on Noelle's life up to this point. Her mother was too self-absorbed to even pretend to listen to her. The last time Noelle remembered trying to talk to her mother, she was about eleven years old and giddy in love with the grocery bagger, John. John had gallantly pushed their cart to the car and, a bit awkwardly, unloaded their bags for them. The grapefruit tumbled out of the bag in the trunk, and when he scrambled to gather them up, his cap fell off his head. Then he stood up too quickly and bumped his head on the trunk lid. "Th-th-there you go," he'd stuttered. So charming. Afterward, Noelle was a warm rosy-peach from head to toe.

"Mom, he's so cute. Did you see the way he smiled at me? It makes me feel good and squishy inside. What does that mean, Mom? Have you ever felt like that? Did Daddy make you feel like that?"

Her mother fidgeted with the car keys. "I hate this key chain with the dangly doofus-thing always banging against my fingers or my knee when I'm driving. Rattle, rattle, rattle. Drives me nuts."

Her mother ripped off the little plastic porpoise and threw it into the shrubs. She whipped her head around and glared at Noelle for a split second and then brightened as she flipped the keys in her hand. "Oh, that's so much better. What people will suffer before they learn to make their lives easier. Remember that, dear."

Noelle had stared at her mother in disbelief. How could she have ever expected to share a moment with her? The warmth of young puppy love quickly froze in her chest, leaving that familiar, unyielding steel chunk where her heart should be. Noelle had bought the key chain for her mother during the family's last visit to Florida's Sea World a few years back. She'd thought the little plastic dolphin was cute and had shyly picked it out, hoping her mother would be pleased. Of course.

Since that single moment of clarity, Noelle had sworn never to engage her mother in any significant conversation ever again.

"Hey, ollie ollie home free."

"What?" Noelle shook herself from her bitter reverie and realized that Gina had put her arm around her and given her a light squeeze.

"Are you OK, kid? You were hiding from me there for a while."

Noelle flung her arms around Gina's neck, kissed her on the cheek, and exclaimed, "Thank you for being my friend."

She turned and walked away.

CHAPTER 51

It was her last day, and Eileen was scheduled for her exit interview. She met with Parnell, the human resources director, who was crisply dressed, even for casual day, in brown seersucker, loose-fitting pants, a white silk blouse, and a snug-fitting vest of matching pattern. The tans cleverly picked up a soupçon of color from the pants. Very well put together. Parnell would have no trouble getting another job.

Parnell had several expressions she carefully practiced for each of these interminable exit interviews. For those wretched employees who would never find another job, she sprouted sincere sympathy and encouragement. For hospital troublemakers, she played solemn and thoughtful. For others, she nodded slowly with concern. For most of the rest, she shook her head and muttered, "Tch, tch tch."

As Eileen entered her office, Parnell decided upon sardonic amusement. Parnell never felt that Eileen conveyed to her the proper fear and respect that, as director of the human resources department of the hospital, was indisputably her due.

"So, Parnell, why exactly is it that I must have an exit interview? Don't you think it's at least a little incongruous under the circumstances?"

Sardonic amusement disappeared. Parnell's lips bobbed at Eileen like a fish underwater, her eyes as blank. Gee, Parnell, you'd look great mounted on a wall, on a nice slab of wood, tastefully slathered with an oak veneer. Have you ever thought about that, now that we *all* must look for another career? A taxidermist's trout—that would be perfect for you, Parnell.

"We all would like to learn something from this, Eileen."

"So, what am I supposed to say? 'Gee, I would have loved to continue working here if only it weren't for that pesky hospital folding thing'?"

Parnell chuckled in spite of herself. It was a chilling sound.

Eileen backed off. She wouldn't dream of telling Parnell about her recent discovery about the hospital. If she knew, Parnell would probably arrange a bonfire outside the morgue and dance in the nude to summon spirits of the dead. *Ick.*

CHAPTER 52

The Ellingsworths started to make plans to go to Atlantic City for Nick's quoits championships. It would be a week-long affair and a bit of a strain for Jenaveev, but she was looking forward to a respite after her torturous weeks of radiation treatments.

Even Nick's parents couldn't dampen his enthusiasm for the upcoming tournament. Generally, he hated for them to come to the competitions because he was embarrassed for them to see him in his element. He played fully exposed, expressing his best self without apology or reservation. For them to see him doing something he honestly loved would be an affirmation of their family unit. If he felt good while they watched, they could extend that to mean he felt good in their presence, therefore the family was doing good.

But Nick figured his parents would both be off doing their own thing: his father doing who-knows-what and his mother checking out all the shops and slots. So hopefully they wouldn't be around to pester and distract him during the competition.

He loved the hard, cold steel of the quoit. His set was specially made in northern England by a master blacksmith to regulation criteria. Slickly smooth, each one weighed exactly five and a quarter pounds. After each play, he carefully cleaned them of dirt, every little nook and cranny, until they gleamed.

This would be a dual-purpose trip for Virgil. It would be his and Jenaveev's fifteenth wedding anniversary, and now the whole family would be together in Atlantic City.

Atlantic City had been the honeymoon destination of many East Coast couples during the '50s, and Virgil hoped this would lend the occasion a romantic, old-fashioned air. Things had changed considerably since then and were not nearly as quaint, but the casinos added a modern decadence that was particularly appealing to Virgil. Nick and Noelle would probably want to swim in the Atlantic Ocean, but he wasn't sure if that was a good idea anymore with all the stories about medical waste debris floating on shore. On some days, the smell alone was enough to curdle one's solar plexus. He would be sure to get a nice room with a pool.

Jenaveev was in a frenzy. The weather forecast grew dimmer and dimmer. Hurricane Frederick was bearing down on the Bahamian coast. It was still far from the Atlantic coast, but at the best, it would produce a lot of rain and wind. At first touched by her concern, Virgil soon realized that she was only worried about the damper this would put on her shopping experience.

"Don't they have the entire boardwalk under a mall yet?" The idea was so obvious to her, and she couldn't understand why the city didn't share her infinite wisdom.

Virgil watched the cloud formation on the Weather Channel. Watching the churning cloud that was the eye of the hurricane made him dizzy with excitement and anticipation, and he couldn't figure out why. What would it be like to be tossed and turned, totally out of control, totally at the mercy of this voracious wind? On the other hand, that was pretty much exactly what his life was like.

The more he watched, he began to change focus. Now the eye of the hurricane looked like one of the grommets the company was currently working on. Since they were having problems with the more technical-use grommets, he'd decided he would change the corporate focus to more pedestrian areas, like the grommets used on computer desks to make room for all the cords. The plastic grommet covered the little round hole cut through the desk, leaving room for just the cord and making a fairly neat desk top. Right now, the grommets were usually black or putty-colored.

He'd come up with a design that would revolutionize the concept of grommets. It was a brightly colored paisley design, swirling with color, manufactured with the same concept of multicolored bowling balls. No longer would the grommet be relegated to its boring, understated role of connecting exciting things to other exciting things; now it would reign supreme on its own. It was something to celebrate, something glorious on its own merit, giving customers another choice. Now people would know exactly what grommets were and would base their choice on the grommet's own beauty. It wouldn't just be that "thing with the hole" anymore, but that "pretty pink/blue/black swirly thing." Now kids and wives would get into the decision-making process. His new grommet would be as important as cup holders in SUVs.

He had patented the formula and expected a financial windfall. He hoped to meet with some financial advisors in Atlantic City who could bankroll the venture.

As he watched the swirling of Hurricane Frederick on the Weather Channel, he took it as a good sign.

———

Nick had wanted to take the train in, as the trip was excruciatingly long and he didn't want to endure it along with his parents' endless banter. He just wanted to kick back and let the rhythmic droning of the engines muffle any attempts at conversation. But there they were, in the family SUV. He planned to look out the window the entire trip. He wished he could read, but that made him a little sick. His mother, always encouraging better life through chemicals, offered a motion sickness pill, but he didn't want anything that might interfere with his concentration. Instead, he thought about the upcoming competition and planned his strategy to kick his opponents' butts. If he put just the right backspin on the quoit, it would land perfectly on a slant against the pin. But if it wasn't just so, it could go sailing off to the far left, nowhere near the pin. He motioned the imaginary quoit movements with his hands, and his mom thought he was doing tai chi.

He watched the world go by along the freeway. He used to love the drive to the beach; they would usually go to Ocean City, New Jersey, when they were kids. Lots of swampy fields and homespun frozen custard joints and hand-painted wooden signs hawking everything from crayfish to LET GOD BE YOUR COPILOT. Now most of those signs were gone, replaced with flashy casino billboards, beginning nearly two hundred miles from Atlantic City. He felt like the trip was one very long commercial. They were surrounded by leap-frogging casino buses, some also slathered with advertising. How could the people traveling in the buses see anything? He knew they could see out a little while the bus was moving, but from the inside those advertisements look like a TV screen up close; lots of little dots making up each image. From the inside it felt like you were looking through a thick-mesh screen. He hoped those people didn't pay too much for their taking part in a huge, moving advertisement. Even if he was with his parents, at least he could look out his window unobstructed.

This time, however, his parents were uncustomarily quiet. Their heavy silence was more disconcerting than their usual bursts of venom. He had heard that hate was close to love, so even the most vituperate outbursts showed some underlying passion. This eerie quiet could only mean indifference, and that was more uncomfortable than anything.

In his mind, Nick flung the quoit toward the pin, but it boinked against the pin on a wayward edge and went jetting off into the array of bystanders, his parents among them. His parents just stood there. They didn't seem to notice the five-pound iron object hurtling toward them, landing squarely at their feet between them. No reaction. Just that glassy stare off into the distance, Mom looking left, Dad looking right.

As soon as the car squeezed into the tiny space in the casino garage, Jenaveev jumped out, yelling back, "I'll see you in a couple of hours," and sprinted toward the elevator that would lead her to the glittering-lights land of slot machines and endless shopping. Nick, Noelle, and Virgil stood there, agog and ashamed that she could still surprise them. If they'd seen the worst, then it could only get better, couldn't it? But the better part about her always eluded them.

"Don't you want to know what room we're in?" Noelle cried out.

Jenaveev just fluttered her hand in response without turning around. She jumped into the elevator marked SKUNK LEVEL with a picture of a furry little rotund ball wiggling away.

Virgil muttered to himself as they lugged in their suitcases. He was tempted to just leave Jenaveev's in the car, but it would only lead to a yelling match later, and he just didn't care enough to want to participate. Better yet, he could stay away until after she decided to come back, probably around eleven o'clock that night. Yeah, maybe he'd do that—take a long walk, check out some girlie shows, and wander back to the room at around midnight or one. He didn't give a rat's patootie if she couldn't find the room. The anniversary idea had never been a good one.

The next morning, although not ordinarily an early riser, Nick bolted upright out of bed the split second before the alarm went off. He hated sharing a room with Noelle and hoped to escape before she awoke. But Noelle was deeply dreaming about something, sighing in soft little whinnies. As he tiptoed out the door, he heard the alarm going off in his parents' room. Apparently, no one budged in response. Sometimes at home, Nick would lie in bed listening to their alarm for forty-five minutes. His mother would often mosey out of bed, finally, and trudge downstairs to the kitchen without even turning off the alarm.

Nick loved Atlantic City early in the morning before the busloads of people swarmed all over the boardwalk. It almost seemed tidy. The winds blew away all the sweat, dirt, seaweed, and garbage from the day before, and the boardwalk seemed almost pristine.

It was cloudy, but the wind felt brisk and clean. He walked past a couple of casinos just to get his blood flowing. And then he headed over to the convention hall where the quoits championships were taking place. He grabbed a couple of slices of pizza at one of the stands along the boardwalk. Here, you could get pizza at all hours and no one thought twice about it. Granted, it wasn't the freshest, and he had to take what was left over, broccoli and mozzarella, but what the heck. There was nothing more satisfying than eating pizza at seven o'clock in the morning.

He looked over the competition. Some of the guys had obviously come as part of a club. There weren't too many individualists like him. It wasn't a loner's game, really, even though Nick preferred to play it that way. He knew that others treated it as another excuse to get together and drink beer and get away from the women and watch football or soccer and burp and belch and act like *men*. Nick knew that, even as a kid, he would eat those guys alive.

For him, it was a game of supreme concentration. First, he emptied his mind of all excess thought. He didn't care about his stupid parents, didn't care what his sister was doing now, didn't care when they would all meet again. School didn't matter, his future didn't matter, whether his parents killed one another didn't matter. He was free to become one with the quoit, to fly in the wind, slice through, and land perfectly for a superior score.

But something happened. He got a headache, painful and grinding. He never got headaches. He wished his parents were watching him and rooting for him. No matter that he was contemptuous about the idea earlier, now he really wanted them to be out there. To be excited, to be involved, to be enthusiastic. To shout, "C'mon, Nick, you can do it!" Suddenly, he wanted the support of his family more than anything.

But wait a minute. Someone was jumping up and down a little, trying to get his attention. Noelle! What was she doing here? He instantly forgot his regret and was annoyed that she would turn up; how embarrassing to have your twin sister attend. But one thing he could say for her was that she never giggled in that high-pitched squeal like a lot of other girls. She never did, had never seemed to go through that stage where she was boy crazy or horse crazy or just plain crazy for whatever reason. Goofy, maybe, but not crazy.

He looked over at her. He didn't wave, but she noticed him and nodded and started to head over toward him. Her clothes were baggy; he guessed that she didn't want to attract attention to herself in this male-dominated crowd. That was all right. She'd never shown any interest in quoits, had never pleaded to play with him or to have him show her how or tagged along to watch, even.

"Did the parents kick or something?" he had to ask.

A slight smile. "No, I couldn't deal with the crowds, so"—she looked around at the sparsely filled arena—"I figured it would be good here."

"Ha, ha, very funny. Don't get too comfortable. People come from miles and miles around to be a part of this big event."

Noelle laughed. "No doubt. But right now, anyway, there seems to be a place or two for me to park my fanny."

Nick looked at her. His twin sister. Their eyes connected and everything felt different. His skin suddenly felt hot. She really wasn't too bad. Something good was going to happen today; maybe he really was going to win.

He grabbed his athletic bag and checked out the list of names on the competitor board. Nick Ellingsworth, pin number six. He would be playing on the last pin, at the end of the field. Easier for him to slink off into the sidelines if he didn't do well. The field was divided into six pits, and competitors were divided by age group. The age categories were fairly broad: youth was ages eight to thirteen, young adult was fourteen to nineteen, and adult was anything over that. They also had an old fogie category for sixty-five and older, but that was more just to humor them.

Once you reached the top level of your age group and won three consecutive matches, you could venture into the next age group. But many couldn't handle the extra pressure of playing against guys a lot bigger and older and better than they were. There had been a couple of young hotshots through the years, though, who'd played in the adult category when they were fifteen or sixteen. The older guys had been pretty peeved about it at first but soon shut up after they saw the kids toss.

Nick, at fourteen, was just beginning the young adult level but already felt as if he was beyond their league. Some of these guys were still aiming for ringers, which were so easy to knock away, instead of going for the gater, with the edge of the quoit up against the hob to block it from subsequent ringers. Anyone getting the first ringer had the risk of losing it to a ringer on top of him. The second ringer negated the first. The best strategy was to block the hob, knock away any close competitors, then aim for a ringer with your last pitch.

This competition wasn't sanctioned by any national quoits group that Nick was aware of. He wanted to change that. He wanted to single-handedly bring the sport into focus again. He was a bit conflicted about it. Deep down he loved the relative obscurity of the sport, loved the fact that it wasn't surrounded by throngs of beer-guzzling, belly-flopping fans bellowing their way to oblivion. The only people who were fans generally played the game. There were no cheerleaders, no high-priced sponsors, no sucking-up groupies following one's every move.

Yet there was another part of him that felt the sport was so underestimated, that so many people could benefit from learning to excel at it. To develop the skill of touch to such an advanced degree that you know the second you pick up the quoit, as soon as your fingers feel the cold smooth steel, whether that one would be the winner. The steel spoke through your fingers, a vital exchange of information from animate to inanimate, from hand to steel, until you thrill at sending it spinning toward its goal and it lands in the clay with a resounding thud.

Nick felt quoits could obtain the fervent followers and achieve the same sort of popularity as martial arts, meditation, and yoga, and add itself to the list of centering activities that lifted the soul. But it would keep out the fluffs and the perpetual sheep-like followers, because you had to have a certain amount of strength and agility to excel at it. Although there were standards of distance required between hobs to be considered official, anyone could set up a game with any distance and progressively spread it out as he or she got better. Commitment to the sport was key. And quoits was hardly elitist; no one could say that about a sport that involved slopping about in mud. The mud was a compelling aspect of it too. It couldn't be substituted with artificial turf or rubberized grass or a polyurethane substance of any sort. Only good thick clay, the redder the better, would do. It was a sport for purists.

"So where should I stand?" Noelle asked her brother. "Are you going to be moving around from field to field?"

"No, I should stay right here. They can't have everyone running around where they might get conked on the head with a heavy steel ring…"

Noelle found herself drifting off from Nick's words. She was always comparing the women she met, sizing them up and seeing how they compared with the women she worked with at the club. She often caught herself doing it, not realizing how rude it was, but she couldn't help herself. She was mesmerized by her friends there and thought all female success could be measured against them. She even wondered about her teachers, how one or the other would look writhing to obscure pop music. It always made her giggle. Few women scattered through the crowd; this was mostly men's business.

Noelle often wondered what kind of woman she would be, or should be, or wanted to be. She observed, calculated, evaluated other ladies around her to see what they looked like, how they acted, and what sort of reactions they inspired in others around them. She compiled, sorted, and culled through all the data and expected someday to come up with the ideal female personality for herself.

As Noelle observed, there was that skinny woman over there, in bursitis-inducing tight jeans and lowcut ruffled rayon camisole, laughing nervously, unnaturally, a little too self-consciously. Noelle didn't hear the joke, but the woman laughed—*cackle, cackle*—until a split second of a shadow fell over her face, then she quickly looked around to see how everyone else was reacting. Oooh, no one else was laughing, so she had better stop. The cackling woman had thought her comment was definitely something that cool people would find funny, Noelle was sure of it, that's why the woman had jumped the gun and started laughing before anyone else. That would be the last time she'd ever try that again, Noelle thought.

And then there was that other woman leaning up against a tree. She was dressed in a gaudy full skirt that flared out over her hips, displaying attractive, tanned legs. She seemed to be standoffish, just leaning against the tree, gazing around her with distraction, her foot up against the trunk bark. But there was something just a bit too posed about her. While she feigned indifference, she wanted people to notice her. She looked over at Noelle, who smiled faintly, and the woman squinted her face in disgust. I'm not interested in a pipsqueak like you checking me out, her face screamed out. Validation, validation, from someone important, that's what she wanted, Noelle could tell.

So few women seemed to have true self-confidence. Not like those women at work. Like Gina.

Nick looked around. He loved everything about this game, including the thick, red clay, watered down just enough to catch a carefully executed quoit. The best throws stuck in the clay up against the pin and blocked all subsequent ringers. If it stuck good and hard in the clay, it was nearly impossible to dislodge. He loved the smell of the clay. He loved the feel of the cool, smooth steel in his hand. He loved being outside. Best of all, he loved the sounds of the game. The soft thud of a quoit hitting the clay, the clanging of quoits hitting one another, the nearly silent *phud* when a quoit sunk into the clay for a perfect block against his competitors. How could computer games ever compare to this? Sure, they provided a great deal of eye candy, but he usually became bored with them after a few plays; there simply wasn't enough tactile stimulation. His father thought he was crazy, his son more old-fashioned than himself. Nick's dad loved playing solitaire and still checked out a Pac-Man if he was lucky enough to find one.

Nick looked around the tournament field, basking in the final moments leading up to the start of the championship. This was the most exciting moment, he thought. Everyone milling around, tending to their personal last-minute details, some doing quick exercises and stretches, jumping jacks, fake arm throws, jogging around the perimeter of the field. One guy was doing yoga. Others sat quietly or spoke softly to their friends or family, taut, tense, focused. Nick was calm. He was ready. He had practiced his heart out until his arm tingled, and he was in top shape. During his practice throws, his competitors had narrowed their eyes when his throws landed flatly on every side of the peg. No surprises there. He would be no threat. He didn't want them to see his strategy. Make them think that he was playing it straight.

His first throw landed close, just short of the peg. His competitor's, F-364, landed on top of his, touching the peg. Great shot. No ringers yet. Nick's second throw was a doozy. It cut deeply into the clay—knocking his competitor's quoit into a back flip away from the peg—and stuck into a solid leaner against the peg. His first quoit had moved to the right a bit. A throw of champions. The only way to beat that would be to somehow dislodge his leaner, but that was not likely. It was solidly stuck in the clay. His other quoit was in a miraculous position. Any attempt to knock it away would probably cause it to sink solidly into a ringer. And this was his competitor's last shot. The best he could hope for was to knock his first quoit to ricochet into Nick's and somehow dislodge it from its winner position.

The action moved in slow motion. F-364's quoit flew from his hand in a tumbling end-over-end motion that Nick had rarely seen. Nick held his breath because once it landed it could do almost anything, including uproot his leaner. But no, the throw was short. A dud. Thudded two-feet clear from the peg.

Nick had made it into the finals. He would be back tomorrow.

―

Nick flushed. Triumph was foreign to him, yet he felt like it was something he was meant to pursue. And capture. He held his head a little higher. He had yet to understand the mechanics of endorphins, but he loved the feeling. It was much better than lying stretched out on an ER litter. Noelle was proud of him, and she shyly took his hand as they headed back to the hotel room.

An Atlantic City jitney would be coming by soon to pick them up. The wind had picked up considerably, and big drops of rain plopped on their heads from time to time.

They didn't even notice.

Nick was excited. "What if they ask me to go to England to practice, learn from the masters? Wouldn't that be something? You could come too, Nellie"—he hadn't called her Nellie since they were five—"and sightsee, check out Big Ben, you know…"

He stopped. He really didn't know what his sister liked to do. He knew she rode her bike a lot, but he hadn't seen her hanging around the house much lately.

He looked puzzled. "What do you do with your time these days? You haven't been hanging around with your friends much lately."

Noelle thought a minute. No, she wasn't ready to divulge her new friendships with the Racy Ta-Ta's girls to her brother. It was too personal, and she hadn't quite figured out yet why she liked them all so much. She didn't want to leave it to him or anyone else to interpret it for her. Boys were always so bossy. They always thought they could figure everything out for you. And she liked this new friendship with her brother; she didn't want to ruin it by opening an area that would turn him into a drooling idiot. He would make fun of her, laugh, and say she couldn't compete with women like that, ask her to sneak him in, all sorts of dreary boy things.

"You know, I saw you get off your bike at Racy Ta-Ta's last week," Nick said.

No question, just a statement of fact. A long moment of silence. She really couldn't lie to him; they were twins after all.

"Well, I help around a little, mopping the floors, helping with their makeup, little stuff like that." She cringed and waited for the onslaught of construction-worker comments.

Pause. "Oh."

That's all he said. Noelle sighed in relief.

Eventually, his enthusiasm died into a calm silence. He was happy. They didn't say much to each other for the rest of the trip.

The wind blew through the open sides of the jitney, and they finally realized that they were surrounded by a strange, dark-green gloom.

Nick said, "This looks pretty bad. Isn't that hurricane supposed to be around here somewhere?"

"Frederick," Noelle said. "They said that it was supposed to stay off the coast, so I guess these are after-effects. Geez…"

Dark, thick clouds were forming, making it look a lot later than the six thirty it actually was.

The jitney driver announced, "It looks like we're in for a doozy of a storm, compliments of Frederick. I hope you two are headed for a safe place."

A feeling of dread hit them simultaneously, as did a big mutual sigh.

"Um, yeah, I guess," Nick said. "We're meeting our parents at one of the casinos. We're staying there."

He turned to Noelle. "We're supposed to meet them at seven, isn't that right?"

"Yes, at the buffet table at our hotel," Noelle said with a grimace.

"Don't you wish we could just set out on our own? Maybe travel to England together, see if we have any long-lost relatives we can stay with…"

Noelle nodded. What a dreamy idea.

They decided to go out and celebrate after dinner. Until the announcement from the casino loudspeaker.

CHAPTER 53

Although the clock was on Jenaveev's side, Virgil rolled out of bed and walked across the room to turn it off. He personally never needed an alarm. He could never understand why Jenaveev did, since she never had to keep to any schedule, yet her nightly routine always included setting the alarm.

Virgil strolled along the boardwalk. It was desolate, by boardwalk standards. Fewer people milled about. The eerie green sky apparently drove them away. Many of the businesses had boarded up early in anticipation of the hurricane, sending the casino-hoppers inside. The broke ones could hang out at the bus terminals if they could stand the cigarette smoke. Jenaveev was undoubtedly in a slobbering frenzy at the slot machines, the sevens machines were her favorite, and the kids were who knows where. *Oh, that's right, Nick's tournament. I wonder how he did?* He hoped everyone remembered they were to meet at seven at the buffet table.

The boardwalk wasn't entirely empty, although it was absent the usual pudgy, squinting, casino-cup carrying tourists, leaving it littered with society's rejects, has-beens, and never-beens. Virgil nearly tripped over a bundle of clothing and turned to kick it off the boardwalk when a dark-skinned arm shot out and grabbed his leg. Bleary eyes blazed at him and a voice croaked, "Just 'cause you're hustlin' along, sonny, don't mean you're gitten' anywheres."

That was Melindy. Her family had owned sixty-four acres of prime Louisiana farmland, earned from rough-strewn skills and hard labor learned from their slavery days. In 1916 her grandfather was lynched, the courthouse holding their real estate records burned down, and their property was confiscated and redistributed to various neighboring white families. Identical incidents had occurred throughout the South after the war. It was said that Melindy's family, and the other blackies, got their comeuppance due to their sin of haughtiness. Melindy released Virgil's leg and moaned, "I'm a hoodoo, you best be careful."

It was almost a lucid moment. He wasn't sure if she'd articulated it or if it had played in his head. The air was thick with the odor of the ocean, and foamy waves left behind slimy green things. He couldn't stand the smell but was compelled to head off of the boardwalk and walk along the beach.

His head down, he watched the sand carefully for sharp shells and repulsive seaweed but also deadwood and starfish and jellyfish. And mystifying black stuff. It was a regular maritime graveyard. As he walked into the water, he remembered how fun it used to be to play in the waves when he was younger. His parents used to vacation here in the summertime. He would rent a raft and ride the waves till his back and shoulders were beet red and he was about a mile from where he started. Now they didn't encourage swimming amid the possible medical waste, so they didn't rent the rafts anymore.

He wondered what would happen if he just kept walking out into the sea, deeper and deeper, until finally one big wave would suck him in and the undertow would batter him on all sides and turn him upside down. What a way to go. He wondered if it would be better if he pretended to swim as far as he could go, down to Wildwood perhaps, and then simply get too tired and disappear?

This evening the ocean was wilder and more menacing. The waves pounded the beach, and the swirling water rushed against his legs like a wet black army. Everything was dark except for the white-capped waves rushing in and crashing down. He walked farther and could barely see the littered beach, although the lights from the attractions on the boardwalk emitted an eerie glow. A few hundred years ago, this coast must have been beautiful—clean and pristine, white sandy beaches, high pitched dunes. Blue water, even? Now the East Coast was lined from Florida to Maine with lime-green, lagooned miniature golf courses, bone-shattering roller coaster rides on rickety wooden frames, fast food, fast food, fast food, boardwalks, and hawkers. God, they did have great pizza, though.

The wind started to pick up. Now feeling chilled, he decided against getting soaked in the wet wind, so he trudged back toward the lights and his dismal life. He bet he looked a mess with sand and saltwater clinging to his clothes. Clammy. He hated that clammy feeling, unless sex was involved.

Off on the new pier he saw the Ferris wheel, which had just opened up that year. Fifty years ago the boardwalk was one big ride attraction, but the casino mentality insisted that the rides had outlived their usefulness. So even though there were still isolated remnants from the old amusement park days, they were constructing new rides. The Ferris wheel was normally gorgeous, with bright yellow, orange, and red lights flashing brightly off all the spokes. The middle part revolved counterclockwise, or opposite from the wheel, or at least that's what the lights made it look like. The wheel was dark now, and the ride wasn't operating, darn it, because of the hurricane watch. Still, Virgil found himself wandering toward it. He loved the Ferris wheel, but his kids laughed at him. They only went for the wilder rides, the newfangled metal fabrications with all the charisma of a zooming computer chip, whereas he still liked the wooden coasters, the *only* true roller coasters with their hair-raising plank rattle.

The hurricane wasn't scheduled to strike the New Jersey coast directly, but it was going to be close enough to cause some heavy rain and wind. Even now, in the dark, he could see the whitecaps on the waves as they pounded against the beach. The wind whipped around in sudden rushes, alternating with thick, black silence. Chilly slivers tickled down his spine. He fingered the crumpled letter in his pocket, the one from the Department of the Interior, and sighed. He felt suddenly glad he'd stopped at his lawyer's office a few weeks ago.

Virgil thought he really should go inside. Jenaveev, despite herself, probably would be wondering where he was. Maybe she forgot her credit card and didn't have any cash on her and wouldn't be able to pay for dinner. Maybe she didn't even realize he was gone.

Virgil noticed his feet were soggy and cold. The waves were reaching him on the beach, crashing down with a thud and spreading their stinky foam in a wide arc across the beach. He had walked quite a bit inland; he had every intention of staying dry. Even if it was suddenly high tide, this was frenetic activity from the sea. He looked up and saw whitecap after whitecap and huge waves that blocked the lighthouse on the southern reef. He heard a loud whooshing sound, worse than the traffic on the Schuylkill Expressway during the height of the commute. The wind whipped around him, blowing in his ears, swirling his hair, and he was struck with the raw power of it.

"Hey!" He knew he said it, but he couldn't hear himself over this cacophony of wild weather.

He saw shadows dancing wildly on the beach. It was the lighting from the pizza places and gift shops on the boardwalk illuminating the amusement park rides, tent flaps, and ropes that cast the gyrating shadows. It was a wild world out here; there could be nothing going on in the casinos right now that could compare with this.

Suddenly, Virgil thought, *Wouldn't it be great to sit on one of the Ferris wheel seats on a night like this? And when no one is around?* Virgil climbed over the tiny metal restraining gate to the ride, hardly even a challenge, certainly not a deterrent. The metal felt cold to his hands; it felt good. It had been a typical August New Jersey day, hot and muggy. He was glad things were cooling off a bit; it would make it more comfortable for the people who slept under the boardwalk.

This is crazy. I should go back, he thought. He watched the chairs rock slightly in the increasing wind. But he just couldn't resist; he had to sit on one of them. Usually they closed up the ride with the seats positioned too high to reach, but this time the chair was set as if ready for its next rider. He took the bait.

The restraining bar was locked into place, but he pulled himself up and over and plopped headfirst into the soft vinyl cushion of the seat. He wrenched himself around so that his butt was in the chair with his legs over the top of the restraining bar. Then he was able to squeeze his legs to his chest and dangle them down underneath the bar. *Whew. What grace.* But there didn't seem to be any onlookers, and Virgil just didn't care. He sat there panting, whether from the excitement of doing something illegal, kid-like, or something else, he just didn't know. His nerve endings seemed live-wired.

He sat there in the Ferris wheel chair tapping his toes on the ground. *This is the ultimate grommet. If only I had discovered and patented this thing, my worries would be over. And people might actually like me.* The wind picked up; he could hear the chairs above him rock with noisy squeaks. The waves were getting wild. Saltwater droplets splashed against his face like icy tears.

He had worked so hard to keep his family together; he wondered what would become of him when they all naturally went their separate ways. Noelle and Nick would both get married and have children of their own someday. He had a feeling they would jet out of the house the first chance they got. Then he and Jenaveev would only have each other. Right now, the kids were a buffer between them. Once the kids were gone, he wondered if he and his wife could sidle up next to each other on the couch, watching TV, snuggling together under a soft down comforter, like, well, never mind. He couldn't recall ever snuggling with Jenaveev anywhere. She was always too brittle and nervous.

He would simply continue his descent into a lecherous old man grasping at affection wherever he could reach it. Maybe he should start riding the bus. He could pretend to be some doddering old guy and cop a sloppy feel now and again from an unsuspecting female. He could picture himself sitting next to some luscious young thing and inadvertently touch her thigh, her shoulder, her breast—well, maybe not all at once, that might be a tad suspicious—maybe make a game of it and check off each accomplishment as he achieved it. One day he'd reach the shoulder, the next day a knee, the next day—oh my good, gracious Lord—a breast. What high ecstasy! He was a friendly guy; he could engage them in conversation and totally win them over so they trusted him and then anything would be fair game. Pretty soon he'd be laughing and touching all sorts of parts of their bodies. And they'd allow it because they were too polite to make a scene. Yes, he believed he could manage a lifelong fulfillment from that.

But perhaps not. He'd tried that during the holiday parties at his company, and the managers had caught him every time. Had really laid into him. Now the older he got, the less of a hard time they gave him. He found that most humiliating. Now he was just a silly old stereotype. Oh, there's old Virgil again, trying to hustle some pookaberra from that hottie in Accounting. Hahahahahahahahaha, what a nutty guy!

The next step in his descent would be regional manager Max working to elicit some flirty behavior from some of the women toward Virgil, just to show him some attention.

"Hey, Sally, could you be a sport? Can you go over to poor old Virge over there and giggle a little and make him think he still has it? It will really mean the world to the poor guy."

So, yes, he would have become a charity case.

Part of his charm had always been his habit of speaking in riddles to people, kinda making fun, like he was such a fun-loving guy. Insinuate, that was the name of the game. Tell people just enough, and let them fill in the blanks themselves, but when they came up wrong, you could laugh in their face. *For heaven's sake, whatever gave you that idea? I never said that! Oh, ha, ha, ha, I was just kidding!* It was verboten to ever commit to anything. Never come right out and say, yes, I love your product, I will pay you anything for it because it is worth it. Instead, tell Mr. Creeds the concept piques your interest, but you'd like to check out the beta phase and evaluate the results. It could be a good idea, but the implementation needs reworking.

Never ever say *I love you.* He'd slipped with Eileen, and what a disaster that turned out to be.

She'd called his bluff, and he'd skittered off into the sunset, like a scared little rabbit. He liked her, he thought she had definite possibilities, but he never expected to have to work for her.

So here he was, scheming for ways to be touched to make his skin tingle. Because it would only happen if he stole it.

Suddenly, to his horror, the Ferris wheel began to move. He figured he should jump right off, but he couldn't believe it was happening. No, it was just more intense rocking. But now his feet could no longer reach the ground. *By God, this thing is airborne!*

He'd thought the ride was somehow locked into place, not just loose like a roulette wheel. It moved backward, slowly at first. When it reached the top, it slowed down a bit. But on the downswing, it picked up speed from its own momentum.

Virgil sat transfixed and then started to panic. It was some sort of macabre payback for his youthful habit of yelling at amusement park attendants that the rides were too short. This wind could keep this thing going for a long time. It was very windy; he could hardly think straight.

Suddenly, something on the boardwalk caught his eye. A woman was jumping up and down and shrieking and waving her arms in the air. The wind carried the sound clearly to his ears. In the dim silhouette, it looked like Jenaveev. He needed to figure out a way to climb out of this thing. Maybe if he reached over and grabbed that sturdy metal bar above him, he could swing over the rail of the chair and fall on the sandy beach.

Virgil realized too late that the sturdy metal bar was actually one of the Ferris wheel's moving parts. As he grasped the bar, it pinched his hands. He lost his grip and hurtled through the bone-crunching maze of cold steel below.

His last split-second thought before losing consciousness was *Maybe she's worried about me.* It surprised him. That fleeting little thought cleared his mind and brought him peace, and he was ready to give himself up to the wind and heavens.

Inside Caesar's, Bethany Delgado was immersed in the nickel slots. She and her best friend, Phoebe Gaitlen, had taken a casino bus from Philadelphia for their usual monthly trip. Eleven dollars got them the hour-or-so bus ride, a ten-dollar voucher at Caesar's, and a five-dollar discount on the buffet. Bethany loved playing the slots all day, six glorious hours of clanging quarters and ringing bells. Phoebe preferred to pocket the cash and check out the sights along the boardwalk and the shopping mall.

Because of the stormy weather, Phoebe had drifted back inside and stepped in line to get her ten-dollar roll of quarters. She always felt a little guilty, lining up to exchange her voucher for the roll of quarters and going directly over to the cash-out area to redeem the quarters for dollars. She would usually meander through the slot machines holding her bucket of exactly ten dollars in quarters, slip a quarter in a machine here and there so it wouldn't seem so obvious, eyes darting right and left, and finally head over to the cash-out window.

It always made her a little nervous, in this place of dubious legitimacy anyway, to redeem her paltry ten-dollar pile of quarters. She felt like a big, gloved hand would swoop down and smack her upside her head and doom her to the realm of other casino bus cheaters. "*You!* You did not play enough! You did not deposit the requisite amount of quarters in order to make your presence worthy to us! Be gone, oh worthless one! You are relegated to spend the remaining five and three-quarter hours of your time in the cigarette-smoke chamber of hell that is the bus waiting room."

Phoebe headed toward the booth and heard the jangling of bells and coins that indicated a big winner. She looked around, hoping it might be Bethany. After all, they were best friends; Bethany would surely flip her a few bucks. But, no, it was someone else. A lady with bushy red hair, probably a wig, dressed in an impeccably tailored lemon-yellow pantsuit. Psssh, someone who didn't really look like she needed the money. Big Red's arms thrust upward, her skinny fingers jutting in bony angles in the air like a dead tree in the moonlight.

Jenaveev won the progressive jackpot: $2.3 million dollars. She screamed and ran out on the boardwalk to proclaim her fortune to the world. She waved her arms. Life was wonderful. Let the hurricane come; she was *rich*! She was already rich, sure, but now she was obscenely rich. Just what she'd always wanted.

She was quickly surrounded by the authorities, who wanted to herd her to safety. As she plodded back to the room, she vaguely wondered where Virgil was. Perhaps he would allow her to keep the winnings all to herself. She dreaded the thought of sharing it.

———

When Virgil's body swept up on shore, his firm little butt kept his pants' pocket tight, saving his wallet. Inside the wallet, under the plastic card and picture holders, was a single shiny Mercury dime.

CHAPTER 54

With Virgil's death, Eileen felt a release of something she never realized she was holding onto. Like a tight rubber band that had been stretched to the breaking point and then suddenly loosened.

Eileen pondered going to the funeral. Most of his friends and relatives would wonder who she was and why she was there; those who might remember "them" would undoubtedly be embarrassed for her. But, she figured, why not go? He had been on the board of the hospital; she worked for the president of the hospital. Why wouldn't it be natural that she pay her respects? Winston and others would probably be there. So what if Virgil contributed to the downfall of the hospital? Deep down they all shared the unity of brotherhood, didn't they? Yes, it was a load of claptrap, but Eileen decided she couldn't miss it. She wanted to see who else cared enough to go.

Eileen dressed carefully, lovingly picking out her funeral attire: a pair of black fishnet stockings and the dainty mauve lingerie Virgil had bought her for her birthday long ago. Her black pants were roomy enough that she could tuck in the lingerie, and she wore a black long-sleeve blouse over top, the one with the violet heart that Neil had bought for her. Topped it off with an antique cameo brooch, a gift from her Mom. It was a nice mix and match of gifts from people she'd loved.

She walked into the funeral home and approached the casket, focusing her eyes forward. She gazed into the casket and smiled a little, although tears welled in her eyes. He looked so waxy. Jenaveev must have had a heavy hand in preparing his makeup. Yes, he'd screwed up the hospital; she'd never understand how all that had happened. But she knew him. She knew that he'd had a spirit that yearned for so many things.

She whispered to him in peace and forgiveness, "It's OK." She caressed the waxy face that, for a little upside-down while, had been the center of her life. He was probably looking down at this entire scene, highly amused by it all. And then she whispered, "I'm wearing one of your gifts, which of course wouldn't be complete without black fishnet stockings. You would be thrilled to death. Well, if you weren't already dead."

She bent down to peck his cheek, and one of her tears dripped on his collar. She instinctively reached down to mop it up with her fingers and noticed the initials VIE embroidered on his collar. *La vie. Life. Ha! Nothing like a little French irony for comic relief.* She swiveled around and left quickly lest she offend the grieving survivors with her guffaws. As she bolted out the front door, she heard someone say, "Who was that?"

A few years ago, the query would have transported her into an hour's worth of musing, conjecture, and humiliation. Now she just thought, *God, I'm glad I don't have to know these people, don't have to share funeral reception hors d'oeuvres of prissy cheese and curious animal entrails.*

Neil watched Eileen leave. Suddenly, he heard loud sobbing inside the funeral home and noticed Jenaveev flailing her arms over her head. An older woman stepped toward her and touched Jenaveev gently on her shoulder. Jenaveev wheeled around and beamed a bright, toothy grin. "Why, Charlene my dear, so glad you could come!"

Neil left and ambled over to Eileen. He put his arm around her, and looked deeply in her eyes to assess her mood.

"I'm fine, I'm fine. I have to go now," she said and turned toward her car. Once she was out of everyone's sight, she cried. It was the end of an era. *Thank goodness for that, and for lotion tissues.*

She couldn't listen to the funeral service, the blowsy diatribes and forced humor of all of those who never knew him, not like she knew him, but who nevertheless had the legitimate roles to dedicate publicly a few words to his memory.

Eileen' car windows steamed up and she got out for some fresh air. She stood under the dogwood trees and marveled at their pink-blossomed beauty. Her easily distracted mind worked in her favor today. It was a beautiful sunny day. In the good times, Virgil would have wanted her to be out playing in weather like this. In his honor, she would make love to Neil this afternoon until his earlobes turned pink.

"You were pretty upset this afternoon," Neil said softly as he curled a little tendril of her hair around his finger. "Are you OK?"

"Yes." She rolled over and hugged his arm to her naked body. "I needed the finality of it. Mmm, this is so much better." She dipped her tongue along the line of his collarbone and then rolled over on her back. "But you know, I think he was truly perplexed at how badly his life turned out. I don't think he ever believed he had a hand in it."

"He made his own choices."

"Yes…" The rest of the sentence hung in an uncertain silence. There was a "but" to her thought; she knew it, and she knew Neil knew it.

Neil was quiet. He didn't know if he should tell her exactly to what extent Virgil had cursed the running of the hospital operations.

She continued, "I knew this guy for a little while. I think for a few fleeting moments, he got a glimpse of what he wanted his life to be. A few moments of clarity. Oh, well. Let's get to the good stuff."

Neil nodded. He knew she was over Virgil, and him being dead and all certainly made it easier, but there was still a wispy cloud over her head with Virgil's name on it.

Days plodded by, one by one, after the funeral. She woke up each morning feeling pretty good for an instant, until she remembered he was gone. Then the pain flashed over her in little lightning sparks, jabbing here and there, all over. She couldn't believe that he was really gone, and she couldn't believe how it hurt. She thought she was *way* over him. He'd really been a bit of a creep, in his own inimitable, rich, handsome, winsome, lying-sack-of-shit kind of way. She knew that somehow, down the line, eventually the pain would subside and she would feel a deep sense of justice.

But right now she had to get through this painful episode stuff. That was another hallmark of cancer. No matter how dreadful you feel, for whatever reason, you learn that it will pass—well, most of it anyway—and you'll feel better. You might not feel as good as you did before, but you will feel better. You're always glad when the pain subsides even a little, because that's progress, and even a little is better. She supposed cancer softened your expectations. You learn to accomplish more because you're not as hard on yourself.

Life had its own amusing way of equalizing things. Falling out of an abandoned Ferris wheel during a hurricane—that was pretty spectacular.

CHAPTER 55

Noelle was still reeling from the news of her father. No one would ever have known what happened to him, except for a couple of winos crouched under the boardwalk. They'd come forward, showing lucidity for the first time in years, and told the cops that they saw a man tumbling out of the chair of the Ferris wheel, which was moving in the wind. The cops were about to dismiss it as another of their wide-eyed exclamations of alien abduction, but they could see the wheel still spinning slowly and ran over to the amusement ride area. Virgil's broken body lay on the beach, strewn with twisted strings of seaweed. It was the first time anyone had heard of the wind making the ride go on its own like that.

Noelle sat heavily on the curb outside her home, her head cradled in her arms. Her father had had his goofy moments, but she'd loved him. How could he be so stupid and selfish to do such an idiotic thing? He had abandoned them intentionally, hated all of them, and wanted to escape. No, she knew that wasn't true. But how were they all going to make it without him?

Her father's parents had hustled up from Baltimore to Maple Leaf, fully prepared for a rip-roaring battle over custody of the kids. Never in a million years would they let that yet-to-evolve red-haired menace be the sole and primary influence over their precious grandchildren, they'd made it clear.

They'd counseled with lawyers and child-development experts, digested all manner of books, letters, and teachings, and arrived well armed, demanding to be heard.

Her mother had merely looked bewildered. "The kids? You'd take them? Gosh, thanks."

So that was that.

One day Noelle stopped over at her mother's home, which she shared with her new podiatrist friend, and peeked in the window. Beyond the filmy chiffon curtain, she saw her mother swiveling in circles on her butt on the slippery marble coffee table, her feet and legs straight up in the air. Her mother wiggled her toes in little pink footies and wore white cotton shorts and a fuschia push-up bra. And that's all. With much delight, her mother giggled and shrieked, "Wheeeeeeee!"

Noelle turned around to meet up with her grandparents at home, and she never stopped by again. That's the day she turned in her resignation at Racy Ta-Ta's. She also called Nick. They made arrangements to get together for lunch.

CHAPTER 56

After a day cleaning out her desk and boxing up Winston's books and a final dusting of the plants, Eileen headed home, showered, and waited for Neil. As soon as Neil walked through the door, Eileen danced in front of him, dangling before his face the letter from the Department of the Interior. He grinned with a lifted eyebrow, and she nodded.

Then she enveloped him in her arms. He traced her lips gently with his finger. What a marvelously sensitive spot! She tried to resist licking and sucking the roaming finger—she just wanted to relish the feeling of his manly finger against her tender lips—but finally she had to relent and drew it into her steamy mouth. Then there was no telling where the tossing stopped and turning started; hands and fingers and legs and arms were everywhere, and it was all so good. She felt more and more comfortable with him. Virgil was no longer a watchful ghoul. Now she was all there for Neil.

"OK, Mr. Salto, help me build a museum," she eventually said.

"Well, first you'll need a lot of money."

Her face drooped.

"We can set up a fund for folks to donate," Neil said. "Or apply for a grant."

"That will take forever."

Patience was not Eileen's virtue. She turned over on her stomach and asked him to rub her back. She had tried so hard, but the path seemed endless.

Neil sensed her angst. "So, I spoke with my brother today. Did I ever tell you about Jack? He lives in upstate New York with my sister-in-law. They've been married for twenty years, and he just opened a historical bookstore that includes genealogical charts and personal stories of the local folks. He might have some advice."

He massaged her back in an offhand manner as he chatted, but his hands held the skin-memory of the favorite spots in her shoulders, neck, and lower back. His ploy worked and she drifted off into the familiar sensual cloud. She noted lazily that her arm didn't hurt at all. This regular caressing was rejoining the blunt and damaged nerve endings from her node surgery, making her arm whole again. Or so it seemed. She loved him. She really did. She thought he maybe had a little crush on her too, one that wasn't just charity.

———

Over the weeks, Hayley inched slowly toward Eileen like a shy sparrow. Eileen felt devotion, like tiny fluffs of down, piling in soft pillows inside her, her heart growing rounder and plumper with it, waiting for the right moment when she could appropriately express and share her love for the girl. Hayley was with her mother most of the time, and she was still quite hesitant around Eileen. Eileen did not want to pry into that family unit; they seemed to have it pretty well together without her intrusion. She didn't mind taking a backseat for a while. Once or twice, however, Hayley had reached for Eileen's hand. Her tender, soft little touch caused Eileen to get a lump in her throat and then quickly admonish herself for overreacting to the tiny gesture.

Kerry Ann's new boyfriend was all right. He imposed a bit more and made Eileen squirm for his lack of sensitivity—"So, you're my squeeze's ex's squeeze, huh? Ha, ha!"—but he would be fine. They would all be fine.

———

Ralph Waters, of the morgue, wondered why his arm hair stood on end after he heard about the discovery of the pathway behind the hospital, and that his getting-high playground was not just his own personal escape from the drudgery of his work day, but also played a central role in the struggle for freedom for a few lucky slave escapees. He couldn't admit it to anyone, but he felt somewhat shamed by Eileen's sarcastic dismissal of his apathy about the hospital's history. No one made fun of cool Ralph! When he reached for his lab coat, that he had tossed on a table in the reception area (to cover aforementioned arm hair), a pamphlet fell off the table. "The Pathway to Geneology," it was called. He was just thinking about the pathway! Wow, cool stuff! This led to a long and feverish study into his own geneology, where he eventually not only discovered his relation to the slave, Zeke and Sadie, Mindah and all the rest, but also discovered, it was highly likely, that Zeke's great-grandfather had been brought over in a slave vessel that was overtaken by Blackbeard himself! And that the slave cargo, including Ralph's great-whatever-grandfather joined forces with the infamous pirate! Now this was more like it. Ralph was really a cooler dude than even he thought possible! He started listening raptly to rap music on his CD Walkman, his head bobbing knowingly.

Jenaveev recovered sufficiently from her scare. She adjusted quite well to life without a uvula. The podiatrist she hooked up with was a mutual friend of the family who'd divorced his wife around the same time as Virgil's death. Apparently, his ex also married another mutual friend who also got divorced around the same time, and so on and so on. Their kind found it best to keep it among themselves. They understood each other.

Nick counted off. One, two, three…seven kids. All eager to learn and join the fellowship of quoits players. He had his own chapter; London eat your heart out. Along with his students, he would bring the game back into the limelight. It would be a challenge; hardly anyone even had a yard anymore.

Prying kids away from their computers was nearly impossible, but somehow Nick was handling it.

―

Noelle scratched her forehead with the tip of her pen. She imagined what Gina's life story must be like. The world blossomed with opportunity for a smart girl like Gina. A smart girl could identify what she wanted, with no bars of prejudice or prudery. She could indeed go far. Gina had opened the book to her life and dived in. The pages would turn when she was ready. Gina had turned down college because the entrepreneurial spirit egged her on. She had figured she could learn stuff anytime. What she needed to learn most was how to make money, a lot of it. Afterward, when she was comfy-cozy in her mahogany-stained library, she could read all the humanities she cared to. Noelle's fingers raced along the keyboard.

After Noelle quit Racy Ta-Ta's, she started writing a teen column in the local newspaper. Her first novel, *A Stripper's Tale*, would be published during her junior year of college. Her father would be proud.

―

One morning Jenaveev marched downtown toward Kitty's Boutique in a frantic hurry. The store opened at ten, and here it was eleven forty-five and she wasn't there yet! The sale of the year and she was missing it. How could she be so negligent? Pace, pace, walk, walk, stomp, stomp, stomp, "I'm late, I'm late, I'm late." Suddenly, *poing!* An orange metal disc soared out of nowhere and clonked her on the noggin and killed her.

No one knew exactly how it happened. It was believed to have come from a nearby work site. The problem was, the entire five-block surrounding area was a hotbed of construction activity with two-hundred-foot high cranes. It was impossible to track the metal disc to any one of the sites. No one claimed responsibility. "No, we're not using anything like that here. Our discs are blue."

Her friend the podiatrist tried for a time to track it down. But they had not been married, and he had nothing to gain, financially or otherwise, from finding the source of liability. Sure, the kids would have benefited, but he had only met them a couple of times and never really warmed up to them, and they, in turn, seemed to loathe him. So there was no point in protecting their interests. Besides, the dratted brats inherited what was left from her casino bonanza. So when lawyers came knocking on his door, he simply waved them away and continued buffing his feet.

CHAPTER 57

They tried to find a buyer for the hospital. Several area hospitals expressed interest until all the press revealed the operations gone awry. The doomed hospital also generated a lot of interest from out-of-state, for-profit type institutions. But once they read its financial picture with the lawsuits and operations gone bad, they ran for the hills and were never heard from again.

So there it was. A beautiful, functional building, once filled with wonderful people who had worked so hard for so long and who really cared about their jobs, their hospital, and the patients. None of them had any say. The decision had been made by people who would easily pick up somewhere else without missing a beat. People who hadn't even been with the hospital that long, who hadn't built up any sense of home around it or loyalty to it. The hospital was just another building to occupy, where they dazzled and amazed their coworkers with their numbers games. Only this numbers game screeched to a halt a little prematurely. The people who cared the most, who would have been willing to do almost anything to keep the hospital afloat, were kept completely out of the decision-making process.

The most recent equipment was sold, and everything else was auctioned off. It was not a happy day.

The big regional hospital chain in Philadelphia, Holy Trinity, decided to build a new branch twelve miles east of Sunrise, a spanking new, shiny-bright building without ghosts, history, or age-old MRSA germs lurking in every crevice. They really didn't want to take on Sunrise's debt.

Eileen could barely stand to look at her empty office and hallways. Such a rush of memories flowed over her, she felt dizzy. She had her landmark designation, but it meant nothing. She was tired. She ran her index finger lightly along the wall. Already the paint looked dingy and drab. Black ink marks were scratched next to the doorframe where she, William, or others had often rushed in and out twiddling a pen like a miniature saber.

Suddenly, a guttural "Ahem" startled her.

"I thought I would find you here." It was Falconne Gordon—of Gordon, Larson & Kammerer.

"Oh, I didn't think anyone was here." She narrowed her eyes. "To what do I owe this honor?"

He shuffled into her office and frowned at the six-foot folding tables piled high with paper. Distracted and nervous, he fanned a small pile of paper as he passed.

"We have something for you."

Eileen gave a lopsided smile. "Do I need to call the cops? No, just kidding. We who?"

"He left something for you. This is a bit distasteful, if you can understand."

She dared not move a muscle. "I'm sorry, you're obviously uncomfortable. But I haven't the foggiest idea…"

He managed a pinched smile. "Neither do we. This is a sealed codicil with your name on it. We were instructed to give it to you, no questions asked."

He handed her an envelope and a form. "Just sign here and I'll notarize it."

Her hand shook as she signed.

She fumbled with the envelope, then finally ripped the top off. Inside was a check. And a note that said, "Tails, you win."

Her first thought was *What the…?* followed by *How dare he?*

But then she thought of his smile, crinkled at the corners; his eyes, bright and moist; his warm hand in hers, cozy yet electrified. Her mind did a rapid-fire rundown of their moments together and the toll it took on her during her most vulnerable time, and she said, "Fuck it. It's mine."

She would have her museum.

———

Bob, now the chief editor of the *Maple Leaf Chronicle*, and reluctant ex-smoker, called Eileen, "OK my dear, check out the front page."

"I did, that's more like it, Bob, thanks."

"No, no, thank *you!*"

Eileen re-read the headline and her eyes welled up:

LOCAL WOMAN SAVES SUNRISE'S HERITAGE—HOSPITAL MORPHS INTO UNDERGROUND RAILROAD HISTORIC LANDMARK

Her breast swelled with life.

EPILOGUE

"So, where's Lovie?" Tanesha, dressed in a plain gingham frock and headscarf, whispered from the small stage of the museum as she bent over a makeshift field, picking cotton. Her mates shushed her.

"Word has it he found the Promised Land. War is coming. It's in the air."

In the Sunrise museum's gift shop, Eileen displayed her artwork for sale, theme-based historic scenes of imagined pre- and post-Civil War day-to-day living and slave and escapee life. She was usually careful not to include anything risqué in this place of hallowed memories, but once in a while she couldn't resist. One might think that's a pipe in the guy's mouth, but…oh, never mind. She chuckled as customers commented on the cuteness and detail of the little images.

A customer looked up at the glass case behind Eileen.

"Oh, that must be the first dollar you made. What's that next to it?"

"That's my lucky Mercury dime, or winged liberty dime."

The woman peered at it. "Why is it lucky?"

"It represents freedom. If you believe in it, anything is possible."

The woman smiled and nodded.

Eileen loved the sound of the building early in the morning before the museum opened to the public. A little bit creaky, a few leftover sighs from ghosts that mingled among the memorabilia. Nothing menacing, very peaceful. As if the wandering restless souls had finally found a suitable resting place.

And the smells too. Eileen had thought it would take forever to rid the building of the musty old smells of hospital-running: the antiseptics, the formaldehyde, the bandages, the clean, pressed laundry, and especially, the smell of illness and death. She'd been afraid those odors would permeate everything and that visitors would see nothing but a closed-off hospital trying to make it as something else.

She was determined that this place would maintain its dignity, rise above its demise as a hospital, and reign supreme in its now equally important role.

Now, scattered with artifacts from family ancestors, donations, and other museums, the smell was completely different. The quilts, books, letters, jewelry, clothing, furniture, and other handicrafts and mementos had found a home here and together melded into an entirely new smell. When Eileen shut her eyes and breathed deeply, she could imagine all the piecemeal objects getting to know one another, shyly, recognizing their common thread and feeling thankful to be together to share this bit of history with the people of the community. It was very intimate. The place reeked with nostalgia, and she remembered her own history, even though she had no connection with slavery. She remembered scents of her childhood: the smell of that grand old willow tree, her dad's new Olds, the books in her favorite childhood library.

Even the memories of her own cancer, her cancer that had been cured here while the place was a hospital, seemed to have blended in with the surroundings, drifting through, weaving in and out of the historic objects, finding peace in their shared past suffering and gaining strength from the present, where things were so much better.

ACKNOWLEDGMENTS

So many special folks, I'll start here:

Judy Corcoran
John, Mary, Erik
Sandra (Sam) Asher
The Stellas
Ray Finnen
Alicia Wells
Brenda Shank Boyer
Gerald Putt
The *Smithsonian*
Dobbin House, Gettysburg
York County Historical Society Museum
F. D. Roosevelt for commissioning the Federal Writers Project and its Slave Narrative Collection under the WPA
And to Dr. Linda Gromko, for scooting me off to that mammogram

Made in the USA
Lexington, KY
02 November 2014